To Olive
from Nelli...

Dec 1, 1921

CAP'N WARREN'S WARDS

" Captain Warren had risen from his chair and was facing her."

[Page 48.]

Cap'n Warren's Wards

By JOSEPH C. LINCOLN

Author of "The Depot Master," "The Woman Haters"
"The Postmaster," "Cap'n Erie,"
"Mr. Pratt," etc.

WITH ILLUSTRATIONS
BY EDMUND FREDERICK

A L. BURT COMPANY

PUBLISHERS   NEW YORK

Printed in the United States of America

CAP'N WARREN'S WARDS

CHAPTER I

O STABLE!" screamed the brakeman, opening the car door and yelling his loudest, so as to be heard above the rattle of the train and the shriek of the wind; "Ostable!"

The brakeman's cap was soaked through, his hair was plastered down on his forehead, and, in the yellow light from the car lamps, his wet nose glistened as if varnished. Over his shoulders the shiny ropes of rain whipped and lashed across the space between the cars. The windows streamed as each succeeding gust flung its miniature freshet against them.

The passengers in the car — there were but four of them — did not seem greatly interested in the brakeman's announcement. The red-faced person in the seat nearest the rear slept soundly, as he had done for the last hour and a half. He had boarded the train at Brockton, and, after requesting the conductor not to "lemme me git by Bayport, Bill," at first favored his fellow travelers with a song and then sank into slumber.

The two elderly men sitting together on the right-hand side of the car droned on in their apparently endless Jeremiad concerning the low price of cranberries, the scarcity of scallops on the flats, the reasons why the fish weirs were a failure nowadays, and similar cheerful topics. And in his seat on the left, Mr. Atwood Graves, junior partner in the New York firm of Sylvester, Kuhn and Graves, lawyers, stirred uneasily on the lumpy plush cushion, looked at his watch, then at the time-table in his hand, noted that the train was now seventy-two minutes late, and for at least the fifteenth time mentally cursed the railway company, the whole of Cape Cod from Sandwich to Provincetown, and the fates which had brought him there.

The train slowed down, in a jerky, hiccoughy sort of way, and crept on till the car in which Mr. Graves was seated was abreast the lighted windows of a small station, where it stopped. Peering through the water-streaked pane at the end of his seat, the lawyer saw dim silhouettes of uncertain outline moving about. They moved with provoking slowness. He felt that it would be joy unspeakable to rush out there and thump them into animation. The fact that the stately Atwood Graves even thought of such an undignified proceeding is sufficient indication of his frame of mind.

Then, behind the door which the brakeman, after announcing the station, had closed again, sounded a big laugh. The heartiness of it grated on Mr. Graves's nerves. What idiot could laugh on such a night as this aboard a train over an hour late?

The laugh was repeated. Then the door was flung briskly open, and a man entered the car. He was a big man, broad-shouldered, inclined to stoutness, wearing a cloth cap with a visor, and a heavy ulster, the collar of which was turned up. Through the gap between the open ends of the collar bristled a short, grayish beard. The face above the beard and below the visor was sunburned, with little wrinkles about the eyes and curving lines from the nostrils to the corners of the mouth. The upper lip was shaved, and the eyebrows were heavy and grayish black. Cap, face, and ulster were dripping with water.

The newcomer paused in the doorway for an instant, evidently to add the finishing touch to a conversation previously begun.

"Well, I tell you, Ezra," he called, over his shoulder, "if it's too deep to wade, maybe I can swim. Fat floats, they tell me, and Abbie says I'm gettin' fleshier every day. So long."

He closed the door and, smiling broadly, swung down the aisle. The pair of calamity prophets broke off their lament over the declining fisheries and greeted him almost jovially.

"Hello, Cap'n!" cried one. "What's the south shore doin' over here in this flood?"

"What's the matter, Cap'n?" demanded the other. "Broke loose from your moorin's, have you? Did you ever see such a night in your life?"

The man in the ulster shook hands with each of his questioners, removing a pair of wet, heavy leather gloves as he did so.

"Don't know's I ever did, Dan," he answered. "Couldn't see much of this one but its color — and that's black. I come over this mornin' to attend to some business at the court-house — deeds to some cranberry bog property I just bought — and Judge Baxter made me go home with him to dinner. Stayed at his house all the afternoon, and then his man, Ezra Hallett, undertook to drive me up here to the depot. Talk about blind pilotin'! Whew! The Judge's horse was a new one, not used to the roads, Ezra's near-sighted, and I couldn't use my glasses 'count of the rain. Let alone that, 'twas darker'n the fore-hold of Noah's ark. Ho, ho! Sometimes we was in the ruts and sometimes we was in the bushes. I told Ez we'd ought to have fetched along a dipsy lead, then maybe we could get our bearin's by soundin's. 'Couldn't see 'em if we did get 'em,' says he. 'No,' says I, 'but we could taste 'em. Man that's driven through as much Ostable mud as you have ought to know the taste of every road in town.'"

"Well, you caught the train, anyhow," observed Dan.

"Yup. If we'd been crippled as *well* as blind we could have done that." He seated himself just in front of the pair and glanced across the aisle at Mr. Graves, to find the latter looking intently at him.

"Pretty tough night," he remarked, nodding.

"Yes," replied the lawyer briefly. He did not encourage conversation with casual acquaintances. The latest arrival had caught his attention because there was something familiar about him. It seemed to Graves that he must have seen him before; and yet that was very improbable. This was the attorney's first visit to Cape Cod, and he had already vowed devoutly that it should be his last. He turned a chilling shoulder to the trio opposite and again consulted the time-table. Denboro was the next station; then — thank the Lord — South Denboro, his destination.

Conversation across the aisle was brisk, and its subjects were many and varied. Mr. Graves became aware, more or less against his will, that the person called "Cap'n" was, if not a leader in politics and local affairs, still one whose opinions counted. Some of those opinions, as given, were pointed and dryly descriptive; as, for instance, when a certain town-meeting candidate was compared to a sculpin —"with a big head that sort of impresses you, till you get close enough to realize it *has* to be big to make room for so much mouth."

4

Graves, who was fond of salt water fishing, knew what a sculpin was, and appreciated the comparison.

The conductor entered the car and stopped to collect a ticket from his new passenger. It was evident that he, too, was acquainted with the latter.

"Evening, Cap'n," he said, politely. "Train's a little late to-night."

"It is — for to-night's train," was the prompt response, "but if it keeps on at the rate it's travelin' now, it'll be a little early for to-morrow mornin's, won't it?"

The conductor laughed. "Guess you're right," he said. "This is about as wet a storm as I've run through since I've been on the road. If we get to Provincetown without a washout we'll be lucky . . . Well, we've made another hitch. So far, so good."

The brakeman swung open the door to shout, "Denboro! Denboro!" the conductor picked up his lantern and hurried away, the locomotive whistled hoarsely, and the train hiccoughed alongside another little station. Mr. Graves, peering through his window, imagined that here the silhouettes on the platform moved more briskly. They seemed almost excited. He inferred that Denboro was a bigger and more wide-awake village than Ostable.

But he was mistaken. The reason for the excitement was made plain by the conductor a moment afterwards. That official entered the car, removed his uniform cap, and rubbed a wet forehead with a wetter hand.

"Well, gentlemen," he said, "I've been expecting it, and here it is. Mark me down as a good prophet, will you? There's a washout a mile further on, and a telegraph pole across the track. It's blowing great guns and raining pitchforks. It'll be out of the question for us to go forward before daylight, if then. Darn a railroad man's job anyhow!"

Five minutes later Mr. Graves descended the steps of the car, his traveling bag in one hand and an umbrella in the other. As soon as both feet were securely planted on the platform, he put down the bag to wrestle with the umbrella and the hurricane, which was apparently blowing from four directions at once. Feeling his hat leaving his head, he became aware that the umbrella had turned inside out. He threw the wreck violently under the train and stooped to pick up the bag. The bag was no longer there.

"It's all right," said a calm voice behind him. "I've got your satchel, neighbor. Better beat for harbor, hadn't we? Here! this way."

The bewildered New Yorker felt his arm seized in a firm grip, and he was rushed across the platform, through a deluge of wind-driven water, and into a small, hot, close-smelling waiting room. When he pushed his hat clear of his eyes he saw that his rescuer was the big man who boarded the train at Ostable. He was holding the missing bag and smiling.

"Dirty weather, hey?" he observed, pleasantly. "Sorry your umbrella had to go by the board. I see you was carryin' too much canvas and tried to run alongside in time to give you a tow; but you was dismasted just as I got there. Here's your dunnage, all safe and sound."

He extended the traveling bag at arm's length. Mr. Graves accepted his property and murmured thanks, not too cordially. His dignity and temper had gone overboard with the umbrella, and he had not yet recovered them.

"Well," went on his companion, "here we are! And

6

I, for one, wanted to be somewheres else. Caleb," turning to the station master, who came in at that moment, " any way of my gettin' home to-night?"

" 'Fraid not, Cap'n," was the answer. " I don't know of any. Guess you'll have to put up at the hotel and wait till mornin'."

" That's right," agreed the passenger called " Dan," who was standing near. " That's what Jerry and I are goin' to do."

" Yes, but you and Jerry are bound for Orham. I'm booked for South Denboro, and that's only seven miles off. I'd *swim* the whole seven rather than put up at Sim Titcomb's hotel. I've been there afore, thank you! Look here, Caleb, can't I hire a team and drive over?"

" Well, I don't know. S'pose you might ring up Pete Shattuck and ask him. He's pretty particular about his horses, though, and I cal'late he —"

" All right. I'll ring him up. Pete ought to get over some of his particularness to oblige me. I've helped *him* once or twice."

He was on his way to the ticket office, where the telephone hung on the wall. But Mr. Graves stepped forward and spoke to him.

" Excuse me, sir," said the lawyer. " Did I understand you to say you were going to South Denboro?"

" Yes. I am, if the powers — and Pete Shattuck —'ll let me."

" You were going to drive over? May I go with you? I'm very anxious to get to South Denboro to-night. I have some very important business there, and I want to complete it and get away to-morrow. I must be back in New York by the morning following."

The captain looked his questioner over. There was a doubtful look on his face, and he smiled quizzically.

7

" Well, I don't know, Mr. ——"

" Graves is my name."

" I don't know, Mr. Graves. This ain't goin' to be a pleasure cruise exactly. You might get pretty wet."

" I don't care. I can get dry again when I get there. Of course I shall share the expense of the livery. I shall be greatly obliged if I may go with you. If not, I must try for a rig myself."

" Oh, if you feel that way about it, why, come ahead and welcome. I was only warnin' you, that's all. However, with me aboard for ballast, I guess we won't blow away. Wait a jiffy till I get after Pete."

He entered the ticket office and raised a big hand to the little crank of the telephone bell.

" Let's see, Caleb," he called; " what's Shattuck's number?"

" Four long and two short," answered the station master.

Graves, wondering vaguely what sort of telephone system was in use on Cape Cod, heard his prospective pilot ring the instrument for a full two seconds, repeating the ring four times altogether. This he followed with two sharp tinkles. Then came a series of shouted " Hellos!" and, at last, fragments of one-half of a dialogue.

" That you, Shattuck? Know who this is, don't you? . . . Yes, that's right . . . Say, how many folks listen every time a bell rings on this line? I've heard no less'n eight receivers come down so far . . . Two of 'em went up then, did you hear 'em? . . . Sartin . . . I want to hire a team to go over home with . . . To-night — Sartin . . . I don't care . . . Yes, you will, too . . . *Yes,* you *will* . . . Send my man back with it to-morrow . . .

8

I don't care *what* it is, so it's got four legs and wheels . . ."

And so on for at least five minutes. Then the captain hung up the receiver and came back to the waiting room.

"Bargain's made, Mr. Graves," he announced. "Pete'll have some sort of a turn-out alongside soon's he can get it harnessed. If you've got any extra storm duds in that satchel of yours, I'd advise you to put 'em on. We're goin' to have a rough passage."

Just how rough it was likely to be, Graves realized when he emerged from the station to board the Shattuck buggy. "Pete" himself had driven the equipage over from the livery stable.

"I wouldn't do this for anybody but you, Cap'n," he vouchsafed, in what might be called a reproachful shout. Shouting was necessary, owing to the noise of the storm.

"Wouldn't do what?" replied the captain, looking first at the ancient horse and then at the battered buggy.

"Let this horse out a night like this."

"Humph! I should think night would be the only time you would let him out. . . . There! there! never mind. Get aboard, Mr. Graves. Put your satchel on the floor between your feet. Here, let me h'ist that boot for you."

The "boot" was a rubber curtain buttoned across the front of the buggy, extending from the dashboard to just below the level of the driver's eyes. The lawyer clambered in behind it, the captain followed, the end of the reins was passed through a slit in the boot, Mr. Shuttuck, after inquiring if they were "all taut," gave the command, "Gid-dap!" and horse and buggy moved around the corner of the station, out into darkness.

9

Of the next hour Graves's memories are keen but monotonous,— a strong smell of stable, arising from the laprobe which had evidently been recently used as a horse blanket; the sound of hoofs, in an interminable "jog, jog — splash, splash," never hurrying; a series of exasperated howls from the captain, who was doing his best to make them hurry; the thunderous roar of rain on the buggy top and the shrieking gale which rocked the vehicle on its springs and sent showers of fine spray driving in at every crack and crevice between the curtains.

The view ahead, over the boot, was blackness, bordered by spidery trees and branches whipping in the wind. Occasionally they passed houses sitting well back from the road, a lighted window gleaming cozily. And ever, as they moved, the storm seemed to gather force.

Graves noticed this and, at length, when his nervousness had reached the breaking point, screamed a question in his companion's ear. They had attempted no conversation during the ride, the lawyer, whose contemptuous opinion of the locality and all its inhabitants was now a conviction, feeling that the result would not be worth the effort, and the captain busy with his driving.

"It is blowing worse than ever, isn't it?" yelled the nervous Graves.

"Hey? No, just about the same. It's dead sou'-west and we're getting out of the woods, that's all. Up on those bare hills we catch the full force of it right off the Sound. Be there pretty soon now, if this Old Hundred of a horse would quit walkin' in his sleep and really move. Them lights ahead are South Denboro."

The lights were clustered at the foot of a long and rather steep hill. Down the declivity bounced and rocked the buggy. The horse's hoofs sounded hollow on the planks of a bridge. The road narrowed and became a village street, bordered and arched by tall trees which groaned and threshed in the hurricane. The rain, as it beat in over the boot, had, so the lawyer fancied, a salty taste.

The captain bent down. "Say, Mister," he shouted, "where was it you wanted to stop? Who is it you're lookin' for?"

"What?"

"I say — Heavens to Betsy! how that wind does screech! — I say where'bouts shall I land you. This is South Denboro. Whose house do you want to go to?"

"I'm looking for one of your leading citizens. Elisha Warren is his name."

"What?"

"Elisha Warren. I —"

He was interrupted. There was a sharp crack overhead, followed by a tremendous rattle and crash. Then down upon the buggy descended what, to Graves, appeared to be an avalanche of scratching, tearing twigs and branches. They ripped away the boot and laprobe and jammed him back against the seat, their sharp points against his breast. The buggy was jerked forward a few feet and stopped short.

He heard the clatter of hoofs and shouts of "Whoa!" and "Stand still!" He tried to rise, but the tangle of twigs before him seemed impenetrable, so he gave it up and remained where he was. Then, after an interval, came a hail from the darkness.

"Hi, there! Mr. Graves, ahoy! Hurt, be you?"

"No," the lawyer's tone was doubtful. "No — o, I — I guess not. That you, Captain?"

"Yes, it's me. Stand still, you foolhead! Quit your hoppin' up and down!" These commands were evidently addressed to the horse. "Glad you ain't hurt. Better get out, hadn't you?"

"I — I'm not sure that I can get out. What on earth has happened?"

"Tree limb carried away. Lucky for us we got the brush end, 'stead of the butt. Scooch down and see if you can't wriggle out underneath. I did."

Mr. Graves obediently "scooched." After a struggle he managed to slide under the tangle of branches and, at length, stood on his feet in the road beside the buggy. The great limb had fallen across the street, its heavy end near the walk. As the captain had said, it was fortunate for the travelers that the "brush" only had struck the carriage.

Graves found his companion standing at the horse's head, holding the frightened animal by the bridle. The rain was descending in a flood.

"Well!" gasped the agitated New Yorker. "I'll be hanged if this isn't —"

"Ain't it? But say, Mr. Graves, *who* did you say you was comin' to see?"

"Oh, a person named Elisha Warren. He lives in this forsaken hole somewhere, I believe. If I had known what an experience I must go through to reach him, I'd have seen him at the devil."

From the bulky figure at the horse's head came a chuckle.

"Humph! Well, Mr. Graves, if the butt of that limb had fetched us, instead of t'other end, I don't know but you *might* have seen him there. I'm Elisha Warren, and that's my house over yonder where the lights are."

CHAPTER II

"THIS is your room, Mr. Graves," said Miss Abigail Baker, placing the lighted lamp on the bureau. "And here's a pair of socks and some slippers. They belong to Elisha — Cap'n Warren, that is — but he's got more. Cold water and towels and soap are on the washstand over yonder; but I guess you've had enough *cold* water for one night. There's plenty hot in the bathroom at the end of the hall. After you change your wet things, just leave 'em spread out on the floor. I'll come fetch 'em by and by and hang 'em to dry in the kitchen. Come right downstairs when you're ready. Anything else you want? No? All right then. You needn't hurry. Supper's waited an hour 'n' a half as 'tis. 'Twon't hurt it to wait a spell longer."

She went away, closing the door after her. The bewildered, wet and shivering New Yorker stared about the room, which, to his surprise, was warm and cozy. The warmth was furnished, so he presently discovered, by a steam radiator in the corner. Radiators and a bathroom! These were modern luxuries he would have taken for granted, had Elisha Warren been the sort of man he expected to find, the country magnate, the leading citizen, fitting brother to the late A. Rodgers Warren, of Fifth Avenue and Wall Street.

But the Captain Warren who had driven him to South Denboro in the rain was not that kind of man at all. His manner and his language were as far removed from those of the late A. Rodgers as the latter's brown stone residence was from this big rambling house, with its deep stairs and narrow halls, its antiquated pictures and hideous, old-fashioned wall paper; as far removed as Miss Baker, whom the captain had hurriedly introduced as "my second cousin keepin' house for me," was from the dignified butler at the mansion on Fifth Avenue. Patchwork comforters and feather beds were not, in the lawyer's scheme of things, fit associates for radiators and up-to-date bathrooms. And certainly this particular Warren was not fitted to be elder brother to the New York broker who had been Sylvester, Kuhn and Graves' client.

It could not be, it *could* not. There must be some mistake. In country towns there were likely to be several of the same name. There must be another Elisha Warren. Comforted by this thought, Mr. Graves opened his valise, extracted therefrom other and drier articles of wearing apparel, and proceeded to change his clothes.

Meanwhile, Miss Abigail had descended the stairs to the sitting room. Before a driftwood fire in a big brick fireplace sat Captain Warren in his shirt-sleeves, a pair of mammoth carpet slippers on his feet, and the said feet stretched luxuriously out toward the blaze.

"Abbie," observed the captain, "this is solid comfort. Every time I go away from home I get into trouble, don't I? Last trip I took to Boston, I lost thirty dollars, and —"

"Lost it!" interrupted Miss Baker, tartly. "Gave it away, you mean."

"I didn't *give* it away. I lent it. Abbie, you ought to know the difference between a gift and a loan."

"I do — when there is any difference. But if lendin'

14

Tim Foster ain't givin' it away, then I miss my guess."

"Well," with another chuckle, "Tim don't feel that way. He swore right up and down that he wouldn't take a cent — as a gift. I offered to make him a present of ten dollars, but he looked so shocked that I apologized afore he could say no."

"Yes, and then *lent* him that thirty. Shocked! The only thing that would shock that good-for-nothin' is bein' set to work. What possessed you to be such a softhead, *I* don't know. When you get back a copper of that money I'll believe the millennium's struck, that's all."

"Hum! Well, I'll help you believe it — that is, if I have time afore I drop dead of heart disease. Abbie, you'd make a good lawyer; you can get up an argument out of a perfect agreement. I said the thirty dollars was lost, to begin with. But I knew Tim Foster's mother when she used to think that boy of hers was the eighth wonder of the world. And I promised her I'd do what I could for him long's I lived . . . But it seems to me we've drifted some off the course, ain't we? What I started to say was that every time I go away from home I get into trouble. Up to Boston 'twas Tim and his 'loan.' To-night it's about as healthy a sou'-wester as I've ever been out in. Dan fetched in the team, has he?"

"Yes. It's in the stable. He says the buggy dash is pretty well scratched up, and that it's a wonder you and that Graves man wa'n't killed. Who is he, anyhow?"

"Land knows, I don't."

"You don't know! Then what's he doin' here?"

"Changin' his duds, I guess. That's what I'd do if I looked as much like a drowned rat as he did."

" 'Lisha Warren! if you ain't the most *provokin'* thing! Don't be so unlikely. You know what I mean. What's he come here, to this house, for?"

" Don't know, Abbie. I didn't know he *was* comin' here till just as we got down yonder by Emery's corner. I asked him who he was lookin' for, he said ' Elisha Warren,' and then the tree caved in on us."

" 'Lisha, you — you don't s'pose 'twas a — *sign,* do you?"

" Sign?"

" Yes, a sign, a prophecy-like, a warnin' that somethin' is goin' to happen."

The captain put back his head and laughed.

" Sign somethin' *had* happened, I should think," he answered. " What's *goin'* to happen is that Pete Shuttuck'll get his buggy painted free-for-nothin', at my expense. How's supper gettin' along? Is it ready?"

" Ready? It's been ready for so long that it'll have to be got ready all over again if . . . Oh! Come right in, Mr. Graves! I hope you're drier now."

Captain Warren sprang from the chair to greet his visitor, who was standing in the doorway.

" Yes, come right in, Mr. Graves," he urged, cordially. " Set down by the fire and make yourself comf'table. Abbie'll have somethin' for us to eat in a jiffy. Pull up a chair."

The lawyer came forward hesitatingly. The doubts which had troubled him ever since he entered the house were still in his mind.

" Thank you, Captain," he said. " But before I accept more of your hospitality I feel I should be sure there is no mistake. I have come on important business, and —"

"Hold on!" The captain held up a big hand. "Don't you say another word," he commanded. "There's just one business that interests me this minute, and that's supper. There's no mistake about *that*, anyhow. Did you say 'Come ahead,' Abbie? or was you just going to? Good! Right into the dinin' room, Mr. Graves."

The dining room was long and low. The woodwork was white, the floor green painted boards, with braided rag mats scattered over them. There were old-fashioned pictures on the walls, pictures which brought shudders to the artistic soul of Atwood Graves. A broad bay window filled one side of the apartment, and in this window, on shelves and in wire baskets, were Miss Baker's cherished and carefully tended plants. As for the dining table, it was dark, old-fashioned walnut, as were the chairs.

"Set right down here, Mr. Graves," ordered the captain. "I'll try to keep you supplied with solid cargo, and Abbie'll 'tend to the moistenin'. Hope that teapot is full up, Abbie. Hot tea tastes good after you've swallered as much cold rain as Mr. Graves and I have . . . Father-we-thank-thee-for-these-mercies-set-before-us-Amen . . . How's your appetite when it comes to clam pie, Mr. Graves?"

Mr. Graves's appetite was good, and the clam pie was good. So, too, were the hot biscuits and the tea and homemade preserves and cake. Conversation during the meal was, for the most part, a monologue by the captain. He gave Miss Baker a detailed and exaggerated account of his adventures in Ostable, on board the train, and during the drive home. The housekeeper listened, fidgeting in her chair.

" 'Lisha Warren," she interrupted, "how you do talk! Rainin' so hard you had to hold the reins taut to keep the horse's head out of water so he wouldn't drown! The idea!"

"Fact," asserted Captain Warren, with a wink at his guest. "And that wa'n't the worst of it. 'Twas so dark I had to keep feelin' the buggy with my foot to be sure I was in it. Ain't that so, Mr. Graves? . . . Here! Abbie won't like to have you set lookin' at that empty plate. She's always afraid folks'll notice the gilt's wearin' off. Pass it over quick, and let me cover it with some more pie."

"Yes, and have some more tea," urged Miss Abbie. "You mustn't pay attention to what he says, Mr. Graves," she went on. "Some day he'll tell the truth by accident, and then I'll know it's time to send for the doctor."

Several times the lawyer attempted to mention the business which had brought him to the Cape, and the probability of his having made a mistake. But neither host nor housekeeper would listen.

"When you've been in South Denboro as long as I have," declared the former, "you'll understand that the time to talk business is when you can't think of anything else. Wait till we get into the settin' room. Abbie, those six or eight biscuits I've ate are gettin' lonesome. I'll take another for sociability, thank you."

But, at last, when all the biscuits but one were gone, and the cake plate looked like the Desert of Sahara, the captain pushed back his chair, rose, and led the way into the next room. Miss Baker remained to clear the table.

"Set down by the fire, Mr. Graves," urged the captain. "Nothin' like burnin' wood to look hot and comf'table, is there? It don't always make you feel that way — that's why I put in hot water heat — but for looks and sociableness you can't beat a log fire. Smoke, do you?"

"Yes. Occasionally. But, Captain Warren —"

"Here, try that. It's a cigar the Judge gave me over to Ostable. He smokes that kind reg'lar, but if you don't like it, throw it away. He ain't here to see you do it, so you won't be fined for contempt of court. I'll stick to a pipe, if you don't mind. Now we're shipshape and all taut, I cal'late. Let's see, you wanted to talk business, I believe."

"Yes, I did. But before I begin I should like to be sure you are the Elisha Warren I came from New York to interview. Is there another of that name in Denboro?"

"Um-hm. There's Warrens a-plenty all through this section of the Cape. Our family blew ashore here a hundred and fifty years ago, or such matter. My dad's name was Elisha; so was my grandfather's. Both sea cap'ns, and both dead. There's another Elisha livin' over on the shore lane."

"Indeed. Then perhaps it is he I want."

"P'raps. He's keeper of the town poorhouse. I can tell you better if you give me an idea what your business is."

"I am an attorney. And now let me ask another question, please. Have you — had you a brother in business in New York?"

"Hey?" The captain turned and looked his guest squarely in the eye. His brows drew together.

"I've got a brother in New York," he answered, slowly. "Did *he* send you here?"

"Was your brother's name A. Rodgers Warren?"

"'A. Rodgers'? No. His name is Abijah Warren,

and — Wait! His middle name is Rodgers, though. Did 'Bije send you to me?"

"A moment, Captain. Was your brother a broker?"

"Yes. His office is — or used to be on Broad Street. What —"

"You have not heard from him for some time?"

"Not for eighteen years. He and I didn't agree as well as we might. Maybe 'twas my fault, maybe 'twas his. I have my own ideas on that. If you're lookin' for 'Bije Warren's brother, Mr. Graves, I guess you've come to the right place. But *what* he sent you to me for, or what he wants — for he wants somethin', or he wouldn't have sent — I don't understand."

"Why do you think he wanted something?"

"Because he's 'Bije Warren, and I was brought up with him. When we was young ones together, he went to school and I went to work. He got the frostin' on the cake, and I got the burnt part next to the pan. He went to college, and I went to sea. He . . . However, you mustn't think I find fault with him for that. I sp'iled him as much as anybody, I guess. 'Twas later on that we . . . Well, never mind that, either. What is it he wants of me, after eighteen years?"

"He wants a good deal of you, Captain Warren. Or *did* want it."

"Did? Don't he want it now?"

"I don't know. Captain, I'm surprised that you haven't heard. It seems that I am the bearer of bad news. Your brother —"

"Is 'Bije *dead?*"

"He died ten days ago very suddenly. In a way it was a great shock to us all, yet we have known that his heart was weak. He realized it, too."

"So 'Bije is dead, hey?" Captain Elisha's face was very grave, and he spoke slowly. "Dead! Well, well, well!"

He paused and looked into the fire. Graves saw again that vague resemblance he'had caught on the train, but had forgotten. He knew now why he noticed it. Unlike as the two brothers were, unlike in almost every way, the trace of family likeness was there. This sun-burned, retired captain *was* the New York financier's elder brother. And this certainty made Mr. Graves's errand more difficult, and the cause of it more inexplicable.

Captain Elisha cleared his throat.

"Well, well!" he sighed. "So 'Bije has gone. I s'pose you think it's odd, maybe," he went on, "that I ain't more struck down by the news. In a way, I am, and, in a way, I'm mighty sorry, too. But, to speak truth, he and I have been so apart, and have had nothin' to do with each other for so long that — that, well, I've come to feel as if I didn't have a brother. And I know he felt that way. Yes, and *wanted* to feel so — I know that."

"I wouldn't say that, if I were you," observed the lawyer, gently. "I think you're mistaken there."

"I ain't mistaken. Why, look here, Mr. Graves! There was a time when I'd have got down on my knees and crawled from here to New York to help 'Bije Warren. I lent him money to start in business. Later on him and I went into partnership together on a — a fool South American speculation that didn't pan out for nothin'. I didn't care for that. I took my chance same as he did, we formed a stock company all amongst ourselves, and I've got my share of the stock somewhere yet. It may come in handy if I ever want to paper the barn. But 'twa'n't business deals of that kind that parted us, 'twas another matter. Somethin' that he did to other folks who'd trusted us and . . . Humph! this don't interest you, of course . . . Well, 'Bije was well off, I know. His wife died way back in the nineties. She was one of them fashionable women, and a hayseed salt-herrin' of a bachelor brother-in-law stuck down here in the sandheaps didn't interest her much — except as somethin' to forget, I s'pose. I used to see her name in the Boston papers occasionally, givin' parties at Newport and one thing a'nother. I never envied 'em that kind of life. I'm as well fixed as I want to be. Got some money put by for a rainy spell, comf'table house and land, best town on earth to live in and work for; I'm satisfied and always have been. I wouldn't change for nothin'. But I'm nine year older than 'Bije was — and yet I'm left alive. Hum!"

"Your brother had two children by his marriage," said Graves, after a moment of silence.

"Hey? Two children? Why, yes, I remember he did. Boy and girl, wa'n't they? I never saw 'em. They've growed up by this time, of course."

"Yes, the eldest, Caroline, is nearly twenty. The boy, Stephen, is a year younger. It is concerning those children, Captain Warren, that I have come to you."

Captain Elisha turned in his chair. "Hey?" he queried. "The children? You've come to me about 'Bije's children?"

Graves nodded. "Yes," he answered, solemnly. "That is what I meant by saying your brother had not forgotten you or wished to forget you. In spite of the estrangement, it is evident that his confidence in your judgment and integrity was supreme. His children

22

were his idols, Captain Warren, and he has left them in your charge."

The captain's pipe fell to the hearth.

"*What?*" he shouted. "Left his children to — to *me!* Mr. Graves, you're — you're out of your head — or I am!"

"No, I'm perfectly sane. I have a copy of the will here, and —"

He was interrupted by Miss Baker, who appeared at the door of the dining room. "Did you want me, 'Lisha?" she asked.

Her employer stared at her in a dazed, uncomprehending way.

"Want you?" he repeated. "Want you?"

"Yes; I heard you holler, and I thought p'raps you was callin' me."

"Hey? No, I don't want you, Abbie. . . . Holler! I shouldn't wonder! If all I did was holler, I'm surprised at myself. No, no! Run along out and shut the door. Yes, shut it. . . . Now, Mr. Graves, say that over again and say it slow."

"I say that your brother has left his two children in your care until the youngest shall become of age — twenty-one. I have a copy of his will here, and —"

"Wait, wait! let me think. Left his children to me! . . . to *me*. Mr. Graves, had 'Bije lost all his money?"

"No. He was not the millionaire that many thought him. Miss Warren and her brother will be obliged to economize somewhat in their manner of living. But, with care *and* economy, their income should be quite sufficient, without touching the principal, to —"

"Hold on again; the income, you say. What is that income?"

"Roughly speaking, a mere estimate, about twenty to twenty-five thousand yearly."

Captain Elisha had stooped to pick up the pipe he had dropped. His fingers touched it, but they did not close. Instead he straightened up in his chair as if suffering from an electric shock.

"Mr. Graves," he began; "Mr. Graves, are you cra —. No, I asked you that before. But — but twenty *thousand* a — a year! For mercy sakes, what's the principal?"

"In the neighborhood of five hundred thousand, I believe. Of course, we had no authority to investigate thoroughly. That will be a part of your duties, but —"

"S-shh! Let me soak this into my brains a little at a time. 'Bije leaves his children five hundred thousand, half a million, and — and they've got to *economize!* And I'm . . . Would you mind readin' me that will?"

The attorney drew a long envelope from his pocket, extracted therefrom a folded document, donned a pair of gold-mounted eyeglasses, and began to read aloud.

The will was short and very concise. "'I, Abijah Rodgers Warren, being of sound mind —'"

"You're sartin that part's true, are you?" broke in the captain.

Graves nodded, rather impatiently, and continued. "'Of sound mind, memory and understanding, do make, publish and declare this to be my last will and testament, in manner following, that is to say: —

"'First: — I direct my executor hereinafter named to pay my just debts and funeral expenses as soon as may be convenient after my decease.'"

"Did he owe much, think likely?" asked Captain Elisha.

" Apparently not. Very little beyond the usual bills of a household."

" Yes, yes. Grocer and butcher and baker and such-like. Well, I guess they won't have to put in a keeper. Heave ahead."

" ' Second : — I give, devise and bequeath all my estate, both real and personal, to my brother, Elisha Warren, if he survive —' "

The captain gasped. " To me? " he cried, in utter amazement. " He leaves it to *me?* 'Bije leaves — say, Mr. Graves, there's some mistake here somewhere, sure! And besides, you said —"

" Just a minute, Captain Warren, if you please. If you'll be patient and not interrupt, I'll try to make the whole matter plain."

" Well, if you can do *that,* you'll have King Solomon and all his wisdom beat a mile, that's all I've got to say. Go on."

" ' To my brother, Elisha Warren, if he survive me, *in trust,* nevertheless, for the following purpose, to wit : —

" ' To invest the same and to use the income thereof for the education and maintenance of my two children, Caroline Edgecombe Warren —' "

" Edgecombe? Named for some of his wife's folks, I presume likely. Excuse me for puttin' my oar in again. Go on."

" ' And Stephen Cole Warren —' "

" *That's* his wife, sartin. She was a Cole. I swan, I beg your pardon."

" ' Until the elder, Caroline Edgecombe Warren, shall have reached her twenty-first birthday, when one-half of the principal of said estate, together with one-half of the accumulated interest, shall be given to her, and the trust continued for the education and maintenance of my son, Stephen Cole Warren, until he shall have reached his twenty-first birthday, when I direct that the remainder be given to him.

" ' Third : — I appoint as testamentary guardian of my said children my said brother, Elisha Warren.

" ' Fourth : — I appoint as sole executor of this, my last will and testament, my said brother, Elisha Warren.

" ' Fifth : — Imposing implicit trust and confidence in Elisha Warren, my brother, I direct that he be not required to give bond for the performance of any of the affairs or trusts to which he has been herein appointed.'

" The remainder," concluded Graves, refolding the will, " is purely formal. It is dated May 15th, three years ago. Your brother, Captain Warren, evidently realized, although no one else seems to have done so, the precarious state of his health, and prepared, as every careful person should, for the great emergency."

The attorney removed his eyeglasses and rubbed them with his handkerchief. Captain Elisha sat silent, staring at the fire. After an interval, Graves spoke again.

" Of course, Captain," he went on, " my errand is now plain. I come to acquaint you with your brother's last wishes and to ascertain whether or not you are willing to accept the trust and responsibility he has laid upon you. As you doubtless know, the state provides a legal rate of reimbursement for such services as yours will — or may — be. Ahem ! "

" May be? You mean I ain't got to do this thing unless I want to ? "

" Certainly. You have the right to renounce the various appointments, in which case another executor, trustee, and guardian will be appointed. I realize, and I'm sure that your brother's children will realize, your hesitance in assuming such a responsibility over persons whom you have never even met."

"Yes, I guess we'll all realize it; you needn't worry about that. Look here, do the children know I'm elected?"

"Yes. Of course, the will has been read to them."

"Hum! I s'pose likely they was overcome with joy, wa'n't they?"

Graves bit his lip. Remembering the comments of Miss Caroline and her brother when they learned of their uncle's appointment, he had difficulty in repressing a smile.

"Well," he replied, slowly, "of course, one could scarcely expect them to rejoice. They have never seen you. In fact, I doubt if either of them knew their father had a brother, living."

"Y-e-e-s. That part don't surprise me. But the rest of it does. By the miracles of the prophets! the rest of it does! That 'Bije — 'Bije — should leave his children and their money to *me* to take care of is passin' human belief, as our old minister used to say — . . . Humph! I s'pose likely, Mr. Graves, you'd like to have me say yes or no to the thing while you're here, hey?"

Graves nodded. "It would be well to do so," he said. "The settlement of the estate must be taken in hand as soon as possible. The law so directs."

"Yes, I see that. Well, what would you advise my doin'?"

To this direct question the lawyer returned a noncommittal answer.

"I'm afraid that must be answered by yourself alone, Captain Warren," he said. "Of course, the acceptance of the trust will necessarily involve much trouble and inconvenience, especially to one of your — er — settled and — er — conservative — I judge merely from what you have said — your conservative habits. The estate is large, the investments are, doubtless, many and varied, and the labor of looking into and investigating them may require some technical skill and knowledge of finance. Yes."

"Um-hm. . . . Well, I judge that that kind of skill and knowledge could be hired, if a feller felt like payin' fair wages; hey?"

"Oh, yes, yes. Any good lawyer could attend to that, under the supervision of the executor, certainly. But there are other inconveniences to a — a —"

"Country jay like me. I understand. Go ahead."

"I mean that you would probably be required to spend much, or all, of the next two or three years in New York."

"Would, hey? I didn't know but bein' as a guardian has entire charge of the children and their money and all — I understand that's what he does have — he could direct the children fetched down to where *he* lived, if he wanted to. Am I wrong?"

"No," the lawyer's hesitancy and annoyance was plainly evident. "No-o. Of course, that *might* be done. Still, I —"

"You think that wouldn't cause no more rejoicin' than some other things have? Yes, yes; I cal'late I understand, Mr. Graves. Well, I guess you'll have to give me to-night to chew over this. I guess you will. It's come on me so sudden, 'Bije's death and all, that I want to be by myself and think. I don't want to seem unsociable or lackin' in hospitality. The whole house is yours. Help yourself to it. But when I'm caught in a clove hitch, I just have to set down and think myself out of it.

I *have* to. I was built and launched that way, I guess, and maybe you'll excuse me."

"Certainly, Captain Warren. You're quite right in wishing to deliberate on so important a matter. And, if you will excuse me in return, I believe I will go to my room. I've had a rather wearing day."

"And a damp evenin'. Yes, I'll excuse and sympathize with you, too. I'll see you to your room, and I'll hope you'll have consider'ble more sleep than I'm likely to get. Abbie! . . . Abbie! . . . Fetch Mr. Graves's lamp, won't you, please?"

It was after two the next morning before Captain Elisha rose from his chair by the fire and entered his bed chamber. Yet, when Atwood Graves came down to breakfast, he found his host in the sitting room awaiting him.

"Afore we tackle Abbie's pancakes and fishballs, Mr. Graves," said the captain, "let's get the rest of that will business off our minds. Then we can have the pancakes to take the taste out of our mouths, as you might say. And let me ask you one more question. This — er — er — Caroline and Stephen, they're used to livin' pretty well — fashionable society, and the like of that, hey?"

"Yes. Their home was on Fifth Avenue, and the family moved in the best circles."

"Hum! I should imagine life on twenty-odd thousand a year must be pretty much all circles, one everlastin' 'turn your partners.' Well, Mr. Graves, my circles down here are consider'ble smaller, but they suit me. I'm worth twenty-odd thousand myself, not in a year, but in a lifetime. I'm selectman and director in the bank and trustee of the church. When I holler 'Boo,' the South Denboro folks — some of them, anyhow — set up and take notice. I can lead the grand march down in this neighborhood once in a while, and I cal'late I'm prettier leadin' it than I would be doin' a solitaire jig for two years on the outside edge of New York's best circles. And I'm mighty sure I'm more welcome. Now my eyesight's strong enough to see through a two-foot hole after the plug's out, and I can see that you and 'Bije's children won't shed tears if I say no to that will. No offense meant, you know; just common sense, that's all."

This was plain speaking. Mr. Graves colored, though he didn't mean to, and for once could not answer offhand.

" So," continued the captain, " I'll ease your and their minds by sayin' that, the way I feel now, I probably sha'n't accept the trust. I *probably* sha'n't. But I won't say sure I won't, because — well, because 'Bije was my brother; he was that, no matter what our diff'rences may have been. And I know — I *know* that there must be some reason bigger than ' implicit trust ' and the other May-baskets for his appointin' me in his will. What that reason is I *don't* know — yet."

" Then you intend —? "

" I don't know what I intend — in the end. But for a beginnin', I cal'late to run down to New York some time durin' the next week, take a cruise 'round, and sort of look things over."

CHAPTER III

I T'S a box of a place, though, isn't it," declared Mr.
Stephen Warren, contemptuously glancing about
the library of the apartment. "A box, by George!
I think it's a blooming shame that we have to put up
with it, Sis."

Mr. Warren sprawled in the most comfortable chair
in the room, was looking out through the window, across
the wind-swept width of Central Park West, over the
knolls and valleys of the Park itself, now bare of foliage
and sprinkled with patches of snow. There was a dis-
contented look on his face, and his hands were jammed
deep in his trousers pockets.

His sister, Caroline, sat opposite to him, also looking
out at the December landscape. She, too, was dis-
contented and unhappy, though she tried not to show
it.

"Why don't you say something," snapped Stephen,
after a moment of silence. "*Isn't* it a box of a place?
Now come."

"Yes," replied the young lady, without looking at her
brother. "Yes, Steve, I suppose it is. But you must
remember that we must make the best of it. I always
wondered how people could live in apartments. Now
I suppose I shall have to find out."

"Well, I maintain that we don't have to. We aren't
paupers, even though father wasn't so well fixed as everyone thought. With management and care, we could
have stayed in the old house, I believe, and kept up ap-

31

pearances, at least. What's the use of advertising that we're broke?"

"But, Steve, you know Mr. Graves said—"

"Oh, yes, I know. You swallowed every word Graves said, Caro, as if he was the whole book of Proverbs. By George, *I* don't; I'm from Missouri."

Mr. Warren, being in the Sophomore class at Yale, was of the age when one is constitutionally "from Missouri." Probably King Solomon, at sixty, had doubts concerning the scope and depth of his wisdom; at eighteen he would have admitted its all-embracing infallibility without a blush.

"I tell you," continued Stephen, "there's no sense in it, Sis. You and I know plenty of people whose incomes are no larger than ours. Do they 'economize,' as Graves is continually preaching? They do not, publicly at least. They may save a bit, here and there, but they do it where it doesn't show and nobody knows. Take the Blaisdells, for instance. When the Sodality Bank went up, and old Blaisdell died, everybody said the family was down and out. They must have lost millions. But did *they* move into 'apartments' and put up a placard, 'Home of the Dead-Brokes. Walk in and Sympathize?' I guess they didn't! They went into mourning, of course, and that let them out of entertaining and all that, but they stayed where they were and kept up the bluff. That's the thing that counts in this world — keeping up the bluff."

"Yes, but everyone knows they are — bluffing, as you call it."

"What of it? They don't really know, they only suspect. And I met Jim Blaisdell yesterday and he shook my hand, after I had held it in front of his eyes where he couldn't help seeing it, and had the nerve to tell me he hoped things weren't as bad with us as he had heard."

"I never liked the Blaisdells," declared Caroline, indignantly.

"Neither did I. Neither do most people. But Jim is just as much in the swim as he ever was, and he's got his governor's place on the board of directors at the bank, now that it's reorganized, and an office down town, and he's hand and glove with Von Blarcom and all the rest. They think he's a promising, plucky young man. They'll help his bluff through. And are his mother and sister dropped by the people in their set? I haven't noticed it."

"Well, Mrs. Corcoran Dunn told me that everyone was talking about the Blaisdells and wondering how long they could keep it up. And the newspapers have been printing all sorts of things, and hinting that young Mr. Blaisdell's appointment as director, after his father wrecked the bank, was a scandal. At least, we haven't *that* to bear up under. Father was honest, if he wasn't rich."

"Who cares for the newspapers? They're all run by demagogues hunting sensations. What makes me feel the worst about all this is that Stock Exchange seat of father's. If I were only of age, so that I could go down there on the floor, I tell you it wouldn't be long before you and I were back where we belong, Sis. But, no, I'm a kid, so Graves thinks, in charge of a guardian — a *guardian,* by gad!"

He snorted, in manly indignation. Caroline, her pretty face troubled, rose and walked slowly across the room. It was a large room, in spite of the fact that it was one of a suite in an apartment hotel, and furnished richly. A. Rodgers Warren spent his money with taste, and spent it freely while he lived. The furniture, the paintings, and bric-a-brac were of the very best, chosen with care, here and abroad.

"Oh, dear!" sighed the girl. "I do hope Mr. Graves will be well enough to call to-day. He expected to. Except for the telephone message telling us that that *man* at Denboro —"

"Our dear Uncle Elisha," put in Stephen, with sarcasm. "Uncle ''Lish!' Heavens! what a name!"

"Hush! He can't help his name. And father's was worse yet — Abijah! Think of it!"

"I don't want to think of it. Neither did the governor; that's why he dropped it, I suppose. Just what did Graves say? Give me his exact words."

"His partner, Mr. Kuhn, telephoned. He said that Mr. Graves had a bad cold, having been wet through in a dreadful storm down there in the country. The doctor forbade his leaving the house for a day or two, but he would call on Tuesday — to-day — if he was sufficiently recovered. And Mr. Kuhn said that everything was satisfactory. This Captain Warren — a ship captain, I suppose he is — would, in all probability, refuse to accept the guardianship and the rest of it —"

"Refuse? I should think so. I'm just as certain father was insane when he made that will as I am that I'm alive. If I thought he wasn't, I'd never forgive him."

"Hush, Steve. You promised me you wouldn't speak in that way."

"Well, all right, I won't. But, Caro, he *must* have been insane. If he wasn't, do you suppose he would have put us and the estate in the care of a Down-East jay? It's inconceivable! It's ridiculous! Think of it. Suppose this uncle of ours had accepted. Suppose he had come to town here and any of our friends had met him. ' This is our guardian, Captain Warren, of Punkin Centre.' ' Please to meet ye,' says Uncle 'Lish. ' How's taters?' Horrors! Say, Caro, you haven't told anyone, Malcolm or his mother, or anyone, have you?"

"Of course not, Steve. You know I wouldn't."

"Well, don't. They needn't know it, now or at any other time. Graves will probably get himself appointed, and he's respectable if he is an old fogy. We'll worry along till I'm twenty-one, and then — well, then I'll handle our business myself."

Evidently there was no question in his mind as to his ability to handle this or any business, no matter how involved. He rose from his chair and yawned.

"It's deadly dull," he complained. "You don't need me, do you, Caro? I believe I'll go out for a while. That is, unless you really care."

His sister hesitated before replying. When she spoke, there was disappointment in her tone.

"Why, Steve," she said, "I did hope you might be here when Mr. Graves came. He will wish to speak of important matters, and it seems to me that both of us should hear what he has to say."

Young Warren, who had started for the door, stopped and kicked impatiently at the corners of the rug.

"Oh, well!" he observed, "if you want me of course I'll stay. But why doesn't old Graves come, if he is coming. Maybe he's under the weather yet," he added, hopefully. "Perhaps he isn't coming at all to-day. I believe I'll call up Kuhn on the 'phone and find out."

He was on his way to the telephone when the doorbell buzzed.

"Gad! there he is now," he exclaimed. "Now I sup-

35

pose I'll have to stay. We'll hear about dear Uncle 'Lish, won't we? Oh, joy!"

But the staid butler, when he entered the library, did not announce the lawyer's name.

"Mrs. Corcoran Dunn and Mr. Malcolm," he said. "Will you see them, Miss Caroline?"

The young lady's face lit up.

"Certainly, Edwards," she said. "Show them — Oh, Mrs. Dunn, I'm so glad to see you! It was *ever* so good of you to come. And Malcolm."

Mrs. M. Corcoran Dunn was tall and, in South Denboro, would have been called "fleshy," in spite of her own and the dressmaker's efforts to conceal the fact. She was elaborately gowned and furred, and something about her creaked when she walked. She rushed into the room, at the butler's heels, and, greeting Caroline with outstretched hands, kissed her effusively on the cheek.

"My dear child," she cried, "how could I stay away? We have spoken of you and Stephen *so* often this morning. We know how lonely you must be, and Malcolm and I decided we *must* run in on you after lunch. Didn't we, Malcolm?"

Mr. Malcolm Corcoran Dunn, her son, was a blond young man, with a rather indolent manner.

"Sure, Mater!" he said, calmly. "How d'ye do, Caroline? 'Lo, Steve!"

The quartette shook hands. Mrs. Dunn sank creakingly into a chair and gazed about the room. Malcolm strolled to the window and looked out. Stephen followed and stood beside him.

"My dear," said Mrs. Dunn, addressing Caroline, "how are you getting on? How are your nerves? Is all the dreadful 'settling' over?"

"Very nearly, thank goodness."

"That's a mercy. I should certainly have been here yesterday to help you in superintending and arranging and so on, but I was suffering from one of my 'hearts,' and you know what *they* are."

Everyone who knew Mrs. Corcoran Dunn was acquainted with her "hearts." The attacks came, so she was accustomed to explain, from an impaired valve, and "some day"— she usually completed the sentence with upturned eyes and a resigned upward wave of the hand.

Her son turned from the window.

"I say, Mother," he explained, wearily, "I do wish you wouldn't speak of your vital organs in the plural. Anyone would imagine you were a sort of freak, like the two-headed boy at the circus. It's positively distressing."

Stephen laughed. He admired young Dunn immensely. Mrs. Dunn sighed.

"Don't, Malcolm, dear," she pleaded. "You sound so unfeeling. One not acquainted with your real kindness of heart —"

"Oh, drop it," interrupted Malcolm. "Let's omit the heart interest. This isn't a clinic. I say, Steve, how do you like the new flat? It is a flat, isn't it?"

Stephen turned red. His sister colored and bit her lip. Mrs. Dunn hastened to the rescue.

"Horrors!" she exclaimed. "Malcolm, you really are insufferable. Flat! Caroline, dear, you mustn't mind him. He will have his joke. Malcolm, apologize."

The command was sharp, and her son obeyed it.

"Beg your pardon, Steve," he said. "Yours, too, Caroline. I was only joking. There's a little beast of a bookkeeper down at the office who is forever talking of his 'nice flat in the Bronx.' It's a standing guy, you know. So far as I can see, these are pretty snug quarters. And attractively arranged, too. Your taste, Caroline, I'm betting."

Miss Warren, slightly mollified, bowed assent.

"I thought so," continued Malcolm. "No one but you would have known exactly the right spot for everything. Show us through, won't you?"

But Mrs. Dunn had other plans.

"Not now, Malcolm," she put in. "Caroline is tired out, I'm sure. A little fresh air will do her good. I was going to suggest that you and she and Stephen go for a short ride. Yes, really you must, my dear," she added, turning to the girl beside her. "Our car is at the door, it's not at all a bad afternoon, and the outing will be just what you need."

"Thank you, Mrs. Dunn," said Caroline, gratefully. "I should like to. Indeed, I should. But we have been expecting a business call from Mr. Graves, father's lawyer, and —"

"Oh, come on, Sis!" interrupted Stephen. "I'm dying to get out of this jail. Let old Graves wait, if he comes. We won't be long; and, besides, it's not certain that he is coming to-day. Come on!"

"I'm afraid I ought not, Steve. Mr. Graves may come, and — and it seems too bad to trouble our friends —"

"It's not trouble, it's pleasure," urged Mrs. Dunn. "Malcolm will be delighted. It was his idea. Wasn't it?" turning to her son.

"Oh, yes! certainly," replied the young gentleman. "Hope you'll come, Caroline. And you, of course, Steve. The blessed machine's been off its feed for a week or more, but Peter says he thinks it's all right again. We'll give it a try-out on the Drive. Hope we have better luck than my last," with a laugh. "They nabbed us for speeding, and I had to promise to be a good boy or to be fined. Said we were hitting it at fifty an hour. We *were* going some, that's a fact. Ha! ha!"

"But he won't be reckless when you're with him, Caroline," put in his mother. "You will go? That's so nice! As for Mr. Graves, I'll explain if he comes. Oh, no! *I'm* not going! I shall remain here in this comfortable chair and rest until you return. It's exactly what my physician orders, and for once I'm going to obey him. My heart, you know, my poor heart—"

She waved her hand and raised her eyes. Miss Warren expostulated, but to no purpose. Mrs. Corcoran Dunn would *not* go, but the others must. So, at last, they did. When Caroline and her brother had gone for their wraps, Mrs. Dunn laid a hand on her son's arm.

"Now mind," she whispered, "see if you can find out anything during the ride. Something more explicit about the size of their estate and who the guardian is to be. There are all sorts of stories, you know, and we *must* learn the truth very soon. Don't appear curious, but merely friendly. You understand?"

"Sure, Mater," was the careless answer. "I'll pump."

The two departed, leaving their lady visitor ensconced in the comfortable chair. She remained in it for perhaps five minutes. Then she rose and sauntered about the room. She drifted into the drawing-room, returning a moment later and sauntering casually toward the open desk by the fireplace. There were papers and letters scattered about this desk, and these she turned over, glancing toward the door to be sure no one was coming. The letters were, for the most part, messages of sympathy from friends of the Warren family. Hearing an approaching step, she hastily returned to the chair.

Edwards, the butler, entered the library and replenished the fire. Mrs. Dunn languidly accosted him.

"Ah — er — Edwards," she said, "you are — er — growing familiar with your new home?"

"Yes, ma'am," replied Edwards, politely.

"It must seem — er — small compared to the other."

"Smaller; yes, ma'am."

"But very snug and comfortable."

"Yes, ma'am."

"It is fortunate that Miss Warren and her brother have the aid of such a — an old servant of the family."

"Thank you, ma'am."

"Is Miss Caroline managing her own affairs?"

"Apparently so. Yes, ma'am."

"I presume, however, a guardian has been appointed? With an estate such as the late Mr. Warren *must* have left, some responsible person would be, of course, necessary."

She paused. Edwards, having arranged the logs to his liking, brushed the dust from his hands.

"I don't know, ma'am, I'm sure," he said. "Neither Miss Caroline nor Mr. Stephen have spoken with me concerning the family affairs."

Mrs. Corcoran Dunn straightened, with hauteur.

"I think that was the doorbell," she remarked, a trifle sharply. "If it should be Mr. Graves, the attorney, you may show him into the library here."

"Yes, ma'am," said Edwards once more, and departed.

The lady visitor heard voices in the passage. She listened, but could hear nothing understandable. Evidently the butler was having an argument with someone. It could not be Graves.

Edwards reappeared, looking troubled.

"It's a — a gentleman to see Miss Caroline," he said.

"He won't give his name, ma'am, but says she's expecting him."

"Expecting him?"

"Yes, ma'am. I told him she was out, but he said he was intending to stay a while anyway, and would wait. I asked his business, but he wouldn't tell it."

"That's odd." Mrs. Dunn was slightly interested. "A tradesman, perhaps; or an agent of the landlord."

"No-o, ma'am. I don't think he's either of them, ma'am."

"What sort of a person is he, Edwards?"

The butler's face twitched for an instant with a troubled smile. Then it resumed its customary respectful calm.

"I hardly know, ma'am. He's an oddish man. He —I think he's from the country."

From behind him came a quiet chuckle.

"You're right, Commodore," said a man's voice; "I'm from the country. You guessed it."

Edwards jumped, startled out of his respectable wits. Mrs. Dunn rose indignantly from her chair.

"I beg your pardon, ma'am," said the intruder, appearing in the doorway. "You mustn't think I'm forcin' my way where I ain't wanted. But it seemed to take so long to make the Admiral here understand that I was goin' to wait until Caroline came back that I thought I'd save time and breath by provin' it to him. I didn't know there was any company. Excuse me, ma'am, I won't bother you. I'll just come to anchor out here in the entry. Don't mind me."

He bowed politely, picked up the large suit-case, plainly bran-new, which he had momentarily placed on the rug at his feet, and, with it in one hand and a big soft felt hat in the other, stepped back into the hall out of sight. The astonished Mrs. Dunn and the paralyzed Edwards heard a chair crack as if a heavy weight had descended upon it. Evidently he had "come to anchor."

The lady was the first to recover the power of speech. "Why!" she exclaimed, in an alarmed whisper. "Why! I never heard of such brazen impertinence in my life. He must be insane. He is a lunatic, isn't he, Edwards?"

The butler shook his head. "I — I don't know, ma'am," he stammered.

"I believe he is." Mrs. Dunn's presence of mind was returning, and with it her courage. Her florid cheeks flamed a more vivid red, and her eyes snapped. "But whether he is or not, he sha'n't bulldoze me."

She strode majestically to the door. The visitor was seated in the hall, calmly reading a newspaper. Hat and suit-case were on the floor beside him.

"What do you mean by this?" demanded the lady. "Who are you? If you have any business here, state it at once."

The man glanced at her, over his spectacles, rose and stood looking down at her. His expression was pleasant, and he was remarkably cool.

"Yes, ma'am," he said, gravely. "I'll be glad to tell you who I am, if you'd like to have me. I'd have done it before, but I thought there weren't any use troublin' you with my affairs. But, just a minute —" he hesitated —" I haven't made any mistake, have I? I understood your steward — the feller with the brass buttons, to say that Abijah Warren's children lived here. That's so, ain't it? If not, then I *am* mistaken."

Mrs. Dunn regarded him with indignation. "You are," she said coldly. "The family of the late Mr.

Rodgers Warren lives here. I presume the slight resemblance in names misled you. Edwards, show the gentleman out."

"Just one moment more, ma'am. It was Rodgers Warren's children I was lookin' for. A. Rodgers Warren he called himself, didn't he? Yes. Well, the A stood for Abijah; that was his Christian name. And he left two children, Caroline and Stephen? Good! I thought for a jiffy I'd blundered in where I had no business, but it's all right. You see, ma'am, I'm their uncle from South Denboro, Massachusetts. My name is Elisha Warren."

Mrs. Dunn gasped. Edwards, peering over her shoulder, breathed heavily.

"You are — their *uncle?*" repeated the lady.

"Yes, ma'am. I'm 'Bije's brother. Oh, don't worry. It's all right. And don't fret yourself about me, either. I'll set right down out here and read my paper and wait till Caroline or Stephen get home. They're expectin' me. Mr. Graves, the lawyer, told 'em I was comin'."

He calmly seated himself and adjusted his spectacles. Mrs. Dunn stared at him, then at Edwards. After an instant's indecision, she stepped back into the library and walked to the window. She beckoned, with an agitated finger, to the butler, who joined her.

"Edwards," she whispered, "did you hear what he said?"

"Yes, ma'am," replied Edwards, wide-eyed and wondering.

"Is it true?"

"I don't know, ma'am."

"Did Mr. Warren have a brother?"

"I didn't know that he had, ma'am."

"Do you — do you think it likely that he would have a brother like — like *that?*"

"I don't know, ma'am."

"Was Miss Caroline expecting him?"

"I don't know, ma'am. She —"

"Oh, you don't know anything! You're impossible. Go away!"

"Yes, ma'am," said Edwards thankfully; and went.

Mrs. Corcoran Dunn stood for some minutes by the window, thinking, or trying to think a way to the truth in this astounding development. Of course the man *might* be a lunatic who had gained his information concerning the Warren family from the papers; but he did not look like a lunatic. On the other hand, he certainly did not look as one would have expected a brother of Rodgers Warren's to look. Oddest of all, if he was such a brother, why had neither Caroline or Stephen mentioned his existence? According to his story, Graves, the Warren lawyer, had warned the children of his coming. Caroline had been very reticent concerning her father's will, the amount of his estate, and the like. And Mrs. Dunn had repeatedly, though discreetly, endeavored to find out these important details. Neither hints nor questions had resulted satisfactorily. Was it possible that this was the reason, this country uncle? If so — well, if so, here was a Heaven-sent opportunity for a little genteel and perfectly safe detective work. Mrs. Dunn creakingly crossed the room and spoke.

"Mr. Warren," she said, "I feel guilty in keeping you out there. Won't you come into the library?"

"Why, thank you, ma'am, I'm all right. Don't you trouble about me. Go right on with your readin' or sewin' or knittin' or whatever you was doin' and —"

44

"I was not — reading," replied Mrs. Dunn, with a slight shudder. "Come in, please. I wish you to."

Captain Elisha folded his paper and put it in his pocket. Entering the library, he stood quietly waiting.

"Won't you sit down?" asked his impromptu hostess, trying hard to be gracious.

"Thank you," said the captain. He sank into an arm-chair and looked curiously about him.

"So you are the late Mr. Warren's brother?" asked the lady, making her first lead in the game.

"Yes, ma'am. His older brother. 'Bije was ten year younger'n I am, Mrs.— er —"

"Dunn. I am an old friend of the family."

"That's good. I'm glad to hear they've got friends. When you're in sickness or trouble or sorrer, friendship counts for consider'ble. How are the young folks — Caroline and Stephen — pretty smart, hey?"

"*Smart?* Why, they are intelligent, naturally. I —"

"No, no. I mean are they pretty well?"

"Very well, indeed, considering the shock of their recent bereavement."

"Yes, yes. Of course. And they've moved, too. Movin's an awful job. They say three movin's are as bad as a fire, but I cal'late I'd rather burn up a set of carpets than *pull* 'em up, 'specially if they was insured. 'Tain't half so much strain on your religion. I remember the last time we took up our carpets at home, Abbie — she's my second cousin, keepin' house for me — said if gettin' down on my knees has that effect on me she'd never ask me to go to prayer-meetin' again. Ho! ho!"

He chuckled. Mrs. Dunn elevated her nose and looked out of the window. Then she led another small trump.

"You say that Miss Caroline and her brother expect you," she said. "You surprise me. Are you sure?"

"Oh, yes, ma'am. I'm sure. When Mr. Graves came down to see me, last week 'twas, I told him to say I'd be up pretty soon to look the ground over. This is a pretty fine place the young folks have got here," he added, gazing admiringly at the paintings and bookcases.

"Yes," assented the lady, condescendingly. "For an apartment it is really quite livable."

"Livable!" Captain Elisha's astonishment got the better of his politeness for the moment. "Um! Yes, I should say a body *might* manage to worry along in it. Was the place where they used to live any finer than this?"

"Certainly!"

"You don't tell me! No wonder they talked about economi — Humph!"

"What were you about to say, Mr. Warren?"

"Oh, nothin', nothin'! Talkin' to myself is a habit I've got. Abbie — my second cousin; I guess I told you about her — says it's a sure sign that a person's rich or out of his head, one or t'other. I ain't rich, so —" He chuckled once more.

"Mr. Graves came to see you at your home, did he?"

"Yes, ma'am. At South Denboro. And he certainly did have a rough passage. Ho! ho! Probably you heard about it, bein' so friendly with the family."

"Ahem! Doubtless he would have mentioned it, but he has been ill."

"Sho! I'm sorry to hear that. I was afraid he'd catch cold."

"Yes. I hope Mr. Graves's errand was successful?"

"Well, sort of so-so."

46

"Yes. He came to see you in connection with your brother's estate — some legacy, perhaps?"

She did not look at the captain when she asked this question. Therefore, she did not notice the glance which he gave her. When he answered, it was in the same deliberate, provokingly deliberate, manner.

"Um-hm. Somethin' of that kind, Mrs. Dunn. I can't help thinkin'," he went on, "how nice it is that Caroline and Steve have such a good friend as you to help 'em. Your husband and 'Bije was chums, I s'pose?"

"No, not exactly. The friendship was on my side of the family."

"So? Want to know! Your husband dead, ma'am?"

Mrs. Dunn changed the subject. Her husband, Mr. Corcoran Dunn — once Mike Dunn, contractor and Tammany politician — was buried in Calvary Cemetery. She mourned him, after a fashion, but she preferred not to talk about him.

"Yes," she answered shortly. "It — it looks as if it might snow, doesn't it?"

"I shouldn't wonder. Have you any children, ma'am?"

"One — a son." The widow's tone was frigid.

"So? He must be a comfort to you. I s'pose likely he's a friend of my nephew and niece, too."

"Certainly."

"That's good. Young folks ought to have young friends. You live in this neighborhood, ma'am?"

The lady did not answer. She gazed haughtily at the trees in the Park. Captain Elisha rubbed a smile from his lips with his hand and remained silent. The tall clock ticked loud.

There came the sound of laughter from the passage

47

outside. The hall door opened. A moment later, Caroline, followed by her brother and young Dunn, entered the library.

The girl's cheeks were rosy from the cold wind. Her hair, beneath the fur auto cap, had blown in brown, rippled disorder across her forehead. She was smiling.

"Oh, Mrs. Dunn!" she cried. "I'm so glad I accepted your — Malcolm's — invitation. We had a glorious ride! I —"

She stopped short. Captain Warren had risen from his chair and was facing her. Mrs. Dunn also rose.

"Caroline," she said, nervously, "this "— pausing on the word —" gentleman is here to see you. He says he is —"

The captain interrupted her. Stepping forward he seized his niece's hands in his. "Well, well!" he exclaimed admiringly. "'Bije's girl, that I ain't seen since you was a little mite of a baby! Caroline, I'm your Uncle Elisha."

"Good *Lord!*" groaned Stephen Warren.

CHAPTER IV

IF the captain heard Stephen's fervent ejaculation, he paid no attention to it. Dropping his niece's hand, he extended his own toward his nephew.

"And this is Stephen?" he said. "Well, Steve, you and me have never met afore, I b'lieve. But that's our misfortune, not our fault, hey? How are you? Pretty smart?"

The boy's face was flaming. He mumbled something to the effect that he was all right enough, and turned away without accepting the proffered hand. Captain Elisha glanced quickly at him, then at his sister.

"Well, Caroline," he said, pleasantly, "I s'pose you've been expectin' me. Mr. Graves told you I was comin', didn't he?"

Miss Warren, also, was flushed with embarrassment and mortified surprise.

"No," she stammered. "He has been ill."

"Sho! you don't say! Mrs. Dunn — your friend here — said he was laid up with a cold, but I didn't realize 'twas as bad as that. So you didn't know I was comin' at all."

"No. We — we have not heard from you since he returned."

"That's too bad. I hope I sha'n't put you out any, droppin' in on you this way. You mustn't treat me as comp'ny, you know. If 'tain't convenient, if your spare room ain't ready so soon after movin', or anything of that kind, I can go to a hotel somewheres for a day or so. Hadn't I better, don't you think?"

Caroline hesitated. If only they might have been spared this public humiliation. If the Dunns had not been there. It was bad enough to have this dreadful country uncle come at all; but to have him come now, before they were prepared, before any explanations had been made! What should she do?

Her brother, fidgeting at her elbow, not daring to look at Malcolm Dunn, who, he knew, was thoroughly enjoying the scene, could stand it no longer.

"Caro," he snapped, "what are you waiting for? Don't you *know* that the rooms are not ready? Of course they're not! We're sorry, and all that, but Graves didn't tell us and we weren't prepared. Certainly he'll have to go to the hotel, for — for the present."

He ventured to raise his eyes and glare indignantly at the captain. Finding the latter looking intently at him, he dropped them again and jammed his clenched fists into his pockets.

Captain Elisha pulled thoughtfully at his beard.

"Humph!" he grunted. "Humph! then I cal'late maybe —" He took a step toward the door, stopped, turned back, and said, with calm decision, "I guess I'd better stay. You won't mind me, Caroline — you and Stephen. You *mustn't*. As I said, I ain't comp'ny. I'm one of the family, your pa's brother, and I've come some consider'ble ways to see you two young folks and talk with you. I've come because your pa asked me to. I'm used to roughin' it, been to sea a good many v'yages, and if a feather bed ain't handy I can get my forty winks on the floor. So that's settled, and you mustn't have me on your conscience. That's sense, ain't it, Mrs. Dunn?"

Mrs. Corcoran Dunn did not deign a reply. Caroline answered for her.

"Very well," she said, coldly. Stepping to the desk she rang a bell. The butler appeared in the doorway.

"Edwards," said Miss Warren, "this gentleman," indicating the captain, "is to be our guest, for the present. You may show him to his room — the blue room, I think. If it is not ready, see that it is made so."

"Yes, Miss Caroline," replied Edwards. Retiring to the hall, he returned with the suit-case.

"Will you wish to go to your room at once, sir?" he asked.

"Why, I guess I might as well, Commodore," answered Captain Elisha, smiling. "Little soap and water won't do no harm. Fact is, I feel's if 'twas a prescription to be recommended. You needn't tote that valise, though," he added. "'Tain't heavy, and I've lugged it so fur already sence I got off the car that I feel kind of lonesome without it."

The butler, not knowing exactly how to answer, grinned sheepishly. Captain Elisha turned to Mrs. Dunn and her son.

"Well, good afternoon, ma'am," he said. "I'm real glad to have made your acquaintance. Yours, too, sir," with a nod toward Malcolm. "Your mother told me what a friend of the young folks you was, and, as I'm sort of actin' pilot for 'em just now, in a way of speakin', any friend of theirs ought to be a friend of mine. Hope to see you often, Mr. Dunn."

The young man addressed smiled, with amusement not at all concealed, and languidly admitted that he was "charmed."

"Your first visit to the city?" he inquired, in a tone which caused Stephen to writhe inwardly.

"No-o. No, not exactly. I used to come here pretty frequent, back in my sea-goin' days, when my ship was in port. I sailed for Osgood and Colton, down on South Street, for a spell. They were my owners. You don't remember the firm, I s'pose?"

"No. The privilege has been denied me. You find some changes in New York, don't you — er — Captain? You are a captain, or a bos'n, or admiral — something of that sort, I presume?"

"Malcolm!" said his mother, sharply.

"Oh, no offense intended. My sea terms are rather mixed. The captain will excuse me."

"Sartin! Cap'n's what they all call me, mostly. Your son ain't ever been to sea, except as passenger, I cal'late, ma'am?"

"Certainly not," snapped Mrs. Dunn.

"Of course, of course. Well, 'tain't a life I'd want a boy of mine to take up, nowadays. But it did have some advantages. I don't know anything better than a v'yage afore the mast to learn a young feller what's healthy for him to unlearn. Good day, ma'am. Good day, Mr. Dunn. I mustn't keep the Commodore waitin' here with that valise. I'll be out pretty soon, Caroline; just as soon as I've got the upper layer of railroad dust off my face and hands. You'll be surprised to see how light-complected I really am when that's over. All right! Heave ahead, Commodore!"

He departed, preceded by Edwards and the suit-case. Stephen Warren threw himself violently into a chair by the window. Young Dunn laughed aloud. His mother flashed an indignant glance at him, and then hurried to Caroline.

"You poor dear!" she exclaimed, putting an arm about the girl's shoulder. "Don't mind us, please don't!

Malcolm and I understand. That is, we know how you feel and —"

" Oh, but you *don't* know, Mrs. Dunn," cried Caroline, almost in tears. " You don't understand! It's so much worse than you think. I — I — Oh, why did father do it? How could he be so inconsiderate?"

" There! there!" purred the friend of the family. " You mustn't, you know. You really mustn't. Who is this man? This uncle? Where does he come from? Why does he force himself upon you in this way? I didn't know your poor father had a brother."

" Neither did we," growled Stephen, savagely. Malcolm laughed again.

" What does it all mean, dear?" begged Mrs. Dunn. " You are in trouble, I'm sure. Don't you think we — Malcolm and I — might be able to help you? We should so love to do it. If you feel that you *can* confide in us; if it isn't a secret —"

She paused expectantly, patting the girl's shoulder. But Caroline had heard young Dunn's laugh, and was offended and hurt. Her eyes flashed as she answered.

" It's nothing," she said. " He has come to see us on a matter of business, I believe. I am nervous and — foolish, I suppose. Mr. Graves will see us soon, and then everything will be arranged. Thank you for calling, Mrs. Dunn, and for the ride."

It was a very plain hint, but Mrs. Dunn did not choose to understand it as such.

" You're sure you hadn't better tell me the whole story, dear?" she urged. " I am old enough, almost, to be your mother, and perhaps my advice might . . . No? Very well. You know best but — You understand that it is something other than mere curiosity which leads me to ask."

"Of course, I understand," said the girl hastily. "Thank you very much. Perhaps, by and by, I can tell you everything. But we must see Mr. Graves first. I — oh, *don't* ask me more now, Mrs. Dunn."

The widow of so astute a politician as Mike Dunn had been in his day could have scarcely failed to profit by his teachings. Moreover, she possessed talent of her own. With a final pat and a kiss, she prepared for departure.

"Good-by, then," she said, "or rather, *au revoir*. We shall look in to-morrow. Come, Malcolm."

"I say, Mal!" cried Stephen, rising hurriedly. "You won't tell anyone about —"

"Steve!" interrupted his sister.

Malcolm, about to utter a languid sarcasm, caught his mother's look, and remained silent. Another meaning glance, and his manner changed.

"All right, Steve, old man," he said. "Good-by and good luck. Caroline, awfully glad we had the spin this afternoon. We must have more. Just what you and Steve need. At your service any time. If there is anything I can do in any way to — er — you understand — call on me, won't you? Ready, Mater?"

The pair were shown out by Edwards. On the way home in the car Mrs. Corcoran Dunn lectured her son severely.

"Have you no common sense?" she demanded. "Couldn't you see that the girl would have told me everything if you hadn't laughed, like an idiot?"

The young man laughed again.

"By Jove!" he exclaimed, "it was enough to make a wooden Indian laugh. The old jay with the barnacles telling us about the advantages of a sailor's life. And Steve's face! Ho! ho!"

His mother snorted disgust. "If you had brains," she

declared, "you would have understood what he meant by saying that the sea was the place to learn what to unlearn. He was hitting at you. Was it necessary to insult him the first time you and he exchanged a word?"

"Insult him? *Him?* Ha, ha! Why, Mater, what's the matter with you? Do you imagine that a hayseed like that would recognize an insult without an introduction? And, besides, what difference does it make? You don't intend putting him on your calling list, do you?"

"I intend cultivating him for the present."

"*Cultivating* him?"

"Yes — for the present. He is Rodgers Warren's brother. That lawyer, Graves, traveled miles to see him. What does that mean? That, in some important way, he is connected with the estate and those two children. If the estate is worth anything, and we have reason to believe it is, you and I must know it. If it isn't, it is even more important that we should know, before we waste more time. If Caroline is an heiress, if she inherits even a moderate fortune —"

She shrugged her shoulders by way of finish to the sentence.

Malcolm whistled.

"But to think of that old Down-Easter being related to the Warren family!" he mused. "It seems impossible."

"Nothing is impossible," observed his mother. Then, with a shudder, "You never met your father's relatives. I have."

When Captain Elisha emerged from his room, after a wash and a change of linen, he found the library untenanted. He strolled about, his hands behind him, inspecting the pictures with critical interest. Caroline, dressed for dinner, found him thus engaged. He turned at the sound of her step.

"Why, hello!" he cried, with hearty enthusiasm. "All rigged up for inspection, ain't you?"

"Inspection?"

"Oh, that's just sailor's lingo. Means you've got your Sunday uniform on, that's all. My! my! how nice you look! But ain't black pretty old for such a young girl?"

"I am in mourning," replied his niece, coldly.

"There! there! of course you are. Tut! tut! How could I forget it. You see, I've been so many years feelin' as if I didn't have a brother that I've sort of got used to his bein' gone."

"I have not." Her eyes filled as she said it. The captain was greatly moved.

"I'm a blunderin' old fool, my dear," he said. "I beg your pardon. Do try to forgive me, won't you? And, perhaps — perhaps I can make up your loss to you, just a little mite. I'd like to. I'll try to, if —"

He laid a hand on her shoulder. She avoided him and, moving away, seated herself in a chair at the opposite side of the desk. The avoidance was so obvious as to be almost brutal. Captain Elisha looked very grave for an instant. Then he changed the subject.

"I was lookin' at your oil paintin's," he said. "They're pretty fine, ain't they? Any of them your work, Caroline?"

"My work?" The girl's astonishment was so great that she turned to stare at her questioner. "My work?" she repeated. "Are you joking? You can't think that I painted them."

"I didn't know but you might. That one over there,

56

with the trees and folks dancin'— sort of picnic scene, I judge — that looks as if you might have done it."

" That is a Corot."

" 'Tis, hey? I want to know! A — a — what did you call it?"

" A Corot. He was a famous French artist. That was father's favorite picture."

" Sho! Well, I like it fust-rate myself. Did 'Bije — did your father know this Mr. Corot well?"

" Know him? Certainly not. Why should you think such a thing as that?"

" Well, he bought the picture of him, and so I s'pose likely he knew him. There was a young feller come to South Denboro three or four year ago and offered to paint a picture of our place for fifteen dollars. Abbie — that's Abbie Baker, she's one of our folks, you know, your third cousin, Caroline; keepin' house for me, she is — Abbie wanted me to have him do the job, but I wa'n't very particular about it, so it never come to nothin'. He done two or three places, though, and I swan 'twas nice work! He painted Sam Cahoon's old ramshackle house and barn, and you'd hardly know it, 'twas so fixed up and fine, in the picture. White paint and green grass and everything just like real. He left out the places where the pickets was off the fence and the blinds hangin' on one hinge. I told Abbie, I says, ' Abbie, that painter's made Sam's place look almost respectable, and if that ain't a miracle, I don't know what is. I would think Sam would blush every time he sees that picture.' Ho, ho! Abbie seemed to cal'late that Sam Cahoon's blushin' would be the biggest miracle of the two. Ho! ho! You'd like Abbie; she's got lots of common sense."

He chuckled at the reminiscence and rubbed his knee.

His niece made no reply. Captain Elisha glanced at the Corot once more and asked another question.

"I presume likely," he said, "that that picture cost consider'ble more than fifteen, hey?"

"Father paid twenty-two thousand dollars for it," was the crushing answer.

The captain looked at her, opened his mouth to speak, shut it again, and, rising, walked across the room. Adjusting his glasses, he inspected the Corot in silence for a few minutes. Then he drew a long breath.

"Well!" he sighed. "*Well.*" Then, after an interval, "Was this the only one he ever painted?"

"The only one? The only picture Corot painted? Of course not! There are many more."

"Did — did this Corot feller get as much for every job as he did for this?"

"I presume so. I know father considered this one a bargain."

"Did, hey? Humph! I ought to know enough by this time not to believe all I hear, but I kind of had an idea that picture paintin' was starvation work. I've read about artists committin' suicide, and livin' in attics, and such. Whew! About two such bargain sale jobs as this, and I'd guarantee not to starve — and to live as nigh the ground as a second-floor bedroom anyhow. How about this next one? This feller in a dory — coddin', I guess he is. Did — did Mr. Corot do him?"

"No. That is by a well-known American artist. It is a good piece of work, but not like the other. It is worth much less. Perhaps five thousand."

"So? Well, even for that I'd undertake to buy consider'ble many dories, and hire fellers to fish from 'em, too. Humph! I guess I'm out of soundin's. When I thought fifteen dollars was a high price for paintin' a

58

view of a house I was slightly mistaken. Next time
I'll offer the paintin' feller the house and ask him what
he considers a fair boot, besides. Sam Cahoon's a better speculator than I thought he was. Hello, Commodore! what's worryin' you now?"

Edwards appeared to announce that dinner was served.
Caroline rose and led the way to the dining room. Captain Elisha followed, looking curiously about him as he
did so. Stephen, who had been sulkily dressing in his
own room, entered immediately after.

The captain surveyed the dining room with interest.
Like the others of the suite, it was sumptuously and
tastefully furnished. He took the chair indicated by the
solemn Edwards, and the meal began.

The butler's sense of humor was not acute, but it was
with considerable difficulty that he restrained his smiles
during the next half hour. A more appreciative ob-
server would have noticed and enjoyed the subtler points.
Stephen's glare of disgust at his uncle when the latter
tucked his napkin in the opening of his waistcoat;
Caroline's embarrassment when the captain complimented
the soup, declaring that it was almost as good as one of
Abbie's chowders; the visitor's obvious uneasiness at
being waited upon attentively, and the like. These Edwards missed, but he could not help appreciating Captain Elisha's conversation.

Caroline said little during dinner. Her brother glow-
ered at his plate and was silent. But the captain talked
and talked.

"Maybe you think I didn't have a time findin' your
new lodgin's," he said. "I come over on the cars, somethin' I don't usually do when there's anything afloat to
carry me. But I had an errand or two to do in Boston,
so I stopped over night at the hotel there and got the

nine o'clock train. I landed here in New York all ship-shape and on time, and started in to hunt you up."

"How did you get our address?" asked his niece. "Mr. Graves couldn't have given it to you, for we only decided on this apartment a few days ago."

"Ho! ho!" chuckled Captain Elisha, rolling in his chair, like a ship in a cross sea. "Ho! ho! You remind me of Abbie, Caroline. That's what she said. 'I never heard of such a crazy cruise,' she says. 'Startin' off to visit folks when you haven't the least idea where they live!' 'Oh, yes, I have,' I says, 'I know where they live; they live in New York.' Well, you ought to have seen her face. Abbie's a good woman — none better — but she generally don't notice a joke until she trips over it. I get consider'ble fun out of Abbie, take her by the large. 'New York!' she says. 'Did anybody ever hear the beat of that? Do you cal'late New York's like South Denboro, where everybody knows everybody else? What are you plannin' to do? run up the fust man, woman or child you meet and ask 'em to tell you where 'Bijah Warren lives? Or are you goin' to trot from Dan to Beersheby, trustin' to meet your nephew and niece on the way? I never in my born days!'

"Well," went on the captain, "I told her that the last suggestion weren't such a bad one, but there was one little objection to it. Considerin' that I hadn't ever laid eyes on Steve and that I hadn't seen you since you was a baby, the chances was against my recognizin' you if we did meet. Ho, ho, ho! Finally I hinted that I might look in the directory, and she got more reconciled to my startin'. Honest, I do believe she'd have insisted on takin' me by the hand and leadin' me to you, if I hadn't told her that.

"The captain talked and talked."

"So I did look in the directory and got the number on Fifth Avenue where you used to be. I asked a policeman the nighest way to get there, and he said take a bus. Last time I was in New York I rode in one of those Fifth Avenue omnibuses, and I never got such a jouncin' in my life. The pavement then was round cobble stones, like some of the roads in Nantucket. I remember I tried to ask a feller that set next to me somethin' or other, and I swan to man I couldn't get nothin' out of my mouth but rattles. 'Metropolitan Museum,' sounded like puttin' in a ton of coal. I thought I was comin' apart, or my works was out of order, or somethin', but when the feller tried to answer he rattled just as bad, so I realized 'twas the reg'lar disease and felt some better. I never shall forget a fleshy woman — somethin' like that Mrs. Dunn friend of yours, Caroline — that set opposite me. It give me the crawls to look at her, her chins shook around so. Ho! ho! she had no less'n three of 'em, and they all shook different ways. Ho! ho! ho! If I'd been in the habit of wearin' false hair or teeth or anything that wa'n't growed to or buttoned on me I'd never have risked a trip in one of those omnibuses.

"So when the police officer prescribed one for me this v'yage, I was some dubious. I'm older'n I was ten year ago, and I wa'n't sure that I'd hold together. I cal'lated walkin' was better for my health. So I found Fifth Avenue and started to walk. And the farther I walked the heavier that blessed satchel of mine got. It weighed maybe ten or twelve pounds at the corner of 42nd Street, but when I got as far as the open square where the gilt woman is hurryin' to keep from bein' run over by Gen'ral Sherman on horseback — that statue, you know — I wouldn't have let that blessed bag go for less'n two ton, if I was sellin' it by weight. So I leaned up against an electric light pole to rest and sort of get my bearin's. Then I noticed what I'd ought to have seen afore, that the street wa'n't paved with cobbles, as it used to be, but was smooth as a stretch of state road down home. So I figgered that a bus was a safe risk, after all. I waited ten minutes or more for one to come, and finally I asked a woman who was in tow of an astrakhan-trimmed dog at the end of a chain, if the omnibuses had stopped runnin'. When I fust see the dog leadin' her I thought she was blind, but I guess she was deef and dumb instead. Anyhow, all she said was 'Ugh!' not very enthusiastic, at that, and went along. Ho! ho! So then I asked a man, and he pointed to a bus right in front of me. You see, I was lookin' for the horses, same as they used to be, and this was an automobile.

"I blushed, I guess, just to show that there was some red underneath the green, and climbed aboard the omnibus. I rode along for a spell, admirin' as much of the scenery as I could see between the women's hats, then I told the skipper of the thing that I wanted to make port at 82nd Street. He said 'Ugh,' apparently suff'rin' from the same complaint the dog woman had, and we went on and on. At last I got kind of anxious and asked him again.

"'Eighty-second!' says he, ugly. 'This is Ninety-first.'

"'Good land!' says I. 'I wanted Eighty-second.'

"'Why didn't you say so?' says he, lookin' as if I'd stole his mother's spoons.

"'I did,' says I.

"'You *did?*' he snarls. 'You did not! If you did, wouldn't I have heard you?'

" Well, any answer I'd be likely to make to that would have meant more argument, and the bus was sailin' right along at the time, so I piled out and did some more walkin', the other way. At last I reached your old number, Stevie, and — Hey? Did you speak? "

" Don't call me ' Stevie,' " growled his nephew, rebelliously.

" Beg your pardon. I keep forgettin' that you're almost grown up. Well, as I was sayin', I got to the house where you used to live, and 'twas shut tight. Nobody there. Ho! ho! I felt a good deal like old Beriah Doane must have on his last ' vacation.' You see, Beriah is one of our South Denboro notorieties; he's famous in his way. He works and loafs by spells until cranberry pickin' time in the fall; then he picks steady and earns thirty or forty dollars all at once. Soon's he's paid off, he starts for Boston on a ' vacation,' an alcoholic one. Well, last fall his married sister was visitin' him, and she, bein' strong for good Templarism, was determined he shouldn't vacate in his regular way. So she telegraphed her husband's brother in Brockton to meet Beriah there, go with him to Boston, and see that he behaved himself and stayed sober. Beriah heard of it, and when his train gets as far as Tremont what does he do but get off quiet and change cars for New Bedford. He hadn't been there for nine years, but he had pleasant memories of his last visit. And when he does get to New Bedford, chucklin' over the way he's befooled his sister and her folks, I'm blessed if he didn't find that the town had gone no-license, and every saloon was shut up! Ho! ho! ho! Well, I felt about the way he did, I guess, when I stood on the steps of your Fifth Avenue house and realized you'd gone away. I wouldn't have had Abbie see me there for somethin'. Ho! ho! "

He leaned back in his chair and laughed aloud. Caroline smiled faintly. Stephen threw down his napkin and sprang to his feet.

"Sis," he cried, "I'm going to my room. By gad! I can't —"

Catching a warning glance from his sister, he did not finish his sentence, but stood sulkily beside his chair. Captain Elisha looked at him, then at the girl, and stopped laughing. He folded his napkin with care, and rose.

"That's about all of it," he said, shortly. "I asked around at two or three of the neighbors' houses, and the last one I asked knew where you'd moved and told me how to get here."

When the trio were again in the library, the captain spoke once more.

"I'm 'fraid I've talked too much," he said, gravely. "I didn't realize how I was runnin' on. Thought I was home, I guess, with the fellers of my own age down at the postoffice, instead of bein' an old countryman, tirin' out you two young city folks with my yarns. I beg your pardon. Now you mustn't mind me. I see you're expectin' company or goin' callin' somewheres, so I'll just go to my bedroom and write Abbie a line. She'll be kind of anxious to know if I got here safe and sound and found you. Don't worry about me, I'll be comf'table and busy."

He turned to go. Caroline looked at him in surprise.

"We are not expecting callers," she said. "And certainly we are not going out to-night. Why should you think such a thing?"

It was her uncle's turn to show surprise.

"Why," he said, with a glance at Stephen, "I see that you're all dressed up, and so I thought, naturally —"

He paused.

Young Warren grunted contemptuously.

"We dressed for dinner, that is all," said Caroline.

"You — you mean you put these clothes on every night?"

"Certainly."

Captain Elisha was plainly very much astonished.

"Well," he observed, slowly. "I — guess I've made another mistake. Hum! Good night."

"Good night," said Stephen, quickly. Caroline, however, seemed embarrassed.

"Captain Warren," she said, "I thought possibly you might wish to talk business with my brother and me. We — we understand that you have come on business connected with father's will. It seems to me that the sooner we — we —"

"Get it over the better, hey? Well, maybe you're right. It's an odd business for an old salt like me to be mixed up in, that's a fact. If it hadn't been so odd, if I hadn't thought there must be some reason, some partic'lar reason, I — well, I guess I'd have stayed to home where I belong. You mustn't think," he added, seriously, "that I don't realize I'm as out of place amongst you and your rich friends as a live fish in a barrel of sawdust. That's all right; you needn't trouble to say no. But you must understand that, realizin' it, I'm not exactly imposin' myself on you for pleasure or — well, from choice. I'm so built that I can't shirk when my conscience tells me I shouldn't, that's all. I'm kind of tired to-night, and I guess you are. To-morrow mornin', if it's agreeable to all hands, we will have a little business talk. I'll have to see Lawyer Graves pretty soon, and have a gen'ral look at your pa's affairs. Then, if everything is all right and I feel my duty's done, I'll probably go back to the Cape and leave you to him, or somebody else able to look out for you. Until then I'm afraid," with a smile which had a trace of bitterness in it; " I'm afraid you'll have to do the best you can with me. I'll try to be no more of a nuisance than I can help. Good night."

When the two young people were left alone, Caroline turned to her brother.

" Steve," she said, " I'm afraid you were a little rude. I'm afraid you hurt his feelings."

The boy stared at her in wonder. " Hurt his feelings!" he exclaimed. "*His* feelings! Well, by Jove! Caro, you're a wonder! Did you expect me to throw my arms around his neck? If he had had any feelings at all, if he was the slightest part of a gentleman, do you suppose he would come here and disgrace us as he is doing? Who invited him? Did we? I guess not!"

" But he is father's brother, and father asked him to come."

" No, he didn't. He asked him — heaven knows why — to look out for our money affairs. That's bad enough; but he didn't ask him to *live* with us. He sha'n't! by gad, he sha'n't! *You* may be as sweet to him as you like, but I'll make it my business to give him the cold shoulder every chance I get. I'll freeze him out, that's what I'll do — freeze him out. Why, Caro! be sensible. Think what his staying here means. Can we take him about with us? Can our friends meet *him* as — as our uncle? He's got to be made to go. Hasn't he now? Hasn't he?"

The girl was silent for a moment. Then she covered her face with her hands. " Oh, yes!" she sobbed. " Oh, yes, he must! he *must!* *Why* did father do it?"

CHAPTER V

THE Warren breakfast hour was nine o'clock. At a quarter to nine Caroline, entering the library, found Stephen seated by the fire reading the morning paper.

"Good morning," she said. Then, looking about the room, asked, "Has — has *he* been here?"

Her brother shook his head. "You mean Uncle 'Lish?" he asked, cheerfully. "No, he hasn't. At least, I haven't seen him and I haven't made any inquiries. I shall manage to survive if he never appears. Let sleeping relatives lie, that's my motto."

He laughed at his own joke and turned the page of the paper. The butler entered.

"Breakfast is served, Miss Caroline," he announced.

"Has Captain Warren come from his room?" asked the young lady.

"No, Miss Caroline. That is, I haven't seen him."

Stephen tossed the paper on the floor and rose.

"I wonder —" he began. Then, with a broad grin, "A sudden thought strikes me, Sis. He has undoubtedly blown out the gas."

"Steve! How can you!"

"Perfectly simple. Absolutely reasonable. Just what might have been expected. 'He has gone, but we shall miss him.' Come on, Caro; I'm hungry. Let the old hayseed sleep. You and I can have a meal in peace. Heavens! you don't care for another experience like last night's, do you?"

"Edwards," said Caroline, "you may knock at Captain Warren's door and tell him breakfast is served."

"Yes," commanded Stephen, "and tell him not to hurry on our account. Come, Caro, come! You're not pining for his society. Well, wait then! *I* won't!"

He marched angrily out of the room. His sister hesitated, her wish to follow complicated by a feeling of duty to a guest, no matter how unwelcome. The butler reappeared, looking puzzled.

"He's not there, miss?" he said.

"Not there? Not in his room?"

"No, Miss Caroline. I knocked, and he didn't answer, so I looked in and he wasn't there. His bed's been slept in, but he's gone."

"Gone? And you haven't seen him?"

"No, miss. I've been up and about since half past seven, and I can't understand where he could have got to."

The door of the hall opened and shut. Edwards darted from the library. A moment afterwards Captain Elisha strolled in. He was wearing his overcoat, and his hat was in his hand.

"Good mornin', Caroline," he hailed, in his big voice. "Surprised to see me, are you? Ho! ho! So was the Commodore. He couldn't understand how I got in without ringin'. Well, you see, I'm used to turnin' out pretty early, and when it got to be most seven o'clock, I couldn't lay to bed any longer, so I got up, dressed, and went for a walk. I fixed the door latch so's I could come in quiet. You haven't waited breakfast for me, I hope."

"No; it is ready now, however."

"Ready now," the captain looked at his watch.

"Yes, I should think so. It's way into the forenoon. You *have* waited for me, haven't you? I'm awfully sorry."

"No, we have not waited. Our breakfast hour is nine. Pardon me for neglecting to tell you that last evening."

"Oh, that's all right. Now you trot right out and eat. I've had mine."

"Had your breakfast?"

"Yes, indeed. When I'm home, Abbie and I usually eat about seven, so I get sort of sharp-set if I wait after that. I cal'lated you city folks was late sleepers, and I wouldn't want to make any trouble, so I found a little eating house down below here a ways and had a cup of coffee and some bread and butter and mush. Then I went cruisin' round in Central Park a spell. This *is* Central Park over across here, ain't it?"

"Yes." The girl was too astonished to say more.

"I thought 'twas. I'd been through part of it afore, but 'twas years ago, and it's such a big place and the paths run so criss-cross I got sort of mixed up, and it took me longer to get out than it did to get in. I had the gen'ral points of the compass, and I guess I could have made a pretty average straight run for home, but every time I wanted to cut across lots there was a policeman lookin' at me, so I had to stick to the channel. That's what made me so late. Now do go and eat your breakfast. I won't feel easy till I see you start."

Caroline departed, and the captain, after a visit to his own room, where he left his coat and hat, returned to the library, picked up the paper which his nephew had dropped, and began reading.

After breakfast came the "business talk." It was a brief one. Captain Elisha soon discovered that his brother's children knew very little concerning their father's affairs. They had always plenty of money, had been indulged in practically every wish, and had never had to think or plan for themselves. As to the size of the estate, they knew nothing more than Mr. Graves had told them, which was that, instead of the several millions which rumor had credited A. Rodgers Warren with possessing, five hundred thousand dollars would probably be the extent of their inheritance, and that, therefore, they must live economically. As a first step in that direction, they had given up their former home and moved to the apartment.

"Yes, yes," mused the captain, " I see. Mr. Graves didn't know about your movin', then? You did it on your own hook, so to speak?"

Stephen answered promptly.

"Of course we did," he declared. "Why not?"

"No reason in the world. A good sensible thing to do, I should say. Didn't anybody advise you where to go?"

"Why should we need advice?" Again it was Stephen who replied. "We aren't kids. We're old enough to decide some things for ourselves, I should think."

"Yes. Sartin. That's right. But I didn't know but p'raps some of your friends might have helped along. This Mrs. Dunn now, she kind of hinted to me that she'd — well, done what she could to make you comf'table."

"She has," avowed Caroline, warmly. "Mrs. Dunn and Malcolm have proved their friendship in a thousand ways. We never can repay them, Stephen and I, never!"

"No. There's some things you can't ever pay, I

know that. Mrs. Dunn found this nice place for you, did she?"

"Why, yes. She and I found it together."

"So? That was lucky, wa'n't it? Advertised in the newspaper, was it; or was there a 'To Let' placard up in the window?"

"No, certainly not. Mrs. Dunn knew that we had decided to move, and she has a cousin who is interested in New York property. She asked him, and he mentioned this apartment."

"One of his own, was it?"

"I believe so. Why are you so particular? Don't you like it?"

Her tone was sharp. Stephen, who resented his uncle's questions as impertinent intrusions upon the family affairs, added one of his own.

"Isn't it as good as those in — what do you call it — South Denboro?" he asked, maliciously.

Captain Elisha laughed heartily.

"Pretty nigh as good," he said. "I didn't notice any better on the way to the depot as I drove up. And I doubt if there's many new ones built since I left. It's a mighty fine lot of rooms, I think. What's the rent? You'll excuse my askin', things bein' as they are."

"Twenty-two hundred a year," answered his niece, coldly.

The captain looked at her, whistled, broke off the whistle in the middle, and did a little mental arithmetic.

"Twenty-two hundred a year!" he repeated. "That's one hundred and eighty odd a month. Say, that cousin of Mrs. Dunn's must want to get his investment back. You mean for just these ten rooms?"

Stephen laughed scornfully.

"Our guardian has been counting, Caro," he remarked.

"Yes. Yes, I counted this mornin' when I got up. I was interested, naturally."

"Sure! Naturally, of course," sneered the boy. "Did you think the twenty-two hundred was the rent of the entire building?"

"Well, I didn't know. I—"

"The rent," interrupted Caroline, with dignity, "was twenty-four hundred, but, thanks to Mrs. Dunn, who explained to her cousin that we were friends of hers, it was reduced."

"We being in reduced circumstances," observed her brother in supreme disgust. "Pity the poor orphans! By gad!"

"That was real nice of Mrs. Dunn," declared Captain Elisha, heartily. "She's pretty well-off herself, I s'pose — hey, Caroline?"

"I presume so."

"Yes, yes. About how much is she wuth, think?"

"I don't know. I never inquired."

"No. Well, down our way," with a chuckle, "we don't have to inquire. Ask anybody you meet what his next door neighbor's wuth, and he'll tell you within a hundred, and how he got it, and how much he owes, and how he gets along with his wife. Ho! ho! Speakin' of wives, is this Mr. Dunn married?"

He looked at his niece as he asked the question. There was no reason why Caroline should blush; she knew it, and hated herself for doing it.

"No," she answered, resentfully, "he is not."

"Um-hm. What's his business?"

"He is connected with a produce exchange house, I believe."

"One of the firm?"

"I don't know. In New York we are not as well

posted, or as curious, concerning our friends' private affairs as your townspeople seem to be."

"I guess that's so. I imagine New Yorkers are too busy gettin' it themselves to bother whether their neighbors have got it or not. Well," he went on, rising, "I guess I've kept you young folks from your work or — or play, or whatever you was going to do, long enough for this once. I think I'll go out for a spell. I've got an errand or two I want to do. What time do you have dinner?"

"We lunch at half past one," answered Caroline. "We dine at seven."

"Oh, yes, yes! I keep forgettin' that supper's dinner. Well, I presume likely I'll be back for luncheon. If I ain't, don't wait for me. I'll be home afore supper — there I go again! — afore dinner, anyhow. Goodby."

Five minutes later he was at the street corner, inquiring of a policeman "the handiest way to get to Pine Street." Following the directions given, he boarded a train at the nearest subway station, emerged at Wall Street, inquired once more, located the street he was looking for, and, consulting a card which he took from a big stained leather pocket-book, walked on, peering at the numbers of the buildings he passed.

The offices of Sylvester, Kuhn, and Graves, were on the sixteenth floor of a new and gorgeously appointed sky-scraper. When Captain Elisha entered the firm's reception room, he was accosted by a wide-awake and extremely self-possessed office boy.

"Who'd you want to see?" asked the boy, briskly.

The captain removed his hat and wiped his forehead with his handkerchief.

"Hold on a jiffy, Sonny," he panted. "Just give me

73

a minute to sort of get myself together, as you might say. I rode up in one of those express elevators of yours, and I kind of feel as if my boots had got tangled up with my necktie. When that elevator feller cast off from the cellar, I begun to shut up like a spyglass. Whew! Say, Son, is Mr. Graves in?"

" No," replied the boy, grinning.

" Hum! Still in the sick bay, is he — hey?"

" He's to home. Got a cold."

" Yup. It's too bad. Mr. — er — Sylvester, is he in?"

" Naw, he ain't. And Mr. Kuhn's busy. Won't one of the clerks do? What do you want to see the firm about?"

" Well, Son, I had reasons of my own. However, I guess I won't disturb Mr. Kuhn, if he's busy's you say. Here! you tell him, or Mr. Sylvester when he comes, that Cap'n Warren, Cap'n Elisha Warren of South Denboro — better write it down — called and will be back about half past twelve or thereabouts. Got it, have you? Hum! is that Elisha? You don't tell me! I've been spellin' it for sixty years, more or less, and never realized it had such possibilities. Lend me your pencil. There! you give Mr. Sylvester that and tell him I'll see him later. So long, Son."

He departed, smiling. The indignant office boy threw the card on the table.

Captain Elisha strolled down Pine Street, looking about him with interest. It had been years since he visited this locality, and the changes were many. Soon, however, he began to recognize familiar landmarks. He was approaching the water front, and there were fewer new buildings. When he reached South Street he was thoroughly at home.

The docks were crowded. The river was alive with small craft of all kinds. Steamers and schooners were plenty, but the captain missed the old square-riggers, the clipper ships and barks, such as he had sailed in as cabin boy, as foremast hand, and, later, commanded on many seas.

At length, however, he saw four masts towering above the roof of a freight house. They were not schooner rigged, those masts. The yards were set square across, and along them were furled royals and upper topsails. Here, at last, was a craft worth looking at. Captain Elisha crossed the street, hurried past the covered freight house, and saw a magnificent great ship lying beside a broad open wharf. Down the wharf he walked, joyfully, as one who greets an old friend.

The wharf was practically deserted. An ancient watchman was dozing in a sort of sentry box, but he did not wake. There was a pile of foreign-looking crates and boxes at the further end of the pier, evidently the last bit of cargo waiting to be carted away. The captain inspected the pile, recognized the goods as Chinese and Japanese, then read the name on the big ship's stern. She was the *Empress of the Ocean,* and her home port was Liverpool.

Captain Elisha, as a free-born Yankee skipper, had an inherited and cherished contempt for British "lime-juicers," but he could not help admiring this one. To begin with, her size and tonnage were enormous. Also, she was four-masted, instead of the usual three, and her hull and lower spars were of steel instead of wood. A steel sailing vessel was something of a novelty to the captain, and he was seized with a desire to go aboard and inspect.

The ladder from ship to wharf was down, of course,

and getting on board was an easy matter. When he reached the deck and looked about him, the great size of the ship was still more apparent. The bulwarks were as high as a short man's head. She was decked over aft, and, as the captain said afterwards, " her cabins had nigh as many stories as a house." From the roof of the " first story," level with the bulwarks, extended a series of bridges, which could be hoisted or lowered, and by means of which her officers could walk from stern to bow without descending to the deck. There was a good-sized engine house forward, beyond the galley and forecastle. Evidently the work of hoisting anchors and canvas was done by steam.

The captain strolled about, looking her over. The number of improvements since his seagoing days was astonishing. He was standing by the wheel, near the companion way, wishing that he might inspect the officers' quarters, but not liking to do so without an invitation, when two men emerged from the cabin.

One of the pair was evidently the Japanese steward of the ship. The other was a tall, clean-cut young fellow, whose general appearance and lack of sunburn showed quite plainly that he was not a seafaring man by profession. The steward caught sight of Captain Elisha, and, walking over, accosted him.

" Want to see skipper, sir? " he asked, in broken English. " He ashore."

" No, Doctor," replied the captain, cheerfully. " I don't want to see him. I've got no business aboard. It's been some time since I trod the quarter-deck of a square-rigger, and I couldn't resist the temptation of tryin' how the planks felt under my feet. This is consider'ble of a clipper you've got here," he added.

" Yes, sir," replied the steward grinning.

"Where you from?" asked Captain Elisha.

"Singapore, sir."

"Cargo all out?"

"Yes, sir."

"Waitin' for another one?"

"Yes, sir. We load for Manila bimeby."

"Manila, hey? Have a good passage across?"

"Yes, sir. She good ship."

"Shouldn't wonder. How d'ye do, sir," to the young man, who was standing near. "Hope you won't think I'm crowdin' in where I don't belong. I was just tellin' the doctor here that it had been some time since I trod a quarter-deck, and I thought I'd see if I'd forgot the feel."

"Have you?" asked the young man, smiling.

"Guess not. Seems kind of nat'ral. I never handled such a whale of a craft as this, though. Didn't have many of 'em in my day. Come over in her, did you?"

"No," with a shake of the head. "No such luck. I'm a land lubber, just scouting round, that's all. She's a bully vessel, isn't she?"

"Looks so. Tell you better after I've seen what she could do in a full-sail breeze. All hands ashore, Doctor?"

"Yes, sir," replied the steward.

"Crew paid off and spendin' their money, I s'pose. Well, if it ain't against orders, I'd kind of like to look around a little mite. May I?"

The steward merely grinned. His companion answered for him.

"Certainly you may," he said. "I'm a friend of one of the consignees, and I'd be glad to show you the ship, if you like. Shall we begin with the cabins?"

Captain Elisha, delighted with the opportunity, expressed his thanks, and the tour of inspection began.

The steward remained on deck, but the captain and his new acquaintance strolled through the officers' quarters together.

"Jerushy!" exclaimed the former, as he viewed the main cabin. "Say, you could pretty nigh have a dance here, couldn't you? A small one. This reminds me of the cabin aboard the *Sea Gull,* first vessel I went mate of — it's so diff'rent. Aboard her we had to walk sittin' down. There wa'n't room in the cabin for more'n one to stand up at a time. But she could sail, just the same — and carry it, too. I've seen her off the Horn with studdin' sails set, when craft twice her length and tonnage had everything furled above the tops'l yard. Hi hum! you mustn't mind an old salt runnin' on this way. I've been out of the pickle tub a good while, but I cal'late the brine ain't all out of my system."

His guide's eyes snapped.

"I understand," he said, laughing. "I've never been at sea, on a long voyage, in my life, but I can understand just how you feel. It's in my blood, I guess. I come of a salt water line. My people were from Belfast, Maine, and every man of them went to sea."

"Belfast, hey? They turned out some A No. 1 sailors in Belfast. I sailed under a Cap'n Pearson from there once — James Pearson, his name was."

"He was my great uncle. I was named for him. My name is James Pearson, also."

"*What?*" Captain Elisha was hugely delighted. "Mr. Pearson, shake hands. I want to tell you that your Uncle Jim was a seaman of the kind you dream about, but seldom meet. I was his second mate three v'yages. My name's Elisha Warren."

Mr. Pearson shook hands and laughed, good-humoredly.

"Glad to meet you, Captain Warren," he said. "And I'm glad you knew Uncle Jim. As a youngster, he was my idol. He could spin yarns that were worth listening to."

"I bet you! He'd seen things wuth yarnin' about. So you ain't a sailor, hey? Livin' in New York?"

The young man nodded. "Yes," he said. Then, with a dry smile, "If you call occupying a hall bedroom and eating at a third-rate boarding-house table living. However, it's my own fault. I've been a newspaper man since I left college. But I threw up my job six months ago. Since then I've been free-lancing."

"Have, hey?" The captain was too polite to ask further questions, but he had not the slightest idea what "free-lancing" might be. Pearson divined his perplexity and explained.

"I've had a feeling," he said, "that I might write magazine articles and stories — yes, possibly a novel or two. It's a serious disease, but the only way to find out whether it's chronic or not is to experiment. That's what I'm doing now. The thing I'm at work on may turn out to be a sea story. So I spend some time around the wharves and aboard the few sailing ships in port, picking up material."

Captain Elisha patted him on the back.

"Now don't you get discouraged," he said. "I used to have an idea that novel writin' and picture paintin' was poverty jobs for men with healthy appetites, but I've changed my mind. I don't know's you'll believe it, but I've just found out, for a fact, that some painters get twenty-two thousand dollars for one picture. For *one*, mind you. And a little mite of a thing, too, that couldn't have cost scarcely anything to paint. Maybe novels sell for just as much. *I* don't know."

79

His companion laughed heartily. "I'm afraid not, Captain," he said. "Few, at any rate. I should be satisfied with considerably less, to begin with. Are you living here in town?"

"Well — we-ll, I don't know. I ain't exactly livin', and I ain't exactly boardin', but — Say! ain't that the doctor callin' you?"

It was the steward, and there was an anxious ring in his voice. Pearson excused himself and hurried out of the cabin. Captain Elisha lingered for a final look about. Then he followed leisurely, becoming aware, as he reached the open air, of loud voices in angry dialogue.

Entrances to the *Empress of the Ocean's* cabins were on the main deck, and also on the raised half-deck at the stern, near the wheel, the binnacle and the officers' corned-beef tubs, swinging in their frames. From this upper deck two flights of steps led down to the main deck below. At the top of one of these flights stood young Pearson, cool and alert. Behind him half crouched the Japanese steward, evidently very much frightened. At the foot of the steps were grouped three rough looking men, foreigners and sailors without doubt, and partially intoxicated. The three men were an ugly lot, and they were all yelling and jabbering together in a foreign lingo. As the captain emerged from the passage to the open deck, he heard Pearson reply in the same language.

"What's the matter?" he asked.

Pearson answered without turning his head.

"Drunken sailors," he explained. "Part of the crew here. They've been uptown, got full, and come back to square a grudge they seem to have against the steward. I'm telling them they'd better give up and go ashore, if they know when they're well off."

The three fellows by the ladder's foot were consulting

together. On the wharf were half a dozen loungers, collected by the prospect of a row.

"If I can hold them off for a few minutes," went on Pearson, "we'll be all right. The wharf watchman has gone for the police. Here! drop it! What are you up to?"

One of the sailors had drawn a knife. The other two reached for their belts behind, evidently intending to follow suit. From the loafers on the wharf came shouts of encouragement.

"Do the dude up, Pedro! Give him what's comin' to him."

The trio formed for a rush. The steward, with a shrill scream, fled to the cabin. Pearson did not move; he even smiled. The next moment he was pushed to one side, and Captain Elisha stood at the top of the steps.

"Here!" he said, sternly. "What's all this?"

The three sailors, astonished at this unexpected addition to their enemies' forces, hesitated. Pearson laid his hand on the captain's arm.

"Be careful," he said. "They're dangerous."

"Dangerous? Them? I've seen their kind afore. Here, you!" turning to the three below. "What do you mean by this? Put down that knife, you lubber! Do you want to be put in irons? Over the side with you, you swabs! Git!"

He began descending the ladder. Whether the sailors were merely too surprised to resist, or because they recognized the authority of the deep sea in Captain Elisha's voice and face is a question. At any rate, as he descended they backed away.

"Mutiny on board a ship of mine?" roared the captain. "What do you mean by it? Why, I'll have you tied up and put on bread and water. Over the side with you! Mutiny on board of *me!* Lively! Tumble up there!"

With every order came a stride forward and a correspondingly backward movement on the part of the three. The performance would have been ridiculous if Pearson had not feared that it might become tragic. He was descending the steps to his new acquaintance's aid, when there rose a chorus of shouts from the wharf.

"The cops! the cops! Look out!"

That was the finishing touch. The next moment the three "mutineers" were over the side and running as fast as their alcoholic condition would permit down the wharf.

"Well, by George!" exclaimed Pearson.

Captain Elisha seemed to be coming out of a dream. He stood still, drew his hand across his forehead, and then began to laugh.

"Well!" he stammered. "Well, I snum! I — I — Mr. Pearson, I wonder what on earth you must think of me. I declare the sight of that gang set me back about twenty years. They — they must have thought I was the new skipper! Did you hear me tell 'em they couldn't mutiny aboard of me? Ho! ho! Well, I am an old idiot!"

Pearson stuck his fist into the palm of his other hand.

"I've got it!" he cried. "I knew your name was familiar. Why, you're the mate that handled the mutinous crew aboard Uncle Jim's bark, the *Pacer,* off Mauritius, in the typhoon, when he was hurt and in the cabin. I've heard him tell it a dozen times. Well, this *is* a lucky day for me!"

Captain Elisha was evidently pleased. "So he told you that, did he?" he began. "That *was* a time and a half, I —"

He was interrupted. Over the rail appeared a blue

helmet, and an instant later a big and very pompous police officer leaped to the deck. He was followed by the wharf watchman, who looked frightened.

"Where's the other one of them?" demanded the policeman. "Oh, it's you, is it? Well, you're too old to be gettin' drunk and fightin'. Come along now, peaceable, and let's have no words about it."

He advanced and laid a hand on the captain's arm.

"You're under arrest," he announced. "Will you come along quiet?"

"I'm under arrest?" repeated Captain Elisha. "Under — My soul and body! Why, I ain't done anything."

"Yes, I know. Nobody's done nothin'. Come on, or shall I — Hello, Mr. Pearson, sir! How d'you do?"

Pearson had stepped forward.

"Slattery," he said, "you've made a mistake. Let me tell you about it." He drew the officer aside and whispered in his ear. After a rather lengthy conversation, the guardian of the peace turned to the watchman.

"What d'you mean by tellin' all them lies?" he demanded.

"Lies?" repeated the astonished watchman. "I never told no lies."

"You did. You said this gentleman," indicating the nervous and apprehensive Captain Elisha, "was fightin' and murderin'. I ask your pardon, sir. 'Twas this bloke's foolishness. G'wan ashore! You make me sick. Good day, Mr. Pearson."

He departed, driving his new victim before him and tongue-lashing him all the way. The captain drew a long breath.

"Say, Mr. Pearson," he declared, "a minute or so ago you said this was a lucky day for you. I cal'late it's a luckier one for me. If it hadn't been for you I'd been

83

took up. Yes, sir, took up and carted off to the lock-up. Whew! that would have looked well in the papers, wouldn't it? And my niece and nephew . . . Je-rushy! I'm mightily obliged to you. How did you handle that policeman so easily?"

Pearson laughed. "Oh," he replied, "a newspaper training and acquaintance has its advantages. Slattery knows me, and I know him."

"Well, I thank you, I do so."

"You needn't. I wouldn't have missed meeting you and seeing you handle those fellows for a good deal. And besides, you're not going to escape so easy. You must lunch with me."

The captain started, hastily pulled out his watch, and looked at it.

"Quarter to one!" he cried. "And I said I'd be back at that lawyer's office at half-past twelve. No, no, Mr. Pearson, I can't go to lunch with you, but I do wish you'd come and see me some time. My address for — for a spell, anyhow — is Central Park West," giving the num-ber, "and the name is Warren, same as mine. Will you come some evenin'? I'd be tickled to death to see you."

The young man was evidently delighted.

"Will I?" he exclaimed. "Indeed I will. I warn you, Captain Warren, that I shall probably keep you busy spinning sea yarns."

"Nothin' I like better, though I'm afraid my yarns'll be pretty dull alongside of your Uncle Jim's."

"I'll risk it. Good-by and good luck. I shall see you very soon."

"That's right; do. So long."

CHAPTER VI

THE boy, Captain Elisha's acquaintance of the morning, was out, regaling himself with crullers and milk at a pushcart on Broad Street, when the captain returned to the officers of Sylvester, Kuhn and Graves. The clerk who had taken his place was very respectful.

"Captain Warren," he said, "Mr. Sylvester was sorry to miss you. He waited until half past twelve and left word for us to telephone if you came. Our Mr. Graves is still ill, and the matter of your brother's estate must be discussed without further delay. Please sit down and I will telephone."

The captain seated himself on the leather-covered bench, and the clerk entered the inner office. He returned, a few moments later, to say:

"Mr. Sylvester is at the Central Club. He wished me to ask if you could conveniently join him there."

Captain Elisha pondered. "Why, yes," he replied, slowly, "I s'pose I could. I don't know why I couldn't. Where is this — er — club of his?"

"On Fifth Avenue, near Fifty-second Street. I'll send one of our boys with you if you like."

"No, no! I can pilot myself, I guess. I ain't so old I can't ask my way. Though —" with a reminiscent chuckle — "if the folks I ask are all sufferin' from that 'Ugh' disease, I sha'n't make much headway."

"What disease?" asked the puzzled clerk.

"Oh, nothin'. I was just thinkin' out loud, that's all. Mr. Sylvester wants to see me right off, does he?"

"Yes, he said he would wait if I 'phoned him you were coming."

"Um-hm. Well, you can tell him I've left the dock, bound in his direction. Say, that young chap that was here when I called the fust time — studyin' to be a lawyer, is he?"

"Who? Tim? No, indeed. He's only the office boy. Why did you ask?"

"Oh, I was just wonderin'. I had a notion he might be in trainin' for a judgeship, he was so high and mighty. Ho! ho! He's got talent, that boy has. Nobody but a born genius could have made as many mistakes in one name as he did when he undertook to spell Elisha. Well, sir, I'm much obliged to you. Good day."

The Central Club is a ponderous institution occupying a becomingly gorgeous building on the Avenue. The captain found his way to its door without much trouble. A brass-buttoned attendant answered his ring and superciliously inquired his business. Captain Elisha, not being greatly in awe of either buttons or brief authority, calmly hailed the attendant as "Gen'ral" and informed him that he was there to see Mr. Sylvester, if the latter was "on deck anywheres."

"Tell him it's Cap'n Warren, Major," he added cheerfully; "he's expectin' me."

The attendant brusquely ushered the visitor into a leather-upholstered reception room and left him. The captain amused himself by looking at the prints and framed letters and autographs on the walls. Then a round, red, pleasant-faced man entered.

"Pardon me," he said, "is this Captain Warren?"

"Yes, sir," was the reply. "That's my name. This is Mr. Sylvester, ain't it? Glad to know you, sir."

"Thanks. Sorry to have made you travel way up here, Captain. I waited until twelve-thirty, but as you didn't come then, I gave you up. Hope I haven't inconvenienced you."

"No, no. Not a mite. Might just as well be here as anywhere. Don't think another thing about it."

"Have you lunched, Captain Warren?"

"No, come to think of it, I ain't. I've been kind of busy this forenoon, and a little thing like dinner — luncheon, I mean — slipped my mind. Though 'tain't often I have those slips, I'm free to say. Ho! ho! Abbie — she's my second cousin, my housekeeper — says I'm an unsartin critter, but there's two things about me she can always count on, one's that my clothes have always got a button loose somewheres, and t'other's my appetite."

He laughed, and Sylvester laughed with him.

"Well," observed the lawyer, "I'm not sure that I couldn't qualify on both of those counts. At any rate I'm sure of my appetite. I had a lunch engagement with an acquaintance of mine, but he hasn't appeared, so you must take his place. We'll lunch together."

"Well, now, I'd like to fust-rate, and it's real kind of you, Mr. Sylvester; but I don't know's I'd better. Your friend may heave in sight, after all, and I'd be in the way."

"Not a bit of it. And I said 'acquaintance,' not 'friend.' Of course you will! You must. We can talk business while we're eating, if you like."

"All right. And I'm ever so much obliged to you. Is there an eatin' house near here?"

"Oh, we'll eat right here at the club. Come."

He led the way, and Captain Elisha followed. The Central Club has a large, exclusive, and wealthy membership, and its quarters correspond. The captain gazed about him at the marble floors and pillars, the paintings and busts, with interest. After checking his hat and coat, as they entered the elevator he asked a question.

"Which floor is your club on, Mr. Sylvester?" he asked.

"Floor? Why, the dining room is on the fourth, if that's what you mean."

"No, I meant how many rooms do you rent?"

"We occupy the entire building. It is our own, and a comparatively new one. We built it three years ago."

"You mean this whole shebang is just one *club?*"

"Certainly."

"Hum! I see. Well, I —"

"What were you going to say?"

"Nothin'. I was wonderin' what fool thing I'd ask next. I'm more used to lodge rooms than I am to clubs, I guess. I'd like to take home a picture of this place to Theophilus Kenney. Theoph's been raisin' hob because the Odd Fellows built on to their buildin'. He said one room was enough for any society. 'Twould be, if we was all his kind of society. Theoph's so small he could keep house in a closet. He's always hollerin' in meetin' about his soul. I asked the minister if it didn't seem ridic'lous for Kenney to make such a big noise over such a little thing. This where we get off?"

The dining room was a large and ornate apartment. Captain Elisha, when he first entered it, seemed about to ask another question, but choked it off and remained silent. Sylvester chose a table in a retired corner, and they sat down.

" Now, Captain Warren," said the host, " what will you eat?"

Captain Elisha shook his head.

" You do the orderin'," he replied dryly; " I'll just set and be thankful, like the hen that found the china doorknob. Anything that suits you will do me, I guess."

The lawyer, who seemed to be thoroughly enjoying his companion, gave his orders, and the waiter brought first a bit of caviar on toast. If Sylvester expected this delicacy to produce astonished comments, he was disappointed.

" Well, well!" exclaimed Captain Elisha. " I declare, you take me back a long ways, Mr. Sylvester. Caviar! Well, well! Why, I haven't ate this since I used to go to Cronstadt. At the American consul's house there we had it often enough. Has a kind of homey taste even yet. That consul was a good feller. He and I were great friends.

" I met him a long spell after that, when I was down in Mexico," he went on. " He'd made money and was down on a vacation. My ship was at Acapulco, and he and I used to go gunnin' together, after wild geese and such. Ho! ho! I remember there was a big, pompous critter of an Englishman there. Mind you, I'm not talkin' against the English. Some of the best men I ever met were English, and I've stood back to back with a British mate on a Genoa wharf when half of Italy was hoppin' around makin' proclamations that they was goin' to swallow us alive. And, somehow or 'nother, they didn't. Took with prophetic indigestion, maybe.

" However, this Englishman at Acapulco was diff'rent. He was so swelled with importance that his back hollered in like Cape Cod Bay on the map. His front bent out to correspond, though, so I cal'late he averaged up all

89

right. Well, he heard about what a good — that I was pretty lucky when it come to shootin' wild geese, and I'm blessed if he didn't send me orders to get him one for a dinner he was goin' to give. Didn't ask — *ordered* me to do it, you understand. And him nothin' but a consignee, with no more control over me than the average female Sunday-school teacher has over a class of boys. Not so much, because she's supposed to have official authority, and he wa'n't. *And* he didn't invite me to the dinner.

"Well, the next time my friend, the ex-consul, and I went out gunnin', I told him of the Englishman's ' orders.' He was mad. ' What are you goin' to do about it? ' he asks. ' Don't know yet,' says I, ' we'll see.' By and by we come in sight of one of them long-legged cranes, big birds you know, standin' fishin' at the edge of some reeds. I up with my gun and shot it. The consul chap looked at me as if I was crazy. ' What in the world did you kill that fish-basket on stilts for? ' he says. ' Son,' says I, ' your eyesight is bad. That's a British-American goose. Chop off about three feet of neck and a couple of fathom of hind legs and pick and clean what's left, and I shouldn't wonder if 'twould make a good dinner for a mutual friend of ours — good *enough,* anyhow.' Well, sir! that ex-consul set plump down in the mud and laughed and laughed. Ho, ho! Oh, dear me! "

"Did you send it to the Englishman? " asked Sylvester.

"Oh, yes, I sent it. And, after a good while and in a roundabout way, I heard that the whole dinner party vowed 'twas the best wild goose they ever ate. So I ain't sure just who the joke was on. However, I'm satisfied with my end. Well, there! I guess you must think I'm pretty talky on short acquaintance, Mr. Sylvester.

You'll have to excuse me; that caviar set me to thinkin' about old times."

His host was shaking all over. "Go ahead, Captain," he cried. "Got any more as good as that?"

But Captain Elisha merely smiled and shook his head.

"Don't get me started on Mexico," he observed. "I'm liable to yarn all the rest of the afternoon. Let's see, we was goin' to talk over my brother's business a little mite, wa'n't we?"

"Why, yes, we should. Now, Captain Warren, just how much do you know about your late brother's affairs?"

"Except what Mr. Graves told me, nothin' of importance. And, afore we go any further, let me ask a question. Do *you* know why 'Bije made me his executor and guardian and all the rest of it?"

"I do not. Graves drew his will, and so, of course, we knew of your existence and your appointment. Your brother forbade our mentioning it, but we did not know, until after his death, that his own children were unaware they had an uncle. It seems strange, doesn't it?"

"It does to me; *so* strange that I can't see two lengths ahead. I cal'late Mr. Graves told you how I felt about it?"

"Yes. That is, he said you were very much surprised."

"That's puttin' it mild enough. And did he tell you that 'Bije and I hadn't seen each other, or even written, in eighteen years?"

"Yes."

"Um-hm. Well, when you consider *that,* can you wonder I was set all aback? And the more I think of it, the foggier it gets. Why, Mr. Sylvester, it's one of them situations that are impossible, that you can prove

7   91

fifty ways *can't* happen. And yet, it has — it sartinly has. Now tell me: Are you, or your firm, well acquainted with my brother's affairs?"

"Not well, no. The late Mr. Warren was a close-mouthed man, rather secretive, in fact."

"Humph! that bein' one of the p'ints where he was different from his nighest relation, hey?"

"I'm not so sure. Have you questioned the children?"

"Caroline and Steve? Yes, I've questioned 'em more than they think I have, maybe. And they know — well, leavin' out about the price of oil paintin's and the way to dress and that it's more or less of a disgrace to economize on twenty thousand a year, their worldly knowledge ain't too extensive."

"Do you like them?"

"I guess so. Just now ain't the fairest time to judge 'em. You see they're sufferin' from the joyful shock of their country relation droppin' in, and —"

He paused and rubbed his chin. His lips were smiling, but his eyes were not. Sylvester noted their expression, and guessed many things.

"They haven't been disagreeable, I hope?" he asked.

"No-o. No, I wouldn't want to say that. They're young and — and, well, I ain't the kind they've been used to. Caroline's a nice girl. She is, sure. All she needs is to grow a little older and have the right kind of advice and — and friends."

"How about the boy?" Mr. Sylvester had met young Warren, and his eyes twinkled as he spoke.

"Steve? Well," there was an answering twinkle in Captain Elisha's eye; "well, Steve needs to grow, too; though I wouldn't presume to tell him so. When a feller's undertakin' to give advice to one of the seven wise men, he has to be diplomatic, as you might say."

The lawyer put back his head and laughed uproariously.

"Ha! ha!" he crowed. "That's good! Then, from your questioning of the children, you've learned —?"

"Not such an awful lot. I think I've learned that — hum! that a good guardian might be a handy thing to have in the house. A reg'lar legal guardian, I mean. Otherwise —"

"Otherwise?"

"Otherwise there might be too many disinterested volunteer substitutes for the job. Maybe I'm wrong, but I doubt it."

"Have you made up your mind to be that guardian?"

"Not yet. I haven't made up my mind to anything yet. Now, Mr. Sylvester, while we're waitin' for what comes next — you've ordered enough grub to victual a ship — s'pose you just run over what your firm knows about 'Bije. That is, if I ain't askin' too much."

"Not at all. That's what I'm here for. You have a right to know. But I warn you my information isn't worth much."

He went on, briefly and with the conciseness of the legal mind, to tell of A. Rodgers Warren, his business and his estate. He had been a broker with a seat on the Stock Exchange.

"That seat is worth consider'ble, ain't it?" interrupted the captain.

"Between eighty and one hundred thousand dollars."

"Yup. Well, it reminds me of a picture I saw once in one of the comic papers. An old feller from the backwoods somewheres — good deal like me, he was, and just about as green — was pictured standin' along with his city nephew in the gallery of the Exchange. And the nephew says, 'Uncle,' says he, 'do you realize that a seat

down there's wuth seventy-five thousand dollars?'
' Gosh!' says the old man, ' no wonder most of 'em are
standin' up.' Ho! ho! Is that seat of 'Bije's part of
the five hundred thousand you figger he's left?"

" Yes, in a way it is. To be truthful, Captain Warren,
we're not sure as to the amount of your brother's tangible assets. Graves made a hurried examination of the
stocks, bonds, and memoranda, and estimated the total,
that's all."

" I see. Well, heave ahead."

The lawyer went on. The dead broker's office had
been on Broad Street. A small office, with but two
clerks. One of the clerks was retained, and the office,
having been leased for a year by its former tenant, was
still open pending the settlement of the estate. A. Rodgers Warren personally was a man who looked older
than he really was, a good liver, and popular among his
companions.

" What sort of fellers were his companions?" asked
Captain Elisha.

" You mean his friends in society, or his companions
down town in Wall Street?"

" The Wall Street ones. I guess I can find out something about the society ones. Anyhow, I can try. These
Wall Streeters that 'Bije chummed with — a quiet lot,
was they?"

Sylvester hesitated. " Why — why — not particularly
so," he admitted. " Nothing crooked about them, of
course. You see, a stock-broker's life is a nerve-racking,
rather exciting one, and —"

" And 'Bije and his chums were excited, too, hey?
All right, you needn't go any further. He was a good
husband while his wife lived, wa'n't he?"

" Yes. Frankly, Captain Warren, so far as I know,

your brother's personal habits were good. There was nothing against his character."

" I'm mighty glad to hear it. Mighty glad. Is there anything else you can tell me?"

" No. Our next move, provided you decide to accept the trust, the executorship, and the rest, is to get together — you and Graves, if he is well enough; you and I if he is not — and begin a careful examination of the stocks, bonds, assets, and debts of the estate. This must be done first of all."

" Graves hinted there wa'n't any debts, to amount to anything."

" So far as we can see, there are none, except a few trifling bills."

" Yes, yes. Hum!" Captain Elisha put down his coffee spoon and seemed to be thinking. He shook his head.

" You appear to be puzzled about something," observed the lawyer, who was watching him intently.

" I am. I was puzzled afore I left home, and I'm just as puzzled now."

" What puzzles you? if I may ask."

" Everything. And, if you'll excuse my sayin' so, Mr. Sylvester, I guess it puzzles you, too."

He returned his host's look. The latter pushed back his chair, preparatory to rising.

" It is all so perfectly simple, on the face of it, Captain Warren," he said. " Your brother realized that he must die, that his children and their money must be taken care of; you were his nearest relative; his trust in your honesty and judgment caused him to overlook the estrangement between you. That's the case, isn't it?"

" Yes. That's the case, on the face of it, as you say. But you've forgot to mention one item."

"What's that?"

"'Bije himself. You knew him pretty well, I can see that. So did I. And I guess that's why we're both puzzled."

Captain Elisha folded his napkin with care and stood up. Sylvester rose, also.

"Come downstairs," he said. "We can enjoy our cigars more comfortably there, and go on with our talk. That is, unless you're in a great hurry."

"No, I ain't in any special hurry. So I get up to Caroline's in season for supper — er, dinner, I mean — I don't care. But I don't want to keep you. You're a busy man."

"This is business. This way, Captain."

The big lounging room of the club, on the first floor, Fifth Avenue side, was almost empty when they entered it. The lawyer drew two big chairs near the open fire, rang the bell, and ordered cigars. After the cigars were lighted and the fragrant clouds of tobacco smoke were rising, he reopened the conversation. And now, in an easy, diplomatic way, he took his turn at questioning.

It was pretty thorough pumping, managed with the skill of an experienced cross-examiner. Captain Elisha, without realizing that he was doing so, told of his boyhood, his life at sea, his home at South Denboro, his position in the village, his work as selectman, as member of the school committee, and as director in the bank. The tone of the questioner expressed nothing — he was too well trained for that — but every item of information was tabulated and appraised.

The tall mahogany-cased clock struck three, then four. The lawyer finished his cigar and lit another. He offered a fresh one to his guest, but the offer was declined.

"No, thank you," observed the captain. "I've been

yarnin' away so fast that my breath's been too busy to keep this one goin'. There's consider'ble left yet. This is a better smoke than I'm used to gettin' at the store down home. I tell Ryder — he's our storekeeper and postmaster — that he must buy his cigars on the reel and cut 'em off with the scissors. When the gang of us all got a-goin' mail times, it smells like a rope-walk burnin' down. Ho! ho! It does, for a fact. Yet I kind of enjoy one of his five-centers, after all. You can get used to most anything. Maybe it's the home flavor or the society. P'raps they'd taste better still if they was made of seaweed. I'll trouble you for a match, Mr. Sylvester. Two of 'em, if you don't mind."

He whittled one match to a point with his pocket knife, impaled the cigar stump upon it, and relit with the other.

Meanwhile the room had been filling up. Around each of the big windows overlooking the Avenue were gathered groups of men, young and old, smoking, chatting, and gazing idly out. Captain Elisha regarded them curiously.

"This ain't a holiday, is it?" he asked, after a while.

"No. Why?"

"I was just wonderin' if all those fellers hadn't any work to do, that's all."

"Who? That crowd?" The lawyer laughed. "Oh, they're doing their regular stunt. You'll find most of them here every afternoon about this time."

"You don't say. Pay 'em wages for it, do you?"

"Not that I know of. Some of them are brokers, who come up after the Exchange closes. Others are business men, active or retired. Some don't have any business — except what they're doing now."

"I want to know! Humph! They remind me of the gang in the billiard room back home. The billiard-roomers — the chronic ones — don't have any business, either, except to keep the dust from collectin' on the chairs. That and talkin' about hard times. These chaps don't seem to be sufferin' from hard times, much."

"No. Most of the younger set have rich fathers or have inherited money."

"I see. They let the old man do the worryin'. That's philosophy, anyhow. What are they so interested in outside? Parade goin' by?"

"No. I imagine an unusually pretty girl passed just then."

"Is that so? Well, well! Say, Mr. Sylvester, the longer I stay in New York the more I see that the main difference between it and South Denboro is size. The billiard-room gang acts just the same way when the downstairs school teacher goes past. Hello!"

"What is it?"

"That young chap by the mizzen window looks sort of familiar to me. The one that stood up to shake a day-day to whoever was passin'. Hum! He's made a hit, ain't he? I expect some unprotected female's heart broke at that signal. I cal'late I know him."

"Who? Which one? Oh, that's young Corcoran Dunn. He is a lady-killer, in his own estimation. How d'ye do, Dunn."

The young man turning grinning from the window, caught a glimpse of the lawyer as the latter rose to identify him. He strolled over to the fire.

"Hello, Sylvester," he hailed, carelessly. "That was a peach. You should have seen her. What? Why, it's the Admiral!"

"How d'ye do, Mr. Dunn," said Captain Elisha.

"Have you two met before?" asked Sylvester in astonishment.

" Yes. I had the pleasure of assisting in the welcoming salute when our seafarin' friend come aboard. How was that, Captain? Some nautical class to that remark? "

" Yup. You done fust rate, considerin' how recent you shipped."

" Thanks. Overwhelmed, I'm sure." Then, with a look of languid amusement at the pair, " What is this — a meeting of the Board of Naval Affairs? Have you bought a yacht, Sylvester? "

" No." The lawyer's tone was sharp.

" Humph! Well, take my advice and don't. Yachts are all right, to have a good time on, but they cost like the devil to keep up. An auto is bad enough. By the way, Sylvester, did you hear about my running over the Irishman this morning? "

" Running over? " repeated the captain, aghast. " You didn't run over nobody, I hope."

" Well, I came devilish near it. Ha! ha! You see, the old tarrier was crossing Saint Nicholas Avenue, with a big market basket full of provisions — the family dinner, I suppose. By Jove, the household appetites must be good ones. It was slippery as the mischief, I was running the car, and I tried to go between the fellow and the curb. It would have been a decent bit of steering if I'd made it. But — ha! ha! — by Jove, you know, I didn't. I skidded. The man himself managed to hop out of the way, but his foot slipped, and down he went. Most ridiculous thing you ever saw. And the street! 'Pon my word it was paved with eatables."

Sylvester, plainly annoyed, did not reply. But Captain Elisha's concern was evident.

" The poor critter! " he exclaimed. " What did you do? "

"The last I saw of him he was sitting in the mud, looking at the upset. I didn't linger. Peters took the wheel, and we beat it. Lucky the cop didn't spot the license number. Might have cost me fifty. They've had me up for speeding twice before. What are you and the Admiral discussing, Sylvester?"

"We were discussing a business matter," answered the lawyer, with significant emphasis.

"Business? Why, sure! I forgot that you were Graves's partner. Settling the family affairs, hey? Well, I won't butt in. Ta, ta! See you later, Captain. You must go for a spin in that car of mine. I'll call for you some day. I'll show you something they don't do on Cape Cod. Regards to Caro and Steve."

He moved off, feeling that his invitation would have met with his mother's approval. She had announced that the country uncle was to be "cultivated."

Captain Elisha's cigar had gone out. He did not attempt to relight it.

"Whew!" he whistled. "Well, when I go for a 'spin,' as he calls it, with *him,* I cal'late my head'll be spinnin' so I won't be responsible for my actions. Whew!"

Sylvester looked curiously at him.

"So you met him before?" he asked.

"Yes. He was at the rooms when I fust landed. Or his mother was there then. He came a little later with Caroline and Stephen."

"I see."

"Yes. Know him and his ma pretty well, do you?"

"Slightly. I've met them, at mutual acquaintances' homes and about town."

"Pretty well fixed, I s'pose, ain't they?"

"I presume so. I don't know."

"Um. He's a sociable young feller, ain't he? Don't stand on any ceremony, hey? Caro and Steve think a lot of him and his mother."

"Yes. Graves has told me the Dunns were very intimate with the Warrens. In fact, just before your brother's death, I remember hearing a rumor that the two families might be even closer connected."

"You mean — er — Caroline and — er — him?"

"There was such a rumor. Probably nothing in it. There is no engagement, I am very sure."

"Yes, yes, I see. Well, Mr. Sylvester, I must be trottin' on. I'll think the whole business over for another day or so and then give you my decision, one way or the other."

"You can't give it now?"

"No-o. I guess I'd better not. However, I think —"

"Yes."

"Well, I think I may take the job. Take it on trial, anyhow."

"Good! I'm glad of it."

"You *are?*"

"I certainly am. And I'm very glad indeed to have made your acquaintance, Captain Warren. Good afternoon. I shall hope to see you again soon."

Captain Elisha left the Central Club in a surprised frame of mind. What surprised him was that a man of such thorough city training and habits as the senior partner of the law firm should express pleasure at the idea of his accepting the charge of A. Rodgers Warren's heirs and estate. Mr. Graves had shown no such feeling.

If he had heard Sylvester's report to Kuhn, at the office next day, he might have been even more surprised and pleased.

"He's a brick, Kuhn," declared the senior partner.

"A countryman, of course, but a keen, able, honest man, and, I think, a mighty good judge of character. If I was as sure of his ability to judge investments and financial affairs, I should be certain the Warren children couldn't be in better hands. And no doubt we can help him when it comes to that. He'll probably handle the girl and boy in his own way, and his outside greenness may jar them a little. But it'll do them good to be jarred at their age. He's all right, and I hope he accepts the whole trust."

"Well," exclaimed Mr. Kuhn; "you surprise me. Graves seemed to be —"

"Graves suffers from the absolute lack of a sense of humor. His path through life is about three feet wide and bordered with rock-ribbed conventionality. If a man has a joke in his system, Graves doesn't understand it and is suspicious. I tell, you, Kuhn, there's more honest common sense and ability in the right hand of this Down-East salt than there ever was in Rodgers Warren's whole body."

CHAPTER VII

DURING the next day Caroline Warren and her brother saw little of their uncle. Not that they complained of this or sought his society. The policy of avoidance and what Stephen called " freezing out " had begun, and the young people kept to themselves as much as possible. At breakfast Caroline was coldly polite, and her brother cold, although his politeness was not overdone. However, Captain Elisha did not seem to notice. He was preoccupied, said but little, and spent the forenoon in writing a second letter to Miss Abigail. In it he told of his experience on board the *Empress of the Ocean* and of the luncheon at the Central Club. But he said nothing concerning his nephew and niece further than the statement that he was still getting acquainted, and that Caroline was a real nice looking girl.

"I suppose you wonder what I've decided about taking the guardianship," he added, just at the close. "Well, Abbie, I'm about in the position of Luther Sylvester when he fell off the dock at Orham. The tide was out, and he went into the soft mud, all under. When the folks who saw him tumble got to the edge and looked over, they saw a round, black thing sticking out of the mire, and, judging 'twas Lute's head, they asked him how he felt. 'I don't know yet,' sputters Lute, 'whether I'm drowned or smothered, but I'm somewheres betwixt and between.' That's me, Abbie, on that guardian business. I'm still betwixt and between. But before this day's over I'll be drowned or smothered, and I'll let you know which next time I write."

After lunch he took a stroll in the Park and passed up and down the paths, thinking, thinking. Returning, he found that Caroline and Stephen had gone for an auto ride with the Dunns and would not be home for dinner. So he ate that meal in solitary state, waited upon by Edwards.

That evening, as he sat smoking in the library, the butler appeared to announce a caller.

"Someone to see you, sir," said Edwards. "Here's his card, sir."

"Eh? Someone to see *me?* Guess you've made a mistake, haven't you, Commodore? I don't know anybody who'd be likely to come visitin' me here in New York. Why, yes! Well, I declare! Tell him to walk right in. Mr. Pearson, I'm glad to see you. This is real neighborly."

The caller was young Pearson, the captain's acquaintance of the previous forenoon. They shook hands heartily.

"Perhaps you didn't think I should accept that invitation of yours, Captain Warren," observed Pearson. "I told you I meant it when I said yes. And calling within thirty-six hours is pretty good proof, isn't it?"

"Suits me fust-rate. I'm mighty glad you came. Set right down. Lonesome at the boardin' house, was it?"

Pearson made a grimace. "Lonesome!" he repeated. "Ugh! Let's talk of something else. Were you in time for your appointment yesterday noon?"

"Why, yes; I was and I wasn't. Say, won't you have a cigar? That's right. And I s'pose, bein' as this is New York, I'd ought to ask you to take somethin' to lay the dust, hey? I ain't made any inquiries myself, but I shouldn't wonder if the Commodore — the feller that let you in — could find somethin' in the spare room closet or somewheres, if I ask him."

The young man laughed. "If you mean a drink," he said, "I don't care for it, thank you."

"What? You ain't a teetotaler, are you?"

"No, not exactly. But —"

"But you can get along without it, hey? So can I; generally do, fur's that goes. But *I'm* from South Denboro. I thought here in New York —"

"Oh, there are many people, even here in New York, who are not convinced that alcohol is a food."

"You don't tell me! Well, I'm livin' and learnin' every day. Judgin' from stories and the yarns in the Boston newspapers, folks up our way have the idea that this town is a sort of annex to the bad place. All right, then we won't trouble the Commodore. I notice you're lookin' over my quarters. What do you think of 'em?"

Pearson had, in spite of himself, been glancing about the room. Its luxury and the evident signs of taste and wealth surprised him greatly.

"Astonish you to find me livin' in a place like this, hey?"

"Why, why, yes, it does, somewhat. I didn't realize you were such an aristocrat, Captain Warren. If I had, I might have been a little more careful of my dress in making my first call."

"Dress? Oh, you mean you'd have put on your Sunday clothes. Well, I'm glad you didn't. You see, *I* haven't got on my regimentals, and if you'd been on dress parade I might have felt bashful. Ho, ho! I don't wonder you are surprised. This is a pretty swell neighborhood, ain't it?"

"Yes, it is."

" These — er — apartments, now. 'Bout as good as any in town, are they?"

" Pretty nearly. There are few better — much better."

" I thought so. You wouldn't call livin' in 'em economizin' to any consider'ble extent, would you?"

" No," with a laugh; " no, *I* shouldn't, but my ideas of economy are — well, different. They have to be. Are you ecomomizing, Captain?"

Captain Elisha laughed and rubbed his knee.

" No," he chuckled, *"I* ain't, but my nephew and niece are. These are their rooms."

" Oh, you're visiting?"

" No, I don't know's you'd call it visitin'. I don't know what you would call it. I'm here, that's about all you can say."

He paused and remained silent. His friend was silent, also, not knowing exactly what remark to make.

" How's the novel comin' on?" asked the captain, a minute later.

" Oh, slowly. I'm not at all sure it will ever be finished. I get discouraged sometimes."

" No use in doin' that. What sort of a yarn is it goin' to be? Give me a gen'ral idea of the course you're tryin' to steer. That is, if it ain't a secret."

" It isn't. But there's mighty little worth telling. When I began I thought I had a good scheme, but it seems pretty weak and dish-watery now."

" Most things do while their bein' done, if you really care about doin' 'em well. Heave ahead! You said 'twas a sea yarn, and I'm a sort of specialist when it comes to salt water. Maybe I might prescribe just the right tonic, though 'tain't very likely."

Pearson began to outline the plot of his novel, speaking slowly at first, but becoming more interested as he continued. Captain Elisha listened meditatively, puffing solemnly at his cigar, and interrupting but seldom.

"I think that's a pretty good idea," he observed, at length. "Yes, sir, that sounds promisin', to me. This cap'n of yours now, he's a good feller. Don't get him too good, though; that wouldn't be natural. And don't get him too bad, neither. I know it's the fashion, judgin' by the sea yarns I've read lately, to have a Yankee skipper sort of a cross between a prize fighter and a murderer. Fust day out of port he begins by pickin' out the most sickly fo'mast hand aboard, mashes him up, and then takes the next invalid. I got a book about that kind of a skipper out of our library down home a spell ago, and the librarian said 'twas awful popular. A strong story, she said, and true to life. Well, 'twas strong — you could pretty nigh smell it — but as for bein' true to life, I had my doubts. I've been to sea, command of a vessel, for a good many years, and sometimes I'd go weeks, whole weeks, without jumpin' up and down on a single sailor. Fact! Got my exercise other ways, I presume likely.

"I tell you," he went on, "the main trouble with that tale of yours, as I see it, is that you're talkin' about things you ain't ever seen. Now there's plenty you have seen, I wouldn't wonder. Let's see, you was born in Belfast, you said. Live there long, did you?"

"Yes, until I went away to school."

"Your father, he went to sea, did he?"

"Yes. But his ship was lost, with all hands, when I was a baby."

"But your Uncle Jim wa'n't lost. You remember him well; you said so. Tell me something you remember."

Before the young man was aware of it, he was telling of his Uncle Jim, of the latter's return from voyages, of his own home life, of his mother, and of the village where he spent his boyhood. Then, led on by the captain's questioning, he continued with his years at college, his experiences as reporter and city editor. Without being conscious that he was doing so, he gave his host a pretty full sketch of himself, his story, and his ambitions.

"Mr. Pearson," said Captain Elisha, earnestly, "don't you worry about that yarn of yours. If you'll take the advice of an old feller who knows absolutely nothin' about such things, keep on rememberin' about your Uncle Jim. He was a man, every inch of him, and a seaman, too. Put lots of him into this hero of yours, and you won't go fur wrong. And when it comes to handlin' a ship, why — well, if you *want* to come to me, I'll try and help you out best I can."

Pearson was delighted.

"You *will?*" he cried. "Splendid! It's mighty good of you. May I spring some of my stuff on you as I write it?"

"Sartin you may. Any time, I'll be tickled to death. I'll be tickled to have you call, too; that is, if callin' on an old salt like me won't be too tirin'."

The answer was emphatic and reassuring.

"Thank you," said Captain Elisha. "I'm much obliged. Come often, do. I — well, the fact is, I'm likely to get sort of lonesome myself, I'm afraid. Yes, I shouldn't wonder if I did."

He sighed, tossed away the stump of his cigar, and added,

"Now, I want to ask you somethin'. You newspaper fellers are supposed to know about all there is to know of everything under the sun. Do you know much about the Stock Exchange?"

Pearson smiled.

"All I can afford to know," he said.

"Humph! That's a pretty good answer. Knowledge is power, they say, but — but I cal'late knowledge of the Stock Exchange is poverty, with a good many folks."

"I think you're right, Captain. It's none of my business, but — were you planning to tackle Wall Street?"

Captain Elisha glanced, under his brows, at his new friend, and his eyes twinkled.

"Didn't know but I might," he replied, solemnly. "Ain't got any — er — tips, any sure things you want to put me on to, have you?"

"I have not. My experience of Wall Street 'sure things' leads me to believe that they're sure — but only for the other fellow."

"Hum! I know a chap down home that made money in stocks. He made it so easy that, as the boys say, 'twas almost a shame to take the money. And 'twas the makin' of him, too."

Pearson was embarrassed and troubled. If this big-hearted, simple-minded countryman had come to New York to buck the stock market, it was time to sound a warning. But had he, on such short acquaintance, the right to warn? The captain was shrewd in his own way. Might not the warning seem presumptuous?

"So — this — this friend of yours was a successful speculator, was he?" he asked. "He was lucky."

"Think so? Well, maybe. His name was Elkanah Chase, and his dad was old man 'Rastus Chase, who made consider'ble in cranberries and one thing or 'nother. The old man brought Elkanah up to be what he called a gentleman. Ho! ho! Hi hum! I ain't sure what

109

'Rastus's idea of a gentleman was, but if he cal'lated to have his son a tramp in go-to-meetin' clothes, he got his wish. When the old man died, he wiiled the boy fifteen thousand dollars. Well, fifteen thousand dollars is a fortune to some folks — if they ain't economizin' in New York — but to Elkanah 'twas just about enough to make him realize his poverty. So, to make it bigger, he got one of them 'tips' from a college friend down here in Wall Street, and put the heft of ten thousand into it. *And,* I swan, if it didn't double his money!"

Captain Elisha's visitor shook his head. He did not even smile.

"He was extremely fortunate," he said. "I give you my word, Captain Warren, that the majority of first speculators don't turn out that way. I hope he was wise enough to keep his profits."

The captain rubbed his chin.

"Jim —" he began. "Excuse me, I should have said Mr. Pearson, but I've got sort of in the habit of callin' folks by their first names. Livin' where you know everybody so well gets you into those habits."

"Jim suits me. I hope you'll cultivate the habit."

"Do you? Well, I will. Now, Jim, referrin' to what I was goin' to say, you, bein' a newspaper man, ought to know everything, but it's pretty plain you don't know Elkanah Chase. Keep his profits! Why, when a feller is all but convinced that he knows it all, one little bit of evidence like that speculation settles it for him conclusive. Elkanah, realizin' that Wall Street was his apple pie, opened his mouth to swaller it at one gulp. He put his profits and every other cent he had into another sure thing tip."

"And won again?"

"No. He lost all that and some more that he borrowed."

"But I thought you said it was the making of him!"

"It was. He had to take a job over at the overalls factory in Ostable. As a fifteen thousand dollar gentleman, he was pretty average of a mess, but they tell me he makes middlin' good overalls. Elkanah convinced me that Wall Street has its good points."

He chuckled. Pearson, relieved, laughed in sympathy.

"Has he paid back the money he borrowed?" he inquired.

"No-o! I guess the creditors'll have to take it out in overalls. However, it's a satisfaction to some of 'em to watch Chase really work. I know that gives me *my* money's worth."

"Oh, ho! You are one of the creditors! Captain Warren, I'm surprised. I sized you up as a shrewder judge of investments."

Captain Elisha colored. "I judged that one correct," he answered. "If I hadn't thought 'twould have turned out that way I never would have plunged. You see, old man Chase was a friend of mine, and — However," he added, hastily changing the subject, "we've strayed some off the course. When I mentioned the Stock Exchange I did it because my brother was a member of it, and I cal'late you might have known him."

Pearson was astonished. "Your brother was a member of the Exchange?" he repeated.

"Um-hm. Never would have guessed it, would you? I s'pose you cal'late all the stock I knew about was on the hoof. Well, I have been acquainted with other breeds in my time. My brother's name was Abijah Warren — A. Rodgers Warren, he called himself."

The effect of this announcement was instantaneous and electric. The young man sat back in his chair.

" A. Rodgers Warren was your brother? " he cried.

" Um-hm. Seems to stagger you some. Contrast between us as big as all that comes to? "

" But — but, Captain Warren — Your brother — Tell me, is Miss Caroline Warren your niece? "

" She is. And Steve is my nephew. 'Tain't possible you're acquainted with them? "

Pearson rose to his feet. " Is — They used to live on the Avenue," he said. " But you said you were visiting. Captain Warren, is this your niece's apartment? "

" Yes, hers and Steve's. Why, what's the matter? Ain't goin', are you? "

" I think perhaps I had better. It is getting late."

" Late! It's only the shank of the evenin'. Jim, I ain't so blind that I can't see through an open window. It ain't the lateness that makes you want to leave so sudden. Is there some trouble between you and Caroline? Course, it's none of my business, and you needn't tell me unless you want to."

The answer was prompt enough.

" No," replied Pearson. " No. I assure you there is nothing of that kind. I — I met Miss Warren. In fact, at one time we were well acquainted. I have the very highest opinion of her. But I think it is best to —"

" Just a minute now. No trouble with Steve? He's a boy and at an age when he's pretty well satisfied with himself and you have to make allowance."

" No. Steve and I were quite friendly. I'm sorry to cut my visit short, but it is late and I *must* go."

He was moving toward the door. Captain Elisha looked at him intently.

"Well, if you must," he said. "But I hope you'll come again soon. Will you?"

"I hope I may. I give you my word, Captain, that I appreciate your invitation, and I do want to know you better."

"Same here. I don't often take sudden fancies, Jim, but I knew your uncle, and I'd bet consider'ble on any member of his family. And I *was* kind of interested in that novel of yours. You haven't said you'd come again. Will you?"

Pearson was much embarrassed.

"I should like to come, immensely," he said, with an earnestness unmistakable; "but — but, to be honest, Captain Warren, there is a reason, one which I may tell you sometime, but can't now — neither Miss Warren nor her brother have any part in it — which makes me reluctant to visit you here. Won't you come and see me at the boarding house? Here's the address. *Will* you come?"

"Sartin! I figured on doin' it, if you gave me the chance."

"Thank you, you'll be welcome. Of course it is *only* a boarding house, and not a very good one. My own room is — well, different from this."

"Yup. Maybe that's why I expect to feel at home in it. Good night, Jim. Thank you for callin'. Shall I ring for the Commodore to pilot you out?"

"No, I can find my way. I — Someone is coming."

From the hall came the clang of the elevator door and the sound of voices. Before the captain or his friend could move, Caroline, Stephen, Mrs. Corcoran Dunn, and Malcolm entered. Caroline was the first to reach the library. Her entrance brought her face to face with Pearson.

"I beg your pardon," she began. "I did not know there was anyone here."

"It's only a friend of mine, Caroline," explained her uncle, quickly. "Just callin' on me, he was."

"Good evening, Miss Warren," said Pearson, quietly.

The girl looked at him for an instant. Then her expression changed, and, with a smile, she extended her hand.

"Why, Mr. Pearson!" she exclaimed. "I'm very glad to see you. You must excuse me for not recognizing you at once. Steve, you remember Mr. Pearson."

Stephen also extended a hand.

"Sure!" he said. "Glad to see you again, Pearson. Haven't met you for an age. How are you?"

Pearson shook both the hands. He was embarrassed and hesitated in his reply.

"It *has* been some time since we met," he said. "This is an unexpected pleasure. Ah, Mr. Dunn, good evening."

"It is Mr. Pearson, the financial writer of the *Planet,* Malcolm," said Caroline. "You used to know him, I think."

"Don't remember, I'm sure. Yes, I do. Met you at the University Club, didn't I?"

"Yes. I was formerly a member."

"And let me present you to Mrs. Corcoran Dunn," went on the girl. "Mr. Pearson used to know father well."

Mrs. Dunn inspected the visitor through her lorgnette, and condescended to admit that she was "delighted."

"I'm very glad you called," continued Caroline. "We were just in time, weren't we? Do sit down. And if you will wait a minute until we remove our wraps — Steve ring for Edwards, please."

"I'm afraid I can't wait, Miss Warren. I dropped in to see your uncle, at his invitation, and, as a matter of fact, I didn't know —"

"To see our *uncle!*" interrupted Stephen, in amazement. "Who?"

"Your uncle, Captain Warren here," explained Pearson, surprised in his turn. "He and I made each other's acquaintance yesterday, and he asked me to call."

"You — you called to see *him?*" repeated Stephen. "Why, what in the world — ?"

"I took the liberty of askin' him, Caroline," observed Captain Elisha quietly, and ignoring the last speaker. "I didn't know you knew him, and I used to sail along with *his* uncle, so he seemed almost like own folks."

"Oh!" Caroline's manner changed. "I presume it was a business call," she said slowly. "I beg pardon for interrupting. We had not seen you since father's death, Mr. Pearson, and I assumed that you had called upon my brother and me. Excuse me. Mrs. Dunn, we will go into the drawing-room."

She led the way toward the apartment. Captain Elisha was about to speak. Pearson, however, explained for him.

"Miss Warren," he said, "if by a business call you mean one in the interest of the *Planet,* I assure you that you are mistaken. I am no longer connected with any paper. I met Captain Warren, under rather unusual circumstances. We discovered that we had mutual friends and mutual interests. He asked me to call on him, and I did so. I did not know, until five minutes ago, that he was your uncle or that you and your brother lived here. I beg you won't leave the room on my account. I was about to go when you came. Good evening."

He bowed and stepped toward the hall. Captain Elisha laid a hand on his arm and detained him.

"Just a minute," he said. "Caroline, I want you and Steve to know that what Mr. Pearson says is exactly true. I ain't the kind to talk to the newspapers about the private affairs of my relations, and, if I'm any judge of character, Mr. Pearson, knowin' you as it seems he does, wouldn't be the kind to listen. That's all. Now, Jim, if you must go."

He and his guest were at the door. Caroline and Mrs. Dunn were at the opposite side of the room. Suddenly the girl halted, turned, and, moving across to where her uncle and the young man were standing, once more extended her hand.

"Mr. Pearson," she said, impulsively, "again I ask your pardon. I should have known. I am very sorry I spoke as I did. Will you forgive me?"

Pearson colored. His embarrassment was more evident than before.

"There is no occasion for apology, Miss Warren," he said. "I don't wonder you thought I had come in my former capacity as reporter."

"Yes, you do. You *must* have wondered. I am very glad you called to see my — my guardian, and I hope you will continue to do so. Father used to speak so highly of you, and I'm sure he valued your friendship. Stephen and I wish to consider his friends ours. Please believe that you are welcome here at any time."

Pearson's reply was brief.

"Thank you, Miss Warren," he said. "You are very kind. Good evening."

In the hall, as they waited for the elevator, Captain Elisha, happier than at any time since his arrival in New York, clapped his friend on the shoulder.

"Jim," he said, "I was beginnin' to doubt my judgment of things and folks. Now I feel better. That niece of mine has got the right stuff in her. After *that* invitation, you will come and see us once in a while. That makes it easier, hey?"

Pearson shook his head. "I'm not sure, Captain," he observed, slowly, "that it doesn't make it harder. I shall look for you at the boarding house very soon. Don't disappoint me. Good night."

The captain's last remark that evening was made to Edwards, whom he met just outside the door of his bedroom.

"Commodore," he said, "a barn full of rats is a nuisance, ain't it?"

"Sir?" stammered the astonished butler.

"I say a barn full of rats is a nuisance."

"Why — why, yes, sir. I should think it might be, sir."

"Yup. Well, I know a worse one. It's a house full of mysteries. By, by, Son. Pleasant dreams."

He sat up until late, meditating profoundly. Then, taking from its envelope the letter yet unsealed, which he had written to Miss Abigail Baker, he added this postscript:

"Eleven o'clock. I have decided, Abbie, to accept the guardianship and the rest of it, for a spell, anyhow. Shall notify the lawyers in the morning. Necessity is one thing, and pleasure is another. I doubt if I find the job pleasant, but I guess it is necessary. Anyhow, it looks that way to me."

CHAPTER VIII

ANNOUNCEMENT of Captain Elisha's decision followed quickly. Sylvester, Kuhn, and Graves received the telephone message stating it, and the senior partner was unqualifiedly delighted. Kuhn accepted his associate's opinion with some reservation. "It is an odd piece of business, the whole of it," he declared. "I shall be curious to see how it works out." As for Mr. Graves, when the information was conveyed to him by messenger, he expressed disgust and dismay. "Ridiculous!" he said. "Doctor, I simply must be up and about within the next few days. It is necessary that a sane, conservative man be at the office. Far be it from me to say a word against Sylvester, as a lawyer, but he is subject to impressions. I imagine this Cape Codder made him laugh, and, therefore, in his opinion, is all right. I'm glad I'm not a joker."

The captain said that he would be down later on to talk things over. Meanwhile, if the "papers and such" could be gotten together, it would "sort of help along." Sylvester explained that there were certain legal and formal ceremonies pertaining to the acceptance of the trust to be gone through with, and these must have precedence. "All right," answered the captain. "Let's have 'em all out at once and get the ache and agony over. I'll see you by and by."

When Mrs. Corcoran Dunn made her daily visit to the Warren apartment that afternoon, she found Caroline alone and almost in tears. Captain Elisha had broken the news at the table during luncheon, after which he went downtown. Stephen, having raved, protested, and made himself generally disagreeable and his sister correspondingly miserable, had departed for the club. It was a time for confidences, and the wily Mrs. Dunn realized that fact. She soothed, comforted, and within half an hour, had learned the whole story. Caroline told her all, the strange will, the disclosure concerning the country uncle, and the inexplicable clauses begging the latter to accept the executorship, the trust, and the charge of her brother and herself. Incidentally she mentioned that a possible five hundred thousand was the extreme limit of the family's pecuniary resources.

" Now you know everything," sobbed Caroline. " Oh, Mrs. Dunn, *you* won't desert us, will you?"

The widow's reply was a triumph, of its kind. In it were expressed sorrow, indignation, pity, and unswerving loyalty. Desert them? Desert the young people, toward whom she had come to feel almost like a mother? Never!

" You may depend on Malcolm and me, my dear," she declared. " We are not fair-weather friends. And, after all, it is not so very bad. Affairs might be very much worse."

" Worse! Oh, Mrs. Dunn, how could they be? Think of it! Stephen and I are dependent upon him for everything. We must ask him for every penny. And whatever he says to do we *must* do. We're obliged to. Just think! if he decides to take us back with him to — South Denboro, or whatever dreadful place he comes from, we shall have to go — and live there."

"But he won't, my dear. He won't. It will take some time to settle your father's affairs, and the business will have to be transacted here in New York."

"I know. I suppose that's true. But that doesn't make it any easier. If he stops here he will stay with us. And what shall we do? We can't introduce him to our friends, or, at least, to any except our best, our understanding friends, like you and Malcolm."

"Why, I'm not sure. He is rather — well — er — countryfied, but I believe he has a good heart. He is not rude or unkind or anything of that sort, is he?"

"No. No-o. He's not that, at all. In fact, he means to be kind in his way. But it's such a different way from ours. He is not used to society; he wouldn't understand that certain things and ways were absolutely essential. I suppose it isn't his fault exactly, but that doesn't help. And how can we tell him?"

"I don't know that you can tell him, but you might hint. Diplomacy, my dear, is one of the necessary elements of life. Whatever else you do remember to be diplomatic. My poor husband used to have a pet proverb — he was interested in politics, my dear, and some of his sayings were a trifle grotesque but very much to the point. He used to say that one could get rid of more flies with molasses than with a club. And I think he was right. Now let me consider. Let's look the situation right in the face. Of course your guardian, as a companion, as an associate for us, for our kind of people, is, to be quite frank, impossible."

"Yes. Yes, I'm sure he is."

"Yes. But he *is* your guardian. Therefore, we can't get rid of him with — well, with a club. He must be endured and made as endurable as possible. And it certainly will not do to offend him."

"Steve says we must do what he calls freezing him out — make him feel that we do not want him here."

"Hum! Well, Stephen is a nice boy — Malcolm adores him — but he isn't a diplomat. If we should — what is it? — freeze out your uncle —"

"Please call him something else."

"Well, we'll call him the encumbrance on the estate; that's legal, I believe, and expresses it nicely. If we should freeze out the encumbrance, we *might* freeze him to his village, and he *might* insist on your going with him, which wouldn't do at *all*, my dear. For one thing, Malcolm would probably insist on going, also, and I, for one, don't yearn for rural simplicity. Ha! ha! Oh, you mustn't mind me. I'm only a doting mamma, dearie, and I have my air castles like everyone else. So, freezing out won't do. No, you and Steve must be polite to our encumbrance."

"I shall not get on my knees to him and beg. That I sha'n't do."

"No one expects you to. If anyone begs it should be he. Condescend to just a little. Make him feel his place. Correct him when he goes too far wrong, and ignore him when he gets assertive. As for getting rid of him at times when it may be necessary — well, I think you may safely leave that to me."

"To you? Oh, Mrs. Dunn, we couldn't think of dragging you into it. It is bad enough that we should be disgraced; but you must not be."

"My dear child, I *think* my position in society is sufficiently established to warrant a risk or two. If *I* am seen in company with — with the encumbrance, people will merely say, 'Oh, it's another of her eccentricities!' that's all. Now, don't worry, and don't fret all that pretty color from your cheeks. Always remember this: it is but for a year or a trifle over. Then you will be of age and can send your encumbrance to the right-about in a hurry."

Caroline, under the spell of this convincing eloquence, began to cheer up. She even smiled.   -

"Well," she said, "I will try to be diplomatic. I really will. But Stephen — I'm not sure what dreadful thing *he* will do."

"He will return to college soon. I will take upon myself the convincing of the encumbrance to that effect. And while he is at home, Malcolm will take charge of him. He will be delighted to do it."

"Mrs. Dunn, how can we ever thank you sufficiently? What should we do without you and Malcolm?"

"I *hope*, my dear, that you will never have to do without me; not for many years, at any rate. Of course, there is always my poor heart, but — we won't worry, will we?"

So, with a kiss and an embrace, this affecting interview ended.

There was another that evening between Mrs. Dunn and her son, which was not devoid of interest. Malcolm listened to the information which his mother gave him, and commented upon it in characteristic fashion.

"Humph!" he observed, "two hundred and fifty thousand, instead of the two million you figured on, Mater! Two hundred and fifty thousand isn't so much, in these days."

"No," replied his parent, sharply, "it isn't so much, but it isn't so little, either."

"I suppose one can get along on it."

"Yes, one can. In fact, I know of two who are managing with a good deal less. Don't be any more of a fool than you can help, Malcolm. The sum itself isn't small, and, besides, the Warrens are a family of standing. To be connected with them is worth a good deal. There are infinite possibilities in it. Oh, if only I might live to see the day when tradespeople meant something other than nuisances to be dodged, I *think* I could die contented."

"Caro's a decent sort of a girl," commented Malcolm, reflectively.

"She's a bright girl and an attractive one. Just now she is in a mood to turn to us, to you. But, for Heaven's sake, be careful! She is delicate and sensitive and requires managing. She likes you. If only you weren't such a blunderer!"

"Much obliged, Mater. You're free with your compliments this evening. What's the trouble? Another ' heart '? "

"No. My heart I can trust, up to certain limits. But I'm afraid of your head, just as I always was of your father's. And here's one more bit of advice: Be careful how you treat that country uncle."

"The Admiral! Ho! ho! He's a card."

"He may be the trump that will lose us the trick. Treat him civilly; yes, even cordially, if you can. And *don't* insult him as you did the first time you and he met."

The young man crossed his legs, and grunted in resignation.

"Well," he said, "it's going to be a confounded bore, but, at the very longest, it'll last but a year. Then Caro will be her own mistress."

"Yes. But there are three hundred and sixty-five days in a year; remember that."

"All right, Mater. You can bet on me. The old hayseed and I will be bosom pals. Wait and see."

The formalities at the lawyers' took some time. Captain Elisha was absent from the apartment the better part of the following two days. The evenings, however, he spent with his niece and nephew, and, if at all sensitive to sudden changes of the temperature, he must have noticed that the atmosphere of the library was less frigid. Caroline was not communicative, did not make conversation, nor was she in the least familiar; but she answered his questions, did not leave the room when he entered, and seemed inclined to accept his society with resignation, if not with enthusiasm. Even Stephen was less sarcastic and bitter. At times, when his new guardian did or said something which offended his highly cultivated sense of the proprieties, he seemed inclined to burst out with a sneer; but a quick "ahem!" or a warning glance from his sister caused him to remain silent and vent his indignation by kicking a footstool or barking a violent order at the unresisting Edwards. Caroline and her brother had had a heart to heart talk, and, as a result, the all-wise young gentleman promised to make no more trouble than he could help.

"Though, by gad, Caro," he declared, "it's only for you I do it! If I had my way the old butt-in should understand exactly what I think of him."

On Thursday, after luncheon, as Captain Elisha sat in his own room, reading a book he had taken from the library, there came a knock at the door.

"Come ahead in!" ordered the captain. Caroline entered. Her uncle rose and put down the book.

"Oh!" he exclaimed, "is it you? Excuse me. I thought 'twas the Commodore — Edwards, I mean. If I'd known you was comin' callin', Caroline, I shouldn't have been quite so bossy. Guess I'd have opened the door for you, instead of lettin' you do it yourself."

"Thank you," answered his niece. "I came to see you on — I suppose you might call it business. At any rate, it is a financial matter. I sha'n't detain you long."

Captain Elisha was a trifle disappointed.

"Oh," he said, "on business, was it? I hoped — I didn't know but you'd come just out of sociability. However, I'm mighty glad to see you, Caroline, no matter what it's for. That's a real becomin' dress you've got on," he added, inspecting her admiringly. "I declare, you look prettier every time I see you. You favor your pa consider'ble; I can see it more and more. 'Bije had about all the good looks there was in our family," with a chuckle. "Set down, do."

The girl seated herself in a rocker, and looked at him for a moment without speaking. She seemed to have something on her mind, and not to know exactly how to express it.

"Captain Warren," she began, "I — I came to ask a favor. I am obliged to ask it, because you are our —" she almost choked over the hated word —" our guardian, and I can no longer act on my own responsibility. I wish to ask you for some money."

Captain Elisha nodded gravely.

"I see," he said. "Well, Caroline, I don't believe you'll find me very close-fisted. I think I told you and Steve that you was to do just as you'd been in the habit of doin'. Of course I *am* your guardian now, and I shall be held responsible for whatever expense comes to the estate. It is quite a responsibility, and I so understand it. As I said to you when I told you I'd decided to take the job on trial, *while* I have it it'll be my pride to see that you or your brother don't lose anything. I intend, if the Almighty spares me so long and I keep on with the trust, to turn over, when my term's out, at least as much to you and Steve as your father left. That's all. Excuse me for mentioning it again. Now, how much do you want? Is your reg'lar allowance too small? Remember, I don't know much about such things here in New York, and you must be frank and aboveboard and tell me if you have any complaints."

"I have no complaints. My allowance is sufficient. It is the same that father used to give me, and it is all I need. But this is a matter outside my personal needs."

"Um-hm. Somethin' to do with the household expenses, hey?"

"No. It is — is a matter of — well, of charity. It may amount to several hundred dollars."

"Yes, yes. I see. Charity, hey? Church?"

"No. One of the maids, Annie, has trouble at home, and I wanted to help her."

The captain nodded once more.

"Annie," he repeated, "that's the rosy-faced one? The Irish one?"

"Yes. Her father was seriously injured the other day and cannot work. His hip is broken, and the doctor's bill will be large. They are very poor, and I thought perhaps —" She hesitated, faltered, and then said haughtily: "Father was very sympathetic and liked to have me do such things."

"Sho! sho! Sartin! Course he did. I like it, too. I'm glad you came to me just as you did, Caroline. How much do you want to start with?"

"I don't know, exactly. I thought I might ask our own doctor to attend to the case, and might send them some delicacies and food."

"Good idea! Go right ahead, Caroline."

"Thank you. I have been over to see them, and they need help — they really do."

"I presume likely. How'd the accident happen? Anybody's fault, was it?"

Caroline's eyes snapped. "Indeed it was!" she said, indignantly. "It was a wet morning, after a rain, and the pavement was slippery. Mr. Moriarty, Annie's father, was not working that day — they were making some repairs at the factory where he is employed, I believe — and he had gone out to do the family marketing. He was crossing the street when an automobile, recklessly driven, so everyone says, drove directly down on him. He tried to jump out of the way and succeeded — otherwise he might have been killed; but he fell and broke his hip. He is an old man, and the case is serious."

"Dear! dear! you don't tell me! Poor old chap! The auto feller — did he help? Seems to me he ought to be the one to be spendin' the money. 'Twas his fault."

"Help! Indeed he didn't! He and the man with him merely laughed, as if it was a good joke, put on speed, and disappeared as quickly as possible."

"Why, the mean swab! Did this Mr. Moriarty or the folks around get the license number of the auto?"

"No. All they know is that it was a big yellow car with two men in it."

"Hey? A yellow car?"

"Yes. Somewhat similar to the one Malcolm — Mr. Dunn drives."

"So, so! Hum! Where did it happen?"

"On Saint Nicholas Avenue, near One Hundred and Twenty-Eighth Street."

"Eh? Saint Nicholas Avenue, you say?"

"Yes." Caroline rose and turned to go. "Thank you, Captain Warren," she said. "I will tell Doctor Henry to take the case at once."

The captain did not answer immediately. With his chin in his hand he was gazing at the floor.

"Good afternoon," said Caroline.

Her uncle looked up.

"Er — Wait just a minute, Caroline," he said. "I guess maybe, if you don't mind, I'd like to think this over a little afore you go too far. You have your doctor go right ahead and see to the old man, and you order the things to eat and whatever's necessary. But afore you give Annie or her father any money, I'd kind of like to figger a little mite."

His niece stopped short, turned and stared at him.

"Oh!" she said, slowly and icily, "I see. Please don't trouble yourself. I should have known. However, my allowance is my own, and I presume I am permitted to do what I please with that."

"Caroline, don't be hasty. I ain't sayin' no about the money. Far from it. I only —"

"I understand — thoroughly. Don't trouble to 'figure,' as you call it. Oh! *why* did I humiliate myself? I should have known!"

"Caroline, please —"

But the girl had gone, closing the door after her. Captain Elisha shook his head, heaved a deep sigh, and then, sinking back into his chair, relapsed into meditation. Soon afterward he put on his hat and coat and went out.

Half an hour later he entered the office of a firm of commission brokers on lower Broad Street, and inquired if a gentleman by the name of Mr. Malcolm Dunn was connected with that establishment. On being answered in the affirmative, he asked if Mr. Dunn were in. Yes, he was.

"Well," said Captain Elisha, "I'd like to speak to

him a minute or so. Just tell him my name's Warren, if you don't mind, young feller."

The clerk objected to being addressed as "young feller," and showed his disapproval by the haughty and indifferent manner in which he departed on the errand. However, he did so depart, and returned followed by Malcolm himself. The latter, who had been misled by the name into supposing his caller to be Stephen Warren, was much astonished when he saw the captain seated outside the railing.

"Good afternoon," said Captain Elisha, rising and extending his hand. "How are you to-day, sir? Pretty smart?"

The young man answered briefly that he was all right. He added he was glad to see his visitor, a statement more polite than truthful.

"Well, what's up?" he inquired, condescendingly. "Nothing wrong with Caro or Steve, I hope."

"No, they're fust-rate, thank you."

"What's doing, then? Is it pleasure or business?"

"Well, a little of both, maybe. It's always a pleasure to see you, of course; and I have got a little mite of business on hand."

Malcolm smiled, in his languid fashion. If he suspected sarcasm in the first part of the captain's reply, it did not trouble him. His self-sufficiency was proof against anything of that sort.

"Business," he repeated. "Well, that's what I'm here for. Thinking of cornering the — er — potato market, were you?"

"No-o. Cranberries would be more in my line, and I cal'late you fellers don't deal in that kind of sass. I had a private matter I wanted to talk over with you, Mr. Dunn; that is, if you ain't too busy."

Malcolm looked at him with an amused curiosity. As he had expressed it in the conversation with his mother, this old fellow certainly was a " card." He seated himself on the arm of the oak settle from which the captain had risen and, lazily swinging a polished shoe, admitted that he was always busy but never too busy to oblige.

" What's on your mind, Captain? " he drawled.

Captain Elisha glanced about him somewhat uneasily.

" I — I don't know as I made it quite clear," he said, " that it was sort of private; somethin' just between us, you understand."

Malcolm hesitated. Sliding from the settle, and impatiently commanding the clerk to open the gate in the railing, he led his caller through the main office and into a small room beyond. On the glass pane of the door was lettered, " Mr. Dunn — Private." A roll-top desk in the corner and three chairs were the furniture. Malcolm, after closing the door, sprawled in the swing chair before the desk, threw one leg over a drawer, which he pulled out for that purpose, and motioned his companion to occupy one of the other chairs.

Captain Elisha took the offered chair and dropped his hat on the floor beside it. Then he inspected the room and its furnishings with interest. Dunn drew out a pocket case, extracted a cigarette, lit it, and waited for him to speak.

" Well," observed the young man, after a moment, " what's the trouble, Admiral? Better get it off your chest, hadn't you? We're private enough here."

The captain answered the last question. " Yes," he said, " this is nice and private. Got a stateroom all to yourself; name on the door, and everything complete. You must be one of the officers of the craft."

" Yes."

"Um-hm. I sort of expected to find your name on the door outside, but there 'twas, ' Smith, Haynes & Co.' I presume likely you're the ' Co.' "

" *I* ' presume likely,' " with mocking impatience. " What about that private matter? "

Captain Elisha did not appear to hear him. His eyes were fixed on several photographs stuck in the rail of Mr. Dunn's desk. The photos were those of young ladies.

" Friends of yours? " inquired the captain, nodding toward the photographs.

" No." Dunn took the photos from the rack and threw them into a pigeon hole. " Look here," he said, pointedly, " I wouldn't hurry you for the world, but — "

He paused. Captain Elisha did not take the hint. His mind was evidently still busy with the vanished photographs.

" Just fancy pictures, I s'pose, hey? " he commented.

" Doubtless. Any other little points I can give you? "

" I guess not. I thought they was fancy ; looked so to me. Well, about that private matter. Mr. Dunn, I come to see you about an automobile."

" An automobile ! " The young man was so astonished that he actually removed his feet from the desk. Then he burst into a laugh. " An automobile? " he repeated. " Captain, has the influence of the metropolis made you a sport already? Do you want to buy a car? "

" Buy one? " It was Captain Elisha's turn to show irritation. " Buy one of them things? Me? I wouldn't buy one of 'em, or run one of 'em, for somethin', *I* tell you! No, I don't want to buy one."

" Why not? Sell you mine for a price."

" Not if I see you fust, thank you. No, Mr. Dunn, 'tain't that. But one of the hired help up to our place

— Caroline's place, I mean — is in trouble on account of one of the dratted machines. They're poor folks, of course, and they need money to help 'em through the doctorin' and nursin' and while the old man's out of work. Caroline was for givin' it to 'em right off, she's a good-hearted girl; but I said — that is, I kind of coaxed her out of it. I thought I'd ask some questions first."

"So you came to me to ask them?" Malcolm smiled contentedly. Evidently the cares and complications of guardianship were already proving too intricate for the unsophisticated countryman. He wished advice, and had come to him for it, possibly at Caroline's suggestion. Affairs were shaping themselves well. Here was an opportunity to act the disinterested friend, as per maternal instructions.

"So you wanted to ask questions, did you, Captain?" he repeated. "Well, fire away. Anything I can do to help you or Caroline will be a pleasure, of course. Smoke?"

He offered the cigarette case. The captain eyed it dubiously and shook his head.

"No," he said; "no, thank you, I commenced smokin' at the butt end, I guess. Begun with a pipe, and them things would seem sort of kindergarten, I'm afraid. No offense meant, you understand. It's all accordin' to what you've been used to. Well, about the questions. Here's the first one: Don't it seem to you that the right one to pay for the doctorin' and nursin' and such of Mr. Moriarty — that's Annie's pa — ought to be the feller who hurt him? That feller, instead of Caroline?"

"Sure thing! If you know who did it, he's your mark."

"He could be held responsible, couldn't he?"

"Certainly."

"Um-hm. So I thought. And if he was a right-minded chap, he'd be glad to help the poor critter, providin' he knew what damage he'd done; wouldn't you think so?"

Malcolm nodded sagely, opened his mouth to speak, and then closed it again. A sudden recollection came to him, an alarming recollection. He turned in his chair and looked at his visitor. Captain Elisha met his gaze frankly.

"Where did this accident happen?" asked Mr. Dunn, his condescending smile absent.

"At the corner of Saint Nicholas Avenue and One Hundred and Twenty-Eighth Street. It happened last Friday mornin', a week ago. And the car that hit him was a yellow one."

Malcolm did not answer. His pale face grew paler, and then flushed a brilliant red. The captain seemed to feel sorry for him.

"Naturally," he went on, "when I heard about it, I remembered what you told Mr. Sylvester and me at the club that afternoon. I understand how 'twas, of course. You never thought you'd done any real harm and just went on, thinkin' 'twas a good joke, much as anything. If you'd known you'd really hurt the poor old man, you'd have stopped to see him. I understand that. But —"

"Look here!" interrupted Dunn, sharply, "did Caroline send you to me?"

"Caroline? No, no! She don't know 'twas your automobile at all. I never said a word to her, 'tain't likely. But afore she spent any of her money, I thought you'd ought to know, because I was sure you wouldn't let her. That's the way I'd feel, and I felt 'twas no more'n honest to give you the chance. I come on my own hook; she didn't know anything about it."

Malcolm drummed on the desk with nervous fingers. The flush remained on his face, his cigarette had gone out, and he threw the stump savagely into the waste-paper basket. Captain Elisha remained silent. At length the young man spoke.

"Well," he growled, pettishly, "how much will it take to square things with the gang? How much damages do they want?"

"Damages? Oh, there won't be any claim for damages, I guess. That is, no lawsuit, or anything of that kind. The Moriartys don't know you did it, and there's no reason why they should. I thought maybe I'd see to 'em and do whatever was necessary; then you could settle with me, and the whole business would be just between us two. Outside the doctor's bills and food and nursin' and such, all the extry will be just the old man's wages for the time he's away from the factory. 'Twon't be very heavy."

More reflection and finger tattoo by his companion. Then:

"All right! I'm in it, I can see that; and it's up to me to get out as easy as I can. I don't want any newspaper publicity. Go ahead! I'll pay the freight."

Captain Elisha arose and picked up his hat.

"That's fust-rate," he said, with emphasis. "I felt sure you'd see it just as I did. There's one thing I would like to say," he added: "that is, that you mustn't think I was stingy about helpin' 'em myself. But it wa'n't really my affair; and when Caroline spoke of spendin' her money and Steve's, I didn't feel I'd ought to let her. You see, I don't know as you know it yet,

Mr. Dunn, but my brother 'Bije left me in charge of his whole estate, and, now that I've decided to take the responsibility, I've got a sort of pride in not wastin' any of his children's inheritance. Good day, Mr. Dunn. I'm much obliged to you."

He opened the office door. Malcolm, frowning heavily, suddenly asked a final question.

"Say!" he demanded, "you'll not tell Caroline or Steve a word of this, mind!"

The captain seemed surprised.

"I guess you didn't catch what I said, Mr. Dunn," he observed, mildly. "I told you this whole business would be just between you and me."

CHAPTER IX

CAPTAIN ELISHA was very far from considering himself a Solomon. As he would have said, he had lived long enough with himself to know what a lot he didn't know. Nevertheless, deep down in his inner consciousness, he cherished a belief in his judgment of human nature. This judgment was not of the snap variety; he took his time in forming it. People and their habits, their opinions and characters, were to him interesting problems. He liked to study them and to reach conclusions founded upon reason, observation, and common sense. Having reached such a conclusion, it disturbed him when the subjects of the problem suddenly upset the whole process of reasoning and apparently proved him wrong by behavior exactly contrary to that which he had expected.

He had been pretty well satisfied with the result of his visit to young Dunn at the latter's office. Malcolm had surrendered, perhaps not gracefully or unconditionally, but he had surrendered, and the condition — secrecy — was one which the captain himself had suggested. Captain Elisha's mental attitude toward the son of the late Tammany leader had been a sort of good-natured but alert tolerance. He judged the young man to be a product of rearing and environment. He had known spoiled youths at the Cape and, in their surroundings, they behaved much as Malcolm did in his. The same disrespect to their elders, the same cock-sureness, and the same careless indifference concerning the effect which their actions might have upon other people — these were natural and nothing but years and the hard knocks of experience could bring about a change. Elkanah Chase, country swell and pampered heir to the cranberry grower's few thousands, and Malcolm Dunn, idol of his set at the Metropolitan Club, were not so very different, except in externals. The similarity confirmed his opinion that New York was merely South Denboro many thousand times magnified.

He knew how young Chase had behaved after an interview not unlike that just described. In Elkanah's case several broken windows and property destroyed on a revel the night before the Fourth had caused the trouble. In Malcolm's it was an automobile. Both had listened to reason and had knuckled under rather than face possible lawsuits and certain publicity. Chase, however, had sulkily refused to speak to him for a month, and regained affability merely because he wished to borrow money. According to the captain's deduction, Dunn should have acted in similar fashion. But he didn't; that was the odd part of it.

For Malcolm, when he next called, in company with his mother, at the Warren apartment, was not in the least sulky. Neither was he over effusive, which would have argued fear and a desire to conciliate. Possibly there was a bit more respect in his greeting of the new guardian and a trifle less condescension, but not much. He still hailed Captain Elisha as " Admiral," and was as mockingly careless as ever in his remarks concerning the latter's newness in the big city. In fact, he was so little changed that the captain was perplexed. A chap who could take a licking when he deserved it, and not hold malice, must have good in him, unless, of course, he was hiding the malice for a purpose. And if that purpose was the wish to appear friendly, then the manner of hiding it proved Malcolm Dunn to possess more brains than Captain Elisha had given him credit for.

One thing seemed sure, the Dunns were not openly hostile. And Caroline was. Since the interview in the library, when the girl had, as she considered it, humiliated herself by asking her guardian for money to help the Moriartys, she had scarcely spoken to him. Stephen, taking his cue from his sister, was morose and silent, also. Captain Elisha found it hard to forgive his dead brother for bringing all this trouble upon him.

His lawyers, so Sylvester informed him, were setting about getting Rodgers Warren's tangible assets together. The task was likely to be a long one. The late broker's affairs were in a muddled state, the books were anything but clear, some of the investments were foreign, and, at the very earliest, months must elapse before the executor and trustee could know, for certain, just how large a property he was in charge of.

He found some solace and forgetfulness of the unpleasant life he was leading in helping the stricken Moriarty family. Annie, the maid at the apartment, he swore to secrecy. She must not tell Miss Caroline of his visits to her parents' home. Doctor Henry, also, though he could not understand why, promised silence. Caroline herself had engaged his services in the case, and he was faithful. But the patient was more seriously hurt than at first appeared, and consultations with a specialist were necessary.

" Goin' to be a pretty expensive job, ain't it, Doctor? " asked the captain of the physician.

" Rather, I'm afraid."

" All right. If expense is necessary, don't be afraid

of it. You do just what you'd ought to, and send the bill to me."

"But Miss Warren insisted upon my sending it to her. She said it was a private matter, and one with which you, as her guardian, had nothing to do."

"I know. Caroline intends to use her own allowance, I s'pose. Well, let her think she will, if 'twill please her. But when it comes to the settlement, call on me. Give her any reason you want to; say a — er — wealthy friend of the family come to life all at once and couldn't sleep nights unless he paid the costs."

"But there isn't any such friend, is there, Captain Warren? Other than yourself, I mean?"

Captain Elisha grinned in appreciation of a private joke. "There is somebody else," he admitted, "who'll pay a share, anyhow. I don't know's he's what you call a bosom friend, and, as for his sleepin' nights — well, I never heard he couldn't do that, after he went to bed. But, anyhow, you saw wood, or bones, or whatever you have to do, and leave the rest to me. And don't tell Caroline or anybody else a word."

The Moriartys lived in a four-room flat on the East Side, uptown, and his visits there gave the captain a glimpse of another sort of New York life, as different from that of Central Park West as could well be imagined. The old man, Patrick, his wife, Margaret, the unmarried son, Dennis, who worked in the gas house, and five other children of various ages were hived somehow in those four small rooms and Captain Elisha marveled greatly thereat.

"For the land sakes, ma'am," he asked of the nurse, "how do they do it? Where do they put 'em nights? That — that closet in there's the pantry and woodshed and kitchen and dinin' room; and that one's the settin'

10   139

room and parlor; and them two dry-goods boxes with doors to 'em are bedrooms. There's eight livin' critters to stow away when it's time to turn in, and one whole bed's took up by the patient. *Where* do they put the rest? Hang 'em up on nails?"

The nurse laughed. "Goodness knows!" she said. "He should have been taken to the hospital. In fact, the doctor and I at first insisted upon his removal there. He would have been much better off. But neither he nor his wife would hear of it. She said he would die sure without his home comforts."

"Humph! I should think more likely he'd die with 'em, or under 'em. I watch that fleshy wife of his with fear and tremblin'. Every time she goes nigh the bed I expect her to trip over a young one and fall. And if she fell on that poor rack-o'-bones," with a wave of the hand toward the invalid, "'twould be the final smash — like a brick chimney fallin' on a lath hencoop."

At that moment the "brick chimney" herself entered the room, and the nurse accosted her.

"Captain Warren here," she said, "was asking where you all found sleeping quarters."

Mrs. Moriarty smiled broadly. "Sure, 'tis aisy," she explained. "When the ould man is laid up we're all happy to be a bit uncomfortable. Not that we are, neither. You see, sor, me and Nora and Rosy sleep in the other bed; and Dinnie has a bit of a shakedown in the parlor; and Honora is in the kitchen; and —"

"There! there!" Captain Elisha interrupted hastily, "don't tell me any more. I'd rather *guess* that the baby bunks in the cookstove oven than know it for sartin. How did the grapes I sent you go?" turning to the sick man.

"Aw, sor! they were foine. God bless you, sor!

Mary be kind to you, sor! Sure the angels'll watch over you every day you live and breathe!"

Captain Elisha bolted for the parlor, the sufferer firing a gatling fusillade of blessings after him. Mrs. Moriarty continued the bombardment, as she escorted him to the door of the flat.

"There! there!" protested the captain. "Just belay! cut it short, there's a good woman! I'll admit I'm a saint and would wear a halo instead of a hat if 'twa'n't so unfashionable. Good day. If you need anything you ain't got, tell the nurse."

The grateful Irish woman did not intend to let him escape so easily.

"Aw, sor," she went on, "it's all right for you to make fun. I'm the jokin' kind, sor, meself. Whin the flats where we used to be got afire and Pat had to lug me down the fire escape in his arms, they tell me I was laughin' fit to kill; that is, when I wasn't screechin' for fear he'd drop me. And him, poor soul, never seein' the joke, but puffin' and groanin' that his back was in two pieces. Ha, ha! Oh, dear! And him in two pieces now for sure and all! Aw, sor, it's all right for you to laugh it off, but what would we do without you? You and Miss Caroline, God bless her!"

"Caroline? She doesn't come here, does she?"

"Indade she does. Sure, she's the perfect little lady! Hardly a day passes — or a week, anyhow — that she doesn't drop in to see how the ould man's gettin' on."

"Humph! Well, see that you don't tell her about me."

Mrs. Moriarty held up both hands in righteous protestation. *She* tell? Might the tongue of her wither between her teeth before it let slip a word, and so on. Captain Elisha waved her to silence.

"All right! all right!" he exclaimed. "So long! Take good care of your husband, and, and — for Heaven's sake, walk careful and don't step on any of the children."

Mrs. Moriarty's tongue did not wither; at all events, it was lively enough when he next met her. The captain's secret was not divulged, and he continued his visits to the flat, taking care, however, to ascertain his niece's whereabouts beforehand. It was not altogether a desire to avoid making his charitable deeds public which influenced him. He had a habit of not letting his right hand know what his left was about in such cases, and he detested a Pharisaical philanthropist. But there was another reason why Caroline must not learn of his interest in the Moriartys. If she did learn it, she would believe him to be helping them on his own responsibility; or, if not, that he was using money belonging to the estate. Of course he would, and honestly must, deny the latter charge, and, therefore, the first would, to her mind, be proven. He intended that Malcolm Dunn should pay the larger share of the bills, as was right and proper. But he could not tell Caroline that, because she must not know of the young man's responsibility for the accident. He could not give Malcolm the credit, and he felt that he ought not to take it himself. It was a delicate situation.

He was lonely, and the days seemed long. Reading the paper, walking in the park, occasionally dropping in at the lawyers' offices, or visiting the shops and other places of interest about town made up the monotonous routine. He breakfasted early, waited upon by Edwards, got lunch at the restaurant nearest to wherever he happened to be at noon, and returned to the apartment for dinner. His niece and nephew dined with him, but when he attempted conversation they answered in monosyllables or not at all. Every evening he wrote a letter to Abbie, and the mail each morning brought him one from her. The Dunns came frequently and seemed disposed to be friendly, but he kept out of their way as much as possible.

Pearson he had not seen since the latter's call. This was a disappointment, for he fancied the young fellow and believed he should like him even better on closer acquaintance. He would have returned the visit, but somehow or other the card with the boarding-house street and number had been lost or mislaid, and the long list of " James Pearsons " in the directory discouraged him. He speculated much concerning the mystery at which the would-be novelist hinted as preventing his accepting Caroline's invitation. Evidently Pearson had once known Rodgers Warren well, and had been esteemed and respected by the latter. Caroline, too, had known him, and was frankly pleased to meet him again. Whatever the trouble might be, she, evidently, was ignorant of it. The captain wondered and pondered, but reached no satisfactory conclusion. It seemed the irony of fate that the one congenial person — Sylvester excepted — whom he had met during his stay in the big city should be scratched from his small list of acquaintances.

With Sylvester he held many familiar and enjoyable chats. The good-natured, democratic senior member of the law firm liked to have Captain Elisha drop in for advice or to spin yarns. Graves, who was well again, regarded the new guardian with respect of a kind, but with distinct disapproval. The captain was, in his opinion, altogether too flippant and jolly. There was nothing humorous in the situation, as Graves saw it, and to laugh when one's brother's estate is in a tangle, indicated unfitness, if nothing worse. Kuhn was a sharp, quick-moving man, who had no time for frivolity if it delayed business.

It was after a long interview with Sylvester that Captain Elisha decided to send Stephen back to college. When he broke the news there was rebellion, brief but lively. Stephen had no desire to continue his studies; he wished to become a stock broker at once, and, as soon as he was of age, take his father's seat on the Exchange.

"Stevie," said Captain Elisha, "one of these days, when you get to be as old as I am or before, you'll realize that an education is worth somethin'."

"Ugh!" grunted the boy, in supreme disgust. "What do you know about that?"

"Why, not much, maybe, but enough."

"Yes?" sarcastically. "What college did you attend?"

"Me? Why, none, more's the pity. What learnin' there was in our family your dad had. Maybe that's why he was what he was, so fur as money and position and society and so on went, and I'm what I am."

"Oh, rubbish! What difference does it make to Malcolm Dunn — now — his going through college?"

"Well, he went, didn't he?"

Stephen grinned. Malcolm had told him some particulars concerning his university career and its termination.

"He went — part way," he answered.

"Ya-as. Well, you've gone part way, so fur. And now you'll go the rest."

"I'd like to know why."

"For one reason, because I'm your guardian and I say so."

Stephen was furiously angry. His father's indulgence and his sister's tolerance had, in most cases, made his will law in the household. To be ordered about in this way by an ignorant interloper, as he considered his uncle, was too much.

"By gad," he shouted, "we'll see!"

"No, we've seen. You run along now and pack your trunk. And take my advice and study hard. You'll be behindhand in your work, so Mr. Sylvester tells me, but you're smart, and you can catch up. Make us proud of you; that's what you can do."

His nephew glanced at him. Captain Elisha was smiling kindly, but there was no sign of change of purpose in his look.

Stephen ground his teeth.

"Oh," he snarled, "if it wasn't for the disgrace! If things weren't as they are, I'd —"

"S-s-s-h! I know; but they are. Maybe I wish they wa'n't 'most as much as you do, but they are. I don't blame you for feelin' mad now; but I'm right and I know it. And some day you'll know it, and thank me."

"When I do, I'll be insane."

"No, you'll be older, that's all. Now pack your trunk — or get the Commodore to pack it for you."

News from the Moriarty sick room continued favorable for a time. Then, with alarming suddenness, a change came. The broken hip was mending slowly, but poor Pat's age was against him, and the shock and long illness were too much for his system to fight. Dr. Henry shook his head dubiously when the captain asked questions. And, one morning at breakfast, Edwards informed him that the old man was dead. Annie had been summoned by telephone at midnight and had gone home.

Captain Elisha, though not greatly surprised, was shocked and grieved. It seemed such a needless tragedy, almost like murder, although there was no malice in it. And the thought of the fatherless children and the poverty of the stricken family made him shudder. Death at any time, amid any surroundings, is terrible; when the dead hands have earned the bread for many mouths it is appalling.

The captain dreaded visiting the flat, but because he felt it to be a duty he went immediately. And the misery and wailing and dismay he found there were worse than his anticipations. He did his best to comfort and cheer. Mrs. Moriarty alternately called upon the saints to bless him and begged to know what she would do now that they were all sure to starve. Luckily, the family priest, a kind-hearted, quiet man who faced similar scenes almost every day of his life, was there, and Captain Elisha had a long talk with him. With Dennis, the oldest son, and Annie, the maid at the Warrens', he also consulted. Money for their immediate needs, he told them, he would provide. And the funeral expenses must not worry them. Afterward — well, plans for the future could be discussed at another time. But upon Dennis and Annie he tried to impress a sense of their responsibility.

"It's up to you, Boy," he said to the former. "Annie's job's sure, I guess, as long as she wants it, and she can give her mother somethin' every month. But you're the man of the house now, and you've got to steer the ship and keep it afloat. That means work, and hard work, lots of it, too. You can do it, if you've got the grit. If I can find a better place and more pay for you,

I will, but you mustn't depend on that. It's up to you, I tell you, and you've got to show what's in you. If you get stuck and need advice, come to me."

He handed the priest a sum of money to cover immediate contingencies, and departed. His letter to Abbie that afternoon was so blue that the housekeeper felt sure he was "coming down" with some disease or other. He had been riding in that awful subway, where the air — so the papers said — was not fit to breathe, and just as like as not he'd caught consumption. His great-uncle on his mother's side died of it, so it "run in the family." Either he must come home or she should come to him, one or the other.

But before evening his blueness had disappeared. He had just returned to his room, after stepping into the hall to drop his letter in the mail chute, when his niece knocked at the door. He was surprised to see her, for she had not spoken to him, except in brief reply to questions, since their misunderstanding in that very room. He looked at her wonderingly, not knowing what to say or what to expect; but she spoke first.

"Captain Warren," she began, hurriedly, "the last time I came to you — the last time I came here, I came to ask a favor, and you — I thought you —"

She was evidently embarrassed and confused. Her guardian was embarrassed, also, but he tried to be hospitable.

"Yes, Caroline," he said, gravely, "I know what you mean. Won't you — won't you sit down?"

To his surprise, she accepted the invitation, taking the same chair she had taken on the occasion of their former interview. But there was a look in her eyes he had never seen there before; at least, not when she was addressing him.

She went on, speaking hastily, as though determined to head off any questioning on his part.

"Captain Warren," she began once more, "the time I came to you in this room you were, so I thought, unreasonable and unkind. I asked you for money to help a poor family in trouble, and you refused to give it to me."

"No, Caroline," he interrupted, "I didn't refuse, you only thought I did."

She held up her hand. "Please let me go on," she begged. "I thought you refused, and I couldn't understand why. I was hurt and angry. I knew that father never would have refused me under such circumstances, and you were his brother. But since then, only to-day, I have learned that I was wrong. I have learned —"

She paused. The captain was silent. He was beginning to hope, to believe once more in his judgment of character; and yet, with his hope and growing joy, there was a trifle of anxiety.

"I have learned," went on his niece, "that I was mistaken. I can't understand yet why you wished to wait before saying yes, but I do know that it must have been neither because you were unkind nor ungenerous. I have just come from those poor people, and they have told me everything."

Captain Elisha started. "What did they tell you?" he asked, quickly. "Who told you?"

"Annie and her mother. They told me what you had done and were doing for them. How kind you had been all through the illness and to-day. Oh, I know you made them promise not to tell me; and you made the doctor and nurse promise, too. But I knew *someone* had helped, and Annie dropped a hint. Then I suspected, and now I know. Those poor people!"

The captain, who had been looking at the floor, and frowning a bit, suddenly glanced up to find his niece's eyes fixed upon him, and they were filled with tears.

"Will you forgive me?" she asked, rising from her chair, and coming impulsively toward him. "I'm sorry I misjudged you and treated you so. You must be a very good man. Please forgive me."

He took her hand, which was swallowed up in his big one. His eyes were moist, also.

"Lord love you, dearie," he said, "there's nothin' to forgive. I realized that I must have seemed like a mean, stingy old scamp. Yet I didn't mean to be. I only wanted to look into this thing just a little. Just as a matter of business, you know. And I . . . Caroline, did that doctor tell you anything more?"

"Any more?" she repeated in bewilderment. "He told me that you were the kindest man he had ever seen."

"Yes, yes. Well, maybe his eyesight's poor. What I mean is did he tell you anything about anybody else bein' in this with me?"

"Anybody else? What do you mean?"

"Oh, nothin', nothin'. I joked with him a spell ago about a wealthy relation of the Moriarty tribe turnin' up. 'Twas only a joke, of course. And yet, Caroline, I — I think I'd ought to say —"

He hesitated. What could he say? Even a hint might lead to embarrassing questions and he had promised Dunn.

"What ought you to say?" asked his niece.

"Why, nothin', I guess. I'm glad you understand matters a little better and I don't intend for the estate nor you to pay these Moriarty bills. Just get 'em off your mind. Forget 'em. I'll see that everything's attended to. And, later on, if you and me can, by puttin' our heads together, help those folks to earnin' a better livin', why, we will, hey?"

The girl smiled up at him. "I think," she said, "that you must be one who likes to hide his light under a bushel."

"I guess likely a two-quart measure'd be plenty big enough to hide mine. There! there! We won't have any more misunderstandin's, will we? I'm a pretty green vegetable and about as out of place here as a lobster in a balloon, but, as I said to you and Steve once before, if you'll just remember I *am* green and sort of rough, and maybe make allowances accordin', this cruise of ours may not be so unpleasant. Now you run along and get ready for dinner, or the Commodore'll petrify from standin' so long behind your chair."

She laughed, as she turned to go. "I should hate to have him do that," she said. "He would make a depressing statue. I shall see you again in a few minutes, at dinner. Thank you — Uncle."

She left Captain Elisha in a curious state of mind. Against his will he had been forced to accept thanks and credit which, he believed, did not rightfully belong to him. It was the only thing to do, and yet it seemed almost like disloyalty to Malcolm Dunn. This troubled him, but the trouble was, just then, a mere pinhead of blackness against the radiance of his spirit.

His brother's daughter had, for the first time, called him uncle.

CHAPTER X

"CAPTAIN WARREN," asked Caroline, as they were seated at the breakfast table next morning, "what are your plans for to-day?" Captain Elisha put down his coffee cup and pulled his beard reflectively. Contrary to his usual desire since he came to the apartment to live, he was in no hurry to finish the meal. This breakfast and the dinner of the previous evening had been really pleasant. He had enjoyed them. His niece had not called him uncle again, it is true, and perhaps that was too much to be expected as yet, but she was cheerful and even familiar. They talked as they ate, and he had not been made to feel that he was the death's head at the feast. The change was marked and very welcome. The bright winter sunshine streaming through the window indicated that the conditions outside were also just what they should be.

"Well," he replied, with a smile, "I don't know, Caroline, as I've made any definite plans. Let's see, to-day's Sunday, ain't it? Last letter I got from Abbie she sailed into me because, as she said, I seemed to have been 'most everywheres except to meetin'. She figgers New York's a heathen place, anyhow, and she cal'lates I'm gettin' to be a backslider like the rest. I didn't know but I might go to church."

Caroline nodded. "I wondered if you wouldn't like to go," she said. "I am going, and I thought perhaps you would go with me."

Her uncle had again raised his cup to his lips. Now

he set it down with a suddenness which caused the statuesque Edwards to bend forward in anticipation of a smash. The captain started to speak, thought better of it, and stared at his niece so intently that she colored and dropped her eyes.

"I know," she faltered, "that I haven't asked you before, but — but —" then, with the impulsiveness which was one of her characteristics, and to her guardian her great charm, she looked him full in the face and added, "but I hoped you would understand that — that *I* understood a little better. I should like to have your company very much."

Captain Elisha drew a long breath.

"Thank you, Caroline," he answered. "I appreciate your askin' me, I sartinly do. And I'd rather go with you than anybody else on earth. But I was cal'latin' to hunt up some little round-the-corner chapel, or Bethel, where I'd feel a little bit at home. I guess likely your church is a pretty big one, ain't it?"

"We attend Saint Denis. It *is* a large church, but we have always been connected with it. Stephen and I were christened there. But, of course, if you had rather go somewhere else —"

"No, no! I hadn't anywhere in particular to go. I'm a Congregationalist to home, but Abbie says I've spread my creed so wide that it ain't more'n an inch deep anywhere, and she shouldn't think 'twould keep me afloat. I tell her I'd rather navigate a broad and shallow channel, where everybody stands by to keep his neighbor off the shoals, than I would a narrow and crooked one with self-righteousness off both beams and perdition underneath.

"You see," he added, reflectively, "the way I look at it, it's a pretty uncertain cruise at the best. Course there's all sorts of charts, and every fleet is sartin it's got the only right one. But I don't know. We're afloat — that much we are sure of — but the port we left and the harbor we're bound for, they're always out of sight in the fog astern and ahead. I know lots of folks who claim to see the harbor, and see it plain; but they don't exactly agree as to what they see. As for me, I've come to the conclusion that we must steer as straight a course as we can, and when we meet a craft in distress, why, do our best to help her. The rest of it I guess we must leave to the Owner, to the One that launched us. I . . . Good land!" he exclaimed, coming out of his meditation with a start, "I'm preachin' a sermon ahead of time. And the Commodore's goin' to sleep over it, I do believe."

The butler, who had been staring vacantly out of the window during the captain's soliloquy, straightened at the sound of his nickname, and asked hastily, "Yes, sir? What will you have, sir?" Captain Elisha laughed in huge enjoyment, and his niece joined him.

"Well," she said, "will you go with me?"

"I'd like to fust-rate — if you won't be too much ashamed of me."

"Then it's settled, isn't it? The service begins at a quarter to eleven. We will leave here at half-past ten."

The captain shaved with extra care that morning, donned spotless linen, including a "stand-up" collar — which he detested — brushed his frock-coat and his hair with great particularity, and gave Edwards his shoes to clean. He would have shined them himself, as he always did at home, but on a former occasion when he asked for the "blackin' kit," the butler's shocked and pained expression led to questions and consequent enlightenment.

He was ready by a quarter after ten, but when his niece knocked at his door she bore a message which surprised and troubled him.

"Mrs. Dunn called," she said, "to ask me to go to church with her. I told her I had invited you to accompany me. Would you mind if she joined us?"

Her guardian hesitated. "I guess," he answered, slowly, "it ain't so much a question of my mindin' her as she mindin' me. Does *she* want me to go along?"

"She said she should be delighted."

"I want to know! Now, Caroline, don't you think I'd be sort of in the way? Don't you believe she'd manage to live down her disappointment if I didn't tag on? You mustn't feel that you've got to be bothered with me because you suggested my goin', you know."

"If I had considered it a bother I should not have invited you. If you don't wish Mrs. Dunn's company, then you and I will go alone."

"Oh, land sakes! I wouldn't have you do that for the world! All right, I'll be out in a jiffy."

He gave his hair a final brush, straightened his tie, turned around once more before the mirror, and walked fearfully forth to meet the visitor. For him, the anticipated pleasure of the forenoon had been replaced by uneasy foreboding.

But Mrs. Corcoran Dunn, as she rose creakingly to greet him, was extremely gracious. She was gowned and furred and hatted in a manner which caused the captain to make hasty mental estimate as to cost, but she extended a plump hand, buttoned in a very tight glove, and murmured her gratification.

"I'm so glad you are to accompany us, Captain Warren," she gushed. "It is a charming winter morning, isn't it?"

Captain Elisha touched the plump glove with his own big finger tips, and admitted that the morning was " fustrate." He was relieved from the embarrassment of further conversation just then by Caroline's appearance in the library. She, too, was richly dressed.

" Are we all ready? " she asked, brightly. " Then we may as well start."

" I'm afraid we're a trifle early, my dear," said Mrs. Dunn, " but we can stroll about a bit before we go in."

The captain looked at the library clock. The time was a quarter to eleven.

" Early? " he exclaimed, involuntarily. " Why, I thought Caroline said —"

He stopped, suddenly, realizing that he had spoken aloud. His niece divined his thought and laughed merrily.

" The service does begin now," she said, " but no one is ever on time."

" Oh! " ejaculated her uncle, and did not speak again until they were at the door of the church. Then Caroline asked him what he was thinking.

" Nothin' much," he answered, gazing at the fashionably garbed throng pouring under the carved stone arch of the entrance; " I was just reorganizin' my ideas, that's all. I've always sort of thought a plug hat looked lonesome. Now I've decided that I'm wearin' the lonesome kind."

He marched behind his niece and Mrs. Dunn up the center aisle to the Warren pew. He wrote his housekeeper afterwards that he estimated that aisle to be " upwards of two mile long. And my Sunday shoes had a separate squeak for every inch," he added.

Once seated, however, and no longer so conspicuous, his common sense and Yankee independence came to his

11

rescue. He had been in much bigger churches than this one, while abroad during his seagoing years. He knew that his clothes were not fashionably cut, and that, to the people about him, he must appear odd and, perhaps, even ridiculous. But he remembered how odd certain city people appeared while summering at South Denboro. Recollections of pointed comments made by boatmen who had taken these summer sojourners on fishing excursions came to his mind. Well, he had one advantage over such people, at any rate, he knew when he was ridiculous, and they apparently did not.

So, saved from humiliation by his sense of humor, he looked about him with interest. When the procession of choir boys came up the aisle, and Mrs. Dunn explained in a condescending whisper what they were, his answer surprised her a trifle. "Yes," whispered the captain in reply, "I know. I've seen the choir in Saint Peter's at Rome."

Only once did he appear greatly astonished. That was when the offering was taken and a certain dignified magnate, whose fame as a king of finance is world-wide, officiated as one of the collectors.

"Heavens and earth!" murmured Captain Elisha, staring wide-eyed at the unmistakable features so often pictured and cartooned in the daily papers; "Caroline — Caroline, am I seein' things or is that — is that —"

"That is Mr. ——," whispered his niece. "He is one of the vestrymen here."

"My soul!" still gazing after the Emperor of Wall Street; "*him* passin' the plate! Well," with a grim smile, "whoever picked him out for the job has got judgment. If *he* can't make a body shell out, nobody can."

He listened to the sermon, the text of which was from

the Beatitudes, with outward solemnity, but with a twinkle in his eye. After the benediction, when Caroline asked how he enjoyed it, the cause of the twinkle became apparent."

"Fine!" he declared, with enthusiasm. "He's a smart preacher, ain't he! And he knew his congregation. You might not guess they was meek perhaps, but they certainly did look as if they'd inherited the earth."

He drew a breath of relief as the trio emerged into the open air. He had enjoyed the novel experience, in a way, but now he felt rather like one let out of jail. The quiet luncheon at home with Caroline was a pleasant anticipation.

But Mrs. Corcoran Dunn smashed his anticipation at a blow. She insisted that he and his niece lunch with her.

"You really must, you know," she declared. "It will be delightful. Just a little family party."

Captain Elisha looked distressed. "Thank you, ma'am," he stammered; "it's awful kind of you, but I wouldn't feel right to go puttin' you to all that trouble. Just as much obliged, but I — I've got a letter to write, you see."

Mrs. Dunn bore his refusal bravely.

"Very well," she said, "but Caroline *must* come with me. I told Malcolm I should bring her."

"Sure! Sartin! Caroline can go, of course."

But Caroline also declined. Having misjudged her guardian in the matter of the Moriarty family, she was in a repentant mood, and had marked that day on her calendar as one of self-sacrifice."

"No, Captain Warren," she said, "I shall not go unless you do."

" Then the captain will come, of course," declared Mrs. Dunn, with decision. " I'm sure he will not be so selfish as to deprive me — and Malcolm — of your company."

So, because he did not wish to appear selfish, Captain Elisha admitted that his letter might be written later in the afternoon, accepted the invitation, and braced his spirit for further martyrdom.

It was not as bad as he expected. The Dunns occupied a small, brown-stone house on Fifth Avenue, somewhat old-fashioned, but eminently respectable. The paintings and bronzes were as numerous as those in the Warren apartment, and if the taste shown in their selection was not that of Rodgers Warren, the connoisseur, they made quite as much show, and the effect upon Captain Elisha was the same. The various mortgages on the property were not visible, and the tradesmen's bills were securely locked in Mrs. Dunn's desk.

The luncheon itself was elaborate, and there was a butler whose majestic dignity and importance made even Edwards seem plebeian by comparison.

Malcolm was at home when they arrived, irreproachably dressed and languidly non-effusive, as usual. Captain Elisha, as he often said, did not " set much store " by clothes; but there was something about this young man which always made him conscious that his own trousers were a little too short, or his boots too heavy, or something. " I wouldn't *wear* a necktie like his," he wrote Abbie, after his first meeting with Malcolm, " but blessed if I don't wish I could *if* I would ! "

Caroline, in the course of conversation during the luncheon, mentioned the Moriartys and their sorrow. The captain tried to head her off and to change the subject, but with little success. He was uncomfortable and kept glancing under his brows at Malcolm, with whom, under the circumstances, he could not help sympathizing to an extent. But his sympathy was wasted. The young man did not appear in the slightest degree nervous. The memory of his recent interview with Captain Elisha did not embarrass him, outwardly at least, half as much as it did the captain. He declared that old Pat's death was beastly hard luck, but accidents were bound to happen. It was a shame, and all that. " If there's anything the mater and I can do, Caroline, call on us, of course."

" Yes, do, Caroline," concurred his mother. " However, one must be philosophic in such cases. It is a mercy that people in their station do not feel grief and loss as we do. Providence, in its wisdom, has limited their susceptibilities as it has their intelligence. Don't you agree with me, Captain Warren?"

" Sartin! " was the prompt reply. " It's always a comfort to me, when I go fishin', to know that the fish ain't got so much brains as I have. The hook hurts, I presume likely, but they ain't got the sense to realize what a mean trick's been played on 'em. The one that's caught's dead, and them that are left are too busy hustlin' for the next meal to waste much time grievin'. That eases my conscience consider'ble."

Caroline seemed to be the only one who appreciated the sarcasm in this observation. She frowned slightly. Mrs. Corcoran Dunn tolerantly smiled, and her son laughed aloud.

" Say, Admiral," he commented, " when it comes to philosophy you go some yourself, don't you?"

" Um-hm. I can be as philosophical about other folk's troubles as anybody I ever see." Then, with an involuntary chuckle of admiration at the young gentleman's coolness, he added, " That is, anybody I ever see afore I come to New York."

Malcolm opened his mouth to reply, but closed it again. The captain, noticing his change of purpose and following the direction of his look, saw Mrs. Dunn shake her head in sharp disapproval. He ate the remainder of his salad in silence, but he thought a good deal.

" And now," said Mrs. Dunn, rising and leading the way to the drawing-room, " we must all go for a motor ride. Everyone rides on Sunday afternoon," she explained, turning to her male guest.

The distressed look returned to Captain Elisha's face. His niece saw it, understood, and came to his rescue.

" I think Captain Warren prefers to be excused," she said, smiling. " He has a prejudice against automobiles."

" No!" drawled Malcolm, the irrepressible. " Not really? Admiral, I'm surprised! In these days, you know!"

" It ain't so much the automobiles," snapped Captain Elisha, irritation getting the better of his discretion, " as 'tis the devilish fools that —"

" Yes? Oh, all right, Mater."

" That are careless enough to get in the way of them," finished the captain, with surprising presence of mind. " Still, if Caroline wants to go —"

" I have it!" exclaimed Mrs. Dunn. " The young people shall go, and the others remain at home. Malcolm shall take you for a spin, Caroline, and Captain Warren and I will stay here and wait until you return. We'll have a family chat, Captain, won't we? Because," with a gay laugh, " in a way we *are* like one family, you see."

And, somewhat to Miss Warren's surprise, her uncle

agreed to this proposition. He did not answer immediately, but, when he did, it was with heartiness.

"Why, yes," he said, "that's a good idea. That's
fust-rate. You young folks go, and Mrs. Dunn and I'll
wait here till you come back. That's the way of the
world — young folks on the go, and the old folks at
home by the fire, hey, Mrs. Dunn?"

The lady addressed did not relish being numbered with
"old folks," but she smiled sweetly, and said she supposed it was. Malcolm telephoned to the garage and to
Edwards at the Warren apartment, ordering the butler
to deliver his mistress's auto cap and cloak to the chauffeur, who would call for them. A few minutes later the
yellow car rolled up to the door.

In the hall Mrs. Dunn whispered a reassuring word
to her departing guest.

"Now enjoy yourself, dear," she whispered. "Have
a nice ride and don't worry about me. If he — if our
encumbrance bores me too much I shall — well, I shall
plead a headache and leave him to his own devices. Besides, he isn't so *very* dreadful, is he?"

Caroline shook her head. "No," she answered, "he
is a good man. I understand him better than I did and
— yes, I like him better, too."

"Oh! . . . Indeed! Well, good-by, dear. *Good-
by.*"

The yellow car roared as the chauffeur cranked it,
then moved off up the crowded avenue. Mrs. Dunn
watched it until it was out of sight. Her brows were
drawn together, and she seemed puzzled and just a bit
disconcerted. However, when she returned to the drawing-room, her gracious smile had returned, and her bland
condescension was again in evidence.

Captain Elisha had been standing by the window.

She begged him to be seated. He thanked her, but looked dubiously at the Louis XVI chair indicated. She noticed the look.

"Suppose we go into the library," she said. "It is much less formal. And there is a fire — for us *old* folks," with a slight accent on the word.

The library was more homelike. Not as many books as at the Warrens', but a great deal of gilt in the bindings and much carving on the cases. The fire was cheery, and the pair sat down before it in big easy chairs. Mrs. Dunn looked intently at the glowing coals.

Captain Elisha cleared his throat. Mrs. Dunn leaned forward expectantly. The captain coughed and sank back in his chair.

"Yes?" purred the lady. "You were about to say?"

"Me? Oh, no, I didn't say anything."

Another period of silence. Mrs. Dunn's foot tapped the rug impatiently. She wished him to begin the conversation, and he would not. At length, in desperation, she began it herself.

"I suppose you find New York rather different from — er — North — er —"

"From South Denboro? Yes, ma'am."

"Do you like the city life?"

"Well, I don't know, ma'am."

"Not as well as you do that of the country, doubtless."

"Well, you see, I ain't had so much of it."

"No, of course not. It does so depend upon what one is accustomed to. Now I fancy I should be perfectly desperate in your village."

One corner of Captain Elisha's mouth curled upward.

"I shouldn't be surprised," he admitted.

"Desperately lonely, I mean."

"Yes'm. I judged that was what you meant. Still, folks can be lonesome in New York."

"Perhaps. But really I don't see how. With all the whirl and the crowds and the glorious excitement. The feeling that one is at the very heart, the center of everything!"

"Yes. If you belong to the machinery, I s'pose it's all right. But if you've been leanin' over the rail, lookin' on, and get pushed in unexpected, maybe you don't care so much about bein' nigh the center."

"Then why stay there? Why not get out?"

"If you're caught in the wheels, gettin' out's somethin' of a job."

"But, as I understand it, Captain Warren — I may be misinformed, for, of course, I haven't been unduly curious concerning your family affairs — as I understand it, you were not obliged to remain among the — among the wheels, as you call them. You could have gotten out quite easily, couldn't you?"

"I presume likely I could. But, you see, ma'am, I had a feelin' that I'd ought to stay."

Mrs. Dunn laughed lightly. "Ah me!" she exclaimed; "you felt it your duty, I suppose. Oh, you New England Puritans!"

She shook her head in playful mockery. Then she added, "But, at all events, it cannot be so very disagreeable — now. I have no doubt it was — well, not comfortable for you at first. Steve and Caroline were quite impossible — really quite furious. Your sudden appearance in the capacity of guardian was too much for them. They were sure you must be a perfect ogre, Captain. I had to use all my eloquence to convince them they would not be devoured alive. But now — what a change! Why, already Caroline accepts you as — well, almost like an old friend, like myself. In the last few days this change in her attitude is quite marked. What *have* you done? Are you a wizard? Do tell me!"

This appeal, delivered with eloquence and most engaging play of brow and eye, should have been irresistible. Unfortunately the captain did not appear to have heard it. Leaning forward, his hands clasped between his knees, he was gazing into the fire. And when he spoke, it was as if he were thinking aloud.

"I s'pose 'tis a sort of disease, this duty business," he mused. "And most diseases ain't cheerful visitations. Still a feller ought not to growl about it in public. I always did hate for a man to be goin' about forever complainin' of his sufferin's — whether they was from duty or rheumatiz."

Mrs. Dunn's lips snapped shut. She pressed them together impatiently. Evidently her questions, and their diplomatic prelude, had been unheard and wasted. However, she did not intend to be sidetracked or discouraged.

"One should not prate of one's duty, of course," she agreed. "Not that you do — far from it. But, as I was saying, our dear Caroline has —"

"Thank you, ma'am. I hope I don't groan too loud. Do you know, I believe climate has a bearin' on duty, same as it has on rheumatics. I s'pose you city folks —" and there was almost contempt in the words —" are sort of Christian Science, and figger it's an ' error ' — hey? Somethin' to be forgot."

The lady resented the interruption, and the contempt nettled her.

"Not at all!" she retorted. "We city dwellers have our duties, also."

"Is that a fact? I want to know!"

"Certainly it is a fact," tartly. "I have my duties and many of them."

"Um! So? Well, I s'pose you do feel you must dress just so, and live just so, and do just such and such things. If you call those duties, why —"

"I do. What else are they, pray?"

Mrs. Dunn was finding it difficult to keep her temper. To be catechised in this contemptuously lofty manner by one to whom she considered herself so immensely superior, was too much. She forgot the careful plan of campaign which she had intended to follow in this interview, and now interrupted in her turn. And Captain Elisha, who also was something of a strategist, smiled at the fire.

"We do have our social duties, our duties to society," snapped the widow, hotly. "They are necessary ones. Having been born — or risen to — a certain circle, we recognize the responsibilities attached to it. We *are* careful with whom we associate; we have to be. As for dress, we dress as others of our friends do."

"And maybe a little better, if you can, hey?"

"If we can — yes. I presume —" with crushing irony —"dress in South Denboro counts but little."

"You wouldn't say that if you ever went to sewin' circle," with a chuckle. "Still, compared to the folks at your meetin'-house this morning, our congregation would look like a flock of blackbirds alongside of a cage full of Birds of Paradise. But most of us — the women folks especial — dress as well as we can."

"As well as you can!" triumphantly. "There! you see? And you live as well as you can, don't you?"

"If you mean style, why, we don't set as much store by it as you do."

"Nonsense! We are obliged to be," with a slight

shudder at the vulgarism, "*stylish*. If we should lapse, if we should become shabby and behind the fashion or live in that way, people would wonder and believe it was because we could not afford to do otherwise."

"Well, s'pose they did, you'd know better yourselves. Can't you be independent?"

"No. Not unless you are very, very rich; then it might be considered an eccentricity. Independence is a costly luxury, and few can afford it."

"But suppose you can't afford the other thing?"

"Then we must pretend we can. Oh, you *don't* understand! So *much* depends upon a proper appearance. Everything depends upon it — one's future, one's children's future — everything."

"Humph!" with the same irritating smile, "I should think that might mean some plannin'. And plans, the best of 'em, are likely to go wrong. You talk about the children in your — in what you call your 'circle.' How can you plan what they'll do? You might when they was little, perhaps; but when they grow up it's different."

"It is not. It *can't* be! And, if they have been properly reared and understand their responsibilities, they plan with you."

"Land sakes! You mean — why, s'pose they take a notion to get married? I'm an old bach, of course, but the average young girl or feller is subject to that sort of ailment, 'cordin' to the records. S'pose one of your circle's daughters gets to keepin' company with a chap who's outside the ring? A promisin', nice boy enough, but poor, and a rank outsider? Mean to say she sha'n't marry him if she wants to."

"Certainly! That sort of marriage is never a happy one, unless, of course, the girl is wealthy enough not to care. And even then it is not advisable. All their customs and habits of thought are different. No! Emphatically, no! And the girl, if she is sensible and well reared, as I have said, will understand it is impossible."

"My soul and body! Then you mean to tell me that she *must* look out for some chap in her crowd? If she ain't got but just enough to keep inside the circle — this grand whirlamagig you're tellin' me about — if she's pretendin' up to the limit of her income or over, then it's her duty, and her ma and pa's duty, to set her cap for a man who's nigher the center pole in the tent and go right after him? Do you tell me that? That's a note, I must say!"

Mrs. Dunn's foot beat a lively tattoo on the rug. "I don't know what you mean by a ' note,' " she commented, with majestic indignation. "I have not lived in South Denboro, and perhaps my understanding of English is defective. But marriages among cultivated people, *society* people, intelligent, ambitious people are, or should be, the result of thought and planning. Others are impossible!"

"How about this thing we read so much about in novels? — Love, I believe they call it."

"Love! Love is well enough, but it does not, of itself, pay for proper clothes, or a proper establishment, or seats at the opera, or any of the practical, necessary things of modern life. You can't keep up a presentable appearance on *love!* If I had a daughter who lacked the brains to understand what I had taught her, that is, her duty as a member of good society, and talked of making a love match, I would . . . But there! You can't understand, I suppose."

She rose and shook the wrinkles from her gown. Captain Elisha straightened in his chair. "Why, yes, ma'am," he drawled, quietly; "yes, ma'am, I guess I understand fust-rate."

And suddenly Mrs. Dunn also understood. Her face, which had grown almost too red for one attached to a member of polite society, grew redder still. She turned away and walked to the window.

" What nonsense we've been talking!" she said, after a moment's silence. " I don't see what led us into this silly discussion. Malcolm and your niece must be having a delightful ride. I almost wish I had gone with them."

She did wish it, devoutly. Captain Elisha still remained by the fire.

" Automobiles are great things for hustlin' around in," he observed. " Pity they're such dangerous playthings. Yet I s'pose they're one of the necessities of up-to-date folks, same as you said, Mrs. Dunn."

" Surely," she asked coldly, " you don't condemn automobiles, Captain Warren? What would you — return to stage coaches?"

" Not a mite! But I was thinkin' of that poor Moriarty man."

" His death was due to an accident. And accidents," she turned and looked directly at him, " when they involve financial damages, may be paid for."

The captain nodded. " Yes," he said.

" And when arrangements for such payment is made, *honorable* people — at least, in the circle of which you and I have been speaking — consider the matter settled and do not refer to it again, either among themselves — or elsewhere."

" Yes, ma'am." He nodded again. She did know; Malcolm, evidently, had told her. " Yes, ma'am. That's the way any decent person would feel — and act — if such a thing happened — even if they hailed from South Denboro."

He pushed back his chair and stood up. She continued

to look him over, much as if she were taking a mental inventory of his character, or revising an old one.

"I hope," she said, lightly, but with deliberation, "our little argument and — er — slight disagreement concerning — er — duty will not make us enemies, Captain Warren."

"Enemies! Land sakes, no! I respect anybody's havin' opinions and not bein' afraid to give 'em. And I think I can understand some of how you feel. Maybe if I was anchored here on Fifth Avenue, same as you are, instead of bein' blown in by an unexpected no'theaster, I'd be feelin' the same way. It's all accordin', as I've said so often. Enemies? No, indeed!"

She laughed again. "I'm so glad!" she said. "Malcolm declares he'd be quite afraid of me — as an enemy. He seems to think I possess some mysterious and quite diabolical talent for making my un-friends uncomfortable, and declares he would compromise rather than fight me at any time. Of course it's ridiculous — just one of his jokes — and I'm really harmless and very much afraid. That's why I want you and me to be friends, Captain Warren."

"Sure!" Captain Elisha nodded emphatically. "That's what I want, too."

But that evening, immediately after his return to the apartment, when — Caroline having gone to her own room to remove her wraps — he and the butler were alone, he characteristically unburdened his mind.

"Mr. Warren, sir," said Edwards, "a young gentleman left a note here for you this afternoon. The elevator man gave it to me, sir. It's on your dressing table, sir."

The captain's answer had nothing whatever to do with the note. He had been thinking of other things.

"Commodore," he said, "I've got the answer."

"To the note? Already, sir? I didn't know you'd seen it."

"I ain't. I've got the answer to the conundrum. It's Mother!"

"Mother, sir? I — I don't know what you mean."

"I do. The answer's Mother. Sonny don't count, though he may think he does. But Mother's the whole team and the dog under the wagon. And, Commodore, we've got to trot some if we want to keep ahead of that team! Don't you forget it!"

He went to his room, leaving the bewildered butler to retire to the kitchen, where he informed the cook that the old man was off his head worse than common to-night.

"Blessed if he don't think he's a trotting horse!" said Edwards.

CHAPTER XI

THE note on the dining room table proved, to the captain's delight, to be from James Pearson. It was brief and to the point.

"Why don't you come and see me?" wrote the young man. "I've been expecting you, and you promised to come. Have you forgotten my address? If so, here it is. I expect to be in all day to-morrow."

The consequence of this was that eleven o'clock the next day found Captain Elisha pulling the bell at a brick house in a long brick block on a West Side street. The block had evidently been, in its time, the homes of well-to-do people, but now it was rather dingy and gone to seed. Across the street the first floors were, for the most part, small shops, and in the windows above them doctors' signs alternated with those of modistes, manicure artists, and milliners.

The captain had come a roundabout way, stopping in at the Moriarty flat, where he found Mrs. Moriarty in a curious state of woe and tearful pride. "Oh, what will I do, sir?" she moaned. "When I think he's gone, it seems as if I'd die, too. But, thanks to you and Miss Warren — Mary make it up to her! — my Pat'll have the finest funeral since the Guinny saloon man was buried. Ah, if he could have lived to see it, he'd have died content!"

The pull at the boarding-house bell was answered by a rather slatternly maid, who informed the visitor that she guessed Mr. Pearson was in; he 'most always was around lunch time. So Captain Elisha waited in a typical boarding-house parlor, before a grate with no fire in it and surrounded by walnut and plush furniture, until Pearson himself came hurrying downstairs.

"Say, you're a brick, Captain Warren!" he declared, as they shook hands. "I hoped you'd come to-day. Why haven't you before?"

The captain explained his having mislaid the address.

"Oh, was that it? Then I'm glad I reminded you. Rather a cheeky thing to do, but I've been a reporter, and nerve is necessary in that profession. I began to be afraid living among the blue-bloods had had its effect, and you were getting finicky as to your acquaintances."

"You didn't believe any such thing."

"Didn't I? Well, perhaps I didn't. Come up to my room. I think we can just about squeeze in, if you don't mind sitting close."

Pearson's room was on the third flight, at the front of the house. Through the window one saw the upper half of the buildings opposite, and above them a stretch of sky. The bed was a small brass and iron affair, but the rest of the furniture was of good quality, the chairs were easy and comfortable, and the walls were thickly hung with photographs, framed drawings, and prints.

"I put those up to cover the wall paper," explained the host. "I don't offer them as an art collection, but as a screen. Sit down. Put your coat on the bed. Shall I close the window? I usually keep the upper half open to let out the pipe smoke. Otherwise I might not be able to navigate without fog signals."

His visitor chuckled, followed directions with his coat and hat, and sat down. Pearson took the chair by the small flat-topped desk.

"How about that window?" he asked. "Shall I shut it?"

"No, no! We'll be warm enough, I guess. You've got steam heat, I see."

"You mean you hear. Those pipes make noise enough to wake the dead. At first I thought I couldn't sleep because of the racket they made. Now I doubt if I could without it. Would you consider a cigar, Captain?"

"Hum! I don't usually stop to consider. But I tell you, Jim — just now you said something about a pipe. I've got mine aboard, but I ain't dared to smoke it since I left South Denboro. If you wouldn't mind —"

"Not a bit. Tobacco in this jar on the desk. I keep a temporary supply in my jacket pocket. Matches? Here you are! What do you think of my — er — state-room?"

"Think it makes nice, snug quarters," was the prompt answer.

"Humph! Snug is a good word. Much like living in an omnibus, but it answers the purpose. I furnished it myself, except for the bed. The original bureau had pictures of cauliflowers painted on each drawer front. Mrs. Hepton — my landlady — was convinced that they were roses. I told her she might be right, but, at all events, looking at them made me hungry. Perhaps she noticed the effect on my appetite and was willing for me to substitute."

The captain laughed. Then, pointing, he asked: "What's that handbill?"

The "handbill" was a fair-sized poster announcing the production at the "Eureka Opera House" of the "Thrilling Comedy-Drama, The Golden Gods." Pearson looked at it, made a face, and shook his head.

"That," he said, "is my combined crusher and comforter. It is the announcement of the first, and next to the last, performance of a play I wrote in my calf days. The 'Eureka Opera House' is — or was, if the 'gods' weren't too much for it — located at Daybury, Illinois. I keep that bill to prevent my conceit getting away with me. Also, when I get discouraged over my novel, it reminds me that, however bad the yarn may turn out to be, I have committed worse crimes."

This led to the captain's asking about the novel and how it was progressing. His companion admitted having made some progress, more in the line of revision than anything else. He had remodeled his hero somewhat, in accordance with his new friend's suggestions during their interview at the Warren apartment, and had introduced other characters, portrait sketches from memory of persons whom he had known in his boyhood days in the Maine town. He read a few chapters aloud, and Captain Elisha waxed almost enthusiastic over them.

Then followed a long discussion over a point of seamanship, the handling of a bark in a gale. It developed that the young author's knowledge of saltwater strategy was extensive and correct in the main, though somewhat theoretical. That of his critic was based upon practice and hard experience. He cited this skipper and that as examples, and carried them through no'theasters off Hatteras and typhoons in the Indian Ocean. The room, in spite of the open window, grew thick with pipe smoke, and the argument was punctuated by thumps on the desk and chair arms, and illustrated by diagrams drawn by the captain's forefinger on the side of the dresser. The effects of oil on breaking rollers, the use of a "sea-anchor" over the side to "hold her to it," whether or not a man was justified in abandoning his ship under certain given circumstances, these were debated pro and con. Always Pearson's "Uncle Jim" was held up as the final authority, the paragon of sea captains, by the visitor, and, while his host pretended to agree, with modest reservations, in this estimate of his relative, he was more and more certain that his hero was bound to become a youthful edition of Elisha Warren himself — and he thanked the fates which had brought this fine, able, old-school mariner to his door.

At length, Captain Elisha, having worked "Uncle Jim" into a safe harbor after a hundred mile cruise under jury jig, with all hands watch and watch at the pumps, leaned forward in triumph to refill his pipe. Having done so, his eyes remained fixed upon a photograph standing, partially hidden by a leather collar box, upon the dresser. He looked at it intently, then rose and took it in his hand.

"Well, I swan!" he exclaimed. "Either what my head's been the fullest of lately has struck to my eyesight, or else — why, say, Jim, that's Caroline, ain't it?"

Pearson colored and seemed embarrassed. "Yes," he answered, "that is Miss Warren."

"Humph! Good likeness, too! But what kind of rig has she got on? I've seen her wear a good many dresses — seems to have a different one for every day, pretty nigh — but I never saw her in anything like that. Looks sort of outlandish; like one of them foreign girls at Geneva — or Leghorn, say."

"Yes. That is an Italian peasant costume. Miss Warren wore it at a fancy dress ball a year ago."

"Want to know! I-talian peasant, hey! Fifth Avenue peasant with diamonds in her hair. Becomin' to her, ain't it."

" I thought so."

" Yup. She looks pretty *enough!* But she don't need diamonds nor hand-organ clothes to make her pretty."

Then, looking up from the photograph, he asked, " Give you this picture, did she?"

His friend's embarrassment increased. " No," he answered shortly. Then, after an instant's hesitation. " That ball was given by the Astorbilts and was one of the most swagger affairs of the season. The *Planet* — the paper with which I was connected — issues a Sunday supplement of half-tone reproductions of photographs. One page was given up to pictures of the ball and the costumes worn there."

" I see. Astonishin' how folks do like to get their faces into print. I used to know an old woman — Aunt Hepsibah Tucker, her name was — she's dead now. The pride of Aunt Hepsy's heart was that she took nineteen bottles of ' Balm of Burdock Tea ' and the tea folks printed her picture as a testimonial that she lived through it. Ho, ho! And society big-bugs appear to have the same cravin'."

" Some of them do. But that of your niece was obtained by our society reporter from the photographer who took it. Bribery and corruption, of course. Miss Warren would have been at least surprised to see it in our supplement. I fancied she might not care for so much publicity and suppressed it."

" Um-hm. Well, I guess you did right. I'll thank you for her. By the way, I told Caroline where I was cal'latin' to go this mornin', and she wished to be remembered to you."

Pearson seemed pleased, but he made no comment. Captain Elisha blew a smoke ring from his pipe.

"And say, Jim," he added, embarrassed in his turn, "I hope you won't think I'm interferin' in your affairs, but are you still set against comin' up to where I live? I know you said you had a reason, but are you sure it's a good one?"

He waited for an answer but none came. Pearson was gazing out of the window. The captain looked at his watch and rose.

"I guess I'll have to be goin'," he said. "It's after twelve now."

His host swung around in his chair. "Sit down, Captain," he said. "I've been doing a lot of thinking since I saw you, and I'm not sure about that reason. I believe I'll ask your advice. It is a delicate matter, and it involves your brother. You may see it as he did, and, if so, our friendship ends, I suppose. But I'm going to risk it."

"Mr. Rodgers Warren and I," he went on, "were well acquainted during the latter part of my newspaper work. I was financial man on the *Planet,* and some articles I wrote took your brother's fancy. At all events, he wrote me concerning them in highly complimentary terms and asked me to call and see him at his office. I did so and — well, we became very friendly, so much so that he invited me to his house. I dined there several times, was invited to call often, and — I enjoyed it. You see, I had few friends in the city, outside my journalistic acquaintances, and I suppose I was flattered by Mr. Warren's kindness and the fancy he seemed to have taken to me. And I liked Miss Warren — no one could help that — and I believed she liked me."

"She does like you," interrupted his companion, with surprise. "Caroline's a good girl."

"Yes, she is. However, she isn't in this story, except as a side-issue. At this time my ambitions were for a newspaper career, and I thought I was succeeding. And her father's marked interest and the things he said to me promised more than an ordinary success. He was a well known man on the street, and influential. So my head began to swell, and I dreamed — a lot of foolishness. And then —"

He paused, put down his empty pipe, and sighed.

"Well, then," he continued, "came the upset. I judged from what you said at our previous conversation, Captain, that you were well enough acquainted with Wall Street to know that queer operations take place there. Did you read about the South Shore Trolley business?"

Captain Elisha considered. "Why, yes," he said, slowly, "seem's if I did. One of those consolidations with 'holdin' companies' and franchises and extensions and water by the hogshead. Wa'n't that it? I remember now; the Boston papers had considerable about it, and I presume likely the New York ones had more. One of those all-accordin'-to-law swindles that sprout same as toadstools in a dark place, but die out if the light's turned on too sudden. This one didn't come to nothin' but a bad smell, if I remember right."

"You do. And I suppose I'm responsible for the smell. I got wind of the thing, investigated, found out something of what was going on, and printed a preliminary story in the *Planet*. It caused a sensation."

He paused once more. Captain Elisha, for the sake of saying something, observed, "I shouldn't wonder."

"It certainly did. And the morning on which it appeared, Mr. Rodgers Warren 'phoned me. He wished to see me at once. I went down to his office. Captain, I dislike to tell you this. Mr. Warren was your brother."

"I know he was. And I'm his executor. Both those reasons make me 'specially anxious to have you tell me the truth. Heave ahead now, to oblige me."

"Well, I found him very polite and cordial, at first. He said that a ridiculous and sensational story concerning the Trolley Combine had appeared in the *Planet*, and he would like to have me contradict it and suppress further falsehoods of the kind. I told him I couldn't do that, because the story was true. I had written it myself. He was angry, and I could see that he was holding himself in by main strength. I went on to explain that it was the duty of an honest paper, as I saw it, to expose such trespass upon the people's rights. He asked me if I knew who was behind the scheme. I said I knew some of the backers. They were pretty big men, too. Then he informed me that he himself was deeply interested.

"I was knocked off my feet by that, you can imagine. And, to be frank, Captain, if I had known it at first I'm not sure that I, personally, would have taken the matter up. Yet I might; I can't tell. But now that I had done it and discovered what I had, I couldn't give it up. I must go on and learn more. And I knew enough already to be certain that the more I learned the more I should write and have published. It was one of those things which had to be made public — if a fellow had a conscience about him and a pride in the decency of his profession.

"All this was going through my head as I sat there in his private office. And he took my surprise and hesitation as symptoms of wavering and went at me, hard. Of course I knew, he said, that the operation was absolutely within the law. I did, but that didn't make it more honest or moral or just. He went on to say that in large financial deals of this nature petty scruples must be lost sight of. Good of the business, rights of stockholders, all that sort of stuff; he rang the changes. All the papers cared for was sensation; to imperil the fortune of widows and orphans whose savings were invested in the South Shore Stock, for the sake of sensation, was a crime. He should have known better than to say that to me; it is such an ancient, worn-out platitude."

"I know. I've been to political meetin's. The widows and orphans are always hangin' on the success of the Republican party — or the Democratic, whichever way you vote. The amount of tears shed over their investments by fellers you wouldn't trust with a brass five-cent piece, is somethin' amazin'. Go on; I didn't mean to interrupt."

"Then he switched to a more personal appeal. He said he had taken a fancy to me; had liked me from the very beginning. He recognized my unusual genius at first sight and had gone as far as to make plans bearing directly on my future. He was associated with men of wealth and business sagacity. Large deals, of which the Trolley Combine was but one, were on foot. He and his friends needed a representative on the press — a publicity agent, so to speak. Some of the greatest corporations employed men of that kind, and the salaries paid were large and the opportunities afforded greater still. Well, that's true enough. I know writers who are doing just that thing and getting rich at it. I suppose they've squared their consciences somehow and are willing to write lies and misleading articles for what there is in it. I can't, that's all; I'm not built that way, and I told him so.

"It ended in an open break. He reminded me of the favors he had done me. He had treated me almost like a son, had introduced me to his family, entertaining me at his table. Where was my gratitude? That was another bad break on his part, for it made me mad. I told him I had not asked to be adopted or fed by him; if I had supposed his kindness had an ulterier motive, I would have seen him at the devil before I accepted a favor. My career as a financial visitor was ended. Get out of his office! I got. But the Trolley Combine did not go through. The *Planet* and the other papers kept up the fight and — and the widows and orphans are bankrupt, I presume."

Captain Elisha's pipe had gone out long since. He absently rubbed the warm bowl between his palms.

"Humph!" he muttered. "So 'Bije was deep in that business, was he?"

"He was. Very deep indeed, I found out afterwards. And, I declare, I almost pitied him at the time. He acted as if his whole fortune was staked on the gamble. His hands shook, and the perspiration stood on his forehead as he talked. I felt as if I had been the means of ruining him. But of course, I hadn't. He lived for some time after that, and, I understand, died a rich man."

"Yes. He left what I'd call a heap of money. My nephew and niece don't seem to think so, but I do."

"So you see, Captain, why I stopped calling on the Warrens, and why I did not accept Miss Warren's invitation."

"I see . . . I see . . . And yet I don't

know. 'Bije may have took to you for business reasons, but the children didn't. They liked you for yourself. Caroline as much as said so. And their father never told 'em a word about the row, neither. Of course you couldn't have called when he was alive, but he's gone, and I'm — well, I'm sort of temporary skipper there now. And *I* want you to come."

"But if Miss Warren did know? She should know, I think."

"I ain't sure that she should. I guess there's consider'ble in her pa's life she ain't acquainted with. And she's as straight and honest and upright as a schooner's fo'mast. You did nothin' to be 'shamed of. It's the other way 'round, 'cordin' to my notion. But leave her out of it now. I've sacrificed some few things to take the job I've got at present, but I can't afford to sacrifice my friends. I count on you as a friend, and I want you to come and see *me*. Will you?"

"I don't know, Captain Warren. I must think it over a while, I guess."

"All right — think. But the invitation stands — *my* invitation. And, if you want to shift responsibility, shift it on to me. Some day, if it'll make you feel better, I'll tell Caroline and Stevie the whole story. But I want them to know you and the world — and me — a little better first. 'Cordin' to my notion, they need education just along that line. They've got teachers in other branches, but . . . There! I've *got* to be goin'. There's the dinner bell now."

The string of Japanese gongs, hung in the lower hall, sounded sonorously. Captain Elisha reached for his coat and hat, but Pearson caught his arm.

"No, you don't!" he declared. "You're going to stay and have lunch with me — here. If you say no, I shall believe it is because you are afraid of a boarding-house meal."

His guest protested, but the protests were overruled, and he and his host went down to the dining room. The captain whispered as they entered, "Land sakes, Jim, this takes me back home. It's pretty nigh a twin to the dinin' room at the Centre House in South Denboro."

All boarding-house dining rooms bear a family likeness, so the comment was not far wrong. A long table, rows of chairs on each side, ancient and honorable pictures on the walls, the landlady presiding majestically over the teapot, the boarders' napkins in rings — all the familiar landmarks were present.

Most of the male "regulars" were in business about the city and therefore lunched elsewhere, but the females were in evidence. Pearson introduced his guest. The captain met Mrs. Hepton, the landlady, plump, gray-haired, and graciously hospitable. She did not look at all like a business woman, but appearances are not always to be trusted; Mrs. Hepton had learned not to trust them — also delinquent boarders, too far. He met Miss Sherborne, whose coiffure did not match in spots, but whose voice, so he learned afterward, had been "cultivated abroad." Miss Sherborne gave music lessons. Mrs. Van Winkle Ruggles also claimed his attention and held it, principally because of the faded richness of her apparel. Mrs. Ruggles was a widow, suffering from financial reverses; the contrast between her present mode of living and the grandeur of the past formed her principal topic of conversation.

There were half a dozen others, including an artist whose aversion to barbers was proclaimed by the luxuriant length of his locks, a quiet old gentleman who kept the second-hand book store two doors below; his wife, a neat, trim little body; and Mr. and Mrs. C. Dickens, no less.

Mr. Dickens was bald, an affliction which he tried to conceal by brushing the hair at the sides of his head across the desert at the top. He shaved his cheeks and wore a beard and mustache. Mrs. Dickens addressed him as " C.," and handed him the sauce bottle, the bread, or whatever she imagined he desired, as if she were offering sacrifice to an idol.

She sat next to Captain Elisha and imparted information concerning her lord and master in whispers, during the intervals between offerings.

" My husband will be pleased to meet you, Captain Warren," she murmured. "Any friend of Mr. Pearson is certain to be an acquisition. Mr. Pearson and my husband are congenial spirits; they are members of the same profession."

" I want to know, ma'am."

" Yes. What is it, 'C.' dear? Oh, the butter! Margaret —" to the waitress —" Mr. Dickens wishes another butter-ball. Yes, Captain Warren, Mr. Dickens is an author. Haven't you noticed the — er — resemblance? It is considered quite remarkable."

Captain Elisha looked puzzled. "Why," he said, " I hadn't noticed it 'special. Jim's — Mr. Pearson's — eyes and his are some the same color, but —"

" Oh, no! not the resemblance to Mr. Pearson. I didn't mean *that*. The resemblance to his more famous namesake. Surely you notice it *now*."

The captain shook his head. "I — I'm afraid I'm thick-headed, ma'am," he admitted. "I'm out of soundin's."

"But the nose, and his beard, and his manner. Don't they remind you of the English Dickens?"

"O-oh!" Captain Elisha inspected the great man with interest. He had a vague memory of a portrait in a volume of "Pickwick" at home. "Oh, I see! Yes, yes."

"Of course you see! Everyone does. Mr. Dickens often says — it is one of his favorite jokes — that while other men must choose a profession, his was chosen for him by fate. How, with such a name, could he do anything except write?"

"I don't know, ma'am. But names are risky pilots, ain't they? I've run against a consider'ble number of Solomons, but there wa'n't one of 'em that carried more'n a deckload of wisdom. They christened me Elisha, but I can't even prophesy the weather with sartinty enough to bet. However, I daresay in your husband's case it's all right."

The lady had turned away, and he was afraid he might have offended her. The fear was groundless; she was merely offering another sacrifice, the sugar this time.

"Yes?" she asked, turning, "you were saying —"

"Why — er — nothin' of account. I cal'late the C. stands for Charles, then."

"No-o. Mr. Dickens's Christian name is Cornelius; but don't mention it before him, he is very sensitive on that point."

The Dickenses "tickled" the captain exceedingly, and, after the meal was over, he spoke of them to Pearson.

"Say," he said, "you're in notorious company, ain't you, Jim? What has Cornelius Charles turned out so far, in the way of masterpieces?"

Pearson laughed. "I believe he is employed by a

subscription house," he replied. "Doing hack work on an encyclopedia. A great collection of freaks, aren't they, Captain Warren?"

"Kind of. But that old book-shop man and his wife seem nice folks. And, as for freaks, the average boardin' house, city or country, seems to draw 'em like flies. I guess most anybody would get queer if they boarded all the time."

"Perhaps so. Or, if they weren't queer, they wouldn't board permanently from choice. There are two or three good fellows who dine and breakfast here. The food isn't bad, considering the price."

"No, it ain't. Tasted more like home than any meal I've had for a good while. I'm afraid I never was cut out for swell livin'."

Mrs. Hepton approached them as they stood in the hall. She wished to know if Mr. Pearson's friend was thinking of finding lodgings. Because Mr. Saks — the artist's name — was giving up the second floor back in a fortnight, and it was a very pleasant room. "We should be delighted to add you to our little circle, Captain Warren."

Pearson told her that his companion was already lodged, and she said good-by and left them. The captain smiled broadly.

"Everything in New York seems to be circles," he declared. "Well, Jim, you come up and circulate with me, first chance you get. I'm dependin' on you to call, remember."

The young man was still doubtful.

"I'll see," he said. "I can't promise yet — perhaps I will."

"You will — after you've thought it out to a finish. And come soon. I'm gettin' interested in that second

edition of your Uncle Jim, and I want to keep along
with him as fast as you write. Good-by. Much
obliged for the dinner — there I go again! — luncheon,
I mean."

CHAPTER XII

PEARSON called. He appeared at the apartment a week after the luncheon at the boarding house and was welcomed by the Captain Elisha, who, hearing his voice, strode into the hall, sent the shocked Edwards to the right-about in a hurry, seized his friend's hand, and ushered him into the library. Pearson said nothing concerning his change of mind, the course of reasoning which led him to make the visit, and the captain asked no questions. He took it for granted that the young fellow's common sense had turned the trick, and, the result being what it was, that was sufficient.

They spent a pleasant afternoon together. Caroline was out, and they had the library to themselves. The newest chapters of the novel were read and discussed, and the salty flavor of the talk was as pronounced as ever. Pearson left early, but promised to come again very soon.

When Caroline returned her uncle told her of his visitor. She seemed unfeignedly pleased, but regretted that she had not been there. "He was such a friend of father's," she said, "that seeing him here would be almost like the old days. And so many of those whom we thought were his friends and ours have left us."

This was true. Rodgers Warren and his children had had many acquaintances, had been active in church and charitable work, and their former home was a center of entertainment and gayety while he lived.

But his death and the rumors of shrinkage in the family fortune, the giving up of the Fifth Avenue residence, the period of mourning which forbade social functions, all these helped to bring about forgetfulness on the part of the many; and Caroline's supersensitiveness and her firm resolve not to force her society where it might be unwelcome had been the causes of misunderstanding in others, whose liking and sympathy were genuine. " I don't see what has come over Caroline Warren," declared a former girl friend, " she isn't a bit as she used to be. Well, I've done my part. If she doesn't wish to return my call, she needn't. *I* sha'n't annoy her again. But I'm sorry, for she was the sweetest girl I knew."

Stephen had never been very popular, and his absence at college still further reduced the number of young people who might be inclined to call. Their not calling confirmed Caroline's belief that she and her brother were deliberately shunned because of their change in circumstances, and she grew more sensitive and proudly resentful in consequence. Naturally she turned for comfort to those who remained faithful, the Dunns in particular. They were loyal to her. Therefore, with the intensity of her nature, she became doubly loyal to them. The rector of St. Denis dropped in frequently, and others occasionally, but she was lonely. She craved the society of those nearer her own age.

Pearson's coming, then, was psychologically apt. When he made his next call upon Captain Elisha, to find the latter out but his niece at home, she welcomed him cordially and insisted upon his waiting until her guardian returned. The conversation was, at first, embarrassing for the ex-reporter; she spoke of her father, and Pearson — the memory of his last interview with the latter fresh in his mind, and painfully aware that she knew nothing of it — felt guilty and like a hypocrite. But soon the subject changed, and when the captain entered the library he found the pair laughing and chatting like old acquaintances, as, of course, they were.

Captain Elisha, paying no attention to his friend's shakes of the head, invited his niece to be present at the reading of the latest addition to what he called "mine and Jim's record-breakin' sea yarn."

"It's really mine, you understand, Caroline," he observed, with a wink. "I'm silent partner in the firm — if you can call the one that does all the talkin' silent — and Jim don't do nothin' but make it up and write it and get the profits. Course, you mustn't mention this to him, 'cause he thinks he's the author, and 'twould hurt his feelin's."

"He's quite right," declared Pearson, emphatically. "If the thing is ever finished and published he will deserve all the credit. His advice had already remade it. This uncle of yours, Miss Warren," he added, turning to her, "is like the admiral Kipling wrote about — he has 'lived more stories' than ever I could invent."

The captain, fearful that his niece might take the statement seriously, hastened to protest.

"He's just foolin', Caroline," he said. "All I've done is set and talk and talk and talk. I've used up more of his time and the surroundin' air than you'd believe was possible. When I get next to salt water, even in print, it's time to muzzle me, same as a dog in July. The yarn is Jim's altogether, and it's mighty interestin' — to me anyhow."

"I'm sure it will be to me, also," declared the young lady. "Captain Warren has told me all about it, Mr.

Pearson, and I'm very eager to hear the new portion."

"There!" Captain Elisha slapped his knee. "There, Jim!" he exclaimed, "you hear that? Now you've *got* to read it. Anchor's apeak! Heave ahead and get under way."

So, because he could not well refuse, the author reluctantly began to read. And, as usual, his nautical friend to interrupt and comment. Caroline listened, her eyes twinkling. When the reading and the arguments were at an end, she declared it was all splendid; "Just like being at sea one's self," she said. "I positively refuse to permit another installment to be submitted unless I am — on deck. That's the proper phrase, isn't it, Captain?"

"Aye, aye, ma'am! Jim, we've shipped a new second mate, and she's goin' to be wuth her salt. You hear *me!*"

She proved to be worth all of that, at least in Pearson's opinion. His calls and the readings and discussions became more and more frequent. Each of the trio enjoyed them greatly, Caroline quite as much as the others. Here was something new and fresh, something to furnish a real interest. The story advanced rapidly, the character of the nautical hero shaped itself better and better, and the heroine, also, heretofore a somewhat shadowy and vague young woman, began to live and breathe. She changed surprisingly, not only in mental but in physical characteristics.

Captain Elisha was first to notice the latter peculiarity.

"Say, Jim!" he interrupted, one afternoon, "what was that you just read about Mary? Her hat blowin' off to leeward and her brown hair blowin' after it? Or somethin' of that sort?"

Caroline laughed merrily. The author turned to the passage mentioned.

"Not exactly, Captain," he replied, smiling. "I said her hat had blown away, and her brown curls tossed in the wind. What's wrong with that? Hats do blow away in a sou'wester; I've seen them."

"Perhaps he thinks she should have been more careful in pinning it on," suggested the feminine member of the advisory board.

Captain Elisha shook his head. "No," he observed calmly, "but why was she wearin' that kind of hair? She's pretty young to use a switch, ain't she?"

"Switch?" repeated "Mary's" creator, with some indignation. "What are you talking about? When I first described her, I said that her hair was luxuriant and one of her chief beauties."

"That's a fact! So you did. What made her dye it?"

"Dye it? What do you think she is — a chorus girl?"

"If I remember right she's a postmaster's daughter. But why is she wearin' brown hair, if it ain't neither false or dyed? Back in the third chapter 'twas *black*, like her eyes."

Caroline burst into another laugh. Pearson blushed to his forehead. "Well, by George!" he admitted, "you're right. I believe I did have it black, at first."

"You sartin did! I ain't got any objections to either color, only it ought to stay put, hadn't it? In a town of the size she's livin' in, a girl with changeable hair is likely to be kind of conspicuous. I tell you! maybe it bleached out in the sun. Ho, ho!"

The writer made a note on the margin of his manuscript and declared that his heroine's tresses and eyes should be made to correspond at all stages. They did, but they remained brown. Captain Elisha chuckled inwardly, but offered no further comments. Caroline, whose own hair and eyes were brown, did not refer to the matter at all.

She and the young man became better acquainted at each succeeding " literary clinic," as the latter called them. When Rodgers Warren first introduced him at their former home he had impressed her favorably, largely because of her desire to like anyone whom her father fancied. She worshiped the dead broker, and his memory to her was sacred. She would have forgiven and did forgive any wrong he might have done her, even his brother's appointment as guardian, though that she could not understand. Unlike Stephen, who fiercely resented the whole affair and said bitter things concerning his parent, she believed he had done what he considered right. Her feeling against Captain Elisha had been based upon the latter's acceptance of that appointment when he should have realized his unfitness. And his living with them and disgracing them in the eyes of their friends by his uncouth, country ways, made her blind to his good qualities. The Moriarty matter touched her conscience, and she saw more clearly. But she was very far from considering him an equal, or other than what Mrs. Corcoran Dunn termed him, an " encumbrance," even yet. She forced herself to be kind and tolerant and gave him more of her society, though the church-going experience was not repeated, nor did she accompany him on his walks or out-of-door excursions.

If Pearson's introductions had been wholly as a friend of her guardian, her feeling toward him might have been tinged with the same condescension or aversion, even. But, hallowed as he was by association with her father, she welcomed him for the latter's sake. And, as she became interested in the novel and found that her suggestions concerning it were considered valuable, she looked forward to his visits and was disappointed if, for any reason, they were deferred. Without being aware of it, she began to like the young author, not alone because he wrote entertainingly and flattered her by listening respectfully to her criticisms, or because her father had liked him, but for himself.

Captain Elisha was much pleased.

"I told you, Jim!" he said. "She's just as glad to see you as I am. Now don't you see how foolish it was to stay away 'cause you and 'Bije had a spat? Think of all the good times we'd have missed! And we needed a female aboard your Uncle Jim's craft, to help with 'Mary' and the rest."

His friend nodded. "She has been a great help, certainly," he answered. "But I can't help feeling guilty every time I come here. It is too much like obtaining her friendship under false pretenses. She should know the whole thing, I believe."

"She shall know it, when I think it's time for her to. But I want her to know you first. Then she'll be able to judge without so much prejudice. I told you I'd take the responsibility. You leave the ship in my charge for a spell."

In spite of this confident assertion, the captain also felt a trifle guilty. He realized that selfishness was involved in his keeping Pearson's secret from his niece. He was thoroughly enjoying himself with these two, and he could not bear to risk the breaking up which might follow disclosure.

One evening, while a "clinic" was in progress and

" She and the young man became better acquainted at each
succeeding 'literary clinic.'"

the three were deep in consultation, Edwards entered to announce Mrs. Corcoran Dunn and Mr. Malcolm. The butler's giving the lady precedence in his announcing showed that he, too, realized who was ranking officer in that family, even though the captain's " conundrum " had puzzled him. Mrs. Dunn and her son entered at his heels.

The lady took in the group by the table at a glance: Pearson, with the manuscript in his hands; Captain Elisha leaning back in his chair, frowning at the interruption; Caroline rising to welcome the guests, and coloring slightly as she did so. All these details Mrs. Dunn noted, made an entry in her mental memorandum-book, and underscored it for future reference.

If she discerned unpleasant possibilities in the situation, she did not allow them to disturb her outward serenity. She kissed Caroline and called her " dear child " as fondly as usual, shook hands graciously with Captain Elisha, and bowed condescending recognition of Pearson.

" And how is the novel coming on? Do tell me! " she begged. " I'm sure we interrupted a reading. It's too bad of us, really! But Malcolm insisted upon coming. He has been very busy of late — some dreadful ' corner ' or other on the exchange — and has neglected his friends — or thinks he has. I told him I had explained it all to you, Caroline, but he *would* come to-night. It is the first call he has made in weeks; so you *see!* But there! he doesn't consider running in here a call."

Call or not, it spoiled the evening for at least two of the company. Pearson left early. Captain Elisha excused himself soon after and went to his room, leaving the Dunns to chat with Caroline for an hour or more. Malcolm joked and was languid and cynical. His mother asked a few carefully guarded questions.

"Quite a clever person, this young author friend of yours seems to be, Caroline," she observed. "Almost brilliant, really."

"He isn't a friend of mine, exactly," replied the girl. "He and Captain Warren are friendly, and father used to know and like him, as I have told you. The novel is great fun, though! The people in it are coming to seem almost real to me."

"I daresay! I was a great reader myself once, before my health — my heart, you know — began to trouble me. The doctors now forbid my reading anything the least bit exciting. Has this — er — Mr. Pearson means?"

"I know very little of him, personally, but I think not. He used to be connected with the *Planet,* and wrote things about Wall Street. That was how father came to know him."

"Live in an attic, does he?" inquired Malcolm. "That's what all authors do, isn't it? Put up in attics and sleep on pallets — whatever they are — and eat crusts, don't they? Jolly life — if you like it! I prefer bucking wheat corners, myself."

Mrs. Dunn laughed, and Caroline joined her, though not as heartily.

"How ridiculous you are, Malcolm!" exclaimed his mother. "Mr. Pearson isn't that kind of an author, I'm sure. But where does he live, Caroline?"

"Somewhere on West 18th Street, I believe. He has rooms there, I think."

"Oh! Really? And how is this wonderful novel of his progressing? When does he expect to favor us with it?"

"I don't know. But it is progressing very well at present. He has written three chapters since last Wednesday. He was reading them to us when you came."

"Indeed! Since last Wednesday? How interesting!"

Malcolm did not seem to find the topic interesting, for he smothered a yawn. His mother changed the subject. On their way home, however, she again referred to it.

"You must make it a point to see her every day," she declared. "No matter what happens, you must do it."

"Oh, Lord!" groaned her son, "I can't. There's the deuce and all on 'Change just now, and the billiard tournament's begun at the Club. My days and nights are full up. Once a week is all she should expect, I think."

"No matter what you think or what she expects, you must do as I say."

"Why?"

"Because I don't like the looks of things."

"Oh, rubbish! You're always seeing bugaboos. Uncle Hayseed is pacified, isn't he? I've paid the Moriarty crowd off. Beastly big bills they were, too!"

"Humph! Uncle Hayseed, as you call him, is anything but a fool. But he isn't the particular trouble at present. He and I understand each other, I believe, and he will be reasonable. But — there is this Pearson. I don't like his calling so frequently."

Malcolm laughed in huge scorn. "Pearson!" he sneered. "Why, he's nothing but a penny-a-liner, without the penny. Surely you're not afraid Caroline will take a fancy to him. She isn't an idiot."

" She's a young girl, and more romantic than I wish she was. At her age girls do silly things, sometimes. He called on Wednesday — you heard her say so — and was there again to-night. I don't like it, I tell you."

" Her uncle is responsible for —"

" It is more than that. She knew him long before she knew her uncle existed. Her father introduced him — her *father*. And to her mind, whatever her father did was right."

" Witness his brilliant selection of an executor. Oh, Mater, you weary me! I used to know this Pearson when he was a reporter down town, and . . . Humph!"

" What is it?"

" Why, nothing, I guess. It seemed as if I remember Warren and Pearson in some sort of mix-up. Some . . . Humph! I wonder."

He was silent, thinking. His mother pressed his arm excitedly.

" If you remember anything that occurred between Rodgers Warren and this man, anything to this Pearson's disadvantage, it may pay us to investigate. What was it?"

" I don't know. But it seemed as if I remembered Warren's . . . or a friend of his telling me . . . saying something . . . but it couldn't be of importance, because Caroline doesn't know it."

" I'm not so sure that it may not be important. And, if you recall, on that day when we first met him at Caroline's, she seemed hurt because he had not visited them since her father died. Perhaps there *was* a reason. At any rate, I should look into the matter."

" All right, Mater, just as you say. Really you ought to join a Don't Worry Club."

"One member in the family is quite sufficient. And I expect you to devote yourself to Caroline from now on. That girl is lonely, and when you get the combination of a lonely romantic young girl and a good-looking and interesting young fellow, even though he is as poor as a church mouse, *anything* may happen. Add to that the influence of an unpractical but sharp old Yankee relative and guardian — then the situation is positively dangerous."

CHAPTER XIII

AN important event was about to take place. At least, it seemed important to Captain Elisha, although the person most intimately concerned appeared to have forgotten it entirely. He ventured to remind her of it.

" Caroline," he said, " Sunday is your birthday, ain't it?"

His niece looked at him in surprise. " Yes," she answered, " it is. How did you know?"

" Why, I remembered, that's all. Graves, the lawyer man, told me how old you and Stevie were, fust time I met him. And his partner, Mr. Sylvester, gave me the date one day when he was goin' over your pa's will. You'll be twenty years old Sunday, won't you?"

" Yes."

It was late in the afternoon, and she had been out since ten o'clock shopping with Mrs. Dunn, lunching down town with the latter and Malcolm, and motoring for an hour or two. The weather for the season was mild and sunny, and the crisp air had brightened her cheeks, her eyes sparkled, her fur coat and cap were very becoming, and Captain Elisha inspected her admiringly before making another remark.

" My! My!" he exclaimed, after an instant's pause. " Twenty years old! Think of it! 'Bije's girl's a young woman now, ain't she? I cal'late he was proud of you, too. He ought to have been. I presume likely *he* didn't forget your birthday."

He rose to help her with the heavy coat. As he lifted it from her shoulders, he bent forward and caught a glimpse of her face.

"There! there!" he said, hastily. "Don't feel bad, dearie. I didn't mean to hurt your feelin's. Excuse me; I was thinkin' out loud, sort of."

She did not answer at once, but turned away to remove her cap. Then she answered, without looking at him.

"He never forgot them," she said.

"Course he didn't. Well, you see I didn't forget, either."

It was an unfortunate remark, inasmuch as it drew, in her mind, a comparison between her handsome, dignified father and his rude, uncultured brother. The contrast was ever present in her thoughts, and she did not need to be reminded of it. She made no reply.

"I was thinkin'," continued the captain, conscious of having made a mistake, "that maybe we might celebrate somehow, in a quiet way."

"No. I am not in the mood for — celebrations."

"Oh, I didn't mean fireworks and the town band. I just thought —"

"Please don't. I remember other birthdays too well."

They had been great occasions, those birthdays of hers, ever since she was a little girl. On the eighteenth she made her *début* in society, and the gown she wore on that memorable evening was laid away upstairs, a cherished memento, to be kept as long as she lived. Each year Rodgers Warren took infinite pains to please and surprise his idolized daughter. She could not bear to think of another birthday, now that he had been taken from her.

Her guardian pulled his beard. "Well," he observed

ruefully, " then my weak head's put my foot in it again, as the feller said. If I ain't careful I'll be like poor cracked Philander Baker, who lives with his sister over at Denboro Centre. The doctor told Philander he was threatened with softenin' of the brain, and the sister thanked him for the compliment. You see, Caroline, I wrote on my own hook and asked Stevie to come home Saturday and stay till Monday. I kind of thought you'd like to have him here."

" Oh, I should like *that!* But will he come? Has he written you?"

" Hey? Yes, I cal'late he'll be on deck. He's — er — yes, he's written me."

He smiled as he answered. As a matter of fact, the correspondence between Stephen and himself had been lengthy and voluminous on the part of the former, and brief and business-like on his own. The boy, on his return to college, had found "conditions" awaiting him, and the amount of hard work involved in their clearance was not at all to his taste. He wrote his guardian before the first week was over, asserting that the whole business was foolishness and a waste of time. He should come home at once, he said, and he notified the captain that such was his intention. Captain Elisha replied with promptness and decision. If he came home he would be sent back, that was all. " I realize you've got a job ahead of you, Son," wrote the captain, " but you can do it, if you will. Fact is, I guess you've got to. So sail in and show us what you're made of."

Stephen's answer was a five page declaration of independence. He refused to be bullied by any living man. He had made arrangements to come to New York on the following Monday, and he was coming. As to being sent back, he wished his uncle to understand that it was one thing to order and another to enforce obedience. To which he received the following note:

"I can't stop you from coming, Steve, except by going to New Haven and holding you by main strength. That I don't propose to do, for two reasons: first, that it is too much trouble, and second that it ain't necessary. You can come home once in a while to see your sister, but you mustn't do it till I say the word. If you do, I shall take the carfare out of your allowance, likewise board while you are here, and stop that allowance for a month as a sort of fine for mutiny. So you better think it over a spell. And, if I was you, I wouldn't write Caroline that I was coming, or thinking of coming, till I had my mind made up. She believes you are working hard at your lessons. I shouldn't disappoint her, especially as it wouldn't be any use.

"Your affectionate uncle,
"ELISHA WARREN."

The result of all this was that Stephen, whose finances were already in a precarious condition, did think it over and decided not to take the risk. Also, conscious that his sister sided with their guardian to the extent of believing the university the best place for him at present, he tore up the long letter of grievance which he had written her, and, in that which took its place, mentioned merely that he was "grinding like blazes," and the only satisfaction he got from it was his removal from the society of the "old tyrant from Cape Cod."

He accepted the tyrant's invitation to return for the week-end and his sister's birthday with no hesitation

14   203

whatever; and his letter of acceptance was so politic as to be almost humble.

He arrived on an early train Saturday morning. Caroline met him at the station, and the Dunns' car conveyed them to the latter's residence, where they were to spend the day. The Dunns and Caroline had been together almost constantly since the evening when Malcolm and his mother interrupted the reading of the novel. The former, while professing to be harassed by business cares, sacrificed them to the extent of devoting at least a part of each twenty-four hours to the young lady's society. She was rarely allowed to be alone with her uncle, a circumstance which troubled her much less than it did him. He missed the evenings which he had enjoyed so much, and the next consultation over the adventures of Pearson's "Uncle Jim" and his "Mary" seemed flat and uninteresting without criticism and advice.

The author himself noticed the difference.

"Rot!" he exclaimed, throwing the manuscript aside in disgust. "It's rot, isn't it! If I can't turn out better stuff than that, I'd better quit. And I thought it was pretty decent, too, until to-night."

Captain Elisha shook his head. "It don't seem quite so shipshape, somehow," he admitted, "but I guess likely it's 'cause my head's full of other things just now. I'm puzzled 'most to death to know what to get for Caroline's birthday. I want to get her somethin' she'll like, and she's got pretty nigh everything under the sun. Say, Jim, you've been workin' too hard, yourself. Why don't you take to-morrow off and cruise around the stores helpin' me pick out a present. Come ahead — do!"

They spent the next afternoon in that "cruise," visiting department stores, jewelers, and art shops innumerable. Captain Elisha was hard to please, and his comments characteristic.

"I guess you're right, Jim," he said, "there's no use lookin' at pictures. Let alone that the walls are so covered with 'em now a fly can't scarcely light without steppin' on some kind of scenery — let alone that, my judgment on pictures ain't any good. I cal'late that's considered pretty fine, ain't it?" pointing to a painting in the gallery where they then were.

"Yes," replied the dealer, much amused. "That is a good specimen of the modern impressionist school."

"Humph! Cookin' school, I shouldn't wonder. I'd call it a portrait of a plate of scrambled eggs, if 'twa'n't for that green thing that's either a cow or a church in the offin'. Out of soundin's again, I am! But I knew she liked pictures, and so . . . However, let's set sail for a jewelry store."

The sixth shop of this variety which they visited happened to be one of the largest and most fashionable in the city. Here the captain's fancy was taken by a gold chain for the neck, set with tiny emeralds.

"That's pretty — sort of — ain't it, Jim?" he asked.

"Yes," replied his companion, with emphasis, "it is. And I think you'll find it is expensive, also."

"That so? How much?" turning to the salesman.

The latter gave the price of the chain. Captain Elisha whistled.

"Whew! Jerushy!" he exclaimed. "And it wouldn't much more than go around my wrist, at that. All the same size, are they?"

"No. Some are longer. The longer ones are higher priced, of course."

"Sartin! They're for fleshy folks, I s'pose. Mrs.

Thoph Kenney down home, she'd have to splice three of 'em together to make the round trip. Thoph's always scared he won't get his money's wuth in a trade, but he couldn't kick when he got her. To give the minister a dollar and walk off with two hundred and eighty pounds of wife is showin' some business sagacity, hey? To do him justice, I will say that *he* seems to be satisfied; she's the one that does the complainin'. I guess this is the most expensive counter in the store, ain't it, Mister?"

The clerk laughed. "No, indeed," he said. "These are all moderate priced goods. I wonder," turning to Pearson, "if your friend wouldn't like to see some of our choice pieces. It is a quiet day here, and I shall be glad to show them."

He led the way to a set of show cases near the door on the Fifth Avenue side. There before Captain Elisha's dazzled eyes were displayed diamond necklaces and aigrettes, tiaras and brooches, the figures on their price tags running high into the thousands. Pearson and the good-natured clerk enjoyed themselves hugely.

"Jim," said the captain after a little of this, "is there a police officer lookin' this way?"

Pearson laughed. "I guess not," he answered. "Why? The temptation isn't getting too much for your honesty, is it?"

"No," with a sigh, "but I'm carryin' a forty dollar watch and wearin' a ring that cost fifteen. I thought they was some punkins till I begun to look at this stuff. Now they make me feel so mean and poverty-struck that I expect to be took up for a tramp any minute. Mister," to the clerk, "you run right along and wrap up that chain I was lookin' at. Hurry! or I'll be ashamed to carry anything so cheap."

"Think she'll like it, do you, Jim?" he asked, when they were once more out of doors with the purchase in his inside pocket.

"She ought, certainly," replied Pearson. "It's a beautiful thing."

"Yes. Well, you see," apologetically, "I wanted to give her somethin' pretty good. 'Bije always did, and I didn't want to fall too fur behind. But," with a chuckle, "you needn't mention the price to anybody. If Abbie — my second cousin keepin' house for me, she is — if Abbie heard of it she'd be for puttin' me in an asylum. Abbie's got a hair breastpin and a tortoise shell comb, but she only wears 'em to the Congregationalist meetin'-house, where she's reasonably sure there ain't likely to be any sneak-thieves. She went to a Unitarian sociable once, but she carried 'em in a bag inside her dress."

Captain Elisha planned to surprise his niece with the gift at breakfast on the morning of her birthday, but, after reflection, decided to postpone the presentation until dinner time. The inevitable Dunns had taken upon themselves the duty of caring for the girl and her brother during the major part of the day. The yellow car appeared at the door at ten o'clock and bore the two away. Caroline assured her guardian, however, that they would return in season for the evening meal.

The captain spent lonely but busy hours until dinner time came. He had done some scheming on his own hook and, after a long argument with the cook, reënforced by a small sum in cash, had prevailed upon that haughty domestic to fashion a birthday cake of imposing exterior and indigestible make-up. Superintending the icing of this master-piece occupied some time. He then worried Edwards into a respectful but stubborn

207

fury by suggesting novelties in the way of table arrangement. Another bestowal of small change quelled the disturbance. Then came, by messenger, a dozen American Beauty roses with Mr. Pearson's card attached. These the captain decided should be placed in the center of the festive board. As a center piece had been previously provided, there was more argument. The cook took the butler's side in the debate, and the pair yielded only when Captain Elisha again dived into his pocket.

"But I warn you, all hands," he observed, "that this is the last time. My right fist's got a cramp in it this minute, and you couldn't open it again with a cold chisel."

At last, however, everything was as it should be, and he sat down in the library to await the coming of the young people. The gold chain in its handsome leather case, the latter enclosed in the jeweler's box, was carefully laid beside Caroline's place at the table. The dinner was ready, the cake, candles and all — the captain had insisted upon twenty candles — was ready, also. There was nothing to do but wait — and he waited.

Six-thirty was the usual dinner hour. It passed. Seven o'clock struck, then eight, and still Captain Elisha sat alone in the library. The cook sent word that the dinner was ruined. Edwards respectfully asked, "What shall I do, sir?" twice, the second time being sent flying with an order to "Go for'ard and keep your hatches closed!" The nautical phraseology was lost upon the butler, but the tone and manner of delivery were quite understandable.

Several times the captain rose from his chair to telephone the Dunn house and ask the reason for delay. Each time he decided not to do so. No doubt there were good reasons; Caroline and her brother had been de-tained; perhaps the automobile had broken down — the things were always breaking down just at the most inconvenient times; perhaps . . . Well, at any rate, he would not 'phone just yet; he would wait a little longer.

At last the bell rang. Captain Elisha sprang up, smiling, his impatience and worry forgotten, and, push-ing the butler aside, hurried to open the door himself. He did so and faced, not his niece and nephew, but Pearson.

" Good evening, Captain," hailed the young man, cheerily. " Didn't expect me, did you? I dropped in for a moment to shake hands with you and to offer congratulations to Miss Warren." Then, noticing the expression on his friend's face, he added, " What's the matter? Anything wrong? Am I intruding?"

" No, no! Course not. You're as welcome as an-other egg in a poor man's hen-house. Come right in and take off your things. I'm glad to see you. Only — well, the fact is I thought 'twas Caroline comin' home. She and Stevie was to be here over two hours ago, and I can't imagine what's keepin' 'em."

He insisted upon his visitor's remaining, although the latter, when he understood the situation, was reluctant to do so.

" Caroline'll be real glad to see you, Jim, I know," the captain said. " And I want you to stay for my sake. Between pacifyin' the Commodore and frettin' over what couldn't possibly happen, I was half dead of the fidgets. Stay and cheer me up, there's a good feller. I'd just about reached the stage where I had the girl and boy stove to flinders under that pesky auto. I'd even begun to figger on notifyin' the undertaker. Tell me

I'm an old fool and then talk about somethin' else. They'll be here any minute."

But a good many minutes passed, and still they did not come. Pearson, aware of his companion's growing anxiety, chatted of the novel, of the people at the boarding house, of anything and everything he could think of likely to divert attention from the one important topic. The answers he received were more and more brief and absent. At last, when Edwards again appeared, appealingly mute, at the entrance to the dining room, Captain Elisha, with a sigh which was almost a groan, surrendered.

"I guess," he said, reluctantly, "I guess, Jim, there ain't any use waitin' any longer. Somethin's kept 'em, and they won't be here for dinner. You and I'll set down and eat — though I ain't got the appetite I cal'-lated to have."

Pearson had dined hours before, but he followed his friend, resolved to please the latter by going through the form of pretending to eat.

They sat down together. Captain Elisha, with a rueful smile, pointed to the floral centerpiece.

"There's your posies, Jim," he observed. "Look pretty, don't they. She ain't seen 'em yet, but she'll like 'em when she does. And that over there is her present from me. Stevie gave her a box of gloves, and I expect, from what Mrs. Dunn hinted, that she and that son of hers gave her somethin' fine. She'll show us when she gets here. What's this, Commodore? Oysters, hey? Well, they ought to taste like home. They're 'Cape Cods'; I wouldn't have anything else."

"We won't touch the birthday cake, Jim," he added, a little later. "She's got to cut that herself."

The soup was only lukewarm, but neither of them

commented on the fact. The captain had scarcely tasted of his, when he paused, his spoon in air.

"Hey?" he exclaimed. "Listen! What's that? By the everlastin', it *is*. Here they are, at *last!*"

He sprang up with such enthusiasm that his chair tipped backwards against the butler's devoted shins. Pearson, almost as much pleased, also rose.

Captain Elisha paid scant attention to the chair incident.

"What are you waitin' for?" he demanded, whirling on Edwards, who was righting the chair with one hand and rubbing his knee with the other. "Don't you hear 'em at the door? Let 'em in!"

He reached the library first, his friend following more leisurely. Caroline and Stephen had just entered.

"Well!" he cried, in his quarter-deck voice, his face beaming with relief and delight, "you *are* here, ain't you! I begun to think . . . Why, what's the matter?"

The question was addressed to Stephen, who stood nearest to him. The boy did not deign to reply. With a contemptuous grunt, he turned scornfully away from his guardian.

"What is it, Caroline?" demanded Captain Elisha. "*Has* anything happened?"

The girl looked coldly at him. A new brooch — Mrs. Corcoran Dunn's birthday gift — sparkled at her throat.

"No accident has happened, if that is what you mean," she said.

"But — why, yes, that was what I meant. You was so awful late, and you know you said you'd be home for dinner, so —"

"I changed my mind. Come, Steve."

She turned to leave the room. Pearson, at that moment, entered it. Stephen saw him first.

"*What?*" he cried. "Well, of all the nerve! Look, Caro!"

"Jim — Mr. Pearson, I mean — ran in a few minutes ago," explained Captain Elisha, bewildered and stammering. "He thought of course we'd had dinner and — and — he just wanted to wish you many happy returns, Caroline."

Pearson had extended his hand and a "Good evening" was on his lips. Stephen's strange behavior and language caused him to halt. He flushed, awkward, surprised, and indignant.

Caroline turned and saw him. She started, and her cheeks also grew crimson. Then, recovering, she looked him full in the face, and deliberately and disdainfully turned her back.

"Come, Steve!" she said again, and walked from the room.

Her brother hesitated, glared at Pearson, and then stalked haughtily after her.

Captain Elisha's bewilderment was supreme. He stared, open-mouthed, after his nephew and niece, and then turned slowly to his friend.

"What on earth, Jim," he stammered. "What's it *mean?*"

Pearson shrugged his shoulders. "I think I know what it means," he said. "I presume that Miss Warren and her brother have learned of my trouble with their father."

"Hey? No! you don't think *that's* it."

"I think there's no doubt of it."

"But how?"

"I don't know how. What I do know is that I should

not have come here. I felt it and, if you will remember, I said so. I was a fool. Good night, Captain."

Hot and furiously angry at his own indecision which had placed him in this humiliating situation, he was striding towards the hall. Captain Elisha seized his arm.

"Stay where you are, Jim!" he commanded. "If the trouble's what you think it is, I'm more to blame than anybody else, and you sha'n't leave this house till I've done my best to square you."

"Thank you; but I don't wish to be 'squared.' I've done nothing to be ashamed of, and I have borne as many insults as I can stand. I'm going."

"No, you ain't. Not yet. I want you to stay."

At that moment Stephen's voice reached them from the adjoining room.

"I tell you I shall, Caro!" it proclaimed, fiercely. "Do you suppose I'm going to permit that fellow to come here again — or to go until he is made to understand what we think of him and why? No, by gad! I'm the man of this family, and I'll tell him a few things."

Pearson's jaw set grimly.

"You may let go of my wrist, Captain Warren," he said; "I'll stay."

Possibly Stephen's intense desire to prove his manliness made him self-conscious. At any rate, he never appeared more ridiculously boyish than when, an instant later, he marched into the library and confronted his uncle and Pearson.

"I — I want to say —" he began, majestically; "I want to say —"

He paused, choking, and brandished his fist.

"I want to say —" he began again.

"All right, Stevie," interrupted the captain, dryly, "then I'd say it if I was you. I guess it's time you did."

"I want to — to tell that fellow *there*," with a vicious stab of his forefinger in the direction of Pearson, "that I consider him an — an ingrate — and a scoundrel — and a miserable —"

"Steady!" Captain Elisha's interruption was sharp this time. "Steady now! Leave out the pet names. What is it you've got to tell?"

"I — my sister and I have found out what a scoundrel he is, that's what! We've learned of the lies he wrote about father. We know that he was responsible for all that cowardly, lying stuff in the *Planet* — all that about the Trolley Combine. And we don't intend that he shall sneak into this house again. If he was the least part of a man, he would never have come."

"Mr. Warren —" began Pearson, stepping forward. The captain interrupted.

"Hold on, Jim!" he said. "Just a minute now. You've learned somethin', you say, Stevie. The Dunns told you, I s'pose."

"Never mind who told me!"

"I don't — much. But I guess we'd better have a clear understandin', all of us. Caroline, will you come in here, please?"

He stepped toward the door. Stephen sprang in front of him.

"My sister doesn't intend to cheapen herself by entering that man's presence," he declared, hotly. "I'll deal with him, myself!"

"All right. But I guess she'd better be here, just the same. Caroline, I want you."

"She sha'n't come!"

214

"Yes, she shall. Caroline!"

The boy would have detained him, but he pushed him firmly aside and walked toward the door. Before he reached it, however, his niece appeared.

"Well?" she said, coldly. "What is it you want of me?"

"I want you to hear Mr. Pearson's side of this business — and mine — before you do anything you'll be sorry for."

"I think I've heard quite enough of Mr. Pearson already. Nothing he can say or do will make me more sorry than I am, or humiliate me more than the fact that I have treated him as a friend."

The icy contempt in her tone was cutting. Pearson's face was white, but he spoke clearly and with deliberation.

"Miss Warren," he said, "I must insist that you listen for another moment. I owe you an apology for —"

"Apology!" broke in Stephen, with a scornful laugh. "Apology! Well, by gad! Just hear that, Caro!"

The girl's lip curled. "I do not wish to hear your apology," she said.

"But I wish you to hear it. Not for my attitude in the Trolley matter, nor for what I published in the *Planet*. Nor for my part in the disagreement with your father. I wrote the truth and nothing more. I considered it right then — I told your father so — and I have not changed my mind. I should act exactly the same under similar circumstances."

"You blackguard!" shouted Stephen. Pearson ignored him utterly.

"I do owe you an apology," he continued, "for coming here, as I have done, knowing that you were ignorant of the affair. I believe now that you are misinformed

as to the facts, but that is immaterial. You should
have been told of my trouble with Mr. Warren. I
should have insisted upon it. That I did not do so is
my fault and I apologize; but for that only. Good
evening."

He shook himself free from the captain's grasp,
bowed to the trio, and left the room. An instant later
the outer door closed behind him.

Caroline turned to her brother. "Come, Steve," she
said.

"Stay right where you are!" Captain Elisha did not
request now, he commanded. "Stevie, stand still.
Caroline, I want to talk to you."

The girl hesitated. She had never been spoken to in
that tone before. Her pride had been already deeply
wounded by what she had learned that afternoon; she
was fiercely resentful, angry, and rebellious. She was
sure she never hated anyone as she did this man who
ordered her to stay and listen to him. But — she stayed.

"Caroline," said Captain Elisha, after a moment of
silence, "I presume likely — of course I don't know
for sartin, but I presume likely it's Mrs. Dunn and that
son of hers who've told you what you think you know."

"It doesn't concern you who told us!" blustered
Stephen, pushing forward. He might have been a fly
buzzing on the wall for all the attention his uncle paid
him.

"I presume likely the Dunns told you, Caroline," he
repeated, calmly.

His niece met his gaze stubbornly.

"Well," she answered, "and if they did? Wasn't it
necessary we should know it? Oh!" with a shudder of
disgust, "I wish I could make you understand how
ashamed I feel — how *wicked* and ashamed I feel that

I — *I* should have disgraced father's memory by . . . Oh, but there! I can't! Yes; Mrs. Dunn and Malcolm did tell us — many things. Thank God that we *have* friends to tell us the truth!"

"Amen!" quietly. "I'll say amen to that, Caroline, any time. Only I want you to be sure those you call friends are real ones and that the truths they tell ain't like the bait on a fishhook, put on *for* bait and just thick enough to cover the barb."

"Do you mean to insinuate —" screamed the irrepressible nephew, wild at being so completely ignored. His uncle again paid not the slightest attention.

"But that ain't neither here nor there now," he went on. "Caroline, Mr. Pearson just told you that his coming to this house without tellin' you fust of his quarrel with 'Bije was his fault. That ain't so. The fault was mine altogether. He told me the whole story; told me that he hadn't called since it happened, on that very account. And I took the whole responsibility and *asked* him to come. I did! Do you know why?"

If he expected an answer none was given. Caroline's lids drooped disdainfully. "Steve," she said, "let us go."

"Stop! You'll stay here until I finish. I want to say that I didn't tell you about the Trolley fuss because I wanted you to learn some things for yourself. I wanted you to know Mr. Pearson — to find out what sort of man he was afore you judged him. Then, when you had known him long enough to understand he wasn't a liar and a blackguard, and all that Steve has called him, I was goin' to tell you the whole truth, not a part of it. And, after that, I was goin' to let you decide for yourself what to do. I'm a lot older than you are; I've mixed with all sorts of folks; I'm past the stage where

217

I can be fooled by — by false hair or soft soap. You can't pour sweet oil over a herrin' and make me believe it's a sardine. I know the Pearson stock. I've sailed over a heap of salt water with one of the family. And I've kept my eyes open since I've run acrost this particular member. And I knew your father, too, Caroline Warren. And I say to you now that, knowin' Jim Pearson and 'Bije Warren — yes, and knowin' the rights and wrongs of that Trolley business quite as well as Malcolm Dunn or anybody else — I say to you that, although 'Bije was my brother, I'd bet my life that Jim had all the right on his side. There! that's the truth, and no hook underneath it. And some day you'll realize it, too."

He had spoken with great vehemence. Now he took a handkerchief from his pocket and wiped his forehead. When he again looked at his niece, he found her staring intently at him; and her eyes blazed.

"Have you quite finished — now?" she demanded. "Steve, be quiet!"

"Why, yes, I guess so, pretty nigh. I s'pose there ain't much use to say more. If I was to tell you that I've tried to do for you and Steve in this — same as in everything else since I took this job — as if you were my own children, you wouldn't believe it. If I was to tell you, Caroline, that I'd come to think an awful lot of you, you wouldn't believe that, either. I did hope that since our other misunderstandin' was cleared up, and you found I wa'n't what you thought I was, you'd come to me and ask questions afore passin' judgment; but perhaps —"

And now she interrupted, bursting out at him in a blast of scorn which took his breath away.

"Oh, stop! stop!" she cried. "Don't say any more.

You have insulted father's memory, and defended the man who slandered him. Isn't that enough? Why must you go on to prove yourself a greater hypocrite? We learned, my brother and I, to-day more than the truth concerning your *friend*. We learned that you have lied — yes, lied — and —"

"Steady, Caroline! be careful. I wouldn't say what I might be sorry for later."

"Sorry! Captain Warren, you spoke of my misjudging you. I thought I had, and I was sorry. To-day I learned that your attitude in that affair was a lie like the rest. *You* did not pay for Mr. Moriarty's accident. Mr. Dunn's money paid those bills. And you allowed the family — and me — to thank *you* for your generosity. Oh, I'm ashamed to be near you!"

"There! There! Caroline, be still. I —"

"I shall not be still. I have been still altogether too long. You are our guardian. We can't help that, I suppose. Father asked you to be that, for some reason; but did he ask you to *live* here where you are not wanted? To shame us before our friends, ladies and gentlemen so far above you in every way? And to try to poison our minds against them and sneer at them when they are kind to us and even try to be kind to you? No, he did not! Oh, I'm sick of it all! your deceit and your hypocritical speeches and your pretended love for us. *Love!* Oh, if I could say something that would make you understand how thoroughly we despise you, and how your presence, ever since you forced it upon Steve and me, has disgraced us! If I only could! I — I —"

She had been near to tears ever since Mrs. Corcoran Dunn, in the kindness of her heart, told her the "truth" that afternoon. But pride and indignation had pre-

15   219

vented her giving way. Now, however, she broke down.

"Oh — oh, Steve!" she cried, and, turning to her brother, sobbed hysterically on his shoulder. "Oh, Steve, what shall we do?"

Stephen put his arm about her waist. "It's all right, Sis," he said soothingly. "Don't cry before *him!* I guess," with a glance at his uncle, "you've said enough to make even him understand — at last."

Captain Elisha looked gravely at the pair. "I guess you have," he said slowly. "I guess you have, Caroline. Anyhow, I can't think offhand of anything you've left out. I could explain some things, but what's the use? And," with a sigh, "you may be right in a way. Perhaps I shouldn't have come here to live. If you'd only told me plain afore just how you felt, I'd — maybe I'd — but there! I didn't know — I didn't know. You see, I thought . . . However, I guess that part of your troubles is over. But," he added, firmly, "wherever I am, or wherever I go, you must understand that I'm your guardian, just the same. I considered a long spell afore I took the place, and I never abandoned a ship yet, once I took command of her. And I'll stick to this one! Yes, sir! I'll stick to it in spite of the devil — or the Dunns, either. Till you and your brother are of age I'm goin' to look out for you and your interests and your money; and nothin' nor nobody shall stop me. As for forcin' my company on you, though, that — well, that's different. I cal'late you won't have to worry any more. Good night."

He thrust his hands into his pockets and walked slowly from the library.

CHAPTER XIV

STEPHEN, the "man of the family," was the only member of the household, servants excepted, who slept soundly that night. Conscious of having done his duty in the affair with Pearson and his guardian, and somewhat fatigued by the disagreeable task of soothing his hysterical sister, he was slumbering peacefully at nine the next morning when awakened by a series of raps on his bedroom door.

"Ah! What? Well, what is it?" he demanded, testily opening his eyes. "Edwards, is that you? What the devil do you mean by making such a row?"

The voice which answered was not the butler's, but Caroline's.

"Steve! Oh, Steve!" she cried. "Do get up and come out! Come, quick!"

"What's the matter?" inquired the young man, sitting up in bed. "Is the house afire?"

"No, no! But do come! I want you. Something has happened."

"Happened? What is it?"

"I can't tell you here. Please dress and come to me as quick as you can."

Stephen, wondering and somewhat alarmed, dressed with unusual promptitude and obeyed. He found his sister standing by the library window, a letter in her hand. She looked troubled and anxious.

"Well, Caro," observed the boy, "here I am. What in the world's up now?"

She turned.

" Oh, Steve! " she exclaimed, " he's gone! "

" Gone? Who? "

" Captain Warren. He's gone."

" Gone? Gone where? Caro, you don't mean he's — *dead?* "

" No, he's gone — gone and left us."

Her brother's expression changed to incredulous joy.

" What? " he shouted. " You mean he's quit? Cleared out? Left here for good? "

" Yes."

" Hurrah! Excuse me while I gloat! Hurrah! We got it through his skull at last! Is it possible? But — but hold on! Perhaps it's too good to be true. Are you sure? How do you know? "

" He says so. See."

She handed him the letter. It was addressed to " My dear Caroline " and in it Captain Elisha stated his intentions succinctly. After the plain speaking of the previous evening he should not, of course, burden them with his society any longer. He was leaving that morning, and, as soon as he " located permanent moorings somewhere else " would notify his niece and nephew of his whereabouts.

" For," he added, " as I told you, although I shall not impose my company on you, I am your guardian same as ever. I will see that your allowance comes to you regular, including enough for all household bills and pay for the hired help and so on. If you need any extras at any time let me know and, if they seem to me right and proper, I will send money for them. You will stay where you are, Caroline, and Stevie must go back to college right away. Tell him I say so, and if he does not I shall begin reducing his allowance according as I wrote

222

him. He will understand what I mean. I guess that is all until I send you my address and any other sailing orders that seem necessary to me then. And, Caroline, I want you and Stevie to feel that I am your anchor to windward, and when you get in a tight place, if you ever do, you can depend on me. Last night's talk has no bearing on that whatever. Good-by, then, until my next.

"ELISHA WARREN."

Stephen read this screed to the end, then crumpled it in his fist and threw it angrily on the floor.

"The nerve!" he exclaimed. "He seems to think I'm a sailor on one of his ships, to be ordered around as he sees fit. I'll go back to college when I'm good and ready — not before."

Caroline shook her head. "Oh, no!" she said. "You must go to-day. He's right, Steve; it's the thing for you to do. He and I were agreed as to that. And you wouldn't stay and make it harder for me, would you, dear?"

He growled a reluctant assent. "I suppose I shall have to go," he said, sullenly. "My allowance is too beastly small to have him cutting it; and the old shark would do that very thing; he'd take delight in doing it, confound him! Well, he knows what we think of him, that's some comfort."

She did not answer. He looked at her curiously.

"Why, hang it all, Caro!" he exclaimed in disgust; "what ails you? Blessed if I sha'n't begin to believe you're sorry he's gone. You act as if you were."

"No, I'm not. Of course I'm not. I'm — I'm glad. He couldn't stay, of course. But I'm afraid — I can't help feeling that you and I were too harsh last night. We said things — dreadful things —"

"Be hanged! We didn't say half enough. Oh, don't be a fool, Caro! I was just beginning to be proud of your grit. And now you want to take it all back. Honestly, girls are the limit! You don't know your own minds for twelve consecutive hours. Answer me now! *Are* you sorry he's gone?"

"No. No, I'm not, really. But I — I feel somehow as if — as if everything was on my shoulders. You're going away, and he's gone, and — What is it, Edwards?"

The butler entered, with a small parcel in his hand.

"I beg your pardon, Miss Caroline," he said. "I should have given you this last evening. It was by your place at the table. I think Captain Warren put it there, miss."

Caroline took the parcel and looked at it wonderingly.

"For me?" she repeated.

"Yes, Miss Caroline. It is marked with your name. And breakfast is served, when you and Mr. Stephen are ready."

He bowed and retired. The girl sat turning the little white box in her hands.

"*He* left it for me," she said. "What can it be?"

Her brother snatched it impatiently.

"Why don't you open it and find out?" he demanded. "Perhaps it's his latch key. Here! I'll do it myself."

He cut the cord and removed the cover of the little box. Inside was the jeweler's leather case. He took it out and pressed the spring. The cover flew up.

"Whew!" he whistled. "It's a present. And rather a decent one, too, by gad! Look, Caro!"

He handed her the open case. She looked at the chain, spread carefully on the white satin lining. Inside the cover was fitted a card. She turned it over and read: "To my niece, Caroline. With wishes for many

224

happy returns, and much love, from her Uncle Elisha Warren."

She sat gazing at the card. Stephen bent down, read the inscription, and then looked up into her face.

"*What?*" he cried. "I believe — You're not *crying!* Well, I'll be hanged! Sis, you *are* a fool!"

The weather that morning was fine and clear. James Pearson, standing by the window of his rooms at the boarding house, looking out at the snow-covered roofs sparkling in the sun, was miserable. When he retired the night before it was with a solemn oath to forget Caroline Warren altogether; to put her and her father and the young cad, her brother, utterly from his mind, never to be thought of again. As a preliminary step in this direction, he began, the moment his head touched the pillow, to review, for the fiftieth time, the humiliating scene in the library, to think of things he should have said, and — worse than all — to recall, word for word, the things she had said to him. In this cheerful occupation he passed hours before falling asleep. And, when he woke, it was to begin all over again.

Why — *why* had he been so weak as to yield to Captain Elisha's advice? Why had he not acted like a sensible, self-respecting man, done what he knew was right, and persisted in his refusal to visit the Warrens? Why? Because he was an idiot, of course — a hopeless idiot, who had got exactly what he deserved! Which bit of philosophy did not help make his reflections less bitter.

He went down to breakfast when the bell rang, but his appetite was missing, and he replied only in monosyllables to the remarks addressed to him by his fellow boarders. Mrs. Hepton, the landlady, noticed the change.

"You not ill, Mr. Pearson, I hope?" she queried. "I do hope you haven't got cold, sleeping with your windows wide open, as you say you do. Fresh air is a good thing, in moderation, but one should be careful. Don't you think so, Mr. Carson?"

Mr. Carson was a thin little man, a bachelor, who occupied the smallest room on the third story. He was a clerk in a department store, and his board was generally in arrears. Therefore, when Mrs. Hepton expressed an opinion he made it a point to agree with her. In this instance, however, he merely grunted.

"I say fresh air in one's sleeping room is a good thing in moderation. Don't you think so, Mr. Carson?" repeated the landlady.

Mr. Carson rolled up his napkin and inserted it in the ring. His board, as it happened, was paid in full to date. Also, although he had not yet declared his intention, he intended changing lodgings at the end of the week.

"Humph!" he sniffed, with sarcasm, "it may be. I couldn't get none in *my* room if I wanted it, so I can't say sure. Morning."

He departed hurriedly. Mrs. Hepton looked disconcerted. Mrs. Van Winkle Ruggles smiled meaningly across the table at Miss Sherborne, who smiled back.

Mr. Ludlow, the bookseller, quietly observed that he hoped Mr. Pearson had not gotten cold. Colds were prevalent at this time of the year. "'These are the days when the Genius of the weather sits in mournful meditation on the threshold,' as Mr. Dickens tells us," he added. "I presume he sits on the sills of open windows, also."

The wife of the Mr. Dickens there present pricked up her ears.

"When did you write that, ' C.' dear?" she asked, turning to her husband. "I remember it perfectly, of course, but I have forgotten, for the moment, in which of your writings it appears."

The illustrious one's mouth being occupied with a section of scorching hot waffle, he was spared the necessity of confession.

"Pardon me," said Mr. Ludlow. "I was not quoting our Mr. Dickens this time, but his famous namesake."

The great " C." drowned the waffle with a swallow of water.

"Maria," he snapped, "don't be so foolish. Ludlow quotes from — er —' Bleak House.' I have written some things — er — similar, but not that. Why don't you pass the syrup?"

The bookseller, who was under the impression that he had quoted from the " Christmas Carol," merely smiled and remained silent.

"My father, the Senator," began Mrs. Van Winkle Ruggles, "was troubled with colds during his political career. I remember his saying that the Senate Chamber at the Capitol was extremely draughty. Possibly Mr. Pearson's ailment does come from sleeping in a draught. Not that father was accustomed to *sleep* during the sessions — Oh, dear, no! not that, of course. How absurd!"

She laughed gayly. Pearson, who seemed to think it time to say something, declared that, so far as he knew, he had no cold or any symptoms of one.

"Well," said Mrs. Hepton, with conviction, "something ails you, I know. We can all see it; can't we?" turning to the rest of the company. "Why, you've scarcely spoken since you sat down at the table. And you've eaten next to nothing. Perhaps there is some trouble, something on your mind which is worrying you. Oh, I *hope* not!"

"No doubt it is the preoccupation of genius," remarked Mrs. Dickens. "I'm sure it must be that. When 'C.' is engaged with some particularly trying literary problem he frequently loses all his appetite and does not speak for hours together. Isn't it so, dear?"

"C.," who was painfully conscious that he might have made a miscue in the matter of the quotation, answered sharply.

"No," he said. "Not at all. Don't be silly, Maria."

Miss Sherborne clasped her hands. "*I* know!" she exclaimed in mock rapture; "Mr. Pearson is in love!"

This suggestion was received with applause and hilarity. Pearson pushed back his chair and rose.

"I'm much obliged for this outburst of sympathy," he observed, dryly. "But, as I say, I'm perfectly well, and the other diagnoses are too flattering to be true. Good morning."

Back in his room he seated himself at his desk, took the manuscript of his novel from the drawer, and sat moodily staring at it. He was in no mood for work. The very sight of the typewritten page disgusted him. As he now felt, the months spent on the story were time wasted. It was ridiculous for him to attempt such a thing; or to believe that he could carry it through successfully; or to dream that he would ever be anything better than a literary hack, a cheap edition of "C." Dickens, minus the latter's colossal self-satisfaction.

He was still sitting there, twirling an idle pencil between his fingers, when he heard steps outside his door. Someone knocked.

"Well, what is it?" he asked.

His landlady answered.

"Mr. Pearson," she said, "may I see you?"

He threw down the pencil and, rising, walked to the door and opened it. Mrs. Hepton was waiting in the hall. She seemed excited.

"Mr. Pearson," she said, "will you step downstairs with me for a moment? I have a surprise for you."

"A surprise? What sort of a surprise?"

"Oh, a pleasant one. At least I think it is going to be pleasant for all of us. But I'm not going to tell you what it is. You must come down and see for yourself."

She led the way downstairs, the young man following her, wondering what the surprise might be, and fairly certain it, nor anything else, could be pleasant on that day.

He supposed, of course, that he must descend to the parlor to reach the solution of the mystery, but he was mistaken. On the second floor Mrs. Hepton stopped and pointed.

"It's in there," she said, pointing.

"There" was the room formerly occupied by Mr. Saks, the long-haired artist. Since his departure it had been vacant. Pearson looked at the closed door and then at the lady.

"A surprise for me in *there?*" he repeated. "What's the joke, Mrs. Hepton?"

By way of answer she took him by the arm, and, leading him to the door, threw the latter open.

"Here he is!" she said.

"Hello, Jim!" hailed Captain Elisha Warren, cheerfully. "Ship ahoy! Glad to see you."

He was standing in the middle of the room, his hat on the table and his hands in his pockets.

Pearson was surprised; there was no doubt of that —

not so much at the sight of his friend — he had expected to see or hear from the captain before the day was over — as at seeing him in that room. He could not understand what he was doing there.

Captain Elisha noted his bewildered expression, and chuckled.

"Come aboard, Jim!" he commanded. "Come in and inspect. I'll see you later, Mrs. Hepton," he added, "and give you my final word. I want to hold officer's council with Mr. Pearson here fust."

The landlady accepted the broad hint and turned to go.

"Very well," she said, "but I do hope for all our sakes that word will be *yes*, Mr. Warren — Excuse me, it is Captain Warren, isn't it?"

"It used to be, yes, ma'am. And at home it is yet. 'Round here I've learned to be like a barroom poll-parrot, ready to answer to most everything. There!" as the door closed after her; "now we can be more private. Set down, Jim! How are you, anyway?"

Pearson sat down mechanically. "I'm well enough — everything considered," he replied, slowly. "But what — what are you in here for? I don't understand."

"You will in a minute. What do you think of this — er — saloon cabin?" with a comprehensive sweep of his arm.

The room was of fair size, furnished in a nondescript, boarding-house fashion, and with two windows overlooking the little back yard of the house and those of the other adjoining it. Each yard contained an assortment of ash cans, and there was an astonishing number of clothes lines, each fluttering a variety of garments peculiarly personal to their respective owners.

"Pretty snug, ain't it?" continued the captain.

230

" Not exactly up to that I've been luxuriatin' in lately, but more fittin' to my build and class than that was, I shouldn't wonder. No Corot paintin's nor five thousand dollar tintypes of dory codders; but I can manage to worry along without them, if I try hard. Neat but not gaudy, I call it — as the architect feller said about his plans for the addition to the county jail at Ostable. Hey? Ho! Ho!"

Pearson began to get a clue to the situation.

" Captain Warren," he demanded, " have you — Do you mean to say you've taken this room to *live* in?"

" No, I ain't said all that yet. I wanted to talk with you a little afore I said it. But that was my idea, if you and I agreed on sartin matters."

" You've come here to live! You've left your — your niece's house?"

" Ya-as, I've left. That is, I left the way the Irishman left the stable where they kept the mule. He said there was all out doors in front of him and only two feet behind. That's about the way 'twas with me."

" Have your nephew and niece —"

" Um-hm. They hinted that my room was better than my company, and, take it by and large, I guess they was right for the present, anyhow. I set up till three o'clock thinkin' it over, and then I decided to get out afore breakfast this mornin'. I didn't wait for any good-bys. They'd been said, or all I cared to hear —" Captain Elisha's smile disappeared for an instant — " last evenin'. The dose was sort of bitter, but it had the necessary effect. At any rate, I didn't hanker for another one. I remembered what your landlady told me when I was here afore, about this stateroom bein' vacated, and I come down to look at it. It suits me well enough; seems like a decent moorin's for an old salt water derelict like me; the price is reasonable, and I guess likely I'll take it. I *guess* I will."

"Why do you guess? By George, I hope you will!"

"Do you? I'm much obliged. I didn't know but after last night, after the scrape I got you into, you might feel — well, sort of as if you'd seen enough of me."

The young man smiled bitterly. "It wasn't your fault," he said. "It was mine entirely. I'm quite old enough to decide matters for myself, and I should have decided as my reason, and not my inclinations, told me. You weren't to blame."

"Yes, I was. If you're old enough, I'm *too* old, I cal'late. But I did think — However, there's no use goin' over that. I ask your pardon, Jim. And you don't hold any grudge?"

"Indeed I don't. I may be a fool — I guess I am — but not that kind."

"Thanks. Well, there's one objection out of the way, then, only I don't want you to think that I've hove overboard that 'responsibility' I was so easy and fresh about takin' on my shoulders. It's there yet; and I'll see you squared with Caroline afore this v'yage is over, if I live."

His friend frowned.

"You needn't mind," he said. "I prefer that you drop the whole miserable business."

"Well, maybe, but — Jim, you've taken hold of these electric batteries that doctors have sometimes? It's awful easy to grab the handles of one of those contraptions, but when you want to drop 'em you can't. They don't drop easy. I took hold of the handles of 'Bije's affairs, and, though it might be pleasanter to drop 'em, I can't — or I won't."

"Then you're leaving your nephew and niece doesn't mean that you've given up the guardianship?"

Captain Elisha's jaw set squarely.

"I don't remember sayin' that it did," he answered, with decision. Then, his good-nature returning, he added, "And now, Jim, I'd like your opinion of these new quarters that I may take. What do you think of 'em? Come to the window and take a look at the scenery."

Pearson joined him at the window. The captain waved toward the clothes-lines and grinned.

"Looks as if there was some kind of jubilee, don't it," he observed. "Every craft in sight has strung the colors."

Pearson laughed. Then he said:

"Captain, I think the room will do. It isn't palatial, but one can live in worse quarters, as I know from experience."

"Yup. Well, Jim, there's just one thing more. Have I disgraced you a good deal, bein' around with you and chummin' in with you the way I have? That is, do you *think* I've disgraced you? Are you ashamed of me?"

"I? Ashamed of *you?* You're joking!"

"No, I'm serious. Understand now, I'm not apologizin'. My ways are my ways, and I think they're just as good as the next feller's, whether he's from South Denboro or — well, Broad Street. I've got a habit of thinkin' for myself and actin' for myself, and when I take off my hat it's to a bigger *man* than I am and not to a more stylish hat. But, since I've lived here in New York, I've learned that, with a whole lot of folks, hats themselves count more than what's underneath 'em. I haven't changed mine, and I ain't goin' to. Now, with that plain and understood, do you want me to live here,

233

in the same house with you? I ain't fishin' for compliments. I want an honest answer."

He got it. Pearson looked him squarely in the eye.

" I do," he said. " I like you, and I don't care a damn about your hat. Is that plain?"

Captain Elisha's reply was delivered over the balusters in the hall.

" Hi!" he called. " Hi, Mrs. Hepton."

The landlady had been anxiously waiting. She ran from the dining room to the foot of the stairs.

" Yes?" she cried. " What is it?"

" It's a bargain," said the captain. " I'm ready to engage passage."

CHAPTER XV

THUS Captain Elisha entered another of New York's " circles," that which centered at Mrs. Hepton's boarding house. Within a week he was as much a part of it as if he had lived there for years. At lunch, on the day of his arrival, he made his appearance at the table in company with Pearson, and when the landlady exultantly announced that he was to be " one of our little party " thereafter, he received and replied to the welcoming salutations of his fellow boarders with unruffled serenity.

" How could I help it? " he asked. " Human nature's liable to temptation, they tell us. The flavor of that luncheon we had last time I was here has been hangin' 'round the edges of my mouth and tantalizin' my memory ever since."

" We had a soufflé that noon, if I remember correctly, Captain," observed the flattered Mrs. Hepton.

" Did you? Well, I declare! I'd have sworn 'twas a biled-dinner hash. Knew 'twas better than any I ever ate afore, but I'd have bet 'twas hash, just the same. Tut! tut! tut! Now, honest, Mrs. Hepton, ain't this — er — whatever-you-call-it a close relation — a sort of hash with its city clothes on, hey? "

The landlady admitted that a soufflé was something not unlike a hash. Captain Elisha nodded.

" I thought so," he declared. " I was sartin sure I couldn't be mistaken. What is it used to be in the song book? ' You can smash — you can —' Well, I don't remember. Somethin' about your bein' able to smash the vase if you wanted to, but the smell of the posies was there yet."

Mr. Ludlow, the bookseller, supplied the quotation.

> " ' You may break, you may shatter
> The vase if you will,
> But the scent of the roses
> Will cling to it still,' "

he said, smiling.

"That's it. Much obliged. You can warm up and rechristen the hash if you will, but the corned beef and cabbage stay right on deck. Ain't that so, Mr. Dickens?"

The illustrious "C." bowed.

"Moore?" he observed, with dignity.

"Yes. That's what *I* said—'More!' Said it twice, I believe. Glad you agree with me. The hymn says that weakness is sin, but there's no sin in havin' a weakness for corned-beef hash."

Miss Sherborne and Mrs. Van Winkle Ruggles were at first inclined to snub the new boarder, considering him a country boor whose presence in their select society was almost an insult. The captain did not seem to notice their hints or sneers, although Pearson grew red and wrathful.

"Laura, my dear," said Mrs. Ruggles, addressing the teacher of vocal culture, "don't you feel quite rural to-day? Almost as if you were visiting the country?"

"I do, indeed," replied Miss Sherborne. "Refreshing, isn't it? Ha! ha!"

"It is if one cares for such things. I am afraid *I* don't appreciate them. They may be well enough in their place, but—"

She finished with a shrug of her shoulders. Captain Elisha smiled.

"Yes, ma'am," he said politely, joining in the conversation; "that's what the boy said about the cooky crumbs in the bed. You don't care for the country, I take it, ma'am."

"I do *not!*"

"So? Well, it's a mercy we don't think alike; even Heaven would be crowded if we did — hey? You didn't come from the country, either?" turning to Miss Sherborne.

The young lady would have liked to answer with an uncompromising negative. Truth and the fact that some of those present were acquainted with it compelled her to forego this pleasure.

"I was born in a — a small town," she answered coldly. "But I came to the city as soon as I possibly could."

"Um-hm. Well, I came when I couldn't possibly stay away. We can agree on one thing — we're all here. Yes, and on another — that that cake is fust-rate. I'll take a second piece, if you've no objection, Mrs. Hepton."

When they were alone once more, in the captain's room, Pearson vented his indignation.

"Why didn't you give them as good as they sent?" he demanded. "Couldn't you see they were doing their best to hurt your feelings?"

"Ya-as. I could see it. Didn't need any specs to see that."

"Then why didn't you answer them as they deserved?"

"Oh, I don't know. What's the use? They've got troubles of their own. One of 'em's a used-to-be, and the other's a never-was. Either disease is bad enough without addin' complications."

Pearson laughed. " I don't get the whole of that, Captain," he said. " Mrs. Van is the used-to-be, I suppose. But what is it that Miss Sherborne never was?"

" Married," was the prompt reply. " Old maiditis is creepin' on her fast. You want to be careful, Jim; a certain kind of female gets desperate about her stage."

Pearson laughed again.

" Oh, get out! " he exclaimed, turning to go.

" All right! I will, when you and she are together and you give me the signal. But I tell you honest, I'd hate to do it. Judgin' by the way she smiles and looks up under her eye-winkers at you, you're in danger of kidnappin'. So long. I'll see you again after I get my dunnage unpacked."

The snubbing and sneering came to an abrupt end. Pearson, in conversation with Mrs. Ruggles, casually imparted the information that Captain Elisha was the brother of A. Rodgers Warren, late society leader and wealthy broker. Also, that he had entire charge of the latter's estate. Thereafter Mrs. Ruggles treated the captain as one whose rank was equal to her own, and, consequently, higher than anyone's else in the boarding-house. She made it a point to publicly ask his advice concerning " securities " and " investments," and favored him with many reminiscences of her distinguished father, the Senator. Miss Sherborne, as usual, followed her lead. Captain Elisha, when Pearson joked him on the altered behavior of the two ladies, merely grinned.

" You may thank me for that, Captain," said the young man. " When I told Mrs. Ruggles who and what you were she almost broke down and sobbed. The fact that she had risked offending one so closely connected with the real thing on Fifth Avenue and Wall Street was too dreadful. But she's yours devotedly now. There's an 18-karat crown on your head."

"Yup. I suppose so. Well, I ain't so sot up with pride over wearin' that crown. It used to belong to 'Bije, and I never did care much for second-hand things. Rather have a new sou'wester of my own, any day in the week. When I buy a sou'wester I know what it's made of."

"Mrs. Ruggles knows what the crown is made of — gold, nicely padded with bonds and preferred stock."

"Humph! Sometimes I wonder if the paddin's waterproof. As for the gold — well, you can make consider'ble shine with brass when you're dealin' with nighsighted folks . . . and children."

To this indirect reference to Miss Warren and her brother Pearson made no reply. The pair conversed freely on other subjects, but each avoided this one. The novel, too, was laid on the shelf for the present. Its author had not yet mustered sufficient courage to return to it. Captain Elisha once or twice suggested a session with "Cap'n Jim," but, finding his suggestions received with more or less indifference, did not press them. His mind was busy with other things. A hint dropped by Sylvester, the lawyer, was one of these. It suggested alarming possibilities, and his skepticism concerning the intrinsic worth of his inherited "crown" was increased by it.

He paid frequent visits to the offices of Sylvester, Kuhn, and Graves in Pine Street. Upon the senior partner, whom he esteemed and trusted not only as a business adviser but a friend, he depended for information concerning happenings at the Warren apartment.

Caroline sent him regular statements of her weekly

expenditures, also bills for his approval, but she had written him but once, and then only a brief note. The note brought by a messenger, accompanied a package containing the chain which he and Pearson selected with such deliberation and care at the Fifth Avenue jeweler's. Under the existing circumstances, the girl wrote, she felt that she did not wish to accept presents from him and therefore returned this one. He was alone when the note and package came and sat by the window of his room, looking out at the dismal prospect of back yards and clothes-lines, turning the leather case over and over in his hands. Perhaps this was the most miserable afternoon he had spent since his arrival in the city. He tried to comfort himself by the exercise of his usual philosophy, but it was cold comfort. He had no right to expect gratitude, so he told himself, and the girl undoubtedly felt that she was justified in her treatment of him; but it is hard to be misunderstood and misjudged, even by one whose youth is, perhaps, an excuse. He forgave Caroline, but he could not forgive those who were responsible for her action.

After Pearson had departed, on the morning when the conversation dealing with Mrs. Van Winkle Ruggles and her change of attitude took place, Captain Elisha put on his hat and coat and started for his lawyer's office. Sylvester was glad to see him and invited him to lunch.

" No, thank you," replied the captain. " I just run down to ask if there was anything new in the offin'. Last time I see you, you hinted you and your mates had sighted somethin' or other through the fog, and it might turn out to be a rock or a lighthouse, you couldn't tell which. Made up your mind yet? "

Sylvester shook his head. " No," he said, slowly; " it

is still foggy. We're busy investigating, but we're not ready to report."

"Humph! Well, what's the thing look like? You must be a little nigher to it by now."

The lawyer tapped his desk with a pencil. "I don't know what it looks like," he answered. "That is to say, I don't — I can't believe it is what it appears, at this distance, to be. If it is, it is the most —"

He paused. Captain Elisha waited for him to go on and, when he did not do so, asked another question.

"The most what?" he demanded. "Is it likely to be very bad?"

"Why — why — well, I can't say even that yet. But there! as I told you, I'm not going to permit it to worry me. And you mustn't worry, either. That's why I don't give you any further particulars. There may be nothing in it, after all."

His visitor smiled. "Say, Mr. Sylvester," he said, "you're like the young-ones used to be when I was a boy. There'd be a gang of 'em waitin' by the school-house steps and when the particular victim hove in sight they'd hail him with, 'Ah, ha! *you're* goin' to get it!' 'Wait till teacher sees you!' and so on. Course the victim would want to know what it meant. All the satisfaction he got from them was, 'That's all right! You'll find out! You just wait!' And the poor feller put in the time afore the bell rung goin' over all the things he shouldn't have done and had, and wonderin' which it was this time. You hinted to me a week ago that there was a surprisin' possibility loomin' up in 'Bije's financial affairs. And ever since then I've been puzzlin' my brains tryin' to guess what could happen. Ain't discovered any more of those Cut Short bonds, have you?"

The bonds to which he referred were those of a defunct Short Line railroad. A large number of these bonds had been discovered among A. Rodgers Warren's effects; part of his "tangled assets," the captain had termed them, differentiating from the "tangible" variety.

"Abbie, my housekeeper, has been writin' me," he went on, "about havin' the sewin' room papered. She wants my advice concernin' the style of paper; says it ought to be pretty and out of the common, but not too expensive. I judge what she wants is somethin' that looks like money but ain't really wuth more than ten cents a mile. I've been thinkin' I'd send her a bale or so of those bonds; they'd fill the bill in those respects, wouldn't they?"

Sylvester laughed. "They certainly would, Captain," he replied. "No, we haven't unearthed any more of that sort. And, as for this mystery of ours, I'll give you the answer — if it's worth giving at all, in a very short time. Meanwhile, you go home and forget it."

"Well, I'll try. But I guess it sticks out on my face, like a four days' toothache. But I won't worry about that. You know best whether to tell me now or not, and — well, I'm carryin' about all the worry my tonnage'll stand, as 'tis."

He drew a long breath. Sylvester regarded him sympathetically.

"You mustn't take your nephew's and niece's treatment too much to heart," he said.

"Oh, I don't. That is, I pretend I don't. And I do try not to. But I keep thinkin', thinkin', and wonderin' if 'twould have been better if I hadn't gone there to live at all. Hi hum! a man of my age hadn't ought to mind what a twenty-year-old girl says, or does; 'specially when her kind, advisin' friends have shown her how

242

she's been deceived and hypocrit-ted. By the way, speakin' of hypocrites, I suppose there's just as much 'Dunnin'' as ever goin' on up there?"

"Yes. A little more, if anything, I'm afraid. Your niece and Mrs. Dunn and her precious son are together now so constantly that people are expecting — well, you know what they expect."

"I can guess. I hope they'll be disapp'inted."

"So do I, but I must confess I'm fearful. Malcolm himself isn't so wise, but his mother is —"

"A whole Book of Proverbs, hey? I know. She's an able old frigate. I did think I had her guns spiked, but she turned 'em on me unexpected. I thought I had her and her boy in a clove hitch. I knew somethin' that I was sartin sure they wouldn't want Caroline to know, and she and Malcolm knew I knew it. Her tellin' Caroline of it, *her* story of it, when I wasn't there to contradict, was as smart a piece of maneuverin' as ever was. It took the wind out of my sails, because, though I'm just as right as I ever was, Caroline wouldn't listen to me, nor believe me, now."

"She'll learn by experience."

"Yup. But learnin' by experience is a good deal like shippin' green afore the mast; it'll make an able seaman of you, if it don't kill you fust. When I was a boy there was a man in our town name of Nickerson Cummin's. He was mate of a ship and smart as a red pepper poultice on a skinned heel. He was a great churchgoer when he was ashore and always preachin' brotherly love and kindness and pattin' us little shavers on the head, and so on. Most of the grown folks thought he was a sort of saint, and I thought he was more than that. I'd have worshiped him, I cal'late, if my Methodist trainin' would have allowed me to worship anybody who wa'n't named in Scriptur'. If there'd been an apostle or a prophet christened Nickerson I'd have fell on my knees to this Cummin's man, sure. So, when I went to sea as a cabin boy, a tow-headed snub-nosed little chap of fourteen, I was as happy as a clam at highwater 'cause I was goin' in the ship he was mate of."

He paused. There was a frown on his face, and his lower jaw was thrust forward grimly.

"Well?" inquired Sylvester. "What happened?"

"Hey? Oh, excuse me. When I get to thinkin' of that v'yage I simmer inside, like a teakettle on a hot stove. The second day out — seasick and homesick and so miserable I wished I could die all at once instead of by lingerin' spasms — I dropped a dish on the cabin floor and broke it. Cummin's was alone with me, eatin' his dinner; and he jumped out of his chair when I stooped to pick up the pieces and kicked me under the table. When I crawled out, he kicked me again and kept it up. When his foot got tired he used his fist. 'There!' says he between his teeth, 'I cal'late that'll learn you that crockery costs money.'

"It did. I never broke anything else aboard that ship. Cummin's was a bully and a sneak to everybody but the old man, and a toady to him. He never struck me or anybody else when the skipper was around, but there was nothin' too mean for him to do when he thought he had a safe chance. And he took pains to let me know that if I ever told a soul at home he'd kill me. I'd learned by experience, not only about the price of crockery, but other things, things that a youngster ought not to learn — how to hate a man so that you can wait years to get even with him, for one. I'm sorry I learned that, and," dryly, "so was Cummin's, later. But I did learn, once and for all, not to take folks on trust, nor to size 'em up by their outside, or the noise they make in prayer-meetin', nor the way they can spread soft soap when they think it's necessary. I'd learned that, and I'd learned it early enough to be of use to me, which was a mercy.

"It was a hard lesson for me," he added, reflectively; "but I managed to come out of it without lettin' it bitter my whole life. I don't mind so much Caroline's bein' down on me. She'll know better some day, I hope; and if she don't — well, I'm only a side-issue in her life, anyhow, hove in by accident, like the section of dog collar in the sassage. But I do hope her learnin' by experience won't come too late to save her from . . . what she'll be awful sorry for by and by."

"It must," declared the lawyer, with decision. "You must see to it, Captain Warren. You are her guardian. She is absolutely under your charge. She can do nothing of importance unless you consent."

"Yup. That's so — for one more year; just one, remember! Then she'll be of age, and I can't say 'Boo!' And her share of 'Bije's money'll be hers, too. And don't you believe that that fact has slipped Sister Dunn's memory. I ain't on deck to head her off now; if she puts Malcolm up to gettin' Caroline to give her word, and Caroline gives it — well, I know my niece. She's honorable, and she'll stick to her promise if it runs her on the rocks. And Her Majesty Dunn knows that, too. Therefore, the cat bein' away, she cal'lates now's the time to make sure of the cheese."

"But the cat can come back. The song says it did, you know."

"Um-hm. And got another kick, I shouldn't wonder. However, my claws'll stay sharp for a year or thereabouts, and, if it comes to a shindy, there'll be some tall scratchin' afore I climb a tree. Keep a weather eye on what goes on, won't you?"

"I will. You can depend on me."

"I do. And say! for goodness' sakes put me out of my misery regardin' that rock or lighthouse on 'Bije's chart, soon's ever you settle which it is."

"Certainly! And, remember, don't worry. It may be a lighthouse, or nothing at all. At all events, I'll report very soon."

CHAPTER XVI

BUT, in spite of his promise, Sylvester did not report during the following week or the next. Meanwhile, his client tried his best to keep the new mystery from troubling his thoughts, and succeeded only partially. The captain's days and evenings were quiet and monotonous. He borrowed a book or two from Mrs. Hepton's meager library, read, walked a good deal, generally along the water front, and wrote daily letters to Miss Baker. He and Pearson were together for at least a portion of each day. The author, fighting down his dejection and discouragement, set himself resolutely to work once more on the novel, and his nautical adviser was called in for frequent consultation. The story, however, progressed but slowly. There was something lacking. Each knew what that something was, but neither named it.

One evening Pearson entered the room tenanted by his friend to find the latter seated beside the table, his shoes partially unlaced, and a pair of big slippers ready for putting on.

" Captain," said the visitor, " you look so comfortable I hate to disturb you."

Captain Elisha, red-faced and panting, desisted from the unlacing and straightened in his chair.

" Whew ! " he puffed. " Jim, your remarks prove that your experience of the world ain't as big as it ought to be. When you get to my age and waist measure you'll realize that stoopin' over and comfort don't go together.

247

I hope to be comfortable pretty soon; but I sha'n't be till them boots are off. Set down. The agony'll be over in a minute."

Pearson declined to sit. "Not yet," he said. "And you let those shoes alone, until you hear what I've got to say. A newspaper friend of mine has sent me two tickets for the opera to-night. I want you to go with me."

Captain Elisha was surprised.

"To the opera?" he repeated. "Why, that's a — a sort of singin' theater ain't it?"

"Yes, you're fond of music; you told me so. And Aïda is beautiful. Come on! it will do us both good."

"Hum! Well, I don't know."

"I do. Get ready."

The captain looked at his caller's evening clothes.

"What do you mean by gettin' ready?" he asked. "You've got on your regimentals, open front and all. My uniform is the huntin' case kind; fits in better with church sociables and South Denboro no'theasters. If I wore one of those vests like yours Abbie'd make me put on a red flannel lung-protector to keep from catchin' pneumonia. And she'd think 'twas sinful waste besides, runnin' the risk of sp'ilin' a clean biled shirt so quick. Won't I look like an undertaker, sittin' alongside of you?"

"Not a bit. If it will ease your mind I'll change to a business suit."

"I don't care. You know how I feel; we had a little talk about hats a spell ago, you remember. If you're willin' to take me ' just as I am, without a plea,' as the hymn-tune says, why, I cal'late I'll say yes and go. Set down and wait while I get on my ceremonials."

He retired to the curtain alcove, and Pearson heard

him rustling about, evidently making a hurried change of raiment. During this process he talked continuously.

"Jim," he said, "I ain't been to the theater but once since I landed in New York. Then I went to see a play named 'The Heart of a Sailor.' Ha! ha! that was a great show! Ever take it in, did you?"

"No. I never did."

"Well, you'd ought to. It's a wonder of it's kind. I learned more things about life-savin' and 'longshore life from that drayma than you'd believe was possible. You'd have got some p'ints for your Cap'n Jim yarn from that play; you sartin would! Yes, indeed! Way I happened to go to it was on account of seein' a poster on a fence over nigh where that Moriarty tribe lived. The poster pictured a bark ashore, on her beam ends, in a sea like those off the Horn. On the beach was a whole parcel of life-savers firin' off rockets and blue lights. Keepin' the Fourth of July, I judged they was, for I couldn't see any other reason. The bark wa'n't more'n a hundred foot from 'em, and if all hands on board didn't know they was in trouble by that time, then they deserved to drown. Anyhow, they wa'n't likely to appreciate the celebration. Ho! ho! Well, when I run afoul of that poster I felt I hadn't ought to let anything like that get away; so I hunted up the theater — it wa'n't but a little ways off — and got a front seat for that very afternoon."

"Was it up to the advertising?" asked Pearson.

"*Was* it? Hi hum! I wish you'd been there. More 'special I wished some of the folks from home had been there, for the whole business was supposed to happen on the Cape, and they'd have realized how ignorant we are about the place we live in. The hero was a strappin' six-footer, sort of a combination fisherman and parson, seemed so. He wore ileskins in fair weather and went around preachin' or defyin' folks that provoked him and makin' love to the daughter of a long-haired old relic that called himself an inventor. . . . Oh, consarn it!"

"What's the matter?"

"Dropped my collar button, as usual. Collar buttons are one of the Old Harry's pet traps. I'll bet their responsible for 'most as many lapses from grace as tangled fishlines. Where . . . Ow! . . . All right; I found it — with my bare foot, and edge up, of course."

A series of grunts and short-breathed exclamations followed, indicating that the sufferer was struggling with a tight collar.

"Go on," commanded Pearson. "Tell me some more about the play."

"Hey? Oh, the play. Where was I?"

"You were saying that the heroine's father was an inventor."

"That's what *he* said he was, though he never furnished any proof. His daughter helped him with his inventions, but if she'd cut his hair once in a while 'twould have been a better way of puttin' in the time, 'cordin' to my notion. And there was a rich squire, who made his money by speculatin' in wickedness, and a mortgage, and — I don't know what all. And those Cape Cod folks! and the houses they lived in! and the way they talked! Oh, dear! oh, dear! I got my money's wuth that afternoon."

"What about the wreck? How did that happen?"

"Don't know. It happened 'cause it had to be in the play, I cal'late. The mortgage, or an 'invention' or somethin', was on board the bark and just naturally took a short cut for home, way I figgered it out. But, Jim, you ought to have seen that hero! He peeled off his ileskin-slicker — he'd kept it on all through the sunshine, but now, when 'twas rainin' and rainin' and wreckin' and thunderin', he shed it — and jumped in and saved all hands and the ship's cat. 'Twas great business! No wonder the life-savers set off fireworks! And thunder! Why, say, it never stopped thunderin' in that storm except when somebody had to make a heroic speech; then it let up and give 'em a chance. Most considerate thunder ever I heard. And the lightnin'! and the way the dust flew from the breakers! I was glad I went. . . . There!" appearing fully dressed from behind the curtains. "I'm ready if you are. Did I talk your head off? I ask your pardon; but that 'Heart of a Sailor' touched mine, I guess. I know I was afraid I'd laugh until it stopped beatin'. And all around the people were cryin'. It was enough sight damper amongst the seats than in those cloth waves."

The pair walked over to Broadway, boarded a street car, and alighted before the Metropolitan Opera House. Pearson's seats were good ones, well down in the orchestra. Captain Elisha turned and surveyed the great interior and the brilliantly garbed audience.

"Whew!" he muttered. "This is considerable of a show in itself, Jim. They could put our town hall inside here and the folks on the roof wouldn't be so high as those in that main skys'l gallery up aloft there. Can they see or hear, do you think?"

"Oh, yes. The accepted idea is that they are the real music lovers. *They* come for the opera itself. Some of the others come because — well, because it is the proper thing."

"Yes, yes; I see. That's the real article right over our heads, I suppose."

"Yes. That's the 'Diamond Horseshoe.'"

"All proper things there, hey?"

"Why — er — yes, I suppose so. What makes you ask?"

"Nothing much. I was thinking 'twas better Abbie wa'n't along on this cruise. She'd probably want to put an 'im' in front of that 'proper.' I envy those women, Jim; *they* didn't have to stop to hunt up collar buttons, did they."

He was silent during the first act of the opera. When the curtain fell his companion asked how he liked it.

"Good singin'," he replied; "best I ever heard. Do you understand what they say?"

"No. But I'm familiar with the story of Aïda, of course. It's a favorite of mine. And the words don't really matter."

"I suppose not. It's the way they say it. I had an Irishman workin' round my barn once, and Tim Bailey drove down from Bayport to see me. I was out and Tim and the Irishman run afoul of each other. Tim stuttered so that he made a noise when he talked like one of these gasoline bicycles goin' by. He watched Mike sweepin' out the horse stall and he says, 'You're a pup — pup . . . I say you're a pup —.' He didn't get any further 'cause Mike went for him with the broom. Turned out later that he was tryin' to compliment that Irishman by sayin' he was a particular sort of feller. These folks on the stage might be sayin' most anythin', and I wouldn't know it. But I sha'n't knock 'em down, for I like the way it's said. When the Almighty give us music he more than made up for makin' us subject to toothache, didn't he."

Pearson bought a copy of the libretto, and the captain followed the performance of the next two acts with interest.

"Say, Jim," he whispered, with a broad grin, "it's a good thing this opera idea ain't carried into real life. If you had to sing every word you said 'twould be sort of distressin', 'specially if you was in a hurry. A fust-rate solo when you was orderin' the crew to shorten sail would be a high old brimstone anthem, I'll bet you. And think of the dinner table at our boardin' house! Mrs. Van and C. Dickens both goin' at once, and Marm Hepton serenadin' the waiter girl! Ho! ho! A cat fight wouldn't be a circumstance."

Between the third and the fourth acts the pair went out into the foyer, where, ascending to the next floor, they made the round of the long curve behind the boxes, Pearson pointing out to his friend the names of the box lessees on the brass plates.

"There!" he observed, as, the half circle completed, they turned and strolled back again, "isn't that an imposing list, Captain? Don't you feel as if you were close to the real thing?"

"Godfreys mighty!" was the solemn reply; "I was just thinkin' I felt as if I'd been readin' one of those muck-rakin' yarns in the magazines!"

The foyer had its usual animated crowd, and among them Pearson recognized a critic of his acquaintance. He offered to introduce the captain, but the latter declined the honor, saying that he cal'lated he wouldn't shove his bows in this time. "You heave ahead and see your friend, Jim," he added. "I'll come to anchor by this pillar and watch the fleet go by. I'll have to write Abbie about all this; she'll want to know how the female craft was rigged."

Left alone, he leaned against the pillar and watched the people pass and repass just behind him. Two young men paused just behind him. He could not help overhearing their conversation.

"I presume you've heard the news?" asked one, casually.

"Yes," replied the other, "I have. That is, if you mean the news concerning Mal Dunn. The mater learned it this afternoon and sprung it at dinner. No one was greatly surprised. Formal announcement made, and all that sort of thing, I believe. Mal's to be congratulated."

"His mother is, you mean. She managed the campaign. The old lady is some strategist, and I'd back her to win under ordinary circumstances. But I understand these were not ordinary; wise owl of a guardian to be circumvented, or something of that sort."

"From what I hear the Dunns haven't won so much after all. There was a big shrinkage when papa died, so they say. Instead of three or four millions it panned out to be a good deal less than one. I don't know much about it, because our family and theirs have drifted apart since they moved."

"Humph! I imagine whatever the pan-out it will be welcome. The Dunns are dangerously close to the ragged edge; everybody has been on to that for some time. And it takes a few ducats to keep Mal going. He's no Uncle Russell when it comes to putting by for the rainy day."

"Well, on the whole, I'm rather sorry for — the other party. Mal is a good enough fellow, and he certainly is a game sport; but —"

They moved on, and Captain Elisha heard no more. But what he had heard was quite sufficient. He sat through the remainder of the opera in silence and answered all his friend's questions and remarks curtly and absently.

As they stepped into the trolley Pearson bought an evening paper, not the *Planet,* but a dignified sheet which shunned sensationalism and devoted much space to the doings of the safe, sane, and ultra-respectable element. Perceiving that his companion, for some reason, did not care to talk, he read as the car moved downtown. Suddenly Captain Elisha was awakened from his reverie by hearing his friend utter an exclamation. Looking up, the captain saw that he was leaning back in the seat, the paper lying unheeded in his lap.

" What's the matter? " asked the older man, anxiously.

Pearson started, glanced quickly at his friend, hesitated, and looked down again.

" Nothing — now," he answered, brusquely. " We get out here. Come."

He rose, picked up the paper with a hand that shook a little, and led the way to the door of the car. Captain Elisha followed, and they strode up the deserted side street. Pearson walked so rapidly that his companion was hard pushed to keep pace with him. When they stood together in the dimly lit hall of the boarding house, the captain spoke again.

" Well, Jim," he asked in a low tone, " what is it? You may as well tell me. Maybe I can guess, anyhow."

The young man reached up and turned the gas full on. In spite of the cold from which they had just come, his face was white. He folded the paper in his hand, and with his forefinger pointed to its uppermost page.

" There it is," he said. " Read it."

Captain Elisha took the paper, drew his spectacle case

from his pocket, adjusted his glasses and read. The item was among those under the head of " Personal and Social." It was what he expected. " The engagement is to-day announced of Miss Caroline Warren, daughter of the late A. Rodgers Warren, the well-known broker, to Mr. Malcolm Corcoran Dunn, of Fifth Avenue. Miss Warren, it will be remembered, was one of the most charming of our season-before-last's débutantes and —" etc.

The captain read the brief item through.

" Yes," he said, slowly, " I see."

Pearson looked at him in amazement.

" You *see!* " he repeated. " You — Why! *Did you know it?* "

" I've been afraid of it for some time. To-night, when you left me alone there in the quarter-deck of that opera house, I happened to hear two young chaps talkin' about it. So you might say I knew — Yes."

" Good heavens! and you can stand there and — What are you going to do about it? "

" I don't know — yet."

" Are you going to permit her to marry that — *that* fellow? "

" Well, I ain't sartin that I can stop her."

" My God, man! Do you realize — and *she* — your niece — why —"

" There! there! Jim. I realize it all, I cal'late. It's my business to realize it."

" And it isn't mine. No, of course it isn't; you're right there."

He turned and strode toward the foot of the stairs.

" Hold on! " commanded the captain. " Hold on, Jim! Don't you go off ha'f cocked. When I said 'twas my business to realize this thing, I meant just that and nothin' more. I wa'n't hintin', and you ought to know it. You do know it, don't you?"

The young man paused. "Yes," he answered, after an instant's struggle with his feelings; "yes, I do. I beg your pardon, Captain."

"All right. And here's somethin' else; I just told you I wasn't sartin I could stop the marriage. That's the truth. But I don't recollect sayin' I'd actually hauled down the colors, not yet. Good night."

"Good night, Captain. I shouldn't have misunderstood you, of course. But, as you know, I respected and admired your niece. And this thing has — has —"

"Sort of knocked you on your beam ends, I understand. Well, Jim," with a sigh, "I ain't exactly on an even keel myself."

They separated, Pearson going to his room. As Captain Elisha was passing through the hall on the second floor, he heard someone calling him by name. Turning, he saw his landlady's head, bristling with curl papers, protruding from behind the door at the other end of the passage.

"Captain Warren," she asked, "is that you?"

"Yes, ma'am," replied the captain, turning back.

"Well, I've got a message for you. A Mr. Sylvester has 'phoned you twice this evening. He wishes to see you at his office at the earliest possible moment. He says it is *very* important."

CHAPTER XVII

NINE o'clock is an early hour for a New York lawyer of prominence to be at his place of business. Yet, when Captain Elisha asked the office boy of Sylvester, Kuhn and Graves if the senior partner was in, he received an affirmative answer.

"Yes, sir," said Tim, respectfully. His manner toward the captain had changed surprisingly since the latter's first call. "Yes, sir; Mr. Sylvester's in. He expects you. I'll tell him you're here. Sit down and wait, please."

Captain Elisha sat down, but he did not have to wait long. The boy returned at once and ushered him into the private office. Sylvester welcomed him gravely.

"You got my message, then," he said. "I spent hours last evening chasing you by 'phone. And I was prepared to begin again this morning."

"So? That's why you're on deck so early? Didn't sleep here, did you? Well, I cal'late I know what you want to talk about. You ain't the only one that reads the newspapers."

"The newspapers? Great heavens! it isn't in the newspapers, is it? It can't be!"

He seemed much perturbed. Captain Elisha looked puzzled.

"Course it is," he said. "But I heard it afore I saw it. Perhaps you think I take it pretty easy. Maybe I act as if I did. But you expected it, and so did I, so we ain't exactly surprised. And," seriously, "I realize that it's no joke as well as you do. But we've got a year to fight in, and now we must plan the campaign. I did cal'late to see Caroline this mornin'. Then, if I heard from her own lips that 'twas actually so, I didn't know's I wouldn't drop in and give Sister Corcoran-Queen-Victoria-Dunn a few plain facts about it not bein' a healthy investment to hurry matters. You're wantin' to see me headed me off, and I come here instead."

The lawyer looked at him in astonishment.

"See here, Captain Warren," he demanded, "what do you imagine I asked you to come here for?"

"Why, to talk about that miserable engagement, sartin. Poor girl! I've been awake ha'f the night thinkin' of the mess she's been led into. And she believes she's happy, I suppose."

Sylvester shook his head. "I see," he said, slowly. "You would think it that, naturally. No, Captain, it isn't the engagement. It's more serious than that."

"More serious than — more serious! Why, what on earth? Hey? Mr. Sylvester, has that rock-lighthouse business come to somethin' after all?"

The lawyer nodded. "It has," he replied.

"I want to know! And I'd almost forgot it, not hearin' from you. It's a rock, too, I judge, by the looks of your face. Humph! . . . Is it very bad?"

"I'm afraid so."

The captain pulled his beard. "Well," he said, wearily, after a moment, "I guess likely I can bear it. I've had to bear some things in my time. Anyhow, I'll try. Heave ahead and get it over with. I'm ready."

Instead of answering, Sylvester pushed an electric button on his desk. The office boy answered the ring.

"Have Mr. Kuhn and Mr. Graves arrived?" asked the lawyer.

"Yes, sir. Both of them, sir."

"Tell them Captain Warren is here, and ask them to join us in the inner room. Remind Mr. Graves to bring the papers. And, Tim, remember that none of us is to be disturbed. Do you understand?"

"Yes, sir," said Tim and departed.

Captain Elisha regarded his friend with some dismay. "Say!" he exclaimed, "this *must* be serious, if it takes the skipper and both mates to handle it."

Sylvester did not smile. "It is," he answered. "Come."

He led the way into the room opening from the rear of his own. It was a large apartment with a long table in the center. Mr. Kuhn, brisk and business-like, was already there. He shook hands with his client. As he did so, Graves, dignified and precise as ever, entered, carrying a small portfolio filled with papers.

"Mornin', Mr. Graves," said the captain; "glad to see you, even under such distressin' circumstances, as the undertaker said to the sick man. Feelin' all right again, I hope. No more colds or nothin' like that?"

"No. Thank you. I am quite well, at present."

"That's hearty. If you and me don't do any more buggy ridin' in Cape Cod typhoons, we'll last a spell yet, hey? What you got there, the death warrant?" referring to the portfolio and its contents.

Mr. Graves evidently did not consider this flippancy worth a reply, for he made none.

"Sit down, gentlemen," said Sylvester.

The four took chairs at the table. Graves untied and opened the portfolio. Captain Elisha looked at his solemn companions, and his lips twitched.

"You'll excuse me," he observed, "but I feel as if I was goin' to be tried for piracy on the high seas. Has the court any objection to tobacco smoke? I'm puttin' the emphasis strong on the 'tobacco,'" he added, "because this is a cigar you give me yourself, Mr. Sylvester, last time I was down here."

"No, indeed," replied the senior partner. "Smoke, if you wish. No one here has any objection, unless it may be Graves."

"Oh, Mr. Graves ain't. He and I fired up together that night we fust met. Hot smoke tasted grateful after all the cold water we'd had poured onto us in that storm. Graves is all right. He's a sportin' character, like myself. Maybe he'll jine us. Got another cigar in my pocket."

But the invitation was declined. The "sporting character" might deign to relax amid proper and fitting surroundings, but not in the sacred precincts of his office. So the captain smoked alone.

"Well," he observed, after a few preliminary puffs, "go on! Don't keep me in suspenders, as the feller said. Where did the lightnin' strike, and what's the damage?"

Sylvester took a card from his pocket and referred to a penciled memorandum on its back.

"Captain Warren," he began, slowly, "as you know, and as directed by you, my partners here and I have been engaged for months in carefully going over your brother's effects, estimating values, tabulating and sorting his various properties and securities, separating the good from the worthless — and there was, as we saw at a glance, a surprising amount of the latter —"

"Um-hm," interrupted the captain, "Cut Short bonds and the like of that. I know. Excuse me. Go on."

"Yes. Precisely. And there were many just as valueless. But we have been gradually getting those out of the way and listing and appraising the remainder. It was a tangle. Your brother's business methods, especially of late years, were decidedly unsystematic and slipshod. It may have been the condition of his health which prevented his attending to them as he should. Or," he hesitated slightly, " it may have been that he was secretly in great trouble and mental distress. At all events, the task has been a hard one for us. But, largely owing to Graves and his patient work, our report was practically ready a month ago."

He paused. Captain Elisha, who had been listening attentively, nodded.

" Yes," he said; " you told me 'twas. What does the whole thing tot up to? What's the final figger, Mr. Graves?"

The junior partner adjusted his eyeglasses to his thin nose.

" I have them here," he said. " The list of securities, et cetera, is rather long, but—"

" Never mind them now, Graves," interrupted Kuhn. " The amount, roughly speaking, is close to over our original estimate, half a million."

The captain drew a breath of relief. " Well," he exclaimed, " that's all right then, ain't it? That's no poorhouse pension."

Sylvester answered. " Yes," he said, " that's all right, as far as it goes."

" Humph! Well, I cal'late *I* could make it go to the end of the route; and then have enough left for a return ticket. Say!" with another look at the solemn faces of the three, " what *is* the row? If the estate is wuth ha'f a million, what's the matter with it?"

" That is what we are here this morning to discuss, Captain. A month ago, as I said, we considered our report practically ready. Then we suddenly happened on the trail of something which, upon investigation, upset all our calculations. If true, it threatened, not to mention its effect upon the estate, to prove so distressing and painful to us, Rodgers Warren's friends and legal advisers, that we decided not to alarm you, his brother, by disclosing our suspicions until we were sure there was no mistake. I did drop you a hint, you will remember —"

" I remember. *Now* we're comin' to the rock!"

" Yes. Captain Warren, I think perhaps I ought to warn you that what my partners and I are about to say will shock and hurt you. I, personally, knew your brother well and respected him as an honorable business man. A lawyer learns not to put too much trust in human nature, but, I confess, this — this —"

He was evidently greatly disturbed. Captain Elisha, regarding him intently, nodded.

" I judge it's sort of hard for you to go on, Mr. Sylvester," he said. " I'll help you all I can. You and Mr. Kuhn and Mr. Graves here have found out somethin' that ain't exactly straight in 'Bije's doin's? Am I right?"

" Yes, Captain Warren, you are."

" Somethin' that don't help his character, hey?"

" Yes."

" Somethin's he's done that's — well, to speak plain, that's crooked?"

" I'm afraid there's no doubt of it."

" Humph!" The captain frowned. His cigar had gone out, and he idly twisted the stump between his fingers. " Well," he said, with a sigh, " our family, gen'rally speakin', has always held its head pretty high. Dad was poor, but he prided himself on bein' straight

263

as a plumb line. And, as for mother, she . . ."
Then, looking up quickly, he asked, "Does anybody outside know about this?"

"No one but ourselves — yet."

"Yet? Is it goin' to be necessary for anybody else to know it?"

"We hope not. But there is a possibility."

"I was thinkin' about the children."

"Of course. So are we all."

"Um-hm. Poor Caroline! she put her father on a sort of altar and bowed down afore him, as you might say. Any sort of disgrace to his name would about kill her. As for me," with another sigh, "I ain't so much surprised as you might think. I know that sounds tough to say about your own brother, but I've been afraid all along. You see, 'Bije always steered pretty close to the edge of the channel. He had ideas about honesty and fair dealin' in business that didn't jibe with mine. We split on just that, as I told you, Mr. Graves, when you and I fust met. He got some South Denboro folks to invest money along with him; sort of savin's account, they figgered it; but I found out he was usin' it to speculate with. So that's why we had our row. I took pains to see that the money was paid back, but he and I never spoke afterwards. Fur as my own money was concerned, I hadn't any kick, but . . . However, I'm talkin' too much. Go on, Mr. Sylvester, I'm ready to hear whatever you've got to say."

"Thank you, Captain. You make it easier for me. It seems that your brother's first step toward wealth and success was taken about nineteen years ago. Then, somehow or other, probably through a combination of luck and shrewdness, he obtained a grant, a concession from the Brazilian Government, the long term lease of a good-sized tract of land on the upper Amazon. It was very valuable because of its rubber trees."

"Hey?" Captain Elisha leaned forward. "Say that again!" he commanded sharply.

Sylvester repeated his statement. "He got the concession by paying twenty thousand dollars to the government of Brazil," he continued. "To raise the twenty thousand he formed a stock company of two hundred and fifty shares at one hundred dollars each. One hundred of these shares were in his own name. Fifty were in the name of one 'Thomas A. Craven,' a clerk at that time in his office. Craven was only a dummy, however. Do you understand what I mean by a dummy?"

"I can guess. Sort of a wooden image that moved when 'Bije pulled the strings. Like one of these straw directors that clutter up the insurance companies, 'cordin' to the papers. Yes, yes; I understand well enough. Go ahead! go ahead!"

"That's it. The fifty shares were in Craven's name, but they were transferred in blank and in Mr. Warren's safe. Together with his own hundred, they gave him control and a voting majority. That much we know by the records."

"I see. But this rubber con — contraption wa'n't really wuth anything, was it?"

"Worth anything! Captain Warren, I give you my word that it was worth more than all the rest of the investments that your brother made during his lifetime."

"No!" The exclamation was almost a shout.

"Why, yes, decidedly more. Does that surprise you, Captain?"

Captain Elisha did not answer. He was regarding

265

the lawyer with a dazed expression. He breathed heavily.

"What's the matter?" demanded the watchful Kuhn, his gaze fixed upon his client's face. "Do you know anything —"

The captain interrupted him. "Go on!" he commanded. "But tell me this fust: What was the name of this rubber concern of 'Bije's?"

"The Akrae Rubber Company."

"I see. . . . Yes, yes. . . . Akry, hey! . . . Well, what about it? Tell me the rest."

"For the first year or two this company did nothing. Then, in March, of the third year, the property was released by Mr. Warren to persons in Para, who were to develop and operate. The terms of his new lease were very advantageous. Royalties were to be paid on a sliding scale, and, from the very first, they were large. The Akrae Company paid enormous dividends."

"Did, hey? I want to know!"

"Yes. In fact, for twelve years the company's royalties averaged $50,000 yearly."

"Whe-e-w!" Captain Elisha whistled. "Fifty thousand a year!" he repeated slowly. "'Bije! 'Bije!"

"Yes. And three years ago the Akrae Company sold its lease, sold out completely to the Para people, for seven hundred and fifty thousand dollars."

"Godfreys mighty! Well," after a moment, "that's what I'd call a middlin' fair profit on a twenty thousand dollar investment — not to mention the dividends."

"Captain," Sylvester leaned forward now; "Captain," he repeated, "it is that sale and the dividends which are troubling us. I told you that the Akrae Company was organized with two hundred and fifty shares of stock. Your brother held one hundred in his own name and fifty

266

transferred to him by his dummy, Craven. What I did not tell you was that there were another hundred shares, held by someone, someone who paid ten thousand dollars for them — we know that — and was, therefore, entitled to two-fifths of every dollar earned by the company during its existence, and two-fifths of the amount received for the sale of the lease. So far as we can find out, this stockholder has never received one cent."

The effect of this amazing announcement upon the uniniated member of the council was not as great as the lawyers expected it to be. "You don't tell me!" was his sole comment.

Graves broke in impatiently: "I think, Captain Warren," he declared, "that you probably do not realize what this means. Besides proving your brother dishonest, it means that this stockholder, whoever he may have been —"

"Hey? What's that? Don't you know who he was?"

"No, we do not. The name upon the stub of the transfer book has been scratched out."

Captain Elisha looked the speaker in the face, then slowly turned his look upon the other two faces.

"Scratched out?" he repeated. "Who scratched it out?"

Graves shrugged his shoulders.

"Yes, yes," said the captain. "You don't know, but we're all entitled to guess, hey? . . . Humph!"

"If this person is living," began Sylvester, "it follows that —"

"Hold on a minute! I don't know much about corporations, of course — that's more in your line than 'tis in mine — but I want to ask one question. You say this what-d'ye-call-it — this Akrae thingamajig — was sold out, hull, canvas and riggin', to a crowd in Brazil? It's gone out of business then? It's dead?"

"Yes. But —"

"Wait! Ain't it customary, when a sale like this is made, to turn over all the stock, certificates and all? Sometimes you get stock in the new company in exchange; I know that. But to complete the trade, wouldn't this extry hundred shares be turned in? Or some sharp questionin' done if 'twa'n't?"

He addressed the query to Sylvester. The latter seemed more troubled than before.

"That," he said with some hesitation, "is one of the delicate points in this talk of ours, Captain Warren. A certificate for the missing hundred shares *was* turned in. It was dated at the time of the original issue, made out in the name of one Edward Bradley, and transferred on the back by him to your brother. That is, it was presumably so transferred."

"Presumably. Pre-sumably? You mean — ?"

"I mean that this certificate is — well, let us say, rather queer. To begin with, no one knows who this Bradley is, or was. His name appears nowhere except on that certificate, unless, of course, it did appear on the stub where the scratching has been done; we doubt that, for reasons. Nobody ever heard of the man; and his transfer to your brother was made, and the certificate signed by him, only three years ago, when the Akrae Company sold out. It will take too long to go into details; but thanks to the kindness of the Para concern, which has offices in this city — we have been able to examine this Bradley certificate. Experts have examined it, also. And they tell us —"

He paused.

"Well, what do they tell?" demanded the captain.

" They tell us that — that, in their opinion, the certificate was never issued at the time when, by this date, it presumes to have been. It was made out no longer ago than five years, probably less. The signature of Bradley on the back is — is — well, I hate to say it, Captain Warren, but the handwriting on that signature resembles very closely that of your brother."

Captain Elisha was silent for some moments. The others did not speak, but waited. Even Graves, between whom and his client there was little in common, felt the general sympathy.

At length the captain raised his head.

" Well," he said slowly, " we ain't children. We might as well call things by their right names. 'Bije forged that certificate."

" I'm afraid there is no doubt of it."

" Dear! dear! dear! Why, they put folks in state's prison for that!"

" Yes. But a dead man is beyond prisons."

" That's so. Then I don't see —"

" You will. You don't grasp the full meaning of this affair even yet. If the Bradley certificate is a forgery, a fraud from beginning to end, then the presumption is that there was never any such person as Bradley. But *someone* paid ten thousand dollars for one hundred Akrae shares when the company was formed. *That* certificate has never been turned in. Some person or persons, somewhere, hold one hundred shares of Akrae Rubber Company stock. Think, now! Suppose that someone turns up and demands all that he has been cheated out of for the past seventeen years! Think of that!"

" Well . . . I am thinkin' of it. I got the scent of what you was drivin' at five minutes ago. And I don't see that we need to be afraid. He could have put 'Bije

269

in jail; but 'Bije is already servin' a longer sentence than he could give him. So that disgrace ain't bearin' down on us. And, if I understand about such things, his claim is against the Akrae Company, and that's dead — dead as the man that started it. Maybe he could put in a keeper, or a receiver, or some such critter, but there's nothin' left to keep or receive. Ain't I right?"

"You are. Or you would be, but for one thing, the really inexplicable thing in this whole miserable affair. Your brother, Captain Warren, was dishonest. He took money that didn't belong to him, and he forged that certificate. But he must have intended to make restitution. He must have been conscience-stricken and more to be pitied, perhaps, than condemned. No doubt, when he first began to withhold the dividends and use the money which was not his, he intended merely to borrow. He was always optimistic and always plunging in desperate and sometimes rather shady speculations which, he was sure, would turn out favorably. If they had — if, for instance, the South Shore Trolley Combine had been put through — You knew of that, did you?"

"I've been told somethin' about it. Go on!"

"Well, it was not put through, so his hopes there were frustrated. And that was but one of his schemes. However, when the sale of the Company was consummated, he did an extraordinary thing. He made out and signed his personal note, payable to the Akrae Company, for every cent he had misappropriated. And we found that note in his safe after his death. That was what first aroused our suspicions. *Now*, Captain Warren, do you understand?"

Captain Elisha did not understand, that was evident. His look of wondering amazement traveled from one face to the others about the table.

"A *note!*" he repeated. "'Bije put his *note* in the safe? A note promisin' to pay all he'd stole! And left it there where it could be found? Why, that's pretty nigh unbelievable, Mr. Sylvester! He might just as well have confessed his crookedness and be done with it."

"Yes. It is unbelievable, but it is true. Graves can show you the note."

The junior partner produced a slip of paper from the portfolio and regarded it frowningly.

"Of all the pieces of sheer lunacy," he observed, "that ever came under my observation, this is the worst. Here it is, Captain Warren."

He extended the paper. Captain Elisha waved it aside.

"I don't want to see it — not yet," he protested. "I want to think. I want to get at the reason if I can. Why did he do it?"

"That is what we've been tryin' to find — the reason," remarked Kuhn, "and we can only guess. Sylvester has told you the guess. Rodgers Warren intended, or hoped, to make restitution before he died."

"Yes. Knowin' 'Bije, I can see that. He was weak, that was his main trouble. He didn't mean to be crooked, but his knees wa'n't strong enough to keep him straight when it come to a hard push. But he made his note payable to a Company that was already sold out, so it ain't good for nothin'. Now, why —"

Graves struck the table with his open hand.

"He doesn't understand at all," he exclaimed, impatiently. "Captain Warren, listen! That note is made payable to the Akrae Company. Against that company some unknown stockholder has an apparent claim for two-fifths of all dividends ever paid and two-fifths of the seven hundred and fifty thousand received for the sale.

With accrued interest, that claim amounts to over five hundred thousand dollars."

" Yes, but —"

" That note binds Rodgers Warren's estate to pay that claim. His own personal estate! And that estate is not worth over four hundred and sixty thousand dollars! If this stockholder should appear and press his claim, *your brother's children would be, not only penniless, but thirty thousand dollars in debt!* There! I think that is plain enough!"

He leaned back, grimly satisfied with the effect of his statement. Captain Elisha stared straight before him, unseeingly, the color fading from his cheeks. Then he put both elbows on the table and covered his face with his hands.

" You see, Captain," said Sylvester, gently, " how very serious the situation is. Graves has put it bluntly, but what he says is literally true. If your brother had deliberately planned to hand his children over to the mercy of that missing stockholder, he couldn't have done it more completely."

Slowly the captain raised his head. His expression was a strange one; agitated and shocked, but with a curious look of relief, almost of triumph.

" At last!" he said, solemnly. " At last! Now it's *all* plain!"

" All?" repeated Sylvester. " You mean —?"

" I mean everything, all that's been puzzlin' me and troublin' my head since the very beginnin'. All of it! *Now* I know why! Oh, 'Bije! 'Bije! 'Bije!"

Kuhn spoke quickly.

" Captain," he said, " I believe you know who the owner of that one hundred shares is. Do you?"

Captain Elisha gravely nodded.

"Yes," he answered. "I know him."

"What?"

"You do?"

"Who is it?"

The questions were blurted out together. The captain looked at the three excited faces. He hesitated and then, taking the stub of a pencil from his pocket, drew toward him a memorandum pad lying on the table and wrote a line upon the uppermost sheet. Tearing off the page, he tossed it to Sylvester.

"That's the name," he said.

CHAPTER XVIII

TWO more hours passed before the lawyers and their client rose from their seats about the long table. Even then the consultation was not at an end. Sylvester and the Captain lunched together at the Central Club and sat in the smoking room until after four, talking earnestly. When they parted, the attorney was grave and troubled.

"All right, Captain Warren," he said; "I'll do it. And you may be right. I certainly hope you are. But I must confess I don't look forward to my task with pleasure. I think I've got the roughest end."

"It'll be rough, there's no doubt about that. Rough for all hands, I guess. And I hope you understand, Mr. Sylvester, that there ain't many men I'd trust to do what I ask you to. I appreciate your doin' it more'n I can tell you. Be as — as gentle as you can, won't you?"

"I will. You can depend upon that."

"I do. And I sha'n't forget it. Good-by, till the next time."

They shook hands. Captain Elisha returned to the boarding house, where he found a letter awaiting him. It was from Caroline, telling him of her engagement to Malcolm Dunn. She wrote that, while not recognizing his right to interfere in any way, she felt that perhaps he should know of her action. He did not go down to supper, and, when Pearson came to inquire the reason, excused himself, pleading a late luncheon and no appetite.

He guessed he would turn in early, so he said. It was a poor guess.

Next morning he went uptown. Edwards, opening the door of the Warren apartment, was surprised to find who had rung the bell.

" Mornin', Commodore! " hailed the captain, as casually as if he were merely returning from a stroll. " Is Miss Caroline aboard ship? "

" Why — why, I don't know, sir. I'll see."

" That's all right. She's aboard or you wouldn't have to see. You and me sailed together quite a spell, so I know your little habits. I'll wait in the library, Commodore. Tell her there's no particular hurry."

His niece was expecting him. She had anticipated his visit and was prepared for it. From the emotion caused by his departure after the eventful birthday, she had entirely recovered, or thought she had. The surprise and shock of his leaving and the consequent sense of loneliness and responsibility overcame her at the time, but Stephen's ridicule and Mrs. Corcoran Dunn's congratulations on riddance from the " encumbrance " shamed her and stilled the reproaches of her conscience. Mrs. Dunn, as always, played the diplomat and mingled just the proper quantity of comprehending sympathy with the congratulations.

" I understand exactly how you feel, my dear," she said. " You have a tender heart, and it pains you to hurt anyone's feelings, no matter how much they deserve to be hurt. Every time I dismiss an incompetent or dishonest servant I feel that I have done wrong; sometimes I cry, actually shed tears, you know, and yet my reason tells me I am right. You feel that you may have been too harsh with that guardian of yours. You remember what you said to him and forget how hypocrit-

275

ically he behaved toward you. I can't forgive him that. I may forget how he misrepresented Malcolm and me to you — that I may even pardon, in time — but to deceive his own brother's children and introduce into their society a creature who had slandered and maligned their father — *that* I never shall forget or forgive. And — you'll excuse my frankness, dear — you should never forget or forgive it, either. You have nothing with which to reproach yourself. You were a brave girl, and if you are not proud of yourself, *I* am proud of you."

So, when her uncle was announced, Caroline was ready. She entered the library and acknowledged his greeting with a distant bow. He regarded her kindly, but his manner was grave.

" Well, Caroline," he began, " I got your letter."

" Yes, I presumed you did."

" Um-hm. I got it. It didn't surprise me, what you wrote, because I'd seen the news in the papers; but I was hopin' you'd tell me yourself, and I'm real glad you did. I'm much obliged to you."

She had not expected him to take this tone, and it embarrassed her.

" I — I gave you my reasons for writing," she said. " Although I do not consider that I am, in any sense, duty bound to refer matters, other than financial, to you; and, although my feelings toward you have not changed — still, you are my guardian, and — and —"

" I understand. So you're really engaged? "

" Yes."

" Engaged to Mr. Dunn? "

" Yes."

" And you're cal'latin' to marry him? "

" One might almost take that for granted," impatiently.

" Almost — yes. Not always, but generally, I will give in. You're goin' to marry Malcolm Dunn. Why?"

" Why?" she repeated the question as if she doubted his sanity.

" Yes. Be as patient with me as you can, Caroline. I ain't askin' these things without what seems to me a good reason. Why are you goin' to marry him?"

" Why — because I choose, I suppose."

" Um-hm. Are you sure of that?"

" Am I sure?" indignantly. " What do you mean?"

" I mean are you sure that it's because you choose, or because *he* does, or maybe, because his mother does?"

She turned angrily away. " If you came here to insult me —" she began. He interrupted her.

" No, no," he protested gently. " Insultin' you is the last thing I want to do. But, as your father did put you in my charge, I want you to bear with me while we talk this over together. Remember, Caroline, I ain't bothered you a great deal lately. I shouldn't now if I hadn't thought 'twas necessary. So please don't get mad, but answer me this: Do you care for this man you've promised to marry?"

This was a plain question. It should have been answered without the slightest hesitation. Moreover, the girl had expected him to ask it. Yet, for a moment, she did hesitate.

" I mean," continued Captain Elisha, " do you care for him *enough?*" Enough to live with him all your life, and see him every day, and be to him what a true wife ought to be? See him, not with his company manners on or in his automobile, but at the breakfast table, and when he comes home tired and cross, maybe. When you've got to be forbearin' and forgivin' and —"

" He is one of my oldest and best friends —" she interrupted. Her uncle went on without waiting for her to end the sentence.

"I know," he said. "One of the oldest, that's sure. But friendship, 'cordin' to my notion, is somethin' so small in comparison that it hardly counts in the manifest. Married folks ought to be friends, sartin sure; but they ought to be a whole lot more'n that. I'm an old bach, you say, and ain't had no experience. That's true; but I've been young, and there was a time when *I* made plans . . . However, she died, and it never come to nothin'. But I *know* what it means to be engaged, the right kind of engagement. It means that you don't count yourself at all, not a bit. You're ready, each of you, to give up all you've got — your wishes, comfort, money and what it'll buy, and your life, if it should come to that, for that other one. Do you care for Malcolm Dunn like that, Caroline?"

She answered defiantly.

"Yes, I do," she said.

"You do. Well, do you think he feels the same way about you?"

"Yes," with not quite the same promptness, but still defiantly.

"You feel sartin of it, do you?"

She stamped her foot. "Yes! yes! *yes!*" she cried. "Oh, *do* say what you came to say, and end it!"

Her uncle rose to his feet.

"Why, I guess likely I've said it," he observed. "When two people care for each other like that, they *ought* to be married, and the sooner the better. I knew that you'd been lonesome and troubled, maybe; and some of the friends you used to have had kind of dropped away — busy with other affairs, which is natural enough — and, you needin' sympathy and companionship, I was sort of worried for fear all this had influenced you more'n it ought to, and you'd been led into sayin' yes without realizin' what it meant. But you tell me that ain't so; you do realize. So all I can say is that I'm awful glad for you. God bless you, my dear! I hope you'll be as happy as the day is long."

His niece gazed at him, bewildered and incredulous. This she had *not* expected.

"Thank you," she stammered. "I did not know — I thought —"

"Of course you did — of course. Well, then, Caroline, I guess that's all. I won't trouble you any longer. Good-by."

He turned toward the door, but stopped, hesitated, and turned back again.

"There is just one thing more," he said solemnly. "I don't know's I ought to speak, but — I want to — and I'm goin' to. And I want you to believe it! I do want you to!"

He was so earnest, and the look he gave her was so strange, that she began to be alarmed.

"What is it?" she demanded.

"Why — why, just this, Caroline. This is a tough old world we live in. Things don't always go on in it as we think they'd ought to. Trouble comes to everybody, and when it all looks right sometimes it turns out to be all wrong. If — if there should come a time like that to you and Steve, I want you to remember that you've got me to turn to. No matter what you think of me, what folks have made you think of me, just remember that I'm waitin' and ready to help you all I can. Any time I'm ready — and glad. Just remember that, won't you, because . . . Well, there! Good-by. Good-by!"

He hurried away. She stood gazing after him, astonished, a little frightened, and not a little disturbed and
touched. His emotion was so evident; his attitude
toward her engagement was so different from that which
she had anticipated; and there was something in his
manner which she could not understand. He had acted
as if he pitied her. Why? It could not be because she
was to marry Malcolm Dunn. If it were that, she resented his pity, of course. But it could not be that, because he had given her his blessing. What was it?
Was there something else; something that she did not
know and he did? Why was he so kind and forbearing
and patient?

All her old doubts and questionings returned. She
had resolutely kept them from her thoughts, but they
had been there, in the background, always. When, after
the long siege, she had at last yielded and said yes to
Malcolm, she felt that that question, at least, was settled. She would marry him. He was one whom she
had known all her life, the son of the dearest friend she
had; he and his mother had been faithful at the time
when she needed friends. As her husband, he would
protect her and give her the affection and companionship
she craved. He might appear careless and indifferent
at times, but that was merely his manner. Had not
Mrs. Dunn told her over and over again what a good
son he was, and what a kind heart he had, and how he
worshiped her? Oh, she ought to be a very happy girl!
Of course she was happy. But why had her uncle looked
at her as he did? And what did he mean by hinting
that when things looked right they sometimes were all
wrong? She wished Malcolm was with her then; she
needed him.

She heard the clang of the elevator door. Then the

bell rang furiously. She heard Edwards hasten to answer it. Then, to her amazement, she heard her brother's voice.

" Caroline ! " demanded Stephen. " Caroline ! Where are you ? "

He burst into the room, still wearing his coat and hat, and carrying a traveling bag in his hand.

" Why, Steve ! " she said, going toward him. " Why, Steve ! what —"

He was very much excited.

" Oh ! " he exclaimed, " you're all right then ! You are all right, aren't you ? "

" All right ? Why shouldn't I be all right ? What do you mean ? And why are you here ? "

He returned her look of surprise with one of great astonishment.

" Why am I here ? " he repeated.

" Yes. Why did you come from New Haven ? "

" Why, because I got the telegram, of course ! You expected me to come, didn't you ? "

" *I* expected you ? Telegram ? What telegram ? "

" Why, the — Good Lord, Caro ! what are you talking about ? Didn't you know they telegraphed me to come home at once ? I've pretty nearly broke my neck, and the taxicab man's, getting here from the station. I thought you must be very ill, or something worse."

" They telegraphed you to come here ? Who . . . Edwards, you may take Mr. Warren's things to his room."

" But, Sis —"

" Just a moment, Steve. Give Edwards your coat and hat. Yes, and your bag. That will be all, Edwards. We sha'n't need you."

When they were alone, she turned again to her brother.

" Now, Steve," she said, " sit down and tell me what you mean. Who telegraphed you?"

" Why, old Sylvester, father's lawyer. I've got the message here somewhere. No, never mind! I've lost it, I guess. He wired me to come home as early as possible this morning. Said it was very important. And you didn't know anything about it?"

" No, not a thing. What can it mean?"

" *I* don't know! That's the bell, isn't it? Edwards!"

But the butler was already on his way to the door. A moment later he returned.

" Mr. Sylvester," he announced.

Captain Elisha scarcely left his room, except for meals, during the remainder of that day and for two days thereafter. He was unusually silent at table and avoided conversation even with Pearson, who was depressed and gloomy and made no attempt to force his society upon his friend. Once, passing the door of the latter's room, he heard the captain pacing back and forth as if he were walking the quarter-deck of one of his old ships. As Pearson stood listening the footsteps ceased; silence, then a deep sigh, and they began again. The young man sighed in sympathy and wearily climbed to his den. The prospect of chimneys and roofs across the way was never more desolate or more pregnant with discouragement.

Several times Captain Elisha descended to the closet where the telephone was fastened to the wall and held long conversations with someone. Mrs. Hepton, who knew that her newest boarder was anxious and disturbed, and was very curious to learn the reason, made it a point to be busy near that closet while these conversations took place; but, as the captain was always careful to close the door, she was disappointed. Once the mysterious Mr. Sylvester called up and asked for "Captain Warren," and the landlady hastened with the summons.

"I hope it's nothing serious," she observed, feelingly.

"Yes, ma'am," replied the captain, on his way to the stairs. "Much obliged."

"It is the same person who was so very anxious to get you the other night," she continued, making desperate efforts not to be left behind in the descent. "I declare he quite frightened me! And — you'll excuse me, Captain Warren, but I take such a real friendly interest in my boarders — you have seemed to me rather — rather upset lately, and I *do* hope it isn't bad news."

"Well, I tell you, ma'am," was the unsatisfactory answer, given just before the closet door closed; "we'll do the way the poor relation did when he got word his uncle had willed him one of his suits of clothes — we'll hope for the best."

Sylvester had a report to make.

"The other party has been here," he said. "He has just gone."

"The other party? Why — you don't mean — *him?*"

"Yes."

"Was he alone? Nobody along to look after him?"

"He was alone, for a wonder. He had heard the news, too. Apparently had just learned it."

"He had? I want to know! Who told him?"

"He didn't say. He was very much agitated. Wouldn't say anything except to ask if it was true. I think we can guess who told him."

"Maybe. Well, what did you say?"

"Nothing of importance. I refused to discuss my clients' affairs."

19   283

" Right you are! How did he take that?"

" He went up like a sky-rocket. Said he had a right to know, under the circumstances. I admitted it, but said I could tell him nothing — yet. He went away frantic, and I called you."

" Um-hm. Well, Mr. Sylvester, suppose you do see him and his boss. See 'em and tell 'em some of the truth. Don't tell too much though; not who was to blame nor how, but just that it looks pretty bad so fur as the estate's concerned. Then say you want to see 'em again and will arrange another interview. Don't set any time and place for that until you hear from me. Understand?"

" I think so, partially. But —"

" Until you hear from me — that's the important part. And, if you can, convenient, I'd have the fust interview right off; this afternoon, if it's possible."

" Captain, what have you got up your sleeve? Why don't you come down here and talk it over?"

" 'Cause I'm stickin' close aboard and waitin' developments. Maybe there won't be any, but I'm goin' to wait a spell and see. There ain't much up my sleeve just now but goose-flesh; there's plenty of that. So long."

A development came that evening. Mrs. Hepton heralded it.

" Captain," she said, when he answered her knock, "there's a young gentleman to see you. I think he must be a relative of yours. His name is Warren."

Captain Elisha pulled his beard. " A young *gentleman?*" he repeated.

" Yes. I showed him into the parlor. There will be no one there but you and he, and I thought it would be more comfortable."

" Um-hm. I see. Well, I guess you'd better send him

up. This is comfortable enough, and there won't be nobody but him and me here, either — and I'll be more sartin of it."

The landlady, who considered herself snubbed, flounced away. Captain Elisha stepped to the head of the stairs.

"Come right up, Steve!" he called.

Stephen came. His uncle ushered him into the room, closed the door, and turned the key.

"Stevie," he said, kindly, "I'm glad to see you. Take off your things and set down."

The boy accepted the invitation only to the extent of throwing his hat on the table. He did not sit or remove his overcoat. He was pale, his eyes were swollen and red, his hair was disarranged, and in all respects he looked unlike his usual blasé and immaculate self. His forehead was wet, showing that he had hurried on his way to the boarding house.

The captain regarded him pityingly.

"Set down, Stevie," he urged. "You're all het up and worn out."

His nephew paid no attention. Instead he asked a question.

"You know about it?" he demanded.

"Yes, Stevie; I know."

"You do? I — I mean about the — the Akrae Company and — and all?"

"Yes. I know all about all of it. Do set down!"

Stephen struck his closed fist into the palm of his other hand. He wore one glove. What had become of the other he could not have told.

"You do?" he shouted. "You do? By gad! Then do you know what it means?"

"Yes, I know that, too. Now, Stevie, be a good boy and set down and keep cool. Yes, I want you to."

He put his hands on his nephew's shoulders and forced him into a chair.

"Now, just calm yourself," urged the captain. "There ain't a mite of use workin' yourself up this way. I know the whole business, and I can't tell you — I can't begin to tell you how sorry I feel for you. Yet you mustn't give up the ship because —"

"Mustn't give up!" Stephen was on his feet again. "Why, what are you talking about? I thought you said you knew! Do you think that losing every cent you've got in the world is a *joke?* Do you think that — See here, do you know who this shareholder is; this fellow who's going to rob us of all we own? Who is he?"

"Didn't Mr. Sylvester tell you?"

"He said that there was such a man and that he had the estate cinched. He told us about that note and all the rest. But he wouldn't tell the man's name. Said he had been forbidden to mention it. Do you know him? What sort of fellow is he? Don't you think he could be reasoned with? Hasn't he got any decency — or pity — or —"

He choked, and the tears rushed to his eyes. He wiped them angrily away with the back of his glove.

"It's a crime!" he cried. "Can't he be held off somehow? Who *is* he? I want to know his name."

Captain Elisha sadly shook his head. "I'm afraid he can't, Stevie," he said. "He's got a legal right to all 'Bije left, and more, too. It may be he won't be too hard; perhaps he'll . . . but there," hastily. "I mustn't say that. We've got to face the situation as 'tis. And I can't tell you his name because he don't want it mentioned unless it's absolutely necessary. And we don't, either. We don't want — any of us — to have this get into the papers. We mustn't have any disgrace."

"Disgrace! Good heavens! Isn't there disgrace enough already? Isn't it enough to know father was a crook as well as an idiot? I've always thought he was insane ever since that crazy will of his came to light; but to steal! and then to leave a paper proving it, so that we've got to lose everything! His children! It's —"

"Now hold on, boy! Your dad didn't mean to take what didn't belong to him — for good, that is; the note proves that. He did do wrong and used another man's money, but —"

"'Then why didn't he keep it? If you're going to steal, steal like a man, I say!'"

"Steve, Steve! steady now!" The captain's tone was sterner. "Don't speak that way. You'll be sorry for it later. I tell you I don't condemn your father ha'f so much as I pity him."

"Oh, shut up! You make me sick. You talk just as Caro does. I'll never forgive him, no matter how much she preaches, and I told her so. Pity! Pity him! How about pity for *me?* I — I —"

His overwrought nerves gave way, and, throwing himself into the chair, he broke down completely and, forgetting the manhood of which he was so fond of boasting, cried like a baby. Captain Elisha turned away, to hide his own emotion.

"It's hard," he said slowly. "It's awfully hard for you, my boy. I hate to see you suffer this way." Then, in a lower tone, he added doubtfully. "I wonder if — if — I wonder —"

His nephew heard the word and interrupted.

"You wonder?" he demanded, hysterically; "you wonder what? What are you going to do about it? It's up to you, isn't it? You're our guardian, aren't you?"

"Yes, Stevie, I'm your guardian."

"Yes, you are! But no one would guess it. When we didn't want you, you wouldn't leave us for a minute. Now, when we need you, when there isn't a soul for us to turn to, you stay away. You haven't been near us. It's up to you, I say! and what are you going to do about it? What are you going to *do?*"

His uncle held up his hand.

"S-shh!" he said. "Don't raise your voice like that, son! I can hear you without that, and we don't want anybody else to hear. What am I goin' to do? Stevie, I don't know exactly. I ain't made up my mind yet."

"Well, it's time you did!"

"Yes, I guess likely 'tis. As for my not comin' to see you, you know the reason for that. I'd have come quick enough, but I wa'n't sure I'd be welcome. And I told your sister only 'tother day that — by the way, Steve, how is she? How is Caroline?"

"She's a fool!" The boy sprang up again and shook his fist. "She's the one I've come here to speak about. If we don't stop her she'll ruin us altogether. She — she's a damned fool, I tell you!"

"There! there!" the captain's tone was sharp and emphatic. "That's enough of that," he said. "I don't want to hear you call your sister names. What do you mean by it?"

"I mean what I say. She *is* a fool. Do you know what she's done? She's written Mal Dunn all about it! I'd have stopped her, but I didn't know until it was too late. She's told him the whole thing."

"She has? About 'Bije?"

"Well, perhaps she didn't tell him father was a thief, but she did tell that the estate was gone — that we were flat broke and worse."

"Hum!" Captain Elisha seemed more gratified than

displeased. "Hum! . . . Well, I kind of expected she would. Knowin' her, I kind of expected it."

"You did?" Stephen glared in wrathful amazement. "You expected it?"

"Yes. What of it?"

"What *of* it? Why, everything! Can't you see? Mal's our only chance. If she marries him she'll be looked out for and so will I. She needn't have told him until they were married. The wedding could have been hurried along; the Dunns were crazy to have it as soon as possible. Now —"

"Hold on, Steve! Belay! What difference does her tellin' him make? Maybe she hasn't mentioned it to you, but I had a talk with your sister the other mornin'. She thinks the world of Malcolm, and he does of her. She told me so herself. Of *course* she'd go to him in her trouble. And he'll be proud — yes, and glad to know that he can help her. As for the weddin', I don't see that this'll have any effect except to hurry it up a little more, maybe."

Steve looked at him suspiciously, but there was no trace of sarcasm in the captain's face or voice. The boy scowled.

"Ugh!" he grunted.

"What's the 'ugh' for? See here, you ain't hintin' that young Dunn was cal'latin' to marry Caroline just for her money, are you? Of course you ain't! Why, you and he are the thickest sort of chums. You wouldn't chum with a feller who would play such a trick as that on your own sister."

Stephen's scowl deepened. He thrust his hands into his pocket, and shifted his feet uneasily.

"You don't understand," he said. "People don't do things here as they do where you come from."

"I understand that, all right," with dry emphasis. "I've been here long enough to understand that. But maybe I don't understand *you*. Heave ahead, and make it plain."

"Well — well, then — I mean this: I don't know that Mal was after Caro's money, but — but he had a right to expect *some*. If he didn't, why, then her not telling him until after they were married wouldn't have made any difference. And — and if her tellin' him beforehand *should* make a difference and he wanted to break the engagement, she's just romantic fool enough to let him."

"Well?"

"*Well?* If she doesn't marry him, who's going to take care of her? What's going to become of *me?* We haven't a cent. What kind of a guardian are you? Do you want us to starve?"

He was shouting again. The captain was calm. "Oh," he said, "I guess it won't reach to the starvation point. I'm a pretty tough old critter, 'cordin' to your estimate, but I shouldn't let my brother's children starve. If the wust comes to the wust, there's always a home and plenty to eat for you both at South Denboro."

This offer did not appear to comfort the young gentleman greatly. His disgust was evident.

"South Denboro!" he repeated, scornfully. "Gad! . . . South Denboro!"

"Yup. But we'll let South Denboro alone for now and stick to New York. What is it you expect me to do? What are you drivin' at?"

Stephen shook a forefinger in his guardian's face.

"I expect you to make her stick to her engagement," he cried. "And make her make him stick. She can, can't she? It's been announced, hasn't it? Everybody knows of it! She's got the right — the legal right to hold him, hasn't she?"

His uncle regarded him with a quizzical smile. "Why, ye-es," he answered, "I cal'late she has, maybe. Course, there's no danger of his wantin' to do such a thing, but if he should I presume likely we could make it uncomfortable for him, anyhow. What are you hankerin' for, Steve — a breach-of-promise suit? I've always understood those sort of cases were kind of unpleasant — for everybody but the newspapers."

The boy was in deadly earnest. "Pleasant!" he repeated. "Is any of this business pleasant? You make her act like a sensible girl! You're her guardian, and you make her! And, after that, if he tries to hedge, you tell him a few things. You can hold him! Do it! *Do* it!"

Captain Elisha turned on his heel and began pacing up and down the room. His nephew watched him eagerly.

"Well," he demanded, after a moment, "what are we going to do? Are we going to make him make good?"

The captain paused. "Steve," he answered, deliberately, "I ain't sure as we are. And, as I've said, if he's got a spark of decency, it won't be necessary for us to try. If it should be — if it should be —"

"Well, *if* it should be?"

"Then we can try, that's all. Maybe you run a course a little different from me, Stevie; you navigate 'cordin' to your ideas, and I do by mine. But in some ways we ain't so fur apart. Son," with a grim nod, "you rest easy on one thing — the Corcoran Dunn fleet is goin' to show its colors."

CHAPTER XIX

CAROLINE sat by the library window, her chin in her hand, drearily watching the sleet as it beat against the panes, and the tops of the Park trees lashing in the wind. Below, in the street, the trolleys passed in their never-ending procession, the limousines and cabs whizzed forlornly by, and the few pedestrians pushed dripping umbrellas against the gale. A wet, depressing afternoon, as hopeless as her thoughts, and growing darker and more miserable hourly.

Stephen, standing by the fire, kicked the logs together and sent a shower of sparks flying.

" Oh, say something, Caro, do! " he snapped testily. " Don't sit there glowering; you give me the horrors."

She roused from her reverie, turned, and tried to smile.

" What shall I say? " she asked.

" I don't know. But say something, for heaven's sake! Talk about the weather, if you can't think of anything more original."

" The weather isn't a very bright subject just now."

" I didn't say it was; but it's *a* subject. I hope to goodness it doesn't prevent Sylvester's keeping his appointment. He's late, as it is."

" Is he? " wearily. " I hadn't noticed."

" Of course you hadn't. You don't notice anything. It doesn't help matters to pull a long face and go moping around wiping your eyes. You've got to use philosophy in times like this. It's just as hard for me as it is for you; and I try to make the best of it, don't I? "

She might have reminded him that his philosophy was a very recent acquisition. When the news of their poverty first came he was the one who raved and sobbed and refused to contemplate anything less direful than slow starvation or quick suicide. She had soothed and comforted then. Since the previous evening, when he had gone out, in spite of her protestations, and left her alone, his manner had changed. He was still nervous and irritable, but no longer threatened self-destruction, and seemed, for some unexplained reason, more hopeful and less desperate. Sylvester had 'phoned, saying that he would call at the apartment at two, and since Stephen had received the message he had been in a state of suppressed excitement, scarcely keeping still for five minutes at a time.

"It is just as hard for me as it is for you, isn't it?" he repeated.

"Yes, Steve, I suppose it is."

"You suppose? Don't you know? Oh, do quit thinking about Mal Dunn and pay attention to me."

She did not answer. He regarded her with disgust.

"You are thinking of Mal, of course," he declared. "What's the use? You know what I think: you were a fool to write him that letter."

"Don't, Steve; please don't."

"Ugh!"

"Don't you know he didn't get the letter? I was so nervous and over-wrought that I misdirected it."

"Pooh! Has he ever stayed away from you so long before? Or his precious mother, either? Why doesn't she come to see you? She scarcely missed a day before this happened. Nonsense! I guess he got it all right."

"Steve, stop! stop! Don't dare speak like that. Do you realize what you are insinuating? You don't believe it! You know you don't! Shame on you! I'm ashamed of my brother! No! not another word of that kind, or I shall leave the room."

She had risen to her feet. He looked at her determined face and turned away.

"Oh, well," he muttered, sullenly, "maybe you're right. I don't say you're not. Perhaps he didn't get the letter. You sent it to his office, and he may have been called out of town. But his mother —"

"Mrs. Dunn was not well when I last saw her. She may be ill."

"Perhaps. But if you're so sure about them, why not let it go at that? What's the use of fretting?"

"I was not thinking of them — then."

As a matter of fact, she had been thinking of her uncle, Elisha Warren. As the time dragged by, she thought of him more and more — not as the uncouth countryman whose unwelcome presence had been forced into her life; nor as the hypocrite whose insult to her father's memory she never could forgive or whose double-dealing had been, as she thought, revealed; but as the man who, with the choke in his voice and the tears in his eyes, bade her remember that, whenever she needed help, he was ready and glad to give it.

She did not doubt Malcolm's loyalty. Her brother's hints and insinuations found no echo in her thoughts. In the note which she had written her fiancé she told of the loss of their fortune, though not of her father's shame. That she could not tell; nor did she ask Malcolm to come to her — her pride would not permit that. She wrote simply of her great trouble and trusted the rest to him. That he had not come was due — so she kept repeating to herself — solely to the fact that he had not received her letter. She knew that was it — she knew it. And yet — and yet he did not come.

So, in her loneliness and misery, her guardian's words returned again and again to her memory: " Sometimes when things look all right they turn out to be all wrong. If ever there comes a time like that to you and Steve, remember you've got me to turn to." The time had come when she must turn to someone.

She would never go to him; she vowed it. She would not accept his help if he came to her. But, if he was sincere, if he meant what he said, why did he not come again to proffer it? Because he was not sincere, of course. That had been proven long before. She despised him. But his face, as she last saw it, refused to be banished from her mind. It looked so strong, and yet gentle and loving, like the face of a protector, one to be trusted through good times and bad. Oh, this wicked, wicked world, and the shams and sorrows in it! " Malcolm, why don't you come to me? "

Stephen uttered an exclamation. Looking up, she saw him hurrying toward the hall.

" Someone's at the door," he explained. " It's Sylvester, of course. I'll let him in."

It was not the lawyer but a messenger boy with a note. Stephen returned to the library with the missive in his hand.

" He couldn't get here, Caro," he said, excitedly. " Wants us to come right down to his office. Hurry up! Get your things on. The cab's waiting. Come! Rush! It may be important."

The cab, an electric vehicle, made good time, and they soon reached the Pine Street offices, where they were ushered at once into the senior partner's presence.

"Step into the other room," said Mr. Sylvester, "and wait there, please. I'll join you shortly."

The room was the large one where the momentous conference between Captain Elisha and the three lawyers had so recently taken place. Caroline seated herself in one of the chairs. Stephen walked the floor.

"Hope he doesn't keep us waiting long," he fumed. "I thought of course he was ready or he wouldn't have sent for us."

"Ready?" his sister looked at him, questioningly. "Ready for what?" she repeated, with sudden suspicion. "Steve, do you know what Mr. Sylvester wishes to see us about?"

Her brother colored and seemed a bit disconcerted. "How should I know?" he muttered.

"Is it something new about the estate or that man who owns it? You do know something! I can see it in your face. What is it?"

"Nothing. How should I know what it is?"

"But you do. I believe you do. Look at me! What does Mr. Sylvester want of us?"

The boy hesitated; then whirled and faced her.

"See here, Caro," he said, "maybe I do know something — or I can guess. Now, whatever happens, you've got to be a sensible girl. Certain things have to be dealt with in a practical way, and we're practical people. Sentiment — and pride — and all that sort of stuff, are well enough, but business is business and an engagement is an engagement. Now it's right up to you and —"

"Steve, what are you talking about?"

"That's all right. I know what I'm talking about. Somebody in the family must use common sense, and when it comes to holding a person to a promise, then — Confound it, Sis, we can't starve, can we?"

"What do you mean?" She rose and advanced toward him. "What do you mean by a promise? What have you been doing?"

His confusion increased. He avoided her eyes and moved sullenly toward the other side of the table.

"I haven't done anything," he grumbled, "that is, I've done what any reasonable fellow would do. I'm not the only one who thinks . . . Look here! We've got a guardian, haven't we?"

"A guardian! a *guardian!* Stephen Warren, have you been to him? Have you — Was *that* where you were last night?"

"Well, I —"

"Answer me!"

"What if I have? Whom else am I to go to? Isn't he —"

"But why did you go to him? What did you say?"

"I said — I said — Never mind what I said. He agrees with me, I can tell you that. You'll thank your stars I did go, before very long. I . . . S-sh! Here's Sylvester."

The door of the room opened. The person who entered, however, was not the lawyer, but the very man of whom they had been speaking, Captain Elisha himself. He closed the door behind him.

"Hello, Stevie," he said, with a nod to the boy. Then, turning to his niece, he stepped forward and held out his hand. "Caroline," he began, "I don't doubt you're some surprised to see me here; but I . . . Why, what's the matter?"

The faces of the pair led him to ask the question. Stephen's was red and he looked embarrassed and guilty. Caroline's was white, and she glanced from her brother to her guardian and back again, with flashing eyes.

" What's the matter ? " repeated the captain. " Steve," sharply, " have you been making a fool of yourself again ? What is it ? "

" Nothing," was the sulky answer; " nothing of consequence. Caro is — well, I happened to mention that I called on you last night and — and she doesn't seem to like it, that's all. As I told her, somebody in the family had to use common sense, and you were our guardian and naturally, under the circumstances . . . Why, I'll leave it to anyone ! " with a burst of righteous indignation. " You *are* our guardian."

He proclaimed it as if he expected a denial. Captain Elisha frowned. " Humph ! " he grunted. " That ain't exactly news, is it, Steve ? Seems to me we've taken up that p'int afore; though, as I remember, you didn't used to be sot on all hands knowin' it," with dry sarcasm. " I don't need even your common sense to remind me of it just at this minute. Caroline, your brother did come to see me last night. I was glad he did."

She ignored him. " Steve," she demanded, still facing the young man, " was this, too, a part of your plan ? Did you bring me here to meet — him ? "

" No, I didn't. Sylvester was to come to see us. You know that; he telephoned. I didn't know —"

The captain interrupted. " There, there, son ! " he exclaimed, " let me say a word. No, Caroline, Stevie didn't know I was to meet you here. But I thought it was necessary that I should. Set down, please. I know you must be worn out, poor girl."

" I don't wish to sit. I want to know what my brother called to see you about."

" Well, there was some matters he wanted to talk over."

"What were they? Concerning the estate?"

"Partly that."

"Partly? What else? Captain Warren, my brother has hinted — he has said — What does he mean by holding someone to a promise? Answer me truthfully."

"I shouldn't answer you any other way, Caroline. Steve seems to be worried about — now you mustn't mind my speakin' plain, Caroline; the time's come when I've got to — Steve seems to be worried about the young man you're engaged to. He seems to cal'late that Mr. Dunn may want to slip out of that engagement."

His niece looked at him. Then she turned to her brother. "You went to *him* and . . . Oh, how *could* you!"

Stephen would not meet her gaze. "Well," he muttered rebelliously, "why wouldn't I? You know yourself that Mal hasn't been near you since it happened. If he wasn't after — if he was straight, he would have come, wouldn't he? Mind, I don't say he isn't — perhaps he doesn't know. But, at any rate, something must be done. We had to face possibilities, and you wouldn't listen to me. I tried —"

"Stop!" she cut him short, imperiously. "Don't make me hate you. And you," turning to her uncle, "did *you* listen and believe such things? Did you encourage him to believe them? Oh, I know what you think of my friends! I heard it from your own lips. And I know why you think it. Because they know what you are; because they exposed you and —"

"There, there! Caroline, you needn't go on. I've heard your opinion of my character afore. Never mind me for the minute. And, if you'll remember, *I* ain't said that I doubted your young man. You told me that you thought the world and all of him and that he did of you.

That's enough — or ought to be. But your brother says you wrote him two days ago and he ain't been near you."

" I misdirected the letter. He didn't receive it."

" Um-hm. I see. That would explain."

" Of course it would. That *must* be the reason."

" Yes, seem's if it must."

" It is. What right have you to doubt it? Oh, how can you think such things? Can you suppose the man I am to marry is so despicable — so *mean* as to — as to — I'm ashamed to say it. Why do you presume that money has any part in our engagement? Such trouble as mine only makes it more binding. Do you suppose if *he* were poor as — as I am, that I would desert *him?* You know I wouldn't. I should be glad — yes, almost happy, because then I could show him — could —"

Her voice failed her. She put her handkerchief to her eyes for an instant and then snatched it away and faced them, her head erect. The pride in her face was reflected in Captain Elisha's as he regarded her.

" No, no," he said gently, " I never supposed you'd act but in one way, Caroline. I knew *you.* And, as Steve'll tell you, I said to him almost the same words you've been sayin'. If Malcolm's what he'd ought to be, I said, he'll be glad of the chance to prove how much he cares for your sister. But Steve appeared to have some misgivin's, and so —"

He paused, turned toward the door, and seemed to be listening. Caroline flashed an indignant glance at her brother.

" And so? " she asked, scornfully.

" And so," continued the captain, with a slight change in his tone, " it seemed to me that his doubts ought to be settled. And," rising, as there came a tap at the door, " I cal'late they're goin' to be."

He walked briskly over and opened the door. Sylvester was standing without.

"Come, have they?" inquired Captain Elisha.

"Yes."

"Fetch 'em right in here. Steve, stand over nigher that corner. This way, Caroline, if you please."

He took his niece by the arm and led her to the side of the room not visible from the doorway. She was too astonished to resist, but asked an agitated question.

"What is it?" she cried. "Who is coming?"

"Some friends of yours," was the quiet reply. 'Nothin' to be frightened about. Steve, stay where you are."

The boy was greatly excited. "Is it they?" he demanded. "Is it? By gad! Now, Sis, be a sensible girl. If he should try to hedge, you hold him. Hold him! Understand?"

"Steve, be quiet," ordered the captain. . . . "Ah, Mrs. Dunn, good afternoon, ma'am. Mr. Dunn, good afternoon, sir."

For the pair who, followed by Sylvester, now entered the room were Mrs. Corcoran Dunn and Malcolm.

They were past the sill before Captain Elisha's greeting caused them to turn and see the three already there. Mrs. Dunn, who was in the lead, stopped short in her majestic though creaking march of entrance, and her florid face turned a brighter crimson. Her son, strolling languidly at her heels, started violently and dropped his hat. The lawyer, bringing up in the rear, closed the door and remained standing near it. Caroline uttered an exclamation of surprise. Her brother drew himself haughtily erect. Captain Elisha remained unperturbed and smiling.

"Good afternoon, ma'am," he repeated. "It's been

some time since you and I run across each other. I hope you're feelin' pretty smart."

Mrs. Dunn had faced some unpleasant situations in her life and had proved equal to them. Usually, however, she had been prepared beforehand. For this she had not been prepared — as yet. She had come to the offices of Sylvester, Kuhn, and Graves, at the senior partner's request, to be told, as she supposed, the full and final details of the financial disaster threatening the Warren family. If those details should prove the disaster as overwhelming as it appeared, then — well, then, certain disagreeable duties must be performed. But to meet the girl to whom her son was engaged, and whom she and he had carefully avoided meeting until the lawyers should acquaint them with the whole truth — to meet this girl, and her brother, and her guardian, thus unexpectedly and unprepared, was enough to shake the composure and nerve of even such a veteran campaigner as Mrs. M. Corcoran Dunn.

But of the three to whom the meeting was an absolute surprise,— Caroline, Malcolm and herself — she was characteristically the first to regain outward serenity. For a moment she stood nonplused and speechless, but only for a moment. Then she hastened, with outstretched arms, to Caroline and clasped her in affectionate embrace.

"My dear child!" she cried; "my dear girl! I'm *so* glad to see you! I've thought of you so much! And I pity you so. Poor Malcolm has — Malcolm," sharply, "come here! Don't you see Caroline?"

Malcolm was groping nervously for his hat. He picked it up and obeyed his mother's summons, though with no great eagerness.

"How d'ye do, Caroline," he stammered, confusedly.

"I — I — It's a deuce of a surprise to see you down here. The mater and I didn't expect — that is, we scarcely hoped to meet anyone but Sylvester. He sent for us, you know."

He extended his hand. She did not take it.

"Did you get my letter?" she asked, quickly. Mrs. Dunn answered for him.

"Yes, dear, he got it," she said. "The poor fellow was almost crazy. I began to fear for his sanity; I did, indeed. I did not dare trust him out of my sight. Oh, if you could but know how we feel for you and pity you!"

Pity was not what Caroline wanted just then. The word jarred upon her. She avoided the lady's embrace and once more faced the embarrassed Malcolm.

"You got my letter?" she cried. "You *did?*"

"Yes — er — yes, I got it, Caroline. I — by Jove, you know —"

He hesitated, stammered, and looked thoroughly uncomfortable. His mother regarded him wrathfully.

"Well," she snapped, "why don't you go on? Caroline, dear, you really must excuse him. The dear boy is quite overcome."

Captain Elisha stepped forward.

"Excuse me for interruptin', ma'am," he said, addressing the ruffled matron; "but I know you're sort of surprised to see us all here and maybe I'd better explain. Mr. Sylvester told me you and your son had an appointment with him for this afternoon. Now there was something we — or I, anyhow — wanted to talk with you about, so I thought we might as well make one job of it. Sylvester's a pretty busy man, and I know he has other things to attend to; so why not let him go ahead and tell you what you come to hear, and then we can take

303

up the other part by ourselves. He's told me what you wanted to see him about, and it's somethin' we're all interested in, bein' as we're one family — or goin' to be pretty soon. So suppose he just tells you now. Ain't that a good idea?"

Mrs. Dunn looked at the speaker, and then at the lawyer, and seemed to have caught some of her son's embarrassment.

"I — we did have an appointment with Mr. Sylvester," she admitted, reluctantly; "but the business was not important. And," haughtily, "I do not care to discuss it here."

The captain opened his eyes. "Hey?" he exclaimed. "Not important? You surprise me, ma'am. I judged 'twas mighty important. 'Twas about the real size of your father's estate, Caroline," turning to the girl. "I thought Mrs. Dunn and Mr. Malcolm must think 'twas important, for I understand they've been telephonin' and askin' for appointments for the last two days. Why, yes! and they come way down here in all this storm on purpose to talk it over with him. Am I wrong? Ain't that so, ma'am?"

It was so, and Mrs. Dunn could not well deny it. Therefore, she took refuge in a contemptuous silence. The captain nodded.

"As to discussin' it here," he went on with bland innocence, "why, we're all family folks, same as I said, and there ain't any secrets between us on *that* subject. So suppose we all listen while Mr. Sylvester tells just what he'd have told you and Mr. Malcolm. It's pretty hard to hear; but bad news is soon told. Heave ahead, Mr. Sylvester."

Mrs. Dunn made one more attempt to avoid the crisis she saw was approaching.

"Surely, Caroline," she said testily, "you don't wish your private affairs treated in this public manner. Come, let us go."

She laid a hand on the girl's arm. Captain Elisha quietly interposed.

"No, no," he said. "We'll all stay here. There's nothin' public about it."

Caroline, crimson with mortification, protested indignantly.

"Mr. Sylvester," she said, "it is not necessary to —"

"Excuse me;" her uncle's tone was sharper and more stern; "I think it is. Go on, Sylvester."

The lawyer looked far from comfortable, but he spoke at once and to the point.

"I should have told you and your son just this, Mrs. Dunn," he said. "I intimated it before, and Miss Warren had already written you the essential facts. A new and unexpected development, the nature of which I am not at liberty to disclose now or later, makes Abijah Warren's estate absolutely bankrupt. Not only that, but many thousand dollars in debt. His heirs are left penniless. That is the plain truth, I'm very sorry to say. There is no hope of anything better. You'll forgive me, Miss Warren, I hope, for putting it so bluntly; but I thought it best to avoid every possible misunderstanding."

It was blunt, beyond doubt. Even Captain Elisha winced at the word "penniless." Stephen muttered under his breath and turned his back. Caroline, swaying, put a hand on the table to steady herself. The Dunns looked at each other.

"Thank you, Mr. Sylvester," said the captain, quietly. "I'll see you again in a few moments."

The lawyer bowed and left the room, evidently glad to escape. Captain Elisha turned to Mrs. Dunn.

"And now, ma'am," he observed, "that part of the business is over. The next part's even more in the family, so I thought we didn't need legal advice. You see just how matters stand. My niece is a poor girl. She needs somebody to support her and look out for her. She's got that somebody, we're all thankful to say. She's engaged to Mr. Malcolm here. And, as you're his ma, Mrs. Dunn, and I'm Caroline's guardian, us old folks'll take our affairs in hand; they needn't listen, if they don't want to. I understand from Steve that Malcolm's been mighty anxious to have the weddin' day hurried along. I can't say as I blame him. And *I* think the sooner they're married the better. Now, how soon can we make it, Mrs. Dunn?"

This unexpected and matter-of-fact query was variously received. Mrs. Dunn frowned and flushed. Malcolm frowned, also. Steve nodded emphatic approval. As for Caroline, she gazed at her guardian in horrified amazement.

"Why!" she cried. "You — you — What do you mean by such —"

"Don't be an idiot, Caro!" cut in her brother. "I told you to be sensible. Captain Warren's dead right."

"Stevie, you stay out of this." There was no misunderstanding the captain's tone. "When I want your opinion I'll ask for it. And, Caroline, I want you to stay out, too. This is my trick at the wheel. Mrs. Dunn, what d'you say? Never mind the young folks. You and me know that marriage is business, same as everything else. How soon can we have the weddin'?"

Mrs. Dunn had, apparently, nothing to say — to him. She addressed her next remark to Caroline.

"My dear," she said, in great agitation, "this is really too dreadful. This — er — guardian of yours appears to think he is in some barbarous country — ordering the savages about. Come! Malcolm, take her away."

"No," Captain Elisha stepped in front of the door. "She ain't goin'; and I'd rather you wouldn't go yet. Let's settle this up now. I ain't askin' anything unreasonable. Caroline's under my charge, and I've got to plan for her. Your boy's just crazy to marry her; he's been beggin' for her to name the day. Let's name it. It needn't be to-morrow. I cal'late you'll want to get out invitations and such. It needn't be next week. But just say about when it can be; then I'll know how to plan. That ain't much to ask, sartin."

Much or little, neither Mrs. Dunn nor her son appeared ready to answer. Malcolm fidgeted with his hat and gloves; his mother fanned herself with her handkerchief. Caroline, frantic with humiliation and shame, would have protested again, but her guardian's stern shake of the head silenced her.

"Well, Mr. Dunn," turning to the groom-to-be; "you're one of the interested parties — what do you say?"

Malcolm ground his heel into the rug. "I don't consider it your business," he declared. "You're butting in where —"

"No, no, I ain't. It's my business, and business is just *what* it is. Your ma knows that. She and I had a real confidential up and down talk on love and marriage, and she's the one that proved to me that marryin' in high society, like yours and the kind Caroline's been circulatin' in, was business and mighty little else. There's a business contract between you and my niece. We want to know how soon it can be carried out, that's all."

The young man looked desperately at the door; but

the captain's broad shoulders blocked the way towards it. He hesitated, scowled, and then, with a shrug of his shoulders, surrendered.

"How can I marry?" he demanded sullenly. "Confound it! my salary isn't large enough to pay my own way, decently."

"Malcolm!" cried his mother, warningly.

"Well, Mater, what the devil's the use of all this? You know . . . By Jove! you *ought* to!"

"Hold on, young feller! I don't understand. Your wages ain't large enough, you say? What do you mean? You was *goin'* to be married, wasn't you?"

Mrs. Dunn plunged to the rescue, a forlorn hope, but desperate, and fighting to the end.

"An outrage!" she blurted. "Malcolm, I forbid you to continue this disgusting conversation. Caroline, my poor child, I don't blame you for this, but I call on you to stop it at once. My dear, I—"

She advanced toward the girl with outstretched arms. Caroline recoiled.

"Don't! don't!" she gasped. Captain Elisha spoke up sharp and stern.

"Excuse me, ma'am," he said, "but I'll be obliged if you'll wait a minute. Caroline, don't you say a word. You say — you —" addressing Malcolm, "that you can't support a wife on your wages. You surprise me some, considerin' the swath you've been cuttin' on 'em — but never mind that. Maybe they won't keep automobiles and — er — other things I've heard you was interested in, but if you cut them out and economize a little, same as young married folks I've known have been glad to do, you could scrape along, couldn't you? Hey? Couldn't you?"

Malcolm's answer was another scornful shrug. "You

belong on Cape Cod," he sneered. "Mater, let's get out of this."

"Wait! Put it plain now. Do I understand that you cal'late to break the engagement because my niece has lost her money? Is that it?"

Mrs. Dunn realized that the inevitable was upon them. After all, it might as well be faced now as later.

"This is ridiculous," she proclaimed. "Every sane person knows — though *barbarians* may not —" with a venomous glare at the captain —"that, in engagements of the kind in which my son shared, a certain amount of — er — financial — er — that is, the bride is supposed to have some money. It is expected. Of course it is! Love in a cottage is — well — a bit *passé*. My son and I pity your niece from the bottom of our hearts, but — there! under the circumstances the whole affair becomes impossible. Caroline, my dear, I'm dreadfully sorry, dreadfully! I love you like my own child. And poor Malcolm will be heartbroken — but — you *see*."

She extended her hand in a gesture of utter helplessness. Stephen, who had been fuming and repressing his rage with difficulty during the scene, leaped forward with brandished fist.

"By gad!" he shouted. "Mal Dunn, you cad —"

His uncle pushed him back with a sweep of his arm.

"Steve," he ordered, "I'm runnin' this ship." He gave a quick glance at his niece, and then added, speaking rapidly and addressing the head of the Dunn family, "I see, ma'am. Yes, yes, I see. Well, you've forgot one thing, I guess. Caroline's lived in high society, too. And I've been in it a spell, myself. And Steve's a boy, but he's got a business head. If there's nothin' in marriage but business, then an engagement is what I just called it, a business contract, and it can't be broke without the consent of both sides. You wanted Caroline's money; maybe she wants yours now. If she does, and there's such a thing as law, why, perhaps she can get it."

"That's the talk!" cried Stephen exultingly.

"Yup; perhaps she can. She may be a business woman, too, you know. If money and style and social position's what counts and she wants to force you to keep your promise, why, I'm her guardian and she can count on me to back her up. What do you say, Caroline? I'm at your service. I —"

But Caroline interrupted him.

"Stop!" she cried wildly. "Oh, stop! Do you think — do you suppose I would marry him now? *Now,* after I've seen what he is? Oh," with a shudder of disgust, "when I think what I might have done, I . . . Thank God that the money has gone! I'm glad I'm poor! I'm *glad!*"

"Caro, you fool!" shrieked Stephen. She did not heed him.

"Let me go!" she cried. "Let me get away from him; from this room! I never want to see him or think of him again. Please! *please* let me go! Oh, take me home! Captain Warren, *please* let me go home!"

Her uncle was at her side in a moment. "Yes, yes, dearie," he said, "I'll take you home. Don't give way now! I'll —"

He would have taken her arm, but she shrank from him.

"Not you!" she begged. "Steve!"

The captain's face clouded, but he answered promptly.

"Of course — Steve," he agreed. "Steve, take your sister home. Mr. Sylvester's got a carriage waitin', and he'll go with you, I don't doubt. Do as I tell you, boy — and behave yourself. Don't wait; go!"

He held the door open until the hysterical girl and her brother had departed. Then he turned to the Dunns.

"Well, ma'am," he said, dryly. "I don't know's there's anything more to be said. All the questions seem to be settled. Our acquaintance wa'n't so awful long, but it was interestin'. Knowin' you has been, as the feller said, a liberal education. Don't let me keep you any longer. Good afternoon."

He stepped away from the door. Malcolm and his mother remained standing, for an instant, where they were when Caroline left.

The young man looked as if he would enjoy choking someone, the captain preferably, but said nothing. Then Mrs. Dunn bethought herself of a way to make their exit less awkward and embarrassing.

"My heart!" she said, gasping, and with a clutch at her breast. "My poor heart! I—I fear I'm going to have one of my attacks. Malcolm, your arm—quick!"

With an expression of intense but patient suffering, and leaning heavily upon her son's arm, she moved past Captain Elisha and from the room.

That evening the captain stood in the lower hall of the apartment house at Central Park West, undecided what to do next. He wished more than anything else in the world to go to his niece. He would have gone to her before—had been dying to go, to soothe, to comfort, to tell her of his love—but he was afraid. His conscience troubled him. Perhaps he had been too brutal. Perhaps he shouldn't have acted as he did. Maybe forcing the Dunn fleet to show its colors could have been done more diplomatically. He had wanted her to see those colors for herself, to actually see them. But he might have overdone it. He remembered how she shrank from him and turned to her brother. She might hate him more than ever now. If so, then the whole scheme under which he was working fell to pieces.

He was worried about Steve, too. That young man would, naturally, be furious with his sister for what he would consider her romantic foolishness. He had been warned to behave himself; but would he? Captain Elisha paced up and down the marble floor before the elevator cage and wondered whether his visiting the apartment would be a wise move or a foolish one.

The elevator descended, the door of the cage opened, and Stephen himself darted out. His face was red, he was scowling fiercely, and he strode toward the street without looking in his guardian's direction.

The captain caught him as he passed.

"Here, boy!" he exclaimed; "where's the fire? Where are you bound?"

His nephew, brought thus unexpectedly to a halt, stared at him.

"Oh, it's you!" he exclaimed. "Humph! I'm bound — I don't know where I'm bound!"

"You don't, hey? Well, you can cruise a long ways on a v'yage like that. What do you mean?"

"Aw, let me alone! I'm going to the club, I guess, or somewhere. Anyhow, I won't stay with her. I told her so. Silly little idiot! By gad, she understands what I think of her conduct. I'll never speak to her again. I told her so. She —"

"Here! Belay! Stop! Who are you talking about?"

"Caro, of course. She —"

"You've run off and left her alone — to-night? Where is she?"

"Upstairs — and crying, I suppose. She doesn't do

anything else. It's all she's good for. Selfish, romantic —"

He got no further, for Captain Elisha sent him reeling
with a push and ran to the elevator.

"Eighth floor," he commanded.

The door of the apartment was not latched. Stephen,
in his rage and hurry, had neglected such trifles. The
captain opened it quietly and walked in. He entered the
library. Caroline was lying on the couch, her head
buried in the pillows. She did not hear him cross the
room. He leaned over and touched her shoulder. She
started, looked, and sat up, gazing at him as though not
certain whether he was a dream or reality.

And he looked at her, at her pretty face, now so white
and careworn, at her eyes, at the tear-stains on her
cheeks, and his whole heart went out to her.

"Caroline, dearie," he faltered, "forgive me for comin'
here, won't you? I had to come. I couldn't leave you
alone; I couldn't rest, thinkin' of you alone in your
trouble. I know you must feel harder than ever towards
me for this afternoon's doin's, but I meant it for the
best. I *had* to show you — don't you see? Can you
forgive me? Won't you try to forgive the old feller that
loves you more'n all the world? Won't you try?"

She looked at him, wide-eyed, clasping and unclasping
her hands.

"*I* forgive *you?*" she repeated, incredulously.

"Yes. Try to, dearie. Oh, if you would only believe
I meant it for your good, and nothin' else! If you could
only just trust me and come to me and let me help you.
I want you, my girl, I want you!"

She leaned forward. "Do you really mean it?" she
cried. "How can you? after all I've done? after the
way I've treated you? and the things I've said? You

must *hate* me! Everyone does. I hate myself! You can't forgive me! You can't!"

His answer was to hold out his arms. Another moment and she was in them, clinging to his wet coat, sobbing, holding him fast, and begging him not to leave her, to take her away, that she would work, that she would not be a burden to him — only take her with him and try to forgive her, for he was real and honest and the only friend she had.

And Captain Elisha, soothing her, stroking her hair, and murmuring words of love and tenderness, realized that his labor and sacrifice had not been in vain, that here was his recompense; she would never misunderstand him again; she was his at last.

And yet, in the midst of his joy, his conscience troubled him more than ever.

CHAPTER XX

IT was April; and May was close at hand. The weather was all that late April weather should be, and so often is not. Trees, bushes, and vines were in bud; the green of the new grass was showing everywhere above the dead brown of the old; a pair of bluebirds were inspecting the hollow of the old apple tree, with an eye toward spring housekeeping; the sun was warm and bright, and the water of the Sound sparkled in the distance. Caroline, sitting by the living-room window, was waiting for her uncle to return from the city.

In the kitchen Annie Moriarty was preparing dinner. Annie was now cook as well as chamber-maid, for, of all the Warren servants, she was the only one remaining. Edwards, the "Commodore," had been dismissed, had departed, not without reluctance but philosophically, to seek other employment. "Yes, miss," observed Edwards, when notified that his services were no longer required; "I understand. I've been expecting it. I was in a family before that met with financial difficulties, and I know the signs. All I can say is that I hope you and Mr. Stephen will get on all right, miss. If there's anything I can do to help you, by way of friendship, please let me know. I'd be glad, for old times' sake. And the cook wanted me to tell you that, being as she's got another job in sight and was paid up to date, she wouldn't wait for notice, but was leaving immediate. She's gone already, miss."

The second maid went also. But Annie, Irish and grateful, refused to go. Her mother came to back her in the refusal.

"Indeed she'll not leave you, Miss Caroline — you nor Captain Warren neither. Lord love him! Sure, d'ye think we'll ever forget what you and him done for me and my Pat and the childer? You've got to have somebody, ain't you? And Annie's cookin' ain't so bad that it'll kill yez; and I'll learn her more. Never mind what the wages is, they're big enough. She'll stay! If she didn't, I'd break her back."

So, when the apartment was given up, and Captain Elisha and his wards moved to the little house in Westchester County, Annie came with them. And her cooking, though not by any means equal to that at Delmonico's, had not killed them yet. Mrs. Moriarty came once a week to do the laundry work. Caroline acted as a sort of inexperienced but willing supervising housekeeper.

The house itself had been procured through the kind interest of Sylvester. Keeping the apartment was, under the circumstances, out of the question, and Caroline hated it and was only too anxious to give it up. She had no suggestions to make. She would go anywhere, anywhere that her guardian deemed best; but might they not please go at once? She expected that he would suggest South Denboro, and she would have gone there without a complaint. To get away from the place where she had been so miserable was her sole wish. And trusting and believing in her uncle as she now did, realizing that he had been right always and had worked for her interest throughout, and having been shown the falseness and insincerity of the others whom she had once trusted implicitly, she clung to him with an appeal al-

most piteous. Her pride was, for the time, broken.
She was humble and grateful. She surrendered to him
unconditionally, and hoped only for his forgiveness and
love.

The captain did not suggest South Denboro. He did,
however, tell Sylvester that he believed a little place out
of the city would be the better refuge for the present.

"Poor Caroline's switched clear around," he said to
the lawyer, "and you can't blame her much. She
cal'lates New York's nothin' but a sham from stern to
stern, manned by liars and swindlers and hypocrites and
officered by thieves. 'Tain't no use to tell her 'tain't,
though she might pretend to believe it, if *I* told her, for
just now the poor girl thinks I'm Solomon and Saint
Peter rolled into one. The way she agrees to whatever
I say and the way she looks at me and sort of holds on
to me, as if I was her only anchor in a gale, I declare
it makes me feel meaner than poorhouse tea — and
that's made of blackberry leaves steeped in memories of
better things, so I've heard say. *Am* I a low down
scamp, playin' a dirty mean trick on a couple of orphans?
What do you think, Sylvester?"

"You know what I think, Captain Warren," replied
the lawyer. "You're handling the whole matter better
than any other man could handle it. No one else would
have thought of it, to begin with; and the results so far
prove that you're right."

"Yup. Maybe. I wish you was around to say that
to me when I wake up nights and get to thinkin'. However, as I said, Caroline believes New York is like a
sailors' dance hall, a place for decent folks to steer clear
of. And when the feller you've been engaged to is
shown up as a sneak and your own dad as a crook —
well, you can't blame a green hand for holdin' prejudice

against the town that raised 'em. She'll get over it; but just now I cal'late some little flat, or, better still, a little home out where the back yards ain't made of concrete, would be a first-class port for us to make for. Don't know of such a place at a reasonable rent, do you?"

" I might find one. And you may be right; your niece might like it better, though it will be somewhat of a change. But how about your nephew? He has no objection to the metropolis, I should judge. What will he say?"

" Nothin', I guess — unless he says it to himself. Steve's goin' back to New Haven with things on his mind. He and I had a mornin' service, and I was the parson. He listened, because when you ain't got a cent except what the society allows you, it ain't good orthodoxy to dodge the charity sermon. Steve'll behave, and what he don't like he'll lump. If he starts to open his mouth his ear'll ache, I cal'late. I talked turkey to that young man. Ye-es," with a slight smile, " I'm sort of afraid I lost patience with Stevie."

When Caroline first saw the little house, with its shingled sides, the dead vines over the porch, and the dry stalks of last year's flowers in the yard, her heart sank. With the wind blowing and the bare branches of the old apple tree scraping the roof and whining dolefully, it looked bleak and forsaken. It was so different, so unhomelike, and so, to her eyes, small and poverty-stricken. She made believe that she liked it, exclaimed over the view — which, on the particular day, was desolate enough — and declared the Dutch front door was " old-fashioned and dear." But Captain Elisha, watching her closely, knew that she was only waiting to be alone to give way to wretchedness and tears. He understood, had expected that she would feel thus, but he was disappointed, nevertheless. However, after the front door was passed and they were inside the house, Caroline looked about her in delighted amazement. The living room was small, but bright and warm and cheery. On its walls, hiding the rather vivid paper, were hung some of the best of Rodgers Warren's pictures — the Corot, the codfisher, and others. The furniture and rugs were those which had been in the library of the apartment, those she had been familiar with all her life. The books, many of them, were there, also. And the dining room, except for size, looked like home. So did the bedrooms; and, in the kitchen, Annie grinned a welcome.

" But how could you? " asked Caroline. " How could you keep all these things, Uncle Elisha? I thought, of course, they must all be sold. I cried when they took them away that day when we were leaving to go to the hotel. I was sure I should never see them again. And here they all are! How could you do it? "

The captain's grin was as wide as Annie's. " Oh," he explained, " I couldn't let 'em all go. Never intended to. That five thousand dollar codder up there seemed like own folks, pretty nigh. I'd have kept *him,* if we had to live in one room and a trunk. And we ain't got to that — yet. I tell you, dearie, I thought they'd make you feel more to home. And they do, don't they? "

The look she gave him was answer sufficient.

" But the creditors? " she asked. " That man who — they belong to him, don't they? I supposed of course they must go with the rest."

Captain Elisha winked. " There's times," he answered, " when I believe in cheatin' my creditors. This is one of 'em. Never you mind that feller you mentioned. He's got enough, confound him! He didn't have the face to ask for any more. Sylvester looked out for that. Five hundred thousand, droppin' in, as you might say, unexpected, ought to soften anybody's heart; and I judge even that feller's got some bowels of mercy."

He changed the subject hastily, but Caroline asked no more questions. She never alluded to the lost estate, never expressed any regrets, nor asked to know who it was that had seized her all. The captain had expected her to ask, had been ready with the same answer he had given Stephen, but when he hinted she herself had forbade his continuing. "Don't tell me about it," she begged. "I don't want to know any more. Father did wrong, but — but I know he did not mean to. He was a good, kind father to me, and I loved him. This man whose money he took had a right to it, and now it is his. He doesn't wish us to know who he is, so Steve says, and I'm glad. I don't want to know, because if I did I might hate him. And," with a shudder, "I am trying so hard not to hate anybody."

Her make-believe liking for the little home became more and more real as spring drew near. She began to take an interest in it, in the flower garden, in the beds beside the porch, where the peonies and daffodils were beginning to show green heads above the loam, and in the household affairs. And she had plans of her own, not connected with these. She broached them to her uncle, and they surprised and delighted him, although he would not give his consent to them entirely.

"You mustn't think," she said, "that, because I have been willing to live on your money since mine went, that I mean to continue doing it. I don't. I've been thinking a great deal, and I realize that I must earn my own way just as soon as I can. I'm not fitted for anything now; but I can be and I shall. I've thought perhaps I might learn stenography or — or something like that. Girls do."

He looked at her serious face and choked back his laugh.

"Why, yes," he admitted, "they do, that's a fact. About four hundred thousand of 'em do, and four hundred thousand more try to and then try to make business men think that they have. I heard Sylvester sputterin' about a couple in his office t'other day; said they was no good and not worth the seven dollars a week he paid 'em."

" Seven dollars a *week!* " she repeated.

" Yes. Course some make three times that and more; but they're the experienced ones, the good ones. And there's heaps that don't. What makes you so sot on earnin' a livin', Caroline? Ain't you satisfied with the kind I'm tryin' to give you? "

She regarded him reproachfully. " Please don't say that," she protested. " You always treat your kindness as a joke, but to me it — it —"

" There! there! " quickly. " Don't let's talk foolish. I see what you mean, dearie. It ain't the livin' but because I'm givin' it to you that troubles you. I know. Well, *I* ain't complainin'; but I understand your feelin's and respect 'em. However, I shouldn't study typewritin', if I was you. There's too much competition in it to be comfortable, as the fat man said about runnin' races. I've got a suggestion, if you want to listen to it."

" I do, indeed. What is it? "

" Why, just this. I've been about everythin' aboard ship, but I've never been a steward. Now I'll say this much for Annie, she tried hard. She tumbled into general housekeepin' the way Asa Foster said he fell into

321

the cucumber frame — with a jolt and a jingle; and
she's doin' her best accordin' to her lights. But sometimes her lights need ile or trimmin' or somethin'. I've
had the feelin' that we need a good housekeeper here.
If Annie's intelligence was as broad and liberal as her
shoes, we wouldn't; as 'tis, we do. I'll hire you, Caroline, for that job, if you say so."

"I? Uncle Elisha, you're joking!"

"No, I ain't. Course I realize you ain't had much
experience in runnin' a house, and I hope you understand
I don't want to hire you as a cook. But I've had a
scheme in the back of my head for a fortni't or more.
Somethin' Sylvester said about a young lady cousin of
his made me think of it. Seems over here at the female
college — you know where I mean — they're teachin' a
new course that they've christened Domestic Science.
Nigh's I can find out it is about what our great gran'-
marms larned at home; that, with up-to-date trimmin's.
All about runnin' a house, it is; how to superintend
servants, and what kind of things to have to eat, and
how they ought to be cooked, and takin' care of children
— Humph! we don't need that, do we? — and, well,
everything that a home woman, rich or poor, ought to
know. At least, she ought to 'cordin' to my old-fashioned notions. Sylvester's cousin goes there, and likes
it; and I judge she ain't figgerin' to be anybody's hired
help, either. My idea was about this: If you'd like to
take this course, Caroline, you could do it afternoons.
Mornin's and the days you had off, you could apply your
science here at home, on Annie. Truly it would save me
hirin' somebody else, and — well, maybe you'd enjoy it,
you can't tell."

His niece seemed interested.

"I know of the Domestic Science course," she said.

"Several of my friends — my former friends, were studying it. But I'm afraid, Uncle, that I don't see where earning my living has any part in it. It seems to me that it means your spending more money for me, paying my tuition."

"No more'n I'd spend for a competent housekeeper. Honest, Caroline, I'd like to do it. You think it over a spell."

She did, visiting the University and making inquiries. What she was told there decided her. She took up the course and enjoyed it. It occupied her mind and prevented her brooding over the past. She might have made many friends among the other students, but she was careful to treat them only as acquaintances. Her recent experience with "friends" was too fresh in her mind. She studied hard and applied her knowledge at home. She and Annie made some odd and funny mistakes at first, but they were not made twice, and Captain Elisha noticed a great improvement in the housekeeping. Also, Caroline's spirits improved, though more slowly.

Most evenings they spent together in the living room. She read aloud to her uncle, who smoked his cigar and listened, commenting on the doings of the story folk with characteristic originality and aptitude. Each night, after the reading was over, he wrote his customary note to Abbie Baker at South Denboro. He made one flying trip to that village: "Just to prove to 'em that I'm still alive," as he explained it. "Some of those folks down there at the postoffice must have pretty nigh forgot to gossip about me by this time. They've had me eloped and married and a millionaire and a pauper long ago, I don't doubt. And now they've probably forgot me altogether. I'll just run down and stir 'em up. Good subjects for yarns are scurce at that postoffice, and they ought to be thankful."

On his return he told his niece that he found everything much as usual. "Thoph Kenney's raised a beard 'cause shavin's so expensive; and the Come-Outer minister called the place the other denominations are bound for 'Hades,' and his congregation are thinkin' of firin' him for turnin' Free-Thinker. That's about all the sensations," he said. "I couldn't get around town much on account of Abbie. She kept me in bed most of the time, while she sewed on buttons and mended. Said she never saw a body's clothes in such a state in *her* life."

A few of the neighbors called occasionally. And there were other callers. Captain Elisha's unexpected departure from Mrs. Hepton's boarding house had caused a sensation and much regret to that select establishment. The landlady, aided and abetted by Mrs. Van Winkle Ruggles, would have given a farewell tea in his honor, but he declined. "Don't you do it," he said. "I like my tea pretty strong, and farewells are watery sort of things, the best of 'em. And this ain't a real farewell, anyhow."

"'Say *au revoir,* but not good-by,'" sang Miss Sherborne sentimentally.

"That's it. Everybody knows what good-by means. We'll say the other thing — as well as we can — and change it to 'Hello' the very first time any of you come out to see us."

They were curious to know his reason for leaving. He explained that his niece was sort of lonesome and needed country air; he was going to live with her, for the present. Consequently Mrs. Ruggles, on the trail of aristocracy, was the first to call. Hers was a stately and ceremonious visit. They were glad when it was over. Lawton, the bookseller and his wife, came and were persuaded to remain and dine. Caroline liked them at sight. The most impressive call, however, was that of Mr. and Mrs. " C." Dickens. The great man made it a point to dress in the style of bygone years, and his conversation was a treat. His literary labors were fatiguing and confining, he admitted, and the "little breath of rural ozone" which this trip to Westchester County gave him, was like a tonic — yes, as one might say, a tonic prescribed and administered by Dame Nature herself.

"I formerly resided in the country," he told Caroline.

"Yes," put in his wife, "we used to live at Bayonne, New Jersey. We had such a pretty house there, that is, half a house; you see it was a double one, and —"

"Maria," her husband waved his hand, "why trouble our friends with unnecessary details."

"But it *was* a pretty house, 'C.,' dear," with a pathetic little sigh. "I've missed it a great deal since, Miss Warren. 'C.' had a joke about it — he's such a joker! He used to call it 'Gad's Hill, Junior.'"

"Named after some of David B.'s folks?" asked Captain Elisha innocently. The answer, delivered by Mr. Dickens, was condescending and explanatory.

Caroline laughed, actually laughed aloud, when the visit was over. Her uncle was immensely pleased.

"Hooray!" he cried. "I'll invite 'em up to stay a week. That's the fust time I've heard you laugh for I don't know when."

She laughed again. "I can't help it," she said; "they are so funny."

The captain chuckled. "Yes," he said, "and they don't know it. I cal'late a person's skull has got room for just about so much in it and no more. Cornelius Charles's head is so jammed with self-satisfaction that his sense of humor was crowded out of door long ago."

One boarder at Mrs. Hepton's did not call, nor did Captain Elisha allude to him. Caroline noticed the latter fact and understood the reason. Also, when the captain went to the city, as he frequently did, and remained longer than usual, she noticed that his explanations of the way in which he spent his time were sometimes vague and hurried. She understood and was troubled. Yet she thought a great deal on the subject before she mentioned it.

On the April afternoon when Caroline sat at the window of the living room awaiting her uncle's return she was thinking of that subject. But, at last, her mind was made up. It was a hard thing to do; it was humiliating, in a way; it might — though she sincerely hoped not — be misconstrued as to motive; but it was right. Captain Elisha had been so unselfish, so glad to give up every personal inclination in order to please her, that she would no longer permit her pride to stand in the way of his gratification, even in little things. At least, she would speak to him on the matter.

He came on a later than his usual train, and at dinner, when she asked where he had been, replied, " Oh, to see Sylvester, and — er — around." She asked him no more, but, when they were together in the living room, she moved her chair over beside his and said without looking at him:

" Uncle Elisha, I know where you've been this afternoon. You've been to see Mr. Pearson."

" Hey?" He started, leaned back and regarded her with astonishment and some alarm.

" You've been to see Mr. Pearson," she repeated, " haven't you?"

" Why — why, yes, Caroline, I have — to tell you the truth. I don't see how you knew, but," nervously, " I

326

hope you don't feel bad 'cause I did. I go to see him pretty often. You see, I think a good deal of him — a whole lot of him. *I* think he's a fine young feller. Course I know you don't, and so I never mention him to you. But I do hope you ain't goin' to ask me not to see him."

She shook her head. "No," she said. "I would have no right to ask that, even if I wished to. And I do not wish it. Uncle Elisha, if you were alone here, he would come to see you; I know he would. Invite him to come, please."

His astonishment was greater than ever.

"Invite him to come *here?*" he asked. "To see you?"

"No," hastily; "to see you. This is your home. I have no right to keep your friends from visiting it. I know you would sacrifice everything for me, even them; but I will not be so selfish as to allow it. Ask him here, please. I really want you to."

He pulled his beard. "Caroline," he answered slowly, "I'm much obliged to you. I understand why you're doin' this, and I thank you. But it ain't likely that I'll say yes, is it? And do you suppose Jim would come if I did ask him? He knows you believe he's a — well, all that's bad. You told him so, and you sent him away. I will give in that I'd like to have him here. He's one of the few men friends I've made since I landed in New York. But, under the circumstances — you feelin' as you do — I couldn't ask him, and he wouldn't come if I did."

She remained silent for a time. Then she said: "Uncle, I want you to tell me the truth about Mr. Pearson and father — just why they quarreled and the real truth of the whole affair. Don't spare my feelings; tell me what you believe is the true story. I know you think Mr. Pearson was right, for you said so."

The captain was much troubled.

"I — I don't know's I'd better, dearie," he answered. "I think I do know the truth, but you might think I was hard on 'Bije — on your father. I ain't. And I sympathize with the way he felt, too. But Jim did right, as I see it. He acted just as I'd want a son of mine to do. And . . . Well, I cal'late we'd better not rake up old times, had we?"

"I want you to tell me. Please do."

"I don't know's I'd better. You have been told the story different, and —"

"I know I have. That is the reason why I ask you to tell it. Oh," with a flash of scorn, "I was told many stories, and I want to forget them. And," sadly, "I can bear whatever you may tell me, even about father. Since I learned that he was a — a —"

"S-sh, Caroline; don't!"

"After that, I can bear anything, I think. This cannot be worse."

"Worse! No, no! This ain't very bad. I will tell you, dearie. This is just what happened."

He told her the exact truth concerning the Trolley Combine, his brother's part in it, and Pearson's. She listened without comment.

"I see," she said when he had finished. "I think I see. Mr. Pearson felt that, as a newspaper man, an honest one, he must go on. He knew that the thing was wrong and that innocent people might lose money in it. It was his duty to expose it, and he did it, even though it meant the loss of influence and of father's friendship. I see."

"That was about it, Caroline. I think the hardest

part for him was when 'Bije called him ungrateful. 'Bije had been mighty kind to him, that's a fact."

" Yes. Father was kind; I know that better than anyone else. But Mr. Pearson was right. Yes, he was right, and brave."

" So I size it up. And I do sympathize with your father, too. This wa'n't such an awful lot worse than a good many stock deals. And poor 'Bije was perfectly desp'rate, I guess. If it had gone through he'd have been able to square accounts with the Rubber Company; and just think what that would have meant to him. Poor feller! poor feller!" He sighed. She reached for his hand and stroked it gently with her own.

After another interval she said: " How I insulted and wronged him! How he must despise me!"

" Who? Jim? No, no! he don't do any such thing. He knows you didn't understand, and who was responsible. Jim's got sense, lots of it."

" But it is my misunderstanding and my insulting treatment of him which have kept you two apart — here, at any rate."

" Don't let that worry you, Caroline. I see him every once in a while, up to the city."

" It does worry me; and it will, until it is made right. And," in a lower tone, but with decision, " it shall be."

She rose and, bending over, kissed him on the forehead. " Good night, Uncle," she said.

Captain Elisha was disappointed. " What!" he exclaimed. " Goin' aloft so soon? We ain't had our readin' yet. Pretty early to turn in, seems to me. Stay a little longer, do."

" Not to-night, dear. I'm going to my room. Please excuse me this time." She turned to go and then, turning back again, asked a final question.

"You're sure," she said, hesitatingly; "you're quite sure he will not come here — to you — if you tell him I understand, and — and you ask him?"

"Well, Caroline, I don't know. You see, I was responsible for his comin' before. He had some scruples against it then, but I talked him down. He's sort of proud, Jim is, and he might — might not want to — to —"

"I see. Good night, Uncle."

The next morning, after breakfast, she came to him again.

"Uncle Elisha," she said, "I have written him."

"What? You've written? Written who?"

"Mr. Pearson. I wrote him, telling him I had learned the true story of his disagreement with father and that he was right and I was wrong. I apologized for my behavior toward him. Now, I think, perhaps, if you ask him, he will come."

The captain looked at her. He realized the sacrifice of her pride which writing that letter must have meant, and that she had done it for him. He was touched and almost sorry she had done it. He took both her hands in his.

"Dearie," he said, "you shouldn't have done that. I didn't expect you to. I know you did it just for my sake. I won't say I ain't glad; I am, in one way. But 'twa'n't necessary, and 'twas too much, too hard for you altogether."

"Don't say that," she begged. "Too much! I never can do enough. Compared to what you have done for me it — it . . . Oh, please let me do what little I can. But, Uncle Elisha, promise me one thing; promise that you will not ask me to meet him, if he should come. That I couldn't do, even for you."

CHAPTER XXI

PROMISES of that kind are easier to make than to keep. The captain promised promptly enough, but the Fates were against him. He made it his business to go to town the very next day and called upon his friend. He found the young man in a curiously excited and optimistic frame of mind, radically different from that of the past few months. The manuscript of the novel was before him on the desk, also plenty of blank paper. His fountain-pen was in his hand, although apparently, he had written nothing that morning. But he was going to — oh, yes, he was going to! He was feeling just in the mood. He had read his manuscript, and it was not so bad; by George, some of the stuff was pretty good! And the end was not so far off. Five or six chapters more and the thing would be finished. He would have to secure a publisher, of course, but two had already expressed an interest; and so on.

Captain Elisha drew his own conclusions. He judged that his niece's letter had reached its destination. He did not mention it, however, nor did Pearson. But when the captain hinted at the latter's running out to the house to see him some time or other, the invitation was accepted.

"That's fine, Jim," declared the visitor. "Come any time. I want you to see what a nice little place I've got out there. Don't stand on ceremony, come — er — next week, say." Then, mindful of his promise, he added, "You and I'll have it all to ourselves. I've been cal'-

latin' to hire a sail-boat for the summer; got my eye on a capable little sloop belongin' to a feller on the Sound shore. If all goes well I'll close the deal in a few days. I'll meet you at the depot and we'll have a sail and get dinner at a hotel or somewheres, and then we'll come up to the house and take a whack at Cap'n Jim's doin's in the new chapters. Just you and I together in the settin' room; hey?"

Pearson did not seem so enthusiastic over this programme, although he admitted that it sounded tip-top.

"How is Miss Warren?" he asked, mentioning the name with a nonchalance remarkable, considering that he had not done so before for weeks. "She is well, I hope?"

"Yes, she's fust-rate, thank you. Very well, everything considered. She keeps to herself a good deal. Don't care to meet many folks, and you can't hardly blame her."

Pearson admitted that, and the remainder of the call was largely a monologue by Captain Elisha.

"Well, then, Jim," said the latter, when he rose to go, "you come up Monday or Tuesday of next week. Will you?"

"Yes. I — I think so."

"Don't think, do it. Let me know what train you're comin' on, and I'll meet you at the depot."

This last remark was what upset calculations. Pearson came on Monday, having written the day before. He did not mail the note himself, but trusted it to Mrs. Hepton, who was going out to attend evening service. She forgot it until the next day. So it happened that when he alighted from the train at the suburban station the captain was not there to meet him. He waited a while, and then, inquiring the way of the station agent, walked up to the house by himself. As he turned in at the front walk, Caroline came out of the door. They met, face to face.

It was a most embarrassing situation, particularly for Caroline; yet, with feminine resourcefulness, she dissembled her embarrassment to some extent and acknowledged his stammered, " Good afternoon, Miss Warren," with a cool, almost cold, " How do you do, Mr. Pearson?" which chilled his pleasure at seeing her and made him wish devoutly that he had not been such a fool as to come. However, there he was, and he hastily explained his presence by telling her of the captain's invitation for that day, how he had expected to meet him at the station, and, not meeting him, had walked up to the house.

" Is he in?" he asked.

No, Captain Elisha was not in. He had gone to see the sail-boat man. Not hearing from his friend, he concluded the latter would not come until the next day. " He will be so sorry," said Caroline.

Pearson was rather thankful than otherwise. The captain's absence afforded him an opportunity to escape from a place where he was plainly unwelcome.

" Oh, never mind," he said. " It is not important. I can run out another day. Just tell him I called, Miss Warren, please; that I wrote yesterday, but my letter must have gone astray. Good afternoon."

He was turning to go, but she stopped him. She had fully made up her mind that, when he came, she would not meet him — remembering how she had treated him on the evening of her birthday, she would be ashamed to look him in the face. Besides, she could not meet him after writing that letter; it would be too brazen; he would think — all sorts of things. When he visited her uncle she would remain in her room, or go to the city or somewhere.

But now she had met him. And he had come in response to her uncle's invitation, given because she herself had pleaded that it should be. To let him go away would be rude and ridiculous; and how could she explain to the captain?

"You mustn't go, Mr. Pearson," she said. "You must come in and wait; Captain Warren will be back soon, I'm sure."

"Thank you; but I think I won't wait. I can come another time."

"But you must wait. I insist. Uncle Elisha will be dreadfully disappointed if you don't. There isn't a train for an hour, and he will return before that, I am sure. Please come in."

Pearson was reluctant, but he could think of no reasonable excuse. So he entered the house, removed his overcoat and hat, and seated himself in the living room to await the captain's return. Caroline excused herself, saying that she had an errand at the shop in the village. She made that errand as long as she could, but when she returned he was still there, and Captain Elisha had not appeared.

The conversation was forced, for a time. Each felt the embarrassment, and Pearson was still resentful of the manner in which she had greeted him on his arrival. But, as he looked at her, the resentment vanished, and the other feeling, that which he had determined to forget, returned. Captain Elisha had told him how brave she had been through it all, and, contrasting the little house with the former home, remembering the loss of friends and fortune, to say nothing of the unmasking of those whom she believed were her nearest and dearest, he

334

wondered and admired more than ever. He understood how very hard it must have been for her to write that letter to him, a letter in which she justified his course at the cost of her own father's honor. He longed to tell her that he understood and appreciated.

At last he could not resist the temptation.

" Miss Warren," he said, " please excuse my speaking of this, but I must; I must thank you for writing me as you did. It was not necessary, it was too much to expect, too hard a thing for you to do. It makes me feel guilty. I —"

" Please don't! " she interrupted. " Don't speak in that way. It was right. It was what I should have done long ago."

" But it was not necessary; I understood. I knew you had heard another version of the story and that you felt I had been ungrateful and mean, to say the least, in my conduct toward your father. I knew that; I have never blamed you. And you writing as you did —"

" I did it for my uncle's sake," she broke in, quickly. " You are his closest friend."

" I know, but I appreciate it, nevertheless. I — I wish you would consider me your friend as well as his. I do, sincerely."

" Thank you. I need friends, I know. I have few now, which is not strange," rather bitterly.

He protested earnestly. " I did not mean it in that way," he said. " It is an honor and a great privilege to be one of your friends. I had that honor and privilege once. May I have it again? "

" Thank you, Mr. Pearson . . . Now tell me about your novel. I remember it all so well. And I am very much interested. You must have it nearly completed. Tell me about it, please."

They were deep in the discussion of the novel when Captain Elisha walked into the living room. He was surprised, stating his feelings at their mildest, to find them together, but he did not express his astonishment. Instead, he hailed Pearson delightedly, demanded to know if they had dared tackle Cap'n Jim without the "head doctor's" being on the scene; and insisted upon the author's admitting him to the "clinic" forthwith. Pearson did not take the next train, nor the next. Instead, he stayed for dinner and well into the evening, and when he did go it was after a prompt acceptance of the captain's invitation to "come again in a mighty little while."

Caroline, when she and her uncle were alone after their visitor's departure, made no protest against the invitation having been given. She did not speak of Pearson at all. Captain Elisha also talked of other things, principally about the sail-boat, the summer lease of which he had arranged that afternoon. He declared the sloop to be an "able craft of her tonnage" and that they would have some good times aboard her or he missed his guess. In his own room, when ready for bed, he favored his reflection in the glass with a broad smile and a satisfied wink, from which proceeding it may be surmised that the day had not been a bad one, according to his estimate.

Pearson came again a week later, and thereafter frequently. The sessions with Cap'n Jim and his associates were once more regular happenings to be looked forward to and enjoyed by the three. As the weather grew warmer, the sloop — Captain Elisha had the name she formerly bore painted out and *Caroline* substituted — proved to be as great a source of pleasure as her new skipper had prophesied. He and his niece — and occa-

336

sionally Pearson — sailed and picnicked on the Sound, and Caroline's pallor disappeared under the influence of breeze and sunshine. Her health improved, and her spirits, also. She seemed, at times, almost happy, and her uncle seldom saw her, as after the removal to the suburb he so frequently used, with tears in her eyes and the sadness of bitter memories in her expression and manner. Her work at the University grew steadily more difficult, but she enjoyed it thoroughly and declared that she would not give it up for worlds.

In June two very important events took place. The novel was finished, and Stephen, his Sophomore year at an end, came home from college. He had been invited by some classmates to spend a part of his vacation with them on the Maine coast, and his guardian had consented to his doing so; but the boy himself had something else to propose. On an evening soon after his return, when, his sister having retired, he was alone with the captain, he broached the idea.

" Say," he said, " I've been thinking a good deal while I've been away this last time."

" Glad to hear it, I'm sure," replied his uncle, dryly.

" Yes. I've been thinking — about a good many things. I'm flat broke; down and out, so far as money is concerned. That's so, isn't it? "

Captain Elisha looked at him keenly for an instant. Then:

" It appears that way, I'm afraid," he answered. " What made you ask? "

" Nothing. I wasn't asking, really; I was just stating the case. Now, the way I look at it, this college course of mine isn't worth while. You're putting up for it, and I ought to be much obliged; I am, of course."

" You're welcome, Stevie."

" I know; but what's the use of it? I've got to go to work when it's over. And the kind of work I want to do doesn't need university training. I'm just wasting time; that's what I'm doing."

" Humph! I ain't so sure about that. But what sort of work do you want to do?"

" I want to be down on the Street, as the governor was. If this Rubber Company business hadn't knocked us out, I intended, as soon as I was of age, to take that seat of his and start in for myself. Well, that chance has gone, but I mean to get in some way, though I have to start at the foot of the ladder. Now why can't I leave college and start now? It will be two years gained, won't it?"

Captain Elisha seemed pleased, but he shook his head.

" How do you know you'd like it?" he asked. " You've never tried."

" No, I never have; but I'll like it all right. I know I shall. It's what I've wanted to do ever since I was old enough to think of such things. Just let me start in now, right away, and I'll show you. I'll make good; you see if I don't."

He was very earnest. The captain deliberated before answering.

" Stevie," he said, doubtfully, " I rather like to hear you talk that way; I own up it pleases me. But, as to your givin' up college — that's different. Let me think it over for a day or two; that is, if you can put off the Maine trip so long as that."

" Hang the Maine trip! You let me get into business, the business I want to get into, and I won't ask for a vacation; you can bet on that!"

" All right then. I'll think, and do some questionin' around, and report soon's I've decided what's best."

He laid the stump of his cigar in the ash receiver and rose from his chair. But his nephew had not finished.

"There was something else I intended to say," he announced, but with less eagerness.

"That so? What?"

"Why — why, just this." He fidgeted with his watch chain, colored and was evidently uneasy. " I guess —" he hesitated —" I guess that I haven't treated you as I ought."

"I want to know! You guess that, hey? Why?"

"Oh, you know why. I've been thinking since I went back to New Haven. I've had a chance to think. Some of the fellows in the set I used to be thick with up there have learned that I'm broke, and they — they aren't as friendly as they were. Not all of them, of course, but some. And I wouldn't chase after them; not much! If they wanted to drop me they could. You bet I didn't try to hang on! I was pretty sore for a while and kept to myself and — well, I did a lot of thinking. I guess Caro is right; you've been mighty decent to her and me."

He paused, but Captain Elisha made no comment.

"I guess you have," continued Stephen, soberly. "When you first came, you know, Caroline and I couldn't understand. We thought you were butting in and weren't our sort, and — and —"

"And a hayseed nuisance generally; I know. Heave ahead, son; you interest me."

"Well, we didn't like it. And Mal Dunn and his mother were always sympathizing and insinuating, and we believed they were our best friends, and all that. So we didn't try to understand you or — or even make it livable for you. Then, after the news came that the money had gone, I acted like a kid, I guess. That business of making Mal stick to the engagement was pretty silly. I was nearly desperate, you see, and — and — you knew it was silly. You never took any stock in it, did you?"

The captain smiled.

" Not a heap," he admitted.

" No. All you wanted was to show them up. Well, you did it, and I'm glad you did. But Caro and I have talked it over since I've been home, and we agree that you've been a great deal better to us than we deserve. You didn't *have* to take care of us at all, any more, after the money went. By gad! considering how we treated you, I don't see why you did. *I* wouldn't. But you did — and you are. You've given us a home, and you're putting me through college and — and —"

" That's all right, son. Good night."

" Just a minute. I — I — well, if you let me, I'd like to thank you and — and ask your pardon."

" Granted, my boy. And never mind the thanks, either. Just keep on thinkin' and actin' as you have to-night, and I'll be satisfied. I want to see my nephew makin' a man of himself — a real man; and, Steve, you talk more like a man to-night than I've ever heard you. Stick to it, and you'll do yet. As for goin' to work, you let me chew on that for a few days."

The next morning he called on Sylvester, who in turn took him to a friend of his, a broker — employing a good-sized staff of clerks. The three had a consultation, followed, the day after, by another. That evening the captain made a definite proposal to Stephen. It was, briefly, that, while not consenting to the latter's leaving college, he did consider that a trial of the work in a broker's office might be a good thing. Therefore, if the young man wished, he could enter the employ of Sylvester's friend and remain during July and August.

" You'll leave about the first of September, Steve," he said, " and that'll give you time for the two weeks vacation that you ought to have. Then you can go back to Yale and pitch in till the next summer, when the same job'll be ready for you. After you're through college for good, if what you've learned about brokerin' ain't cured you of your likin' for it — if you still want to go ahead with it for your life job, then — well, then we'll see. What do you say?"

Stephen had a good deal to say, principally in the line of objection to continuing his studies. Finding these objections unavailing, he agreed to his guardian's proposition.

" All right," said the captain; " then you can go to work next Monday. But you'll *have* to work, and be just the same as any other beginner, no better and no worse. There'll be no favoritism, and, if you're really wuth your salt, you won't want any. Show 'em, and me, that you're wuth it."

The novel, the wonderful tale which Captain Elisha was certain would make its author famous, was finished that very day in June when Stephen came back from New Haven. The question of title remained, and the " clinic," now reënforced by Steve — whose dislike for Pearson had apparently vanished with others of his former likes and dislikes — considered that at several sessions. At last " The Man at the Wheel " was selected, as indicating something of the hero's profession and implying, perhaps, a hint of his character. Then came the fateful task of securing a publisher. And the first to whom it was submitted — one of the two firms which had already expressed a desire to read the manuscript — accepted it, at what, for a first novel, were very fair terms. During the summer there was proof to be read and illustrations to be criticized. Captain Elisha did not wholly approve of the artist's productions.

"Jerushy!" he exclaimed, "look at that mainmast! Look at the rake of it! More like a yacht than a deepwater bark, she is enough sight. And the fust mate's got a uniform cap on, like a purser on a steamboat. Make that artist feller take that cap off him, Jim. He's got to. I wish he could have seen some of my mates. They wa'n't Cunarder dudes, but they could make a crew hop 'round like a sand-flea in a clam bake."

Or, when the picture happened to be a shore view:

"What kind of a house is that? Did you ever see a house like that Down-East? I'll leave it to anybody if it don't look like a sugar man's plantation I used to know down Mobile way. All that feller standin' by the door needs is to have his face blacked; then he'd start singin' 'S'wanee River.' This ain't 'Uncle Tom's Cabin.' Bah!"

The advance copy, the first one, was ready early in September, and the author, of course, brought it immediately to his friends. They found the dedication especially interesting: "To C. W. and E. W., consulting specialists at the literary clinics, with grateful acknowledgments." Probably Captain Elisha was never prouder of anything, even his first command, than of that dedication.

And the story, when at last it appeared for sale, was almost from the beginning a success. The reviewers praised it, the reading public — that final court of appeal which makes or unmakes novels — took kindly to it, and discussed and recommended it; and, most important of all, perhaps, it sold and continued to sell. There was something in it, its humanity, its simplicity, its clearly marked characters, which made a hit. Pearson no longer needed to seek publishers; they sought him. His short stories were bid for by the magazines, and his prices climbed and climbed. He found himself suddenly planted in the middle of the highway to prosperity, with a clear road ahead of him, provided he continued to do his best.

In September Stephen gave up his work at the broker's office, spent the weeks with his friends in Maine, and then returned to Yale. He gave up the position on the Street with reluctance. He was sure he liked it now, he declared. It was what he was fitted for, and he meant, more than ever, to take it up permanently as soon as he was free. And his employer told Captain Elisha that the youngster was bright, clever, and apt. "A little conceited, needs taking down occasionally, but that is the only trouble. He has been spoiled, I should imagine," he said.

"Yup," replied the captain, with emphasis; "your imagination's a good one. It don't need cultivatin' any."

The novel being out of the way, and its successor not yet far enough advanced in plot or general plan for much discussion, the "literary clinics" were no longer as frequent. But Pearson's visits to the Warren house were not discontinued. All summer long he had been coming out, once, and usually twice, a week. Captain Elisha had told him not to stand on formality, to come any time, and he did. On most of these occasions he found the captain at home; but, if only Caroline was there, he seemed quite contented. She did not remark on the frequency of his visits. In fact, she mentioned him less and less in conversation with her uncle. But, as the autumn came and moved towards its prime she seemed, to the captain's noticing eye, a trifle more grave, a little more desirous of being by herself. Sometimes he found her sitting by the open fire — pleasant in the cool October evenings — and gazing very soberly at the blaze. She had been in good spirits, more merry and light-hearted than he had ever seen her, during the latter part of the summer; now her old sadness seemed to be returning. It would have troubled him, this change in her mood, if he had not believed he knew the cause.

He was planning a glorious Thanksgiving. At least, it would be glorious to him, for he intended spending the day, and several days, at his own home in South Denboro. Abbie Baker had made him promise to do it, and he had agreed. He would not leave Caroline, of course; she was going with him. Steve would be there, though he would not come until Thanksgiving Day itself. Sylvester, also, would be of the party; he seemed delighted at the opportunity.

" I'm curious to see the place where they raise fellows like you," the lawyer said. " It must be worth looking at."

" Graves don't think so," chuckled the captain. " I invited him, and he said, ' No, thank you ' so quick that the words was all telescoped together. And he shivered, too, when he said it; just as if he felt that sou'west gale whistlin' between his bones even now. I told him I'd pretty nigh guarantee that no more trees would fall on him, but it didn't have any effect."

Pearson was asked and had accepted. His going was so far a settled thing that he had commissioned Captain Elisha to purchase a stateroom for him on the Fall River boat; for of course the captain would not consider their traveling the entire distance by train. At an interview in the young man's room in the boarding house, only three days before the date set for the start, he had been almost as enthusiastic as the Cape Codder himself. The pair had planned several side excursions, time and weather permitting, among them a trip across the Sound to Setuckit Point, with the possibility of some late sea-fowl shooting and a long tramp to one of the life-saving stations, where Pearson hoped to pick up material for his new book. He was all anticipation and enthusiasm when the captain left him, and said he would run out to the house the following day, to make final arrangements.

That day Sylvester 'phoned, asking Captain Elisha to come to his office on a matter of business. When, having done so, the captain, returning, alighted at his home station, he was surprised to see Pearson standing on the platform.

"Why, hello, Jim!" he exclaimed. "What are you doing here? Just come, have you?"

His friend shook his head. "No, Captain Warren," he said; "I'm just going."

"Goin'? What for? Been up to the house, of course? Caroline told you where I'd gone and that I was cal'latin' to hurry back, didn't she?"

"Yes"

"Well, then, course you ain't goin'! You're goin' to stay to dinner. I've got some things to tell you about that life-savin' station cruise. I've been thinkin' that I know the cap'n and most of the crew on the lightship off back of the Point. How'd you like to go aboard of her? You could get some yarns from those fellers that might be wuth hearin'."

"I have no doubt I should. But I'm afraid I can't go. The fact is, Captain, I've decided not to spend Thanksgiving with you, after all."

"Hey?" Captain Elisha could scarcely believe he had heard correctly. "You can't go — to South Denboro?"

"No."

"Why not, for the land sakes?"

"Well, I've decided — I've decided not to."

"But, Jim! Why, I can't have it so! I'm dreadful disappointed. I've counted on your goin'. So has Abbie. She's read your book, and she says she's crazy to see the feller that wrote it. She's told the minister and a whole lot more, and they're all comin' in to look at you. 'Tain't often we have a celebrated character in our town. You've *got* to go."

"Thank you, Captain. I appreciate the invitation and your kindness, but," with decision, "I can't accept."

"Can't you come later? Say Thanksgivin' mornin'? Or even the day after?"

"No."

"But why not? What's the matter with you all of a sudden? Come here! let me look at you."

He took the young man by the arm and led him, almost by main strength, close to the lighted window of the station. It was late, and the afternoon was gloomy. Here, by the lamplight streaming through the window, he could see his face more clearly. He looked at it.

"Humph!" he grunted, after a moment's scrutiny. "You've made up your mind; I can see that. Have you told Caroline? Does she know?"

"Yes. You'll have to excuse me, Captain Warren; my train is coming."

"What did she say?"

Pearson smiled, but there was little mirth in the smile. "I think she agrees with me that it is best," he observed.

"Humph! She does, hey? I want to know! Look here, Jim! have you and she —"

346

He got no further, for Pearson broke away, and, with a hurried " Good night," strode up the platform to meet the city-bound train. Captain Elisha watched it go and then walked slowly homeward, his hands in his pockets, troubled and wondering.

He entered the house by the back door, a remnant of South Denboro habit, and found Annie in the kitchen.

" Where's Caroline? " he asked.

" She's in the living room, sir, I think. Mr. Pearson has been here and just gone."

" Um-hm. So I heard. Say, Annie, you needn't hurry dinner; I ain't ready for it yet awhile."

He hung his coat and hat in the back hall and quietly entered the living room. The lamp was not lighted, and the room was dark, but he saw his niece, a shadowy figure, seated by the window. He crossed to her side.

" Well, Caroline," he said, cheerfully, " I'm home again."

She turned. " I see you are," she answered.

" Humph! your eyes must be better than mine then. I can't see anything in here. It's darker than a nigger's pocket. Suppose we turn on the glim."

He struck a match as he said it. By its light he saw her face. The match burned down to his finger tips and then he extinguished it.

" I don't know but the dark is just as good and more economical," he observed. " No use of encouragin' the graspin' ile trust unless it's necessary. Let's you and me sit here in the dark and talk. No objection to talkin' to your back country relation, have you? "

" No."

" That's good. Well, Caroline, I'm goin' to talk plain again. You can order me to close my hatch any time you feel like it; that's skipper's privilege, and you're boss of this craft, you know. Dearie, I just met Jim Pearson. He tells me he's decided not to go on this Cape cruise of ours. He said you agreed with him 'twas best he shouldn't go. Do you mind tellin' me why?"

She did not answer. He waited a minute and then continued.

"Course, I know I ain't got any real right to ask," he went on; "but I think more of you and Jim than I do of anybody else, and so maybe you'll excuse me. Have you and he had a fallin' out?"

Still she was silent. He sighed. "Well," he observed, "I see you have, and I don't blame you for not wantin' to talk about it. I'm awful sorry. I'd begun to hope that . . . However, we'll change the subject. Or we won't talk at all, if you'd rather not."

Another pause. Then she laid her hand on his.

"Uncle," she said, "you know I always want to talk to you. And, as for the right to ask, you have the right to ask anything of me at any time. And I should have told you, of my own accord, by and by. Mr. Pearson and I have not quarreled; but I think — I think it best that I should not see him again."

"You do? Not see him — any more — at all? Why, Caroline!"

"Not for a long, long time, at least. It would only make it harder — for him; and it's of no use."

Captain Elisha sighed again. "I guess I understand, Caroline. I presume likely I do. He — he asked somethin' of you — and you couldn't say yes to him. That was it, I suppose. Needn't tell me unless you really want to, you understand," he added, hastily.

"But I do. I ought to tell you. I should have told you before, and perhaps, if I had, he would not have

. . . Uncle Elisha, Mr. Pearson asked me to be his wife."

The captain gave no evidence of surprise.

"Yes," he replied, gravely, "I judged that was it. And you told him you couldn't, I suppose. Well, dearie, that's a question nobody ought to answer but the one. She's the only one that knows what that answer should be, and, when other folks interfere and try to influence, it generally means trouble. I'm kind of disappointed; I'll own up to that. I think Jim is a fine, honest, able young man, and he'd make a good husband, I'm sure. And, so far as his business, or profession, or whatever you call it, goes, he's doin' pretty well and sartin to do better. Of course, 'twa'n't that that kept you from ——"

"Uncle Elisha! Am *I* so rich that I should —"

"There! there, my girl! I know 'twa'n't that, of course. I was only thinkin' out loud, that's all — tryin' to find reasons. You didn't care for him enough, I suppose. Caroline, you don't care for anybody else, do you? You don't still care for that other feller, that —"

"Uncle!" she sprang up, hurt and indignant. "How can you?" she cried. "How could you ask that? What must you think of me?"

"Please, Caroline," he protested; "please don't. I beg your pardon. I was a fool! I knew better. Don't go. Tell me the real reason. Sit down again and let's talk this out. Do sit down! that's it. Now tell me; was it that you couldn't care for Jim enough?"

She hesitated.

"Was it?" he repeated.

"I — I like Mr. Pearson very much. I respect and admire him."

"But you don't love him. I see. Well," sadly,

"there's another one of my dreams gone to smash. However, you did just right, dearie. Feelin' that way, you couldn't marry him, of course."

He would have risen now, and she detained him.

"That was not the reason," she said, in a low tone.

"Hey?" he bent toward her. "What?" he cried. "That wa'n't the reason, you say? You do care for him?"

She was silent.

"Do you?" he repeated, gently. "And yet you sent him away. Why?"

She faltered, tried to speak, and then turned away. He put his arm about her and stroked her hair.

"Don't you cry, dearie," he begged. "I won't bother you any more. You can tell me some other time — if you want to. Or you needn't tell me at all. It's all right; only don't cry. 'Cause if you do," with sudden determination, "I shall cry, too; and, bein' as I ain't used to the exercise, I may raise such a row that Annie'll send for the constable. You wouldn't want that to happen, I know."

This unexpected announcement had the desired effect; Caroline laughed hysterically and freed herself from his arm.

"I mustn't be so silly," she said. "I had made up my mind to tell you everything, and I shall. My not caring for Mr. Pearson was not my reason for refusing him. The reasons were two — you and Steve."

"Me and Steve? What in the world have we got to do with it?"

"Everything. He would marry me, poor as I am; and perhaps I — perhaps I should say yes if things were different. Oh, there is no use my deceiving you, or trying to deceive myself! I know I should say yes, and be very, very happy. But I can't! and I won't! I *won't!*"

"But why? And where, for mercy's sake, do Steve and I come in?"

"Uncle Elisha, I suppose you think I have been perfectly satisfied to let you take care of me and of my brother, and give us a home and all that we needed and more. No doubt you thought me selfish enough to be contented with that and go on as I am — as we are — living on your bounty. You had reason to think so. But I have not been contented with that, nor has Steve. He and I have made our plans, and we shall carry them out. He will leave college in two years and go to work in earnest. Before that time I shall be ready to teach. I have been studying with just that idea in view."

"Good land! Why, no, you ain't! You've been studyin' to help me and Annie run this house."

"That was only part of it — the smallest part. I haven't told you before, Uncle, but one of the Domestic Science teachers at the University is a girl I used to know slightly. She is going to be married next year, and, if all goes well, I may be appointed to her position when she leaves. I have a conditional promise already. If I am, why, then, you see, I shall really be earning my own living; you will not have to give up your own home and all your interests there to make me comfortable: you can —"

"Here! here!" Captain Elisha put in, desperately; "don't talk so ridiculous, Caroline. I ain't givin' up anything. I never was more happy than I've been right here with you this summer. I'm satisfied."

"I know, but I am not. And neither is Steve. He and I have planned it all. His salary at first will be small, and so will mine. But together we can earn enough to live somehow and, later on, when he earns more, perhaps we may be able to repay a little of all that you have given us. We shall try. *I* shall insist upon it."

"Caroline Warren, is *that* the reason you sent Jim away? Did you tell him that? Did you tell him you wouldn't marry him on account of me?"

"No, of course I did not," indignantly. "I told him — I said I must not think of marriage; it was impossible. And it is! You *know* it is, Uncle Elisha!"

"I don't know any such thing. If you want to make me happy, Caroline, you couldn't find a better way than to be Jim Pearson's wife. And you would be happy, too; you said so."

"But I am not thinking of happiness. It is my duty — to you and to my own self-respect. And not only that, but to Steve. Someone must provide a home for him. Neither he nor I will permit you to do it a day longer than is necessary. I am his sister and I shall not leave him."

"But you won't have to leave him. Steve's future's all fixed. I've provided for Steve."

"What do you mean?"

"What I say." The captain was very much excited and, for once, completely off his guard. "I've had plans for Steve all along. He's doin' fust-rate in that broker's office, learnin' the trade. Next summer he'll have another whack at it and learn more. When he's out of college I'm goin' to turn over your dad's seat on the Stock Exchange to him. Not give it to him, you know — not right off — but let him try; and then, if he makes a good fist at it, he'll have it permanent. Steve's got the best chance in the world. He couldn't ask much better, seems to me. You ain't got to fret yourself about Steve."

He paused, almost out of breath. He had been speaking rapidly so as to prevent interruption. Caroline's astonishment was too great for words, just then. Her uncle anxiously awaited her reply.

"You see, don't you?" he asked. "You understand. Steve's goin' to have the chance to make a good livin' at the very thing he declares he's set on doin'. I ain't told him, and I don't want you to, but it's what I've planned for him and —"

"Wait! wait, Uncle, please! The Stock Exchange seat? Father's seat? I don't see . . . I don't understand."

"Yes, yes!" eagerly; "your pa's seat. I've meant it for Steve. There's been chances enough to sell it, but I wouldn't do that. 'Twas for him, Caroline; and he's goin' to have it."

"But I don't see how . . . Why, I thought —"

The door of the dining room opened. Annie appeared on the threshold.

"Dinner is served," she announced.

"Be right there, Annie. Now you see that you ain't got to worry about Steve, don't you, Caroline?"

His niece did not answer. By the light from the doorway he saw that she was gazing at him with a strange expression. She looked as if she was about to ask another question. He waited, but she did not ask it.

"Well," he said, rising, "we won't talk any more just now. Annie's soup's gettin' cold, and she'll be in our wool if we don't have dinner. Afterwards we can have another session. Come, Caroline."

She also rose, but hesitated. "Uncle Elisha," she said, "will you excuse me if I don't talk any more to-night? And, if you don't mind, I won't dine with you. I'm not hungry and — and my head aches. I'll go to my room, I think."

"Yes, yes," he said, hastily, "of course. I'm afraid I've talked too much as 'tis. You go up and lie down, and Annie can fetch you some toast and tea or somethin' by and by. But do just answer me this, Caroline, if you can: When you told Jim marryin' was out of the question for you, did he take that as final? Was he contented with that? Didn't he say he was willin' to wait for you, or anything?"

"Yes, he said he would wait, always. But I told him he must not. And I told him he must go and not see me again. I couldn't see him as I have been doing; Uncle, I couldn't!"

"I know, dearie, I know. But didn't you say anything more? Didn't you give him *any* hope?"

"I said," she hesitated, and added in a whisper, "I said if I should ever need him or — or change my mind, I would send for him. I shouldn't have said it. It was weak and wicked of me, but I said it. Please let me go now, Uncle dear. Good night."

She kissed him and hurried away. He ate his lonely dinner absent-mindedly and with little appetite. After it was finished he sat in the living room, the lamp still unlighted, smoking and thinking.

And in her chamber Caroline, too, sat thinking — not altogether of the man she loved and who loved her. She thought of him, of course; but there was something else, an idea, a suspicion, which over and over again she dismissed as an utter impossibility, but which returned as often.

The Stock Exchange seat had been a part of her father's estate, a part of her own and Steve's inheritance.

354

Sylvester had told her so, distinctly. And such a seat was valuable; she remembered her brother reading in the paper that one had recently sold for ninety thousand dollars. How could Captain Warren have retained such a costly part of the forfeited estate in his possession? For it was in his possession; he was going to give it to her brother when the latter left college. But how could he have obtained it? Not by purchase; for, as she knew, he was not worth half of ninety thousand dollars. Surely the creditor, the man who had, as was his right, seized all Rodgers Warren's effects, would not have left that and taken the rest. Not unless he was a curiously philanthropic and eccentric person. Who was he? Who was this mysterious man her father had defrauded? She had never wished to know before; now she did. And the more she pondered, the more plausible her suspicion became. It was almost incredible, it seemed preposterous; but, as she went back, in memory, over the events since her father's death and the disclosure of his astonishing will, little bits of evidence, little happenings and details came to light, trifles in themselves, but all fitting in together, like pieces of an inscription in mosaic, to spell the truth.

CHAPTER XXII

NOVEMBER weather on Cape Cod is what Captain Elisha described as "considerable chancey." "The feller that can guess it two days ahead of time," he declared, "is wastin' his talents; he could make a livin' prophesyin' most anything, even the market price of cranberries." When Caroline, Sylvester, and the captain reached South Denboro after what seemed, to the two unused to the leisurely winter schedule of the railroad, an interminable journey from Fall River, the girl thought she had never seen a more gloomy sky or a more forbidding scene. Gray clouds, gray sea, brown bare fields; the village of white or gray-shingled houses set, for the most part, along the winding main street; the elms and silver-leaf poplars waving bare branches in the cutting wind; a picture of the fag end of loneliness and desolation, so it looked to her. She remembered Mr. Graves's opinion of the place, as jokingly reported by Sylvester, and she sympathized with the dignified junior partner.

But she kept her feelings hidden on her uncle's account. The captain was probably the happiest individual in the state of Massachusetts that morning. He hailed the train's approach to Sandwich as the entrance to Ostable County, the promised land, and, from that station on, excitedly pointed out familiar landmarks and bits of scenery and buildings with the gusto and enthusiasm of a school boy.

"That's Ostable court-house," he cried, pointing.

"And see — see that red-roofed house right over there, just past that white church? That's where Judge Baxter lives; a mighty good friend of mine, the Judge is. I stopped to his house to dinner the night Graves came."

A little further on he added, "'Twas about here that I spoke to Graves fust. I noticed him sittin' right across the aisle from me, with a face on him sour as a sasser of green tamarind preserves, and I thought I'd be sociable. 'Tough night,' I says. 'Umph,' says he. 'Twa'n't a remark cal'lated to encourage conversation, so I didn't try again — not till his umbrella turned inside out on the Denboro platform. Ho! ho! I wish you'd have seen his face *then*."

At Denboro he pointed out Pete Shattuck's livery stable, where the horse and buggy came from which had been the means of transporting Graves and himself to South Denboro.

"See!" he cried. "See that feller holdin' up the corner of the depot with his back! the one that's so broad in the beam he has to draw in his breath afore he can button his coat. That's Pete. You'd think he was too sleepy to care whether 'twas to-day or next week, wouldn't you? Well, if you was a summer boarder and wanted to hire a team, you'd find Pete was awake and got up early. If a ten-cent piece fell off the shelf in the middle of the night he'd hear it, though I've known him to sleep while the minister's barn burned down. The parson had been preachin' against horse-tradin'; maybe that sermon was responsible for some of the morphine influence."

Sylvester was enjoying himself hugely. Captain Elisha's exuberant comments were great fun for him. "This is what I came for," he confided to Caroline. "I don't care if it rains or snows. I could sit and listen to your uncle for a year and never tire. He's a wonder. And I'm crazy to see that housekeeper of his. If she lives up to her reputation there'll be no disappointment in my Thanksgiving celebration."

Dan, the captain's hired man, met them with the carriage at the station, and Miss Baker met them at the door of the Warren home. The exterior of the big, old-fashioned, rambling house was inviting and homelike, in spite of the gloomy weather, and Caroline cheered up a bit when they turned in at the gate. Five minutes of Miss Abigail's society, and all gloom disappeared. One could not be gloomy where Miss Abbie was. Her smile of welcome was so broad that, as her employer said, " it took in all outdoor and some of Punkhorn Neck," a place which, he hastened to add, "was forgot durin' creation and has sort of happened of itself since."

Abbie conducted Caroline to her room — old-fashioned, like the rest of the house, but cozy, warm, and cheery — and, after helping in the removal of her wraps, seized her by both hands and took a long look at her face.

"You'll excuse my bein' so familiar on short acquaintance, dearie," she said, "but I've heard so much about you that I feel's if I knew you like own folks. And you are own folks, ain't you? Course you are! Everyone of 'Lisha's letters have had four pages of you to one of anything else. I begun to think New York was nothin' but you and a whole lot of ten-story houses. He thinks so much of you that I'd be jealous, if I had that kind of disposition and the time to spare. So I must have a good look at you . . . I declare! you're almost prettier than he said. May I kiss you? I'd like to."

She did, and they were friends at once.

" ' I declare! you're almost prettier than he said.
May I kiss you? ' "

The rest of that day and evening were busy times. Captain Elisha showed his visitors about the place, the barn, the cows, the pigpen — the pig himself had gone to fulfill the unhappy destiny of pigs, but they would meet him by sections later on, so the captain assured them. The house and buildings were spotless in paint and whitewash; the yard was raked clean of every dead leaf and twig; the whole establishment was so neat that Caroline remarked upon it.

" It looks as if it had been scoured," she said.

" Um-hm," observed her uncle, with a gratified nod; " that's Abbie. She hates dirt worse than she does laziness, and that ain't sayin' a little. I tell her she'd sand-soap the weather vane if she could climb up to it; as 'tis, she stays below and superintends Dan while he does it. If godliness wants to stay next to cleanliness when she's around it has to keep on the jump. I always buy shirts two degrees heavier'n I need, 'cause I know she'll have 'em scrubbed thin in a fortni't. When it comes to *real* Domestic Science, Caroline, Abbie ain't in the back row of the primer class, now I tell you."

Miss Baker had planned that her young guest should sit in state, with folded hands, in the parlor. She seemed to consider that the proper conduct for a former member of New York's best society. She was shocked when the girl volunteered to help her about the house.

" Course I sha'n't let you," she said. " The idea — and you company! Got more help than I know what to do with, as 'tis. 'Lisha was determined that I should hire a girl to wash dishes and things while you was here. Nothin' would do but that. So I got Annabel Haven's daughter, Etta G. There's fourteen in that family, and the land knows 'twas an act of charity takin' one appetite out of the house. Pay her fifty cents a day, I do, and she's out in the kitchen makin' believe wash windows. They don't need washin', but she was lookin' out of 'em most of the time, so I thought she might as well combine business with pleasure."

But Caroline refused to sit in the parlor and be " company." She insisted upon helping. Miss Baker protested and declared there was nothing on earth to be done; but her guest insisted that, if there was not, she herself must sit. As Abbie would have as soon thought of attending church without wearing her jet earrings as she would of sitting down before dinner, she gave in, after a while, and permitted Caroline to help in arranging the table.

" Why, you do fust-rate ! " she exclaimed, in surprise. " You know where everything ought to go, just as if you'd been settin' table all your life. And you ain't, because 'Lisha wrote you used to keep hired help, two or three of 'em, all the time."

Caroline laughed.

" I've been studying housekeeping for almost a year," she said.

" Studyin' it ! Why, yes, now I remember 'Lisha wrote you'd been studyin' some kind of science at college. 'Twa'n't settin' table science, I guess, though. Ha ! ha ! "

" That was part of it." She explained the course briefly. Abigail listened in amazement.

" And they teach that — at school? " she demanded. " And take money for it? And call it *science?* My land ! I guess I was brought up in a scientific household, then. I was the only girl in the family, and mother died when I was ten years old."

After dinner she consented to sit for a time, though

not until she had donned her Sunday best, earrings and all. Captain Elisha and Sylvester sat with them, and the big fireplace in the sitting room blazed and roared as it had not since its owner left for his long sojourn in the city. In the evening callers came, the Congregational minister and his wife, and some of the neighbors. The latter were pleasant country people, another retired sea captain among them, and they all seemed to have great respect and liking for Captain Elisha and to be very glad to welcome him home. The two captains spun salt water yarns, and the lawyer again decided that he was getting just what he had come for. They left a little after nine, and Caroline said good night and went to her room. She was tired, mentally and physically.

But she did not fall asleep at once. Her mind was still busy with the suspicion which her uncle's words concerning his future plans for Steve had aroused. She had thought of little else since she heard them. The captain did not mention the subject again; possibly, on reflection, he decided that he had already said too much. And she asked no more questions. She determined not to question him — yet. She must think first, and then ask someone else — Sylvester. He knew the truth and, if taken by surprise, might be driven into confession, if there should be anything to confess. She was waiting for an opportunity to be alone with him, and that opportunity had not yet presented itself.

The captain would have spoken further with her concerning James Pearson. He was eager to do that. But her mind was made up; she had sent her lover away, and it was best for both. She must forget him, if she could. So, when her uncle would have spoken on that subject, she begged him not to; and he, respecting her feelings and believing that to urge would be bad policy, refrained.

But to forget, she found, was an impossibility. In the excitement of the journey and the arrival amid new surroundings, she had managed to keep up a show of good spirits, but now alone once more, with the wind singing mournfully about the gables and rattling the windows, she was sad and so lonely. She thought what her life had once promised to be and what it had become. She did not regret the old life, that life she had known before her father died; she had been happy in it while he lived, but miserable after his death. As for happiness, she had been happy that summer, happy with her uncle and with — him. And with him now, even though they would be poor, as she was used to reckoning poverty, she knew she could be very happy. She wondered what he was doing then; if he was thinking of her. She ought to hope that he was not, because it was useless; but she wished that he might be, nevertheless. Then she told herself that all this was wicked; she had made up her mind; she must be true to the task she had set, duty to her brother and uncle.

Her uncle! why had her uncle done all this for her? And why had her father made him their guardian? These were old questions, but now she asked them with a new significance. If that strange suspicion of hers was true it would explain so much; it would explain almost everything. But it could not be true; if it was, why had he not told her when the discovery of her father's dishonesty and of the note forfeiting the estate was made? Why had he not told her then? That was what troubled her most. It did not seem like him to do such a thing — not like his character at all. Therefore, it could not be true. Yet she must know. She resolved to question Sylvester the next day, if possible. And, so resolving, she at last fell asleep.

Her opportunity came the following morning, the day before Thanksgiving. After breakfast Captain Elisha went downtown to call on some acquaintances. He invited Caroline and the lawyer to accompany him, but they refused, the latter because he judged his, a stranger's, presence during the calls would be something of a hindrance to good fellowship and the discussion of town affairs which the captain was counting on, and Caroline because she saw her chance for the interview she so much desired.

After the captain had gone, Sylvester sat down before the fire in the sitting room to read the Boston *Transcript*. As he sat there, Caroline entered and closed the door behind her. Miss Abigail was in the kitchen, busy with preparations for the morrow's plum pudding.

The girl took the chair next that occupied by the lawyer. He put down his paper and turned to her.

" Well," he asked, " how does this Cape Cod air effect your appetite, Caroline? I'm ashamed of mine. I'm rather glad to-morrow is Thanksgiving; on that day, I believe, it is permissible, even commendable, to eat three times more than a self-respecting person ordinarily should."

She smiled, but her answer was in the form of another question, and quite irrelevant.

" Mr. Sylvester," she said, " I wish you would tell me something about the value of a seat on the Stock Exchange. What is the price of one?"

The lawyer looked at her in surprise.

" The value of a seat on the Stock Exchange?" he repeated.

" Yes; what does it cost to buy one?"

He hesitated, wondering why she should be interested in that subject. Captain Elisha had not told him a word of the interview following Pearson's last visit. He wondered, and then surmised a reason — Stephen, of course. Steve's ambition was to be a broker, and his sister was, doubtless, with sisterly solicitude and feminine ignorance of high prices, planning for his future.

"Well," he replied, smiling, "they're pretty expensive, I'm afraid, Caroline."

"Are they?" innocently.

"Yes. I think the last sale was at a figure between ninety and one hundred thousand dollars."

"Indeed! Was father's seat worth as much as that?"

"Yes."

"But," with a sigh, "that, I suppose, went with the rest of the estate."

"Yes."

"Into the hands of the man who took it all?"

"Yes; the same hands," with a sly smile at his own private joke.

"Then how does it happen that my uncle has it in his possession?"

The lawyer smiled no more. He turned in his chair and gazed quickly and keenly at the young lady beside him. And her gaze was just as keen as his own.

"What did you say?" he asked.

"I asked you how it happened that my uncle now has father's Stock Exchange seat in his possession."

"Why! . . . Has he?"

"Yes. And I think you know he has, Mr. Sylvester. I know it, because he told me so himself. *Didn't* you know it?"

This was a line shot from directly in front and a

364

hard one to dodge. A lie was the only guard, and he was not in the habit of lying, even professionally.

"I — I cannot answer these questions," he declared. "They involve professional secrets and —"

"I don't see that this is a secret. My uncle has already told me. What I could not understand was how he obtained the seat from the man to whom it was given as a part of father's debt. Do you know how he obtained it?"

"Er — well — er — probably an arrangement was made. I cannot go into details, because — well, for obvious reasons. You must excuse me, Caroline."

He rose to go.

"One moment more," she said, "and one more question. Mr. Sylvester, who *is* this mysterious person — this stockholder whom father defrauded, this person who wishes his name kept a secret, but who does such queer things? Who is he?"

"Caroline, I tell you I cannot answer these questions. He does wish to remain unknown, as I told you and your brother when we first learned of him and his claim. If I were to tell you I should break my faith with him. . . . You must excuse me; you really must."

"Mr. Sylvester, perhaps you don't need to tell me. Perhaps I can guess. Isn't he my —"

"Caroline, I cannot —"

"*Isn't he my uncle, Elisha Warren?*"

Sylvester was half way to the door, but she was in his path and looking him directly in the face. He hesitated.

"I thought so," she said. "You needn't answer, Mr. Sylvester; your face is answer enough. He is."

She turned away, and, walking slowly to the chair from which she had arisen, sank into it.

"He is," she repeated. "I knew it. I wonder that I didn't know it from the very first. How could I have been so blind!"

The lawyer, nervous, chagrined, and greatly troubled, remained standing by the door. He did not know whether to go or stay. He took his handkerchief from his pocket and wiped his forehead.

"Whew!" he exclaimed. "Well, by — *George!*"

She paid no attention to him, but went on, speaking, apparently, to herself.

"It explains everything," she said. "He was father's brother; and father, in some way, took and used his money. But father knew what sort of man he was, and so he asked him to be our guardian. Father thought he would be kind to us, I suppose. And he has been kind — he has. But why did he keep it a secret? Why did he . . . I don't understand that. Of course the money was his; all we had was his, by right. But to say nothing . . . and to let us believe . . . It does not seem like him at all. It . . ."

Sylvester interrupted quickly. "Caroline! Caroline!" he said, "don't make any mistake. Don't misjudge your uncle again. He is a good man; one of the best men I ever knew. Yes, and one of the wisest. Don't say or think anything for which you may be sorry. I am speaking as your friend."

She turned toward him once more, the distressed, puzzled look still on her face. "But I don't understand," she cried. "He . . . Oh, Mr. Sylvester, please, now that I do know — now that you have told me so much — won't you tell me the rest; the reason and — all of it? Please!"

The lawyer shook his head, regarding her with an expression of annoyance and reluctant admiration.

"Now that *I've* told you!" he repeated. "I don't remember that I've told you anything."

"But you have. Not in words, perhaps, but you have told me. I know. Please go on and tell me all. If you don't," with determination, "I shall make Uncle Elisha tell me as soon as he comes. I shall!"

Sylvester sighed. "Well, by George!" he repeated, feelingly. "I'll tell you one thing, young woman, you're wasting your talents. You should be a member of the bar. Anyone who can lead a battle-scarred veteran of cross-examination like myself into a trap and then spring it on him, as you have done, is gifted by Providence."

"But will you tell me?"

He hesitated, perplexed and doubtful.

"I ought not to say another word on the subject," he declared, emphatically. "What Captain Warren will say to me when he finds this out is unpleasant to consider. But . . . But yet, I don't know. It may be better for you to learn the real truth than to know a part and guess wrongly at the rest. I . . . What is it you want me to tell you?"

"Everything. I want you to sit down here by me and tell me the whole story, from the beginning. Please."

He hesitated a moment longer and, then, his mind made up, returned to his chair, crossed his legs and began. "Here it is," he said.

"Caroline, about twenty years ago, or such matter, your father was a comparatively poor man — poor, I mean, compared to what he afterward became. But he was a clever man, an able business man, one who saw opportunities and grasped them. At that time he obtained a grant in South America for —"

" I know," she interrupted; "the Akrae Rubber Company was formed. You told Steve and me all about that. What I want to know is —"

" Wait. I did not tell you all about it. I said that another man invested ten thousand dollars with your father to form that company. That man, so we now know, was your uncle, Captain Elisha Warren."

" I guessed that. Of course it must have been he."

" It was. The captain was older than your father, had lived carefully, and had saved some money. Also, at that time, he idolized his brother and believed in his shrewdness and capability. He invested this ten thousand on Rodgers Warren's word that the investment was likely to be a good one. That, and to help the latter in business. For a few years the company did nothing; during that time your father and uncle disagreed — concerning another matter, quite unconnected with this one — and they did not see each other again while Rodgers lived. In that long period the Akrae Company made millions. But Elisha supposed it to be bankrupt and worthless; because — well, to be frank, because his brother wrote him to that effect."

He paused, fearful of the effect which this announcement might have upon the girl. But she had guessed this part of her father's dishonor and was prepared for it. She made no comment, and he continued.

" Now we come to the will. Your father, Caroline, was not a bad man at heart. I knew him well, and I believe that may be said truthfully. He realized what he had done, how he had defrauded the brother who had been so kind to him, and he meant, he kept promising himself, to some day repay the money he had taken. To insure that, he put that note with the other papers of the Company. If he did repay, it could be destroyed.

If he did not, if he should die, it would be there to prove — what it did prove. But always in his mind was the thought of you and Steve, the children he loved. He had quarreled with his brother it is true; he had cheated him, but restitution for that cheat he had provided. But what would become of you, left — in case he died without making restitution — penniless? He knew his brother, as I said; knew his character, respected his honesty, and believed in his conscientiousness and his big heart. So he made his will, and in it, as you know, he appointed Elisha your guardian. He threw his children and their future upon the mercy and generosity of the brother he had wronged. That is his reason, as we surmise it, for making that will."

He paused again. Caroline did not speak for a moment. Then she asked:

" And no one knew — you or my uncle or anyone — of all this until last March? "

" No. Graves had, with his usual care and patience, pieced together the evidence and investigated until we were sure that a stockholder in the Akrae Company existed and that all of your father's estate belonged to him. Who that stockholder was we did not know until that day of the meeting at our office. Then Captain Warren told us."

" But he did not know, either? "

" Not until then. He supposed his Akrae stock worthless, and had practically forgotten it. When we told him of its value, of the note, and of the missing shareholder, he knew, of course."

" What did he say? "

" Say? Caroline, he was the most distressed and conscience-stricken man in the city. One would have thought he was the wrongdoer and not the wronged.

369

He would have gone straight to you and asked your pardon, if we would have permitted it."

"But, Mr. Sylvester, now we are coming to the part I cannot understand. Of course the estate belonged to him, I know that. It is his. But why didn't he tell Steve and me the truth then, at once? Why did he let us believe, and employ you to lead us to believe, that it was not he but someone else? Did he think we would blame him? Why has he —"

"Caroline! Caroline! don't you understand yet? Do you imagine for one moment that your uncle intends keeping that money?"

She stared at him in utter amazement.

"Keeping it?" she repeated. "Why not? It is his. It belongs to him."

"Caroline, I'm afraid you don't know him, even yet. He was for going to you at once and destroying the note in your presence. He would have done it, but we persuaded him to wait and think it over for a day or two. He did think and then decided to wait a little longer, for your sake."

"For my sake? For mine?" she passed her hand in a bewildered way across her forehead. "Mr. Sylvester, I don't seem to understand even now. I —"

"For your sake, Caroline. Remember, at that time you were engaged to Malcolm Dunn."

Her intent gaze wavered. She drew a long breath. "I see," she said, slowly. "Oh . . . I see."

"Yes. Captain Warren is one of the best judges of character I ever met. The Dunns did not deceive him for one moment. He was certain Malcolm intended marrying you because of your money; for that matter, so was I. But his was the plan entirely which showed them to you as they were. He knew you were too honest and straightforward to believe such things of the man to whom you were engaged if they were told you; you must see the proof with your own eyes. And he showed it to you."

"But then," she begged, distractedly, "why couldn't he tell me after that? I — I am so stupid, I suppose — but, Mr. Sylvester, all this is — is —"

"He might have told you then, but he did not think it best. Caroline, your uncle has always believed in you. Even when you sent him from your home he did not blame you; he said you were deceived, that was all. But, too, he has always declared that you had been, as he expressed it, 'brought up wrong.' Your money had, in a way, warped your estimate of people and things. He believed that, if you were given the opportunity, you would learn that wealth does not, of itself, mean happiness. So he decided not to tell you, not to give you back your share of your father's money — he refuses to consider it his — until another year, until you were of age, at least. And there was Steve. You know, Caroline, that money and what it brought was spoiling Steve. He has never been so much a man as during the past year, when he thought himself poor. But your uncle has planned for him as well as for you and, when he believes the time has come, he —"

"Please," she interrupted, falteringly; "please don't say any more. Let me think. Oh, please let me think, Mr. Sylvester . . . You say that Uncle Elisha intends giving us all that father took from him? All of it?"

"Yes, all. He considers himself merely your guardian still and will accept only his expenses from the estate."

"But — but it is wonderful!"

"Yes, it is. But I have learned to think him a wonderful man."

She shook her head.

"It is wonderful!" she repeated, brokenly. "Even though we cannot take it, it is wonderful."

"What? Cannot take it?"

"Of course not! Do you suppose that either my brother or I will take the fortune that our father stole — yes, *stole* from him? After he has been living almost in poverty all these years and we in luxury — on *his* money? Of course we shall not take it!"

"But, Caroline, I imagine you will have to take it. I understand your feelings, but I think he will compel you to take it."

"I shall *not!*" she sprang to her feet. "Of course I shall not! Never! never!"

"What's that you're never goin' to take, Caroline? Measles? or another trip down in these parts? I hope 'tain't the last, 'cause I've been cal'latin' you'd like it well enough to come again."

Caroline turned. So did Sylvester. Captain Elisha was standing in the doorway, his hand on the knob. He was smiling broadly, but as he looked at the two by the fire he ceased to smile.

"What's all this?" he asked, suspiciously. "Caroline, what — Sylvester, what have you been tellin' her?"

Neither answered at once. The captain looked from one to the other.

"Well, what's up?" he demanded. "What's the matter?"

The lawyer shrugged his shoulders.

"What's up?" he repeated. "Humph! well, I should say the jig was up. The murder's out. The cat is no longer in the bag. That's about the size of it."

"Sylvester!" Caroline had never seen her uncle thoroughly angry before; "Sylvester," he cried, "have you — Have you dast to tell her what you shouldn't? Didn't you promise me? If you told that girl, I'll — I'll —"

His niece stepped forward. "Hush, Uncle Elisha," she said. "He didn't tell me until I knew already. I guessed it. Then I asked for the whole truth, and he told me."

"The whole truth? *Caroline!*"

He wrung his hands.

"Yes, Uncle, the whole truth. I know you now. I thought I knew you before; but I didn't — not half. I do now."

"Oh, Caroline!" he stepped toward her and then stopped, frantic and despairing. "Caroline! Caroline!" he cried again, "can you ever forgive me? You know — you must know I ain't ever meant to keep it. It's all yours. I just didn't give it to you right off because . . . because . . . Oh, Sylvester, tell her I never meant to keep it! Tell her!"

The lawyer shook his head. "I did tell her," he said, with another shrug, "and she tells me she won't accept it."

"What?" the captain's eyes were starting from his head. "What? Won't take it? Why, it's hers — hers and Steve's! It always has been! Do you cal'-late I'd rob my own brother's children? *Don't* talk so foolish! I won't hear such talk!"

Caroline was close to tears, but she was firm.

"It isn't ours," she said. "It is yours. Our father kept it from you all these years. Do you suppose we will keep it any longer?"

Captain Elisha looked at her determined face; then at

the lawyer's — but he found no help there. His chin thrust forward. He nodded slowly.

"All right! all right!" he said, grimly. "Sylvester, is your shop goin' to be open to-morrer?"

"Guess not, Captain," was the puzzled reply. "It's Thanksgiving. Why?"

"But Graves'll be to home, won't he? I could find him at his house?"

"I presume you could."

"All right, then! Caroline Warren, you listen to me: I'll give you till two o'clock to make up your mind to take the money that belongs to you. If you don't, I swear to the Lord A'mighty I'll take the fust train, go straight to New York, hunt up Graves, make him go down to the office and get that note your father made out turnin' all his property over to that Akrae Company. I'll get that note and I'll burn it up. Then — *then* you'll have to take the money, because it'll be yours. Every bit of evidence that'll hold in law is gone, and nobody but you and Steve'll have the shadow of a claim. I'll do it, so sure as I live! There! now you can make up your mind."

He turned, strode to the door and out of the room. A moment later they heard a scream from Miss Baker in the kitchen: "'Lisha Warren, what ails you? Are you crazy?" There was no answer, but the back door closed with a tremendous bang.

Half an hour after his dramatic exit Captain Elisha was pacing up and down the floor of the barn. It was an old refuge of his, a place where he was accustomed to go when matters requiring deliberation and thought oppressed him. He was alone. Dan had taken the horse to the blacksmith's to be shod.

374

The captain strode across the floor, turned and strode back again. Every few moments he looked at his watch. It was a long way to two o'clock, but each additional moment was another weight piled upon his soul. As he turned in his stride he saw a shadow move across the sill of the big, open door. He caught his breath and stopped.

Caroline entered the barn. She came straight to him and put her hands upon the lapels of his coat. Her eyes were wet and shining.

" Caroline? " he faltered, eagerly.

" You good man! " she breathed, softly. " Oh, you *good* man! "

" Caroline! " his voice shook, but there was hope in it. " Caroline, you're goin' to take the money? "

" Yes, Uncle Elisha. Mr. Sylvester has shown me that I must. He says you will do something desperate if I refuse."

" I sartin would! And you'll take it, really? "

" Yes, Uncle Elisha."

" Glory be! And — and, Caroline, you won't hold it against me, my makin' you think you was poor, and makin' you live in that little place, and get along on just so much, and all that? Can you forgive me for doin' that? "

" Forgive you? Can I ever thank you enough? I know I can't; but I can try all my life to prove what —"

" S-s-h-h! s-s-h! . . . There! " with a great sigh, almost a sob, of relief, " I guess this'll be a real Thanksgivin', after all."

But, a few minutes later, another thought came to him.

" Caroline," he asked, " I wonder if, now that things are as they are, you couldn't do somethin' else — somethin' that would please me an awful lot? "

375

"What is it, Uncle?"

"It's somethin' perhaps I ain't got any right to ask. You mustn't say yes if you don't want to. The other day you told me you cared for Jim Pearson, but that you sent him away 'cause you thought you had to earn a livin' for you and Steve. Now you know that you ain't got to do that. And you said you told him if you ever changed your mind you'd send for him. Don't you s'pose you could send for him now — right off — so he could get here for this big Thanksgivin' of ours? Don't you think you could, Caroline?"

He looked down into her face, and she looked down at the barn floor. But he saw the color creep up over her forehead.

"Send for him — now?" she asked, in a low tone.

"Yes. Now — right off. In time for to-morrow!"

"He could not get here," she whispered.

"Yes, he could. If you send him a telegram with one word in it: 'Come'—and sign it 'Caroline'— he'll be here on to-morrow mornin's train, or I'll eat my hat and one of Abbie's bonnets hove in. Think you could, Caroline?"

A moment; then in a whisper, "Yes, Uncle Elisha."

"Hooray! But — but," anxiously, "hold on, Caroline. Tell me truly now. You ain't doin' this just to please me? You mustn't do that, not for the world and all. You mustn't send for him on my account. Only just for one reason — because *you* want him."

He waited for his answer. Then she looked up, blushing still, but with a smile trembling on her lips.

"Yes, Uncle Elisha," she said, "because *I* want him."

The clouds blew away that night, and Thanksgiving day dawned clear and cold. The gray sea was now blue;

376

the white paint of the houses and fences glistened in the sun; the groves of pitchpine were brilliant green blotches spread like rugs here and there on the brown hills. South Denboro had thrown off its gloomy raiment and was "all dolled up for Thanksgivin'," so Captain Elisha said.

The captain and Sylvester were leaning on the fence by the gate, looking up the road and waiting for Dan and the "two-seater" to heave in sight around the bend. The hired man had harnessed early and driven to the station at least thirty minutes before train time. Captain Elisha was responsible for the early start. Steve was coming on that train; possibly someone else was coming. The captain did not mean they should find no welcome or vehicle at the station.

The whistle had sounded ten minutes before. It was time for Dan to appear at the bend.

"I hope to thunder Jim got that telegram," observed the captain for the twentieth time, at least, since breakfast.

"So do I," replied his friend. "There's no reason why he shouldn't, is there?"

"No, no sensible one; but I've scared up no less than a couple of hundred of the other kind. If he shouldn't come — my, my! she'd be disappointed."

"You wouldn't feel any disappointment yourself, of course," said the lawyer, with sarcasm.

"Who? Me? Oh, I'd be sorer'n a scalded wharf rat in a barrel of pepper. But I don't count. There's the real one up there."

He motioned with his head toward the window of Caroline's room. Sylvester nodded. "Yes," he said, "I suppose so. Captain, I'm somewhat surprised that you should be willing to trust that niece of yours to another man. She's a pretty precious article, according to your estimate."

"Well, ain't she accordin' to yours?"

"Yes. Pretty precious and precious pretty. Look at her now."

They turned in time to catch a glimpse of the girl as she parted the curtains and looked out on the road. She saw them looking at her, smiled, blushed, and disappeared. Both men smoked in silence for a moment. Then the captain said:

"Waitin'. Hi hum! nothin' like it, when you're waitin' for *the* one, is there?"

"No, nothing."

"Yup. Well, for a pair of old single hulks our age, strikes me we're gettin' pretty sentimental. You say you wonder I'd trust Caroline to another man; I wouldn't to the average one. But Jim Pearson's all right. You'll say so, too, when you know him as well as I do."

"I'll trust your judgment, any time. So you won't tell Steve yet awhile that he's not broke?"

"No. And Caroline won't tell him, either. Steve's doin' fust-rate as he is. He's in the pickle tub and 'twill do him good to season a spell longer. But I think he's goin' to be all right by and by. Say, Sylvester, this New York cruise of mine turned out pretty good, after all, didn't it?"

"Decidedly good. It was the making of your niece and nephew. Caroline realizes it now; and so will Steve later on."

"Hope so. It didn't do *me* any harm," with a chuckle. "I wouldn't have missed that little beat up the bay with Marm Dunn for a good deal. For a spell there we was bows abreast, and 'twas hard to tell who'd turn the mark first. Heard from the Dunns lately?"

"No. Why, yes, I did hear that they were in a tighter box than ever, financially. The smash will come pretty soon."

"I'm sorry. The old lady'll go down with colors nailed to the mast, I'll bet; and she'll leave a lot of suds where she sank. Do you know, I never blamed her so much. She was built that way. She's consider'ble like old Mrs. Patience Blodgett, who used to live up here to the Neck; like her — only there never was two people more different. Pashy was the craziest blue-ribboner you ever saw. Her one idea in life was gettin' folks to sign the pledge. She married Tim Blodgett, who was the wust soak in the county — he'd have figgered out, if you analyzed him, about like a bottle of patent medicine, seventy-two per cent alcohol. Well, Pashy married him to reform him, and she made her brags that she'd get him to sign the pledge. And she did, but only by puttin' it in front of him when he was too drunk to read it."

The lawyer laughed heartily. "So you think Mrs. Corcoran Dunn resembles her, do you," he observed.

"In one way — yes. Both of 'em sacrifice everything else to one idea. Pashy's was gettin' that pledge signed, and never mind ways and means. Mrs. Dunn's is money and position — never mind how they come. See what I'm drivin' at?"

Sylvester laughed again. "I guess so," he said. "Captain Warren, I never saw you in better spirits. Do you know what I think? I think that, for a chap who has just given away half of a good-sized fortune and intends giving away the other half, you're the most cheerful specimen I ever saw."

The captain laughed, too. "I am, ain't I," he said. "Well, I can say truthful what I never expected to say in my life — that *once* I was wuth ha'f a million dollars. As for the rest of it, I'm like that millionaire — that . . Hi! Look! There comes Dan! See him!"

They peered eagerly over the fence. The Warren "two-seater" had rounded the bend in the road. Dan was driving. Beside him sat a young fellow who waved his hand.

"Steve!" cried the captain, excitedly. "There's Steve! And — and — yes, there's somebody on the back seat. It's Jim! He's come! Hooray!"

He was darting out of the gate, but his friend seized his coat.

"Wait," he cried. "I don't want to lose the rest of that sentence. You said you were like some millionaire. Who?"

"Don't bother me," cried Captain Elisha. "Who? Why, I was goin' to say I was like that millionaire chap who passes out a library every time he wakes up and happens to think of it. You know who I mean. . . . Ahoy there, Jim! Ahoy, Steve!"

He was waving his hand to the passengers in the approaching vehicle.

"Yes," prompted his friend, hastily, "I know who you mean — Carnegie."

"That's the feller. I've come to feel about the way he says he does — that 'twould be a crime for me to die rich."

(6)

THE END.